Bestselling science and science ~~reinvents fantasy with the insigh~~ ... inside jokes you expect from the author of *The Time Weavers*, *The God Patent*, *The Left Brain Speaks The Right Brain Laughs*, and *The Sensory Deception*.

"*The Book of Bastards* combines a riveting, intense plot of righteous vengeance with tongue-in-cheek banter that will keep you turning the page with eager anticipation. With settings that make you wish they were real, characters you can't help but cheer for, and twists that keep you guessing, Ransom Stephens has crafted an engaging tale that makes every minute of reading, time well spent. I don't often reread a book, but I think I'll make an exception. Loads of fun. Highly recommended."

–Brian D Anderson, bestselling author of
The Bard's Blade

"A delightful, detailed tale about morality, being honest with yourself, and self-reflection, even when you don't like what the glass has to show. A perfect treat for lovers of rich fantasy worldbuilding, gory battles, and the kind of thoughtful, character-driven stories that make your brain whirl, your imagination dance, and your heart surge."

—J.M. Frey, bestselling author of
The Accidental Turn Series

The band played the old songs that never failed, songs of bawdiness washed down with a sip of moral justice: serious enough to bring forth a tear and silly enough to raise a smile.

The Book of

bastards

Volume 1

Ransom Stephens

the intoxicating page

Published in 2021 by The Intoxicating Page.

www.theintoxicatingpage.com

Text copyright © 2021 by Ransom Stephens

All rights reserved.

ISBN: 978-1734635423

Cover design copyright © 2021 by Lance Buckley

FICTION / Fantasy / Humorous
FICTION / Fantasy / Dragons & Mythical Creatures
FICTION / Fantasy / Coming of Age
FICTION / Fantasy / Arthurian
FICTION / Fantasy / Swords & Sorcery
FICTION / Fantasy / Epic

No faeries were harmed in the production of this book, though one or two may reside herein.

For the tiny beings that flit and flutter about and amuse us

Contents

Map of The Fist of God

Glomaythea

Glo Bay

Faer Reef

Great Beach

N

Crescent Cove

A note from your Faithful Tale Faery

I apologize for possessing your brain. At some point you must have clicked "Agree" but still.

Dewey asked me to include a list of the Bastards' names because he can never remember them. I've expanded the list to include most of Dewey's friends, but there isn't enough paper or cyberspace for a complete list of his enemies.

A note on pronunciation: since I enchanted this book with a Phonetic Faery, you already know how to pronounce everything. Whatever comes to mind is correct. Trust me, I'm right here between your ears checking.

-Your faithful Tale Faery

Kingdom of Glomaythea
- Gledig, King of Glomaythea
- Dafina, a.k.a., Daffy, Queen of Glomaythea, and First Princess of Nantesse
- Crisiant, King Gledig's Wizard and Truthteller, also a wizard on the frets

The people of Crescent Cove
- Dewey Nawton, halfling proprietor of The Gold Piece Inn
- Lylli, Dewey's daughter, a druid who has a nice cauldron
- Loretta, staff manager and mother of Rustin and Kaetie
- Kaetie, Loretta's daughter
- Rustin, a.k.a., Rusty, Loretta's son
- The gang-of-five: Aennie, Caeph, Macae, Naelth, Raenny
- Taevius, the oldest Bastard
- Pirates: Madog Grwn, Baertha Dread, Aerrol, Jon-Jay
- Elfs: Conifaer the woodweaver, Lapidae the coldsmith,

Quercus the historian, Naerium

The First Human and his Volunteers
- Lukas of Glomae, the First Human, a.k.a., the Liberator, a.k.a., the illegitimate usurper
- Maedegan, Lukas's righthand man
- Major Blechk, governor of Crescent Cove

PART I

The Innkeeper

1.

Dewey walked between sailors, fishers, and merchants along the wharf, a wooden dock that fronted the rough-water port of Crescent Cove. Everyone gawked at a three-mast frigate anchored in the harbor. Crescent Cove was no stranger to tall ships, but atop that center mast flew the red and black flag of Lukas, The First Human. Dewey had heard of the so-called Flying Anvil but had never seen one: a red flag adorned with a black hammer striking a gray anvil. He'd expected something with a bit more panache.

Some whispered, some scoffed, and a few even voiced support for the Liberation, but everyone wondered how their worlds were about to change. As is common for the long-lived, Dewey had no problem with change—sometimes he even welcomed it. He looked across the harbor and noticed that the freelance ships on both sides of the law, such as it was, had dropped their flags altogether. Dewey considered steadfast neutrality a reasonable response to uncertain times. He pulled his knit cap down to cover his ears and not just to fend off the thinning fog. While Dewey didn't mind change, he despised surprises. He preferred to have news come to him first and worked hard to assure that it would.

Waves rocked the harbor, throwing salty foam onto the wharf. He crossed the street, appreciating the fresh layer of sand that softened the cobblestones for horse's feet as well as his own. He nodded to a woman dressed in oilskins pushing a cart.

"Fine catch this morning," she said, swatting away seagull poachers.

"Good morning to you, Codae," he spoke to her but watched the salmon flopping about in her cart. "I'll give you a silver ohzee for the lot of them."

"Please, Dewey, you and me both know is worth five ohzees." She looked away and added, "Maybe I put them in my own smoker, maybe you pay me a gold ohzee come winter."

Dewey knew her to be a woman of kind heart but a worthy ne-gotiator. Still, he went with the obvious. "Don't need 'em anyway. Trade you one fish for a chord of seasoned apple wood, perfect for smoking,"

"Me fish are five ohzees."

"I do not pay full retail."

But then, Dewey heard a familiar voice from behind, "I'll pay a copper more than whatever the halfling offers!"

Dewey groaned. He'd been haggling with Spaedlie for the last twenty years. Their first time at it, she'd gotten him to pay retail but never again.

Codae slowed enough for Spaedlie to catch up. "The price is now five silver ohzees and one copper."

Dewey narrowed his eyes at Spaedlie who countered with three silvers. Spaedlie had been master of the local shipping guild for the last decade, a merchant queen. Codae waited for Dewey to up his offer, but he knew better than to negotiate with another bidder.

After a few beats of silence, Codae asked about the ship that flew the red and black flag. Dewey told her enough to support his reputation for having all the answers but provided few facts. He didn't know her loyalties, but he had a good idea of Spaedlie's, so he baited them. "You'll have to reckon with the usurper's power."

A look of worry crossed Codae's face, and she pushed her cart a bit faster. A sea lion reared up and barked. She tossed him an anchovy.

"For free?" Dewey pretended to be aghast. "And I once re-spected you."

"His domain, he has a right. And denying him could bring bad luck."

"Bad luck?" Spaedlie said. "From denying a seal the fruit of *your* labor? No. I think not. But I'll tell you what, calling Lukas the 'usurper,' that's where you'll get a case of bad luck."

Dewey resisted the urge to comment. Instead, he pulled off his cap and wiggled his big pointy ears.

"Show 'em off while you can," Spaedlie said. "Though, how you can stand the veiny things, I'll never know."

Dewey said, "Not only are they beautiful, but I can hear for miles—you'd be surprised what I've heard about you, the guilds, Lukas, …"

"And that's why you and your kind can't be trusted." She reached up and pinched one of Dewey's ears. In reply, he swung his hip into hers. They had one of those special relationships among rivals: a healthy dose of animosity built on mutual respect and the ability to share a laugh over drinks after haggling.

Dewey said, "The *usurper* threatens your income more than he does mine." Like most of the people who built Crescent Cove's peculiar success, Spaedlie had always been a vocal opponent of any recognized establishment, excepting her shipping guild, of course.

They heard yelling from across town and then the cracking groan of a barge hitting a dock—buyers from the city of Glomaythea here to acquire goods.

"The beautiful sound of increasing prices," Codae said and doubled her speed.

"You'll want to put that cap back on!" Spaedlie said. She gripped his shoulder and added, "Now, before the Volunteers see you."

Her tone startled him, it bordered on genuine concern. "Volunteers," he said, while replacing his cap. "As if they work for free."

She let go of him. "Another example of Lukas's brilliance. Calling them Volunteers gives the impression that they're lining up to support him."

"Gods help us," Dewey said, "if *impressions* are all it takes to raise a human rabble."

"We're very enthusiastic." Spaedlie jogged ahead with Codae.

Dewey turned up the Broad Way to the marketplace. Now a block uphill from the wharf, the fog was thinner and the sun stronger. He stepped onto the flagstone plaza, passed a herd of goats, ignored the opening offer of the goatherd, stepped around a basket maker, weaved his way through a display of bright new sails ruffling in the sea breeze, and then slowed to a disinterested stroll as he approached the row of brewers and vintners. He needed at least two barrels of ale, a cask of white, a cask of red, some cider— he flicked out a finger for each item he hoped to procure and flipped out a thumb because Codae's salmon looked perfect, and he had that applewood ready. She'd take a silver and a half, unless that damn Spaedlie had already scooped him.

Aside from Spaedlie's burst of concern, it was like any other day in the long life of Dewey Nawton, half-elf proprietor of The Gold Piece Inn.

Two children ran in front of Dewey, a girl and boy dressed in rags. He looked at them again. Their clothes were stained and faded but in a way that didn't set quite right. A tall, thin woman dressed in similar mock rags herded the children. She stepped with the precision and confidence of a dancer, her head high and eyes steady. Her pale skin and long black hair looked as though sunlight had never touched them. But that's not what gave her away. No, the soles of her feet looked like they'd never touched the ground, hardly the tough, blackened feet of anyone who has spent more than a day without shoes—hers were as pink as a newborn's.

An old man in gray robes followed, bent over, and leaning on a staff, but he moved just a hint too smoothly and scanned the marketplace with eyes a bit too sharp for the codger he tried to portray. The eyes caught on Dewey, widening with recognition. Dewey returned the insinuation.

Dewey knew the man who followed this false troupe: the tallest human that Dewey had ever known, save perhaps the man's father, or maybe his grandfather. Dewey stepped out of the way and onto a fine rug. A round, swarthy man moved forward to negotiate or perhaps shoo him away, Dewey would never know which.

Six soldiers dressed in the red and black leather of the Liberator's Volunteer Navy advanced from separate directions, converging on the royal family. Vendors and their customers struggled against each other to get out of the way.

The graceful woman stopped. Dewey had never seen Queen Dafina before. A woman of contrasts, she had wild brown eyes and a reputation for being a weakling, a bit character in the royal court. She knelt to the ground and gathered her youngsters. To her credit, she didn't cry out, and she didn't beg for mercy. She knelt and pulled her children close, instructing them. They stepped behind her, arms around her legs, and she faced the soldiers with her hands on her hips.

The giant man pulled a sword from a scabbard hidden beneath the cape on his back. The smooth sound of metal rubbing the leather scabbard slowed the Volunteers to a cautious walk.

Someone in the crowd called out, "It's King Gledig!" The crowd noises merged into a collective gasp. A profiteer in a black headscarf pulled a dagger from his belt with one hand and a throwing knife from inside his vest with the other. Dewey was struck with admiration for a king who could count on the loyalty of outlaws, but the numbers weren't right for a good fight and profiteers tend to go with the odds.

The King stood with his back to his family. He said nothing but, by checking his footing and grip on his sword, conveyed that he was in no mood to surrender.

The Volunteers exchanged hand signals and inched closer. The one nearest Dewey pulled a crossbow from the holster mounted over his shoulder, inserted a bolt, and wound it tight.

A vendor knocked over a table and hid behind it.

The King held his sword before him and stepped toward the

Volunteer, movements that balanced his arms, legs, and back with the leverage of his sword, the movements of a seasoned warrior.

The false old man had to be Crisiant, the King's Wizard. He raised his staff in the direction of the Queen, Princess, and Prince. A Volunteer gripping an enormous sword with two hands stepped toward him.

The crossbow launched with the leathery sound of a heavy whip slicing the air.

The bolt hit the King's wrist. His sword fell. The sound of heavy metal bouncing on stone echoed through the silent square. Even the seagulls were quiet above the rhythm of the surf.

The King picked up the sword with his uninjured hand.

Volunteers moved in.

The Wizard brought his staff down. Chunks of flagstone broke loose. A single loud pop blasted from the head of the staff. His clothes billowed like a sail in a monsoon, and his staff disintegrated into a dark cloud.

The cloud whirled around the Queen and her children, concealing them. Its surface flickered with flashes of light that looked like sparks but were actually faery wings reflecting sunlight.

The King, with his sword in his off hand, stepped away from the cloud and flicked his blade in a trial figure eight. Blood dripped from the crossbow bolt embedded in his other wrist. He cocked his head, cracking his neck, and beckoned the six fully armed soldiers to battle him with one hand effectively tied behind his back. He launched at the Volunteer with the two-handed sword.

A crossbow bolt hit the King in a thigh. He staggered but didn't fall.

The Volunteer swung his sword into the flashing cloud of faeries that concealed the Queen and heirs. The children's wails penetrated Dewey's tiny heart.

Queen Dafina snarled and emerged to face the man who threatened her children. She grabbed the soldier's sword arm. He shrugged her off, but she came back for more, like a goldfish irritating a shark. Dafina might have been a bit character in court, but Dewey would bet gold to silver that she'd star in her next role. If she had one.

The King wheeled around, raising his sword, building momentum. The Queen pulled on the Volunteer's arm with enough force that, when she let go, he stumbled into the King's path. The King's sword came down, penetrated the Volunteer's forehead first, and then carved a helix down his neck and across his chest, finishing with a thrust to his belly.

The Volunteer fell to the ground, nicely butchered.

Another Volunteer sliced his sword into the dissipating cloud. The children faltered, confused by their wounds. The Queen dove for her children and pulled them to her.

The Wizard rewound his spell. The swarm of faeries coiled around him for an instant, exposing the fallen Prince and Princess and the Queen wrapped around them.

The Wizard cast the faery swarm into a cloud that shrouded the children, Queen, and himself.

Dewey keyed in on one faery, a pointy eared little thing with a head of puffy hair and lacy black butterfly wings. He'd never seen a faery so angry. Everyone knew what happened to those who offended the faer. These soldiers would not be winning any bets for some time. Dewey hoped he could entice them into a game of chance at The Gold Piece Inn.

The King swung on another Volunteer. Biting through the leather and deep into his torso, the sword wedged between ribs. In the instant it took the King to dislodge his sword, the other four Volunteers surrounded him. One poked a rapier into the King's arm and his sword clattered to the bricks again. Another Volunteer kicked the King's legs out from under him.

The King lay on the ground. Three Volunteers held him. The fourth dropped her crossbow and pulled her sword.

Dewey heard a pop, and the faeries flew in every direction, revealing the corpses of the Princess and Prince but no sign of the Queen or Wizard. The King howled his anguish, pain, and regret.

The Volunteer now had her sword clear of its scabbard, a six-foot broadsword. She raised it over her head until it pointed straight up, and then she brought it down.

2.

Dewey could not comprehend why or how the ambitions of human beings drove them to destroy their own children. The human blood that flowed through his veins helped him perceive why Lukas would rid himself of King Gledig, an impediment to his ambition, fair enough. But Dewey's elfin blood would not permit him to accept that the deaths of two innocents could serve any purpose. He knew of only one way to deal with this feeling of outrage. Fortunately, the separation of the King's head from his neck didn't just cast a pall over the marketplace, it diminished the vendors' bargaining skills.

Dewey took advantage of brewers, vintners, and distillers, farmers, shepherds, and butchers. He got Codae down to half a silver ohzee for her cart of salmon. Dewey was certainly a callous, greedy jerk, and the King's death should have affected him, but you have to see it from his perspective. Dewey had already been proprietor of The Gold Piece Inn for 160 years. To a halfling who could expect a lifespan of over five hundred years, the rotation from one ruler to the next seemed less significant than getting a good deal on beer. "First Human," "Liberator," "usurper," none of the titles meant any more to Dewey than "distant annoyance."

The murder of children, though. That, he would carry with him.

With his orders paid for and deliveries arranged, Dewey headed back to The Gold Piece Inn. He passed a row of shops—cobbler, chandler, weaver—and looked up at the mountains. They were called The Fist of God because their four peaks looked like the knuckles of a fist with clenched fingers descending to the cove.

Dewey took his usual shortcut up the steep grade of a narrow alley between buildings that housed wares. Two steps into the alley, he felt that something was off. The shade transformed into shadows that moved from side to side, not dancing but prowling. He turned around. A short, bearded fellow in a green outfit with a black hat and a big toothy grin twirled a cane so as to block Dewey's path out of the alley.

Dewey calculated the money remaining in his purse: the difference between what he'd expected to pay at the market and the bargain rates he'd negotiated. All things considered, he'd rather lose money to thieves than to poor negotiation.

As he reached into his cloak for his purse, the shadows converged, sinking him into a pool of darkness. He heard ruffling and then felt something brush against him. Flickers of light passed between tiny wings, and he could make out the silhouette of someone in robes holding a staff. That someone said, "You could have saved them."

"What could I do?" Dewey said. "In a battle between a king and a usurper, I'm as useful as nipples on a Billy goat."

"You are a greater fool than I." The shadows tightened around Dewey. "The world will suffer for your inaction. You knew it and you did nothing. Nothing!"

It was true enough. Dewey could have warned the King with a short message tied to a seagull's leg, and none of this would have happened.

"Maybe you have me confused with someone powerful?" Dewey said. "I'm just an innkeeper."

The Wizard gave him a sincere chuckle. "More people know of your power than you think."

"Good sir, I assure you that if I'd had a card to play, I'd have offered my support."

"You dare lie to me?"

"I can offer you a drink, a room, a song, a game, perhaps someone to dine with or for comfort, but how could that help our King?"

The Wizard held up his staff and sang in a language that Dewey had heard but never learned. The lyrics rhymed in a simple cadence, and Dewey felt its charm. A path opened in the faery cloud. The Wizard held out his hand with one finger outstretched. A ladybug flew from his fingernail. Caught in the melody, Dewey couldn't pull away. When she was inches from Dewey's face, the ladybug shed her shiny red shell the way that you might drop your robe. Dewey felt a tingling that started in his ear and worked its way into his mind and ever deeper into the core of his being.

"From now and forward in time, Dewey Nawton ..."

The words vibrated the air. White, yellow, blue, and green Glo-Faeries trailed sparks in the darkness between them.

"... when someone asks you for help, you will give it."

The Gold Piece Inn

3.

Dewey rose to his feet. He heard seagulls and crows, waves in the harbor and an auction in the marketplace, all as it should be. He looked around the alley and dusted off his shirt. Other than grief from losing the silver in his purse, he felt fine. He had his share of rivals. If someone wanted to scare him, they'd succeeded. Fair enough. Besides, he was cursed on an almost hourly basis. Why would this be any different?

He continued up to High Street and took in the harbor and the cliffs that form the crescent-shaped cove. Farther off, he saw the lighthouse out on the point, and the many rocky crags that jabbed out of the ocean, dotting the horizon with ship hazards. The rocky sea floor made Crescent Cove a difficult port to navigate. Reputable ships tended to sail farther down the coast and up Glo Bay to deliver their wares to the huge market in Glomaythea.

Alternatively, for the price of negotiating the tricky seas and intermediate merchants, Crescent Cove gave those with something to hide indirect access to Glomaythea. The modest sea traffic kept the town manageable, and the profiteers kept it profitable, the ideal business climate for a greedy but not particularly ambitious fellow like Dewey.

He took a breath of cool sea air and approached his grand three-story building—maroon façade with gold highlights, blue gargoyles, and black shutters, open to welcome the breeze. Dewey passed the stable, glanced in and saw a horse in every stall. One boy forked in hay and another shoveled out manure. He stepped through The Gold Piece Inn's open doors and into an early afternoon ruckus.

More unsettled than he could admit to himself, he overlooked the fresh but unevenly dispensed straw and sawdust on the floor, stepped around three children who had chores to do but were playing on the stairs, and ignored an unpolished banister. He did glance up at the balustrade to see if any of the upstairs rooms were occupied but didn't take any joy at the sight of two closed doors. He scowled at a cat lounging on the chandelier that hung above the saloon.

A regular at a table near the small stage said, "We've got trouble, Dewey." Her name was Baeswax, the chandler who ran a shop down the street. She smelled of tallow and her arms were dotted with burn marks. "Death of the King bodes ill for all of us."

"It doesn't!" said a man next to her, a blacksmith named Ferrous. His face was marked by hundreds of tiny craters. "The First Human is just what we need. He'll set this kingdom aright."

"'First Human'?" Baeswax replied, "You stupid son of a carp, he's a usurper plain and simple. No right to the crown, no interest in peace or prosperity, just old-school conquering. It bodes ill, I tell you."

A serving-lad carrying an armload of foam-topped wooden mugs passed by, and Dewey helped himself. He quaffed the ale in a single gulp.

The miller, a compact man named Grindaer who had close-set black eyes, hair the color of a riverbank, and frown lines that spoke more of conniving than advanced age, said, "First Human or usurper, whatever you call him, he's got what it takes. I've had enough of 'em. Damn faer cost me a fortune."

"You say that out loud?" the baker said. A waft of flour drifted from his bonnet like extreme dandruff. "Baeswax is right, Lukas is an ill-boder."

Dewey tried to overlook the chatter. At least it wouldn't reduce his profits or harm his investments, unlike the goatherd at the corner table. Caepra wore drab gray robes and sat bent over a book with no drink or meal before him. A pair of goats perched on the chair at his side, and a tiny cloven-hoofed Crook Faery reclined in the arc of his shepherd's crook. One goat, a nanny, slurped ale from the mug of a guest at the next table. With ale foam in her beard, she bleated at Dewey.

Dewey replied, "Get in the damn barn." A border collie on the stage between a harp and a bass drum emphasized Dewey's request with a rumbling growl that sent the goats scrambling under the table.

A tall, rangy boy pushed the goats out of the room. The dog curled up and closed his eyes as though the boy had responded to his command.

"Not through the kitchen," Dewey said. "They're farqin goats, Rusty, don't be daft." He spun around and yelled, "Loretta!"

A chair across the saloon, near the casino entrance, scraped the floor. Loretta sat on the lap of a man with wild eyes and a wilder grin. He had three days of beard, wore a red bandana on his head, and smiled with teeth two shades too bright. He supported Loretta as she leaned into Dewey's line of sight.

Dewey said, "Madog, unless you've paid, get your hands off those knockers!"

Loretta tossed Dewey a copper ohzee.

He caught the coin, looked at it, and then at Loretta. "Don't sell yourself short." And to Madog, "Those are the finest, firmest, roundest, plumpest mammalian monuments this side of The Fist—if your willy is worth a copper, they're worth a silver."

With Loretta on his lap, Madog struggled to reach into the fold of his belt. He pulled out another copper ohzee and nestled it carefully, painstakingly, in Loretta's cleavage. She laughed and leaned back so that her bosom engulfed his face.

Dewey stepped over, reached in, and took the coin. "All right, but for that you don't get to touch the pointy bits." His eyes narrowed in disdain. "You disgust me."

From the saloon, he heard his favorite nemesis say, "Dewey was there! He'll tell you. Things are going to change." He looked back and saw Spaedlie, Crescent Cove's merchant queen, looming between arguing tables. She said, "Go on, tell them what happened."

Baeswax said, "We heard about the King's assassination."

"And his heirs," a whaler named Fin said. "But the Wizard got away and the Queen disappeared."

"Lukas will eliminate the Queen and then make *real* changes," Spaedlie said. "Am I right, Dewey?"

Dewey pretended not to listen. Participating in arguments was bad for business.

Spaedlie spoke loud enough for everyone in the inn to hear. "Lukas will liberate us! Humans will finally get a fair shot." Dewey wondered what angle Spaedlie was playing. He had it from reliable sources that she and Lukas were childhood friends.

A tiny figure wearing a suit and bowler hat—he looked like a dapper banker—flitted on the wings of a swallowtail butterfly from a window behind Spaedlie, and then over the rafters to Dewey's shoulder—his Truth Faery. The little guy was Dewey's best friend, and he looked worried.

Spaedlie said, "I'll say it to the face of any faer-lover I meet." She pointed her index finger at Dewey. "That includes you, ya pointy-eared bastard. I look forward to the day that a full-blooded human being runs this place."

Baeswax said, "Then why do you come here?"

"You think your candles make it to Glomaythea if I don't want them to?" Spaedlie said. And then to Dewey, "Your food and drink are good, made by humans for humans, but you immortals, you do nothing but steal from us, steal our very souls."

Despite being born of a human mother and elfin father, Dewey wasn't accustomed to being counted as faer. Elfs certainly didn't count him among their own. He scratched the tip of his right ear, massaging it upright to make it look more elfin and said, "You're in luck Spaedlie. While I am indeed a Bastard, I'm not immortal, and if I'm stealing from you, I'm doing a piss poor job of getting rich."

Dewey turned away and whispered to the Truth Faery, "Is he telling the truth?"

The Truth Faery said, "He believes that what he says is true." The little guy's voice quivered.

Dewey whispered back, "But is it?"

The faery said, "If I could judge absolute truths, would I work at The Gold Piece Inn?"

Dewey saw through the little guy's bluster. There was fear in his wings.

Dewey stepped on Madog's bare foot and continued to a card table where four merchants sat but weren't playing cards. "Bob! Get a card dealer in here."

Bob stood behind the bar toweling wine horns. He had a hunched back as though he made a practice of studying his navel, long gray hair, and droopy eyes behind spectacles with round, blue-tinted lenses. He mumbled, "I'm busy, boss, get off my case."

The Truth Faery flew up to Dewey's nose and indicated that Bob would do as he was told. Bob the bartender made a lot of rebellious noise but liked it here. With everything in order, Dewey turned to his office.

The last he heard of the argument came from Baeswax, "Your damn mill wouldn't turn without the help of the faer—hear this, Dewey? The idiots will kill the goose that lays our golden eggs."

Baeswax knew how to drive a point home. Dewey dreamt of enticing just such a goose to his employ, and the thought of killing one went so against his grain that the image left him grieving as though he'd lost a loved one.

He stepped into his office, and the Truth Faery fluttered back to his windowsill. Dewey exhaled a sigh that started in his feet, went up his spine, and nearly blew out the room's low-burning lantern. Pondering the cold truth—that Lukas had widespread support, even right here at The Gold Piece Inn—spoke louder to him than the beheading of a decent enough king. To control the situation, maybe even profit from it, he would need information. What was Lukas's actual goal? And his strategy, tactics, and resources? More than that, what were his weaknesses? Dewey told himself that he wanted the odds, the over-under on how long it would take for him to win or lose, but what really permeated his cold little heart was a different question altogether: how much of this anti-faer bluster was true?

The faer, Dewey thought, *humans come and go, a generation every couple of decades, but the faer. Without the faer*—he shuddered and then decided, at least until he learned otherwise, that Lukas was just another human conqueror. There was a time that you could set your hourglass by idiot invaders shuffling the decks of empire. *Ahh, that's it, I've just gotten soft these last two centuries. Peace, prosperity—hogwash, nothing but false security.*

He settled at his desk and took out ink, quill, and a sheaf of cheap, rough paper.

* * *

By the time he finished composing the letters, the evening tide had brought in a good crowd. The inn's redwood walls reflected the purple glow of the sunset. The fire was lit, and the fog would soon roll in. It smelled of spilled beer, steaming salmon, and sweaty sailor. Dewey loved the smell of a packed tavern, though now it just felt crowded and uncertain.

Loretta passed with an armload of ale steins and wine horns. She'd grown up at The Gold Piece Inn. Like Dewey, she was a genuine Gold Piece Inn Bastard. Unlike Dewey, the lush, freckled redhead had the big laugh, soft smile, and warm eyes that make humans worth having around. Loretta attracted customers and enjoyed her following almost as much as she treasured her two children. Kaetie was fourteen and Rusty fifteen. He'd never worried about Loretta. She had a place in the world and knew how to keep it. He'd never worried before, anyway.

She circled around the roulette wheel to the card table where five leather-clad, tattooed, spike-studded profiteer sailors appeared to be playing a card game to the death. Loretta set a mug next to her favorite guest, Madog Grwn, and kissed his forehead. Madog wore an evil sneer that meant he would either win the hand or start breaking things—not much of a bluffer, the threat in his tell improved his winnings.

The man next to Madog jumped up, knocked over his chair, and yelled, "Cheat!" His name was Aerrol, the captain of the profiteer ship *Avarice*. He wore a black leather vest that hardly contrasted his skin tone, opened enough to show the fine gold chains that connected his pierced ears to pierced nipples.

Dewey hurried over, prepared to make peace if it didn't cost too much.

Across the table, a woman whose sun-cured flesh threatened to escape the confines of a purple leather bodice dropped her cards as though they'd burned her. "A Card Faery?" She pointed at Dewey. "I wasn't told there was a Card Faery—it's an outrage!"

Aerrol leaned back and laughed in a deep baritone. "Truly, Baertha? And with no Card Faery, cheating is part of the game?"

Dewey tossed a grain of quartz, and a tiny lady of a certain age dressed in lace with black and red paisley wings flew from the deck of cards, caught it, and, before disappearing back into the deck, blew Dewey a kiss. He couldn't avoid thinking of what might come of the Card Faery if Lukas had his way. Cheating would run rampant. He filed the thought under ways to monetize the problem.

He turned to Loretta and said, "Fetch Kaetie and Rusty and try to get Madog to stop playing cards."

"I could take him upstairs."

"Not if he loses all his money."

"Or I can wait for him to lose and then watch him break every glass you own." She gave him a sarcastic curtsy. "Your choice."

He reached onto the table and swept two silver ohzees from Baertha's stack into Aerrol's.

"Loretta," he said, "get your Bastards in my office."

"What's got you so ornery?"

A few minutes later she led Rusty, a lanky, rapidly growing lad with bright blue eyes and an easy but mischievous smile, into the office. Kaetie arrived seconds later, a pudgy girl, nearly a young woman, who had endless waves of dark auburn hair and curious, consuming, brown eyes. She closed the door behind her. Neither of the children had Loretta's pale, freckled coloring, though Rusty shared her gregarious personality and dimples when he smiled.

Dewey said, "Can either of you read?"

Rusty said, "No," and Kaetie said, "We could if you'd teach us."

"Good." Dewey handed a small scroll to Rusty. "Take this to the candle shop and deliver it to Baeswax by hand."

"I'll give it to her right now, she's at a table by the stage."

"Did you hear what I said?" Dewey paused long enough for Rusty to begin a response and then interrupted, "What you'll do is what I tell you to do or you'll be forking night soil in mud for a month." Rusty ducked out so fast that he nearly ran into the door.

Dewey handed Kaetie a dozen tiny rolled up pieces of paper, one by one. "The destinations are written along the edge, here." He pointed at the small script.

Kaetie looked at each one and sorted them.

"Aha!" Dewey said, "You can read."

"Barely. I have to sound out every word. Maybe if I had a book …"

"Books. Horrible, tedious things. You'll learn more in bars

listening to drunks and minstrels." Dewey pointed at each little roll. "These two by gull to Nantesse and Puaepuae, this by raven to Custaello, and all of these to Glomaythea by robin or whatever is in the aviary."

"Seriously? I hate that raven. Last time he pecked at my belly and I swear he scorned me—it could affect my body image, you know—and if you need to send anything by robin, it has to be waterproof because they take baths like constantly."

"What did I tell you to do?" Again, he waited for her to respond so he could interrupt, but Kaetie was wise to him and remained silent. "Uh huh," he said, "then use a Water-Proofing Faery."

"All we have is a Water-Resistant Faery."

"What part of 'do what I tell you' don't you understand?"

"They'll never get the message."

"If they don't get the message, then you'll have plenty of time to pull weeds in the orchard."

She mumbled under her breath, "Illiteracy is the tool of tyrants and pricks."

"And Kaetie," Dewey said, "don't let that raven or anyone else define you. Except for me."

She sorted the rolled-up messages and then pointed at two of them. "These have to be enchanted, seagulls never listen to me, and that farqin raven …"

"No." Dewey stopped in his tracks. "Deliver them tonight."

"Who bit your arse?"

"Trust me, Kaetie." He looked down at her and a million horrible prophecies came to mind. Before he could stop himself, he pulled her up into his arms and buried his face in her hair.

Kaetie pushed away. "What the hell is wrong with you?"

He set her down. "I don't know."

"That was weird." She sounded concerned, which bothered Dewey more than anything he'd experienced yet today.

"They have to be delivered tonight. Focus, Kaetie, focus!"

She looked at the tiny scrolls. "We don't have enough Messenger Faeries for all of these."

"Then get someone to enchant some." But he realized the problem.

Kaetie said, "I think I can do it."

Dewey heard uncertainty in her voice. "You *think*?" It was worth the risk.

"I've seen Lylli do it and I know the words, but I need help from someone who has affinity with the faer. It must be someone who can do what I tell him. Of course, a full-blooded elf would be best. Do you know anyone?"

"Kaetie? One of these days …" Dewey blew out the lantern, shut the door, and followed her through the saloon, nagging her with his doubts.

She shrugged. "If it doesn't work, it doesn't work. We'll get Lylli to do it next week."

"No. Can't waste a day." He walked into Maeggie, a pregnant serving-lass who carried a tray of food in one hand and a half dozen mugs in the other. Kaetie caught the tray in time. One mug sloshed ale across his arm. Maeggie stopped, ready for Dewey to blame her for the mess, but he pulled Kaetie through the kitchen and out to the faery garden.

She counted the scrolls and said, "I need two."

The smells of honeysuckle, lavender, rose, and mint wafted through the garden among milkweed, pansies, chamomile, and the fungi, puddles, and stones that attract faeries. Dewey nodded to a nymph lounging on a piece of quartz centered in a ray of sunlight and scowled at a pair of pixies plotting beneath a nasturtium. He saw several toddler faeries lounging among purple amethyst crystals.

Kaetie leaned over his shoulder. Being a halfling, Dewey's scent didn't frighten the wild faer as much as Kaetie's. A little boy's wings started buzzing like a honeybee. He hadn't taken clothing yet, of course. Dewey whispered, "Back off, Kaetie, you're freaking him out." She shuffled a few steps away and the faery buzzed up and perched on Dewey's finger.

"There's a good one on this daisy," Kaetie said and Dewey repeated the process for a girl Stem Faery with elegant but dusty gold wings. With the little fellow already on his finger, the lass was less hesitant.

They passed the barn and bunkhouse and crossed a field to the aviary, a wooden structure next to a brook. Dewey could hear laughter from the spring that fed the brook. For no reason he could discern, he hated that the teenaged Bastards hung out at his spring.

Kaetie set out bread crusts to attract seagulls. From a dark corner of the aviary, a raven gurgled. A robin hopped around the stream, pigeons cooed from their perches, and grackles complained on the aviary's roof. Seagulls arrived in seconds, grabbed the bread, and flew away.

"See what I mean?" She unrolled the little scrolls with overseas destinations. "Hold the faeries over these."

"Hurry!"

"You want to do it?"

Dewey groaned. The faeries looked down at the curled papers and then at each other. The boy shrugged. The girl crossed her arms. "Kaetie, this is the most important thing you've ever done."

"You always say that."

"Well, this time I mean it."

Kaetie started singing a song in Maegic with a gentle, nasal voice.

"What are you telling them?"

Kaetie ignored him. She dropped her pitch and held her hand over the little boy faery.

The faery grimaced. Kaetie lowered her hand and sang a still lower note. The faery looked at Dewey with fear and determination as though the little guy wasn't sure he could accomplish his mission but meant to try.

Kaetie brought her lips together, drew her hand away, and blew at the faery. He dropped from Dewey's finger and disappeared into the scroll. The other faery watched the process. She held up a tiny finger to Kaetie, took a breath, pinched her nose, and jumped into the other message.

"I did it!" Kaetie said. "Wait 'til I tell Lylli."

"Thank the gods," Dewey said and hugged her.

She struggled out of his arms. "What the hell, Dewey? Is the world ending?"

"Send the damn messages!"

"Hand me that seagull."

"Hand you a seagull?"

"Never mind." Kaetie held up one of the freshly enchanted scrolls, and the seagull swooped down and held out a leg.

4.

Dewey took his seat between the fireplace and the only glazed window in the building. He could see the street, the saloon, the casino, the red-carpeted stairway, and the balconies and rooms on the second and third floors. He listened to the minstrel's ballad of a heartbroken pirate on a desert isle, ate salmon grilled in rosemary and served on sourdough bread, felt the warmth of the fire on one side and the cool evening fog on the other—and none of it soothed Dewey's worries.

Then he saw her on the porch. She fell through the door but not the way drunks fall. She reached up as though climbing from an abyss, and wailed, "Oh gods, please help me. Anyone, please!"

Loretta got to her first, dropped to her knees, and took the woman's hands.

The woman grabbed at Loretta, tears cascading down her face, sobs racking her from head to toe. "Please!"

"It'll be all right, dear. We'll care for you." She looked up at Dewey and added, "We will care for her."

Dewey stood over them. Children accumulated. Teen-aged Aennie said, "She's the cleanest beggar I've ever seen."

Another kid plopped down next to the woman and held his worn black feet up to her clean pink soles. "Somefin wrong wit her feet."

"What the?" Loretta said. "Feet don't come that clean. I've tried." She held the woman at arm's length and examined her. "She's a bag of bones, must be starving—Macae, fetch salted bread."

"Get her out of sight," Dewey said.

"You know her?"

"To the barn. Now!"

Loretta lifted her, muttered, "She weighs nothin'," and guided her back outside.

The screech owl that lived in the barn announced to everyone within a mile that a stranger had arrived.

Dewey looked back at his inn. The minstrel had switched to a light ditty about a horny woman who carried drunk men into a field and took advantage of them—the sort of song that's mostly chorus so anyone can sing along. Children were underfoot and some of the goats had found their way back inside. Bob was pouring ale and wine, the servers who weren't delivering food and drink were lounging on the laps of smiling patrons. A serving-lad named Faernando slipped off a sinewy woman, the profiteer sailor and card-cheat named Baertha. She threw the lad over her shoulder and carried him to the stairs just as the chorus returned to "she threw the boy down, he popped up, and she made him a man." The crowd erupted. Baertha took a bow, the lad waved, and Dewey held out his hand. As she passed, Baertha dug into her belt and tossed a silver ohzee. Dewey said, "You give him two of those when you're through. If you hurt him, it'll piss off the wrong kinds of faeries."

In other words, it was just another night at The Gold Piece Inn, and no one had noticed the beggar at the door.

Dewey rushed through the kitchen and out to the barn. He dodged sheep, rabbits, a sleeping cow, nearly stepped on the tail of an old bloodhound, and climbed the ladder. The loft was covered in straw and cordoned into sections by blankets of differing color and quality. The woman lay on a brown blanket next to an unshuttered window that let in the last light of the day. Loretta appeared to be threatening her with a baguette.

"She's lovely but there's nothin' to her," Loretta said to Dewey. And then to the woman. "You faer?"

"I require your aid," the woman said. "Please, my children …"

Loretta took a bite of the baguette dripping with salty olive oil and then offered it to the woman again. "Never seen a beggar who won't eat. She elfin? Your kind?"

"No, she's as human as you are."

Loretta leaned forward and sniffed the woman's neck. "She don't smell like a human."

"She bathes. Some people do that, you should try it." Dewey helped the woman up.

Loretta examined her hands, no scars or calluses. She ran her fingers through her long, straight black hair and mumbled, "Fine as silk."

Dewey said, "When have you ever touched silk?"

Loretta said. "I didn't think skin got that pale."

The woman's eyes lost focus, and she fainted.

"Farqin shite!" Dewey said, "Get some water—nay, a blast of brandy."

Loretta dropped down the ladder in a fluid, practiced motion.

Dewey waited a few more seconds and then whispered, "Queen Dafina, what are you doing here?"

She sat up straight, dabbed her eyes, and said, "I require your help."

"You have to get out of here."

"You must assemble the bodies of my husband and children." Her voice cracked. "They require decent burial."

"The usurper has them. There's nothing I can do."

"I can pay you more than you can imagine."

"Maybe so but pay means nothing to a dead man."

"Think of the favors I can grant, I can—" and then she went quiet and looked down, blubbering out the words, "My children, my husband, everyone is dead."

"I'm not, and don't plan to be any time soon."

She looked up at him and then around. She fondled the rough threads of the blanket and pulled a piece of straw through a gap in the weave. A lamb bleated below, and a mouse scurried across a rafter overhead.

"Surely you don't want to watch more people die."

The Queen stood and bumped her head on a beam. Dust sprinkled onto her face. "No," she said. "No, anything but that."

"I'd like to help," he said. "Dozens of good people, your subjects and their children, live here—you're duty bound to protect them, and you know what Lukas will do if you're found here."

"Right." She started down the ladder and Dewey held her steady. "I'll go." She stepped toward the barn door and Dewey nudged her, gently at first and then with a bit of authority to the side exit that led to an alley out of view of High Street.

He put two silver ohzees in her hand and said, "Take the morning barge back to Glomaythea or get passage on a ship to Nantesse—isn't that your home?"

"It was."

He gripped her shoulders and rotated her to face him. He waited for her to look up and said. "You asked for my help and I have helped you. Right?"

"Yes, thank you good sir."

He oriented her downhill and gave her a shove. She staggered into the dark alley and down the hill that would take her back to the marketplace if she followed it. She said, "My babies are dead. They're all dead."

Dewey shut the gate just as Loretta appeared with a goblet of brandy.

"Just in time," he said. He took it and drank.

5.

Dewey returned to his seat between the window and fireplace, but it wasn't as comfortable now. The children argued, patrons complained, and his favorite chair poked his back. He went upstairs.

Dewey's bedroom was on the third floor where sea breezes blew away the smells of humanity. He left the shutter open and lay down on his feather bed, staring out at the stars through gaps in the clouds. A mosquito roared past his ear. Laughter and fighting from downstairs jarred him. He got up and closed the shutter.

Dewey had a daughter named Lylli, a druid who lived in a cottage up on The Fist of God. Since half-elfs aren't particularly fertile, he thought of her as a miracle—his miracle. A quarterling druid, and if Lukas found her—he tried to think of something else, anything else.

He drifted off, and his mind found the children who lived in the barn: inquisitive Kaetie and bold Rusty, devious Caeph, conniving Macae, philosophical Naelth, nimble Aennie, clever Raenny, bully Vaence, and girly-girl Viviaen. Had he treated them well enough? He sat up with a start—what was wrong with him? *Did I ever give a farq what the damn Bastards thought of me before? And how do I know all their names?*

He rolled over and images of the two pregnant serving-lasses appeared on his closed eyelids, Laetifah and Maeggie. A mother hadn't died in childbirth since Lylli enchanted a Midwife Faery, but now he was sure that they were doomed. Thoughts of the hundreds of Gold Piece Inn Bastards who had grown up, gone off, had their own children, experienced their many adventures, and died—had they known how much he cared? *No, no, I don't care!* But now he feared that it was all a lie. Never, not even once, had he uttered those three words. *I don't love them. I barely tolerate them!*

He saw his Truth Faery pinned to a wall by his wings, and hundreds of Farq Faeries in a row, marching into a fire, and then Lylli. *No, it's just a dream!*

He stood and opened the shutter to the cold, salty air. It was true, what Crisiant the Wizard said, he could have stopped Lukas in his tracks—*but why? Nothing in it for me, was there? No!*

In the dark of night, conviction overcame him: Lukas already knew. Knew of the Bastards, knew of his network, and was coming to The Gold Piece Inn.

He hurried downstairs. *It's nothing, I'll just check and then I can sleep.* The inn was quiet, empty, and smelled like revelry—had they been celebrating his imminent demise? He stepped into his office, lit a lamp, and shut the door. Then he slid open a panel in the wall behind his desk and crawled through the opening.

Dewey's secret sanctuary was in the precise center of the building. A room six feet square with sound-canceling tapestries on each wall. He let loose a gust of relief. The book was still open on the desk. He turned the gilt-edged pages and found the date he was looking for. *Nothing out of sort, all as it should be.*

Back in his bed, he clenched his eyes shut. Fragments of images passed through his mind: the note he'd taken from a gull's leg months ago, letters falling into words on parchment that he could have sent to the King but hadn't. A five-minute task. A one-day trip by dove that would have cost nothing. Again, he jolted upright—the King was dead, and the Queen suffered because of him.

The lighthouse howled in the distance, a rooster announced the sunrise, and feet shuffled across the floor below. He heard a man moan and a woman laugh, and then he heard children whine.

He sat on the bed wondering if he'd taken ill, and then it hit him. Dewey built his life around knowing the odds and how to set his expectations. He might lack information, but he never lacked the ability to acquire it.

So, this is what a curse feels like. Well, she did offer money and favors— the favors of royalty! You makes your bed, you pays your dues, and if you do it right, you makes a tidy profit.

She couldn't have gotten far.

6.

There had always been a king in Dafina's life who made sure that everything turned out right, someone who would do anything to protect "The First Princess of Nantesse."

A question plagued her: why was she alive?

The Wizard Crisiant could have rescued any of them, why her? She was the least significant of all, the very least.

After leaving The Gold Piece Inn, she'd walked away from the sound of people, away from the harbor, to a place where waves punished the wooden dock. She tripped on a board, fell, and let her sobs put her to sleep. Visions of her little Princess and tiny Prince encompassed in a faery cloud, swords slashing through, screaming, bleeding, dying—she jerked awake surrounded by sea oats bowing to the wind.

Had it happened like that? Had she even tried to protect her children? Or had she run away?

Sunrays shone down from above The Fist of God, burning away the fog. For only the second time in her life, no one watched over her.

But why? Why was she alive?

She let herself stumble down to the soft, cold sand and walked along the beach. Seals lounged along the sandbar at the point where the river emptied into the sea.

Two days ago, she'd been a queen in the Castle of Glomaythea, and not just any queen, her King was the finest man she'd ever known. The sort of man who made every person in a room feel that they were the most important, and he cared about the wellbeing of everyone in his kingdom, both human and faer, friend and foe. Dafina believed to the marrow of her bones that even his enemies had loved him as she did. As she had.

Except for Lukas.

Her blood boiled at the thought of Lukas. She'd avoided him for all these years. It hadn't been difficult. Lukas was well known, but just a smith and merchant who rarely attended royal functions. He must have seen her from afar—King Gledig loved to show her off—but he couldn't have recognized her. She'd been a child of fifteen on that foolish spring day.

Why did her mind go there?

She chased a receding wave and let the foam of the next wash her legs, and one disturbing thought was replaced by another.

Why had Gledig commanded the Wizard Crisiant to save her?

He'd pulled Crisiant aside, leaned down and whispered, "You must save my Queen. For me to fight with honor, I must know that my love will survive." Crisiant had replied with a puzzled look and motioned to the children. Gledig ordered him at full volume, "Promise that you'll preserve Dafina. Promise it now!"

A mistake. As big of a mistake as overlooking the threat of Lukas.

And why had Gledig led them to a gods-forsaken outlaw port? Was the insurrection so complete that they couldn't have found passage to an allied capital and then made their way to Nantesse on a legitimate ship? He couldn't possibly have believed that they'd be safer on a ship of dubious reputation, could he? Was everything she'd believed of him a lie?

Yesterday he'd died in the market square of an outlaw port. She pushed against the memory, but it wouldn't let go. She wondered about his last thoughts. Had she seen relief on his face when he pulled his sword? He'd known he was outnumbered, knew it was over. Had he found relief in suicide? Her anger built. He chose the worst possible time to let her down, and their children. The budding rage dwindled into the hopeless acceptance of fate.

What would she do next?

With no one to assign her a role in the world, a troubling but glorious feeling washed over her. Freedom?

She'd only tasted it once before. There'd always been someone to give her a script and a costume, and without them, she didn't know who she was. Why did it feel glorious?

She hated herself for it. In the face of total ruin, destruction of not just her husband and children, but the country she'd sworn her life to protect, what sort of person would feel free? The pain of loss fought with the sense that she'd been released from a prison.

She wasn't worthy.

* * *

Queen Dafina walked into the sea. A rip-current pulled her feet out from under her and she sank.

Instinct took hold. She fought the current and pulled herself up for a breath. The current dragged her into the path of the river. Whirlpools spun their vortices where the river meets the sea, dragging her down. Grains of sand sparkled in the sunbeams, bubbles and foam rubbed against her. The demands of her lungs forced her to inhale water. She fell to the river bottom.

An arm wrapped around her stomach. She fought back. It tightened against her and flipped her over. Sharp fins along its forearm scraped the back of her neck. A mouth closed over hers and blew air into her lungs. Golden hair surrounded her, streaming and mingling with her own jet-black hair. In one burst of acceleration, she surfaced.

Eyes the size and color of abalone shells peered into hers from inches away.

Dafina choked and sputtered. Locked in the embrace, powerful thrusts held her above water. The woman smiled back, lips red against light bluish green skin, soft feminine cheekbones and the smile of a nurse determined to give her another chance.

Dafina caught her breath, and the maermaid nibbled at her ear and swam ever faster across the river. They broke the surface with enough momentum to fly up onto a sandbar.

The maermaid smoothed the Queen's dress and sang. She sang notes without words, a sweeping melody, and as she sang, thousands of tiny glowing lights swarmed to them. The little lights covered her like a thick wool blanket that had spent the day baking in the sun.

7.

Knowing he was cursed did nothing to reduce the panic. Dewey bolted downstairs. He ran through the kitchen without stopping for a cinnamon roll or tea, so he didn't complain that there was too much or too little cinnamon or that the tea needed more or less steeping.

At the back door, he nearly collided with Rusty who was carrying a huge jug of water in from the spring. He said, "Set that down and round up all the teenage Bastards."

The idea was to send them out to search for the Queen—Rusty and his sister Kaetie, Caeph, Macae, Naelth, Raenny, Aennie, and Vaence and Viviaen. *How do I remember all their names?* That foreign feeling welled back up.

"Oh no," he said. "Never mind, can't risk it. Too dangerous, I'll do it myself."

Not risk it? What was he saying? Why house and feed these

Bastards if not to risk them? Do it himself? The very concept was as foreign as this feeling of—of what? Responsibility? This damn curse was ruining his life!

Rusty said, "Dewey, what's wrong with you?"

"Get out of here, Bastard."

He went to the alley where he'd last seen her and headed downhill. He checked the marketplace first. The merchants he'd taken advantage of the day before glared, but he couldn't find it within himself to gloat. They seemed almost disappointed. He skirted the pile of brown sand that marked the spot where King Gledig and his heirs died. He went to the harbor and asked if any ships had taken passengers. None had. Of course, the ships that frequented Crescent Cove weren't the sort to share such information.

Dewey feared that he'd missed her, that she must have taken to sea with one of the profiteer ships. Hysterical, he ran up a path that led to the cliffs. The Volunteer frigate *Humaenity* still stood at anchor. The Queen probably walked straight down the hill and into the Volunteer's arms. Why hadn't he warned her?

He walked every street and alley. Someone lay passed out or dead in front of The Crab and Anchor. He went in. No one bothered to look up from their drinks. Serving-lasses and lads wore blank expressions and offered patrons exhausted resignation as a substitute for seduction. No music played, no one danced, and no children, dogs, or even goats cluttered the floor.

He searched the shoreline and the bluffs. Every sleeping seal looked like her corpse. Waves smashed into the rocks and blew salt in his eyes. He turned and ran back through town. At the River Adductor, two flatbed stages were parked at the turning basin, neither had horses in their bridles nor stevedores nearby.

Seals barked from the shoreline. A maermaid splashed in the water below. She winked and flipped her tail at him. A few drops hit his nose, and then she wiggled away.

Dewey blocked the late afternoon sun with his hand and

searched the rocky tide pools and small islands on the other side of the river. An endless faery garden, Faer Reef stretched down the coast for miles. Algae and anemone covered rocks in the shallow breakwater. Waves rolled in, erupting against the rocks in bright white showers that filled a million pools, some as small as your palm, others an acre wide and every color from yellow-tinted green to that color of blue that the night sky achieves hours after sunset on moonless nights. She could be anywhere.

He turned and looked up at The Fist of God: rolling hills that looked like clenched fingers covered with the green grass of spring. Trees grew in the valleys between the fingers. If he didn't find her near the river, then he'd have to search the entire Fist of God, miles of hills, forests, and peaks, even if it took the rest of his life. Knowing that he was obsessed and knowing why he was obsessed did nothing to comfort him.

He passed a man sitting on a raft chewing a piece of grass and dangling his feet in the water. The man tipped his hat and offered a ferry ride across the river. Dewey turned him down and continued walking until he reached the point where The Fist's thumb wrapped over the river. It formed a short tunnel called The Haunted Passage because no barge captain would pass through it at night. Dewey knew better, after all he started the rumor of flesh-eating ghosts on night tides—a joke that a certain family of leprechauns appreciated enough to provide sufficient special effects.

He chuckled to himself and realized that he no longer carried the burden he had seconds ago. He wondered why he hadn't sent the Bastards to do this work. Then, without thinking, removing his coat, or securing his purse, he dove into the river, swam across, stepped up a rock, and walked right up to her. Had the curse seen her? He hadn't.

She lay among sea oats. GloFaeries covered her in a blanket of light flickering in different colors. A thousand faeries rose and swarmed around him in a perfect circle. The wings hummed, "We hope you're not too late." She lay unconscious, sunburned, and caked in sand.

Confidence and his comfortable assumption of superiority returned. To test it, he started away from the Queen. The doubts and shame simmered. He knelt over her and took her hand. Her cold fingers clenched his and her eyes opened.

She looked around and started to cry. She mumbled, "They're gone," or something like that, and let her head fall back in the sand.

"It's okay, Queen Dafina, it will be okay." Her eyes opened again, and he added, "Life might not seem worth living right now. And maybe it's not, but you won't know for sure until you've lived a little longer."

"Leave me alone." She looked around, and a smile tugged at her lips. "The faeries, I didn't know how kind they could be. I can lie here, and they'll let me die, free me of this shame."

"I should have helped you last night. I'm sorry." The apology tasted foreign.

She reached into her dress, around torn, muddy rags—it occurred to Dewey that she could now pass for a peasant—and dug out the two silver ohzees he'd given her. "You can have these back. I forgot to thank you for them."

"No, your majesty, I need you to have them." In the back of his mind, Dewey couldn't believe he'd said it. Nearly pure silver. So close to his hand.

He helped her sit up. She held out her index finger and a row of GloFaeries alighted on it. Dewey took her other hand and pulled her up. "I'm taking you back to the inn."

"I'd prefer to stay here."

He reached one arm around her back and the other under her knees and lifted her. She put her arms around his neck and faeries line-danced along her legs. He said, "I can't leave you here." She looked up, pathetic as a wounded animal. He wanted to end her suffering. "You can stay at The Gold Piece Inn until you feel that your life is worth living or you decide that it's not. And if not, I'll carry you back here, set you down, and let you die. Promise."

She relaxed her head against Dewey's shoulder. He walked along the sandbar until he caught the ferryman's attention. The man poled his raft across the river.

"Aye, Dewey, a trip for two across the Adductor: four copper ohzees."

"You know my name but obviously not who I am. One copper."

"Fearful currents in the Adductor right now and greater risks this time of night."

"Night? The sun is two hours from setting."

"Tell that to the ghosts. Three coppers."

"Uh huh," Dewey set the Queen down. "Last chance for a whole copper ohzee, my offer falls with every lie you tell. We can swim."

"A haunted river, vicious currents—you'd force me to risk my life for two coppers?"

"Half a copper for both of us."

"But Dewey, my fishing boat was ruined in a storm. Pirates stole my wife and made her their slave. My children rely on me. Would you have me fail them?" He listed these woes in an uninspired monotone, like a script often recited but never rewarded. "I can't charge less than two coppers." And then he said the maegic words, "Please help me."

"Your children?" Dewey said.

"Ferryman pay isn't enough to support my boy and two girls." He sniffed and rubbed his eyes, but they were several drops short of a tear. "My son has to work as a rent-boy at the Crab and Anchor and my daughter—"

The words came out of Dewey's mouth unbidden. "I'll pay a silver ohzee."

The ferryman's eyes blossomed. "A silver? Why yes sir, thank you sir. Please, this way, madam." He jumped into the water and bent over so that the Queen could step from the land, onto his back, and to the raft.

Dewey struggled against the words, tried to restrain his mouth and vocal cords, but said, "No, no, I'll pay two silvers, one for each of us." Every syllable abused his self-esteem. His hand reached into his purse, took out the two silvers and gave them to the man. And the worst part of it? The instant those coins left his hand, all the anxiety vanished in a puff of remorse. Gone. The silvers were gone forever. Dewey's eyes welled up. How he'd miss their gentle jingle, the way they shined in the sunlight when he counted them. He even mourned the tarnish they'd never get a chance to experience in the warmth of his purse.

The smile on the ferryman's face was something to behold, but Dewey couldn't. He collapsed onto the raft. The Queen took his hand in hers and said, "That was very kind of you." Dewey curled into himself, mumbling, "I'm ruined. I'll never know profit again. Financial devastation awaits."

The Queen, sand still caked over her sunburn, and GloFaeries dropping from her and drifting back to Faer Reef, comforted Dewey.

The ferryman poled them across the river in a matter of seconds.

Dewey stepped off the raft and waited for the Queen. "Do you think he even has children? Farqin curse better be equipped with a Truth Faery."

The Crying Lady

8.

Once the Queen was safe, Dewey couldn't think of a single reason for protecting her. Sure, she had royalty in her blood, but blood couldn't repay a debt in cash or in kind. She couldn't serve or clean or shovel and, with a body like that—too willowy by half, guests of The Gold Piece Inn preferred stout men and round women.

She straggled along behind, tiptoeing across the cobblestones on scratched, bleeding feet. Pure liability—she'd be recognized, and he'd be dead.

"Listen, Dafina—that's your name, right? If anyone finds out who you are, we're all dead. Everyone, the kids, the servers, you, me, even the animals and faeries. They'll burn everything. So, try not to, uh, try not to act royal. And don't answer to your name. We'll call you, um, Daffy? Sure, we'll call you Daffy, all right? Close enough to your actual name that you can cover when you slip up. Maybe if we dress you like a boy, people will think you're just another kid named Daeffid. Can't spit without hitting a Daeffid around here."

He guided her past the inn's entrance. The smells of spilled ale, fresh bread, roasting goat, and herb smoke wafted out the door.

Either he had to assure her safety, which could be expensive, or he had to get rid of this curse, which seemed impossible. He asked, "You hungry?"

She surrendered to his prodding and walked into the barn. He helped her up the ladder, and she plopped down in that same spot by the window. The screech owl gave her a welcoming hoot. Dewey headed for the inn. He looked back at something he'd never expected to see: a queen sitting in his hay loft. Even with the sand and salt in her hair, she looked regal.

He expected to be dead by sunrise.

9.

Queen Dafina stared at the horizon, over the ocean, in the direction of the Nantesse Isles. Her father had brought her to Glomaythea seven years ago. She remembered how he took her hand and led her off the ship. He told her she had a duty to her people, that she'd been training her entire life to work a king's court, that she was ready.

Her marriage to King Gledig secured an alliance and opened trade routes from the continent to the islands of her home. She met him the day they married. He was the biggest man she'd ever seen. When she walked into the Temple of Maentanglement and saw those long arms and giant hands, she'd worried that he'd break her. She stepped up to the altar, and he looked down at her. His kind face and warm eyes belied his physical prowess. She remembered trying to hide behind her eyelashes.

It hadn't been a faery-book wedding. Though the faer were represented, no spell had wrapped them together in passionate romance. They'd found their way together. He had been so tender that first night, sensitive to how she responded to his caresses. It was when he'd asked her desires that he won her. A whisper of respect that had grown through their time together into a bond of trust and understanding, and love. Oh yes, she'd loved him. And if she were granted one wish, she would speak to him across the divide of quick and dead and thank him for loving her.

She heard a chicken complain and then a goat bleat, followed by steps up the ladder. A woman's face emerged, Loretta, the one with great tangles of crimson hair and full red lips. She carried a bucket and a towel in one hand and a basket that smelled of savory meat and bread in the other, and she climbed that ladder like she'd done it a thousand times a day for a hundred years.

"Oh dear," she said. "Let's get you cleaned up. After you've had some food, you'll feel a world better." She knelt and wiped a damp cloth across her forehead. "I'll help you settle in."

"Thank you, madam, I am Dafi-ee, yes, please call me Daffy."

Loretta reached into the bucket and wrapped a wet towel around her neck. "There you go—better?"

"Somewhat." She looked across the hay loft. Blankets of many sizes and colors lay atop an even layer of straw, a few thin tapestries hung from the rafters. She wondered how long she'd be known as Daffy. "Am I to sleep here?"

"Don't worry, you won't be alone."

"Surely there is a room for me."

"Well, there could be." Loretta looked her over and ran her hands along the dirty rags of Daffy's disguise. "I've never seen so many pieces of cloth sewn together. With all that thread—why not sew the pieces into a proper dress?"

"People sleep here? In this barn with the animals?"

"They keep us warm." Loretta gave her another second glance, the fourth in a continuing series. "Where you from?"

"Nantesse, just visiting."

"Oh. Sure. *Visiting* from Nantesse. Right. Me too." Her eyes narrowed. "Sure, you're not faer? Not even a little?"

"Me? No, I'm not faer." Daffy pulled her hair away from her ears. "See?"

"Then for gods' sakes, eat." Loretta offered her a bowl filled with chunks of roasted goat, a few oysters, and a big crusty roll.

"May I have a fork?"

"A fork. Good one, Daffy. A fork! That's ripe. Nanny and Bill? Be dear goats and fetch the stemware and bone china for Daffy, will you?" Loretta's laugh was big and hearty. Her breasts jiggled and her hips wiggled with every guffaw.

Daffy used the bread to scoop meat and broth. After one bite, her appetite took over, and she ate until she felt like she'd burst.

"You're not gonna finish? You'll need more meat on you to get along here."

Daffy licked her fingers and everything she lost came back to her. She felt dizzy, nauseous, but knew that those feelings didn't come from her loss, they came from the other thing.

"No, I take it back, dear!" Loretta hugged her. "You're a fine lass. You have a special beauty, oh Daffy, please—"

"My babies are gone. My husband ..." Daffy tried to swallow back the sobs, tried to push back the wicked sense of independence. She felt her face crumple, and tears poured down but for all the wrong reasons.

Loretta set her gently on her side, curled into the fetal position, and pulled the blanket around her. She reached under the blanket, brought out a short stick, and nestled it between Daffy's belly and her knees. It felt warm, more like smooth stone than wood, and it had a dozen polished pebbles embedded at the tip and around the rim.

Loretta stroked her face and said, "There, there, love, it'll all be better in the morning."

"In the morning?" Daffy sat straight up. "In the morning, my husband will still be dead. My son and my daughter will still be waiting for their burial—better in the morning?!"

Loretta rubbed her shoulders. "You're safe here and we're a kind group, except for Dewey, but you'll get used to him. He has a certain charm, he's an acquired taste, but you'll be warm and safe here. Anything I can do—"

"My husband, the King of Glomaythea, was assassinated yesterday and tonight I have to sleep in a barn? On straw like some sort of common ..." Daffy looked at Loretta and her rage collapsed into what her mother would call real indignity. She hoped against hope that her words hadn't made sense through her sobs. Daffy had grown up in the luxury of a thousand-year-old castle, slept on feather beds, read the great works of literature, and been taught to respect people and faer at every level of society. As Queen, she'd accepted responsibility for their care and that included caring for their self-worth. "Loretta, please, I'm sorry. I didn't mean ..." but she wasn't sure what she meant.

"The King?" Loretta's eyes widened to the bursting point. She stuttered and stood and backed away and leapt down the ladder.

* * *

Daffy's grief came in waves, sometimes so close it overwhelmed her, other times far off, as if yesterday was a decade past, and she could look forward to a new life free of her royal burdens, but no matter where in the cycle, she felt a tremendous desire to sleep and never wake.

Something fluttered between her knees, and then again. She reached down and pulled out the stick that Loretta had given her. It glowed reddish, nearly pink. When she touched the tip, it throbbed, startling her into tossing it away. It clattered down to the barn floor. A donkey brayed and a rabbit thumped, and a hummingbird flew up, hovered in front of her and chirped before darting out the window.

The sounds of the inn—music and singing, yells of joy and outrage, and laughter, mostly laughter—eventually faded away and people started coming up the ladder. She pulled her blanket tight and listened. At first, she thought they were talking about her, but then she realized that they were children, dozens of children cuddling into bed for the night. Still later, she heard more people climb the stairs, mostly women, but a few men tiptoeing their way to blankets set over the straw. She didn't know how to feel about sharing her bed with so many people, but she knew that she didn't like sleeping with fleas.

10.

Dewey went downstairs early the next morning more surprised than happy to be alive. He took his seat between the fireplace and window. The sunrise revealed a rare spring morning without fog. A seagull landed on the gold piece marquee—a thick wooden disk painted shiny gold with ribbed edges that hung from a chain over the entrance to the inn. It started swinging, and the seagull flew off. Dewey thought he saw a scroll on its leg, but that was impossible. Kaetie had just sent the messages yesterday.

Serving-lasses prodded their sleepy children into doing their morning chores. Soon the inn had a fresh layer of sawdust and straw across the floor, the fixtures were polished, and tables scrubbed. Normally, Dewey would take pleasure in criticizing their efforts. Pots and pans clanked onto the stove over the great kitchen fire and soon the smells of baking bread, burning butter, and simmering bacon made their way to Dewey. Normally, he'd pop into the kitchen to claim the finest rasher of bacon for himself. Out beyond the barn, the teenage Bastards weeded, planted, harvested, or carried huge clay jugs of fresh water in from the spring. Others raked the spring's sandy filter and sang to the Water Faeries. Normally, he'd provide advice for discriminating between ripe and rotten fruit and techniques for preventing the sweetest water in Crescent Cove from sloshing onto his floor. Normally, but today a royal pain in his arse was asleep in his barn.

Something bounced against Dewey's window—the damn seagull. And it carried a message.

Dewey went outside. The seagull held out his leg and Dewey took the message. With the Messenger Faery detached, the seagull took off. Dewey palmed the little scroll and looked both ways. Four fishers and a hunter had just come in from the bunkhouse. The serving-lass Laelith set steaming plates at a table for them. No one gave Dewey a second glance. He wondered how long he'd have to question the loyalties of every person he passed.

Profit motive forced a smile on his face, and he paused at the table to report the times of ship departures and weather conditions. He finished with, "The Gold Piece Inn is known as the place 'where great quests begin' because we get sailors to their ships, trappers to their forests, profiteers to their treasure, and heroes to their dragons on time, every day." The men, mouths now full, responded with appropriate amusement and Dewey beelined to his chair.

His back to the room, he unrolled the scroll: "The usurper is sending a thousand Volunteers to Crescent Cove ..." the rest was covered in seagull droppings. Kaetie needed to learn the finer points of Messenger Faery enchantment.

A thousand Volunteers? To search for the Queen and the King's Wizard? A would-be king who took things that personally soured Dewey's stomach—or maybe it was the curse. Everything felt unsettled.

Loretta shot down the red velvet stairs, her red curls bouncing in every direction, and stopped in front of Dewey, hands on her hips and finger pointing. "Keep her away from my kids!"

Why would Lukas waste a thousand troops on an outlaw port? Dewey knew it was too soon to guess. He could barely see his own cards, much less predict Lukas's hand. He looked up into the dragon-lady's flames. "Who? What are you talking about?"

"Don't play dumb with me, Dewey Nawton. What's she doing here?"

"It's complicated. Get used to it."

"I will not." She stomped her foot with each word. "Do you know who she is?" Her face now matched her hair.

"We're stuck with her," Dewey said, and then, more to himself than to her, "If we play it right, it could pay off long term."

"Not for me, it won't. Get her out of here. If you're that smitten, she can stay with Lylli. Far away from us."

An obvious idea, he wondered why it hadn't occurred to him. Blame it on the curse? Lylli's cottage was in a redwood forest between the ring and middle fingers of The Fist of God. "Nope."

Loretta started to shake. With her hair so disheveled, it looked like her head could spin right off. One of the things Dewey liked most about humans was their ability to release great torrents of emotion for almost any slight, perceived or real, and Loretta had the temper of a dozen savages.

She turned to storm off but got caught between her temper and her guest. She forced a grin and held out her hand. The man kissed it and then put something in it. Her girlish giggle came out as an irritated cough. He wore the felt cape and wool breeches of a merchant from the northlands.

"Good morning, sir," Dewey said. "Please take a seat." He indicated a chair next to the window, in front of his own. Loretta disappeared through the kitchen door.

"I have to be off, though I'll compliment you on a wonderful evening, excellent food and spirits and such special companionship."

"Just a quick word and we'll have you fed and on your way in plenty of time—are you sailing today?"

The man dropped into the chair known to those who lived here as Dewey's hot seat. The smile still plastered on his face, he reached into a vest pocket and gave Dewey half a gold ohzee. "I would live here!"

"Kind of you to say, mister …?"

A raven caught Dewey's attention. It swooped down and perched on a gargoyle's tongue. He ran outside. It dropped to the porch and held out its leg. Dewey took the message.

The merchant stepped out and said, "I really must be going."

"I'll be right there, please go back in and sit down." Dewey looked at the message and recognized Jaenet's perfect script. She was a Bastard who'd left The Gold Piece Inn a decade ago. Last he'd heard, she'd joined the Royal Guard. The message confirmed that a thousand troops were indeed on their way to "quell any hint of rebellion," the words "any hint" were underlined. It continued: "and protect hard-working humans from faer tyranny."

Faer tyranny? The faer could be tricky and if mistreated a bit malicious—but tyranny?

The man said, "Good day," and stepped off the porch.

As if reading his thoughts—and he probably was—Dewey's Truth Faery emerged from the windowsill behind the merchant. The little fellow yawned and straightened his hat. The sight warmed the mostly frozen cockles of Dewey's heart.

Dewey tucked the message into his belt. "That's a shame, good sir. If I can't speak with you, I'm afraid you can't visit Loretta again, a safety precaution, you understand, but if it's more important to—"

"Not see Loretta?" He stepped back into the inn and sat in the hot seat.

Dewey returned to his chair. The message felt like it was burning his side, but business was business.

As usual, the man tried to avoid sharing his name and title. Hovering behind him, the Truth Faery tapped his tiny wand on the man's forehead.

The man eventually identified himself as the first son of the second daughter of a noble land-owning family, which made it conceivable that the fellow could inherit a minor barony. The Truth Faery confirmed the validity of most of the claims. When the semi-minor Baron left, Dewey rubbed his Truth Faery's little belly and gave him a tiny ruby grain.

Then he took out the message. Written on actual vellum, not the crappy paper he'd sent, and returned by raven in half a day. "Quell any hint of rebellion" was standard usurper policy, but "protect hard-working humans from faer tyranny"? He looked at a Monitor Faery up on the balustrade and saw a Grain Faery weaving splinters back into a redwood beam. Protect them from what? Could a sane man prefer a world without faeries? No way to test lies or cheats? *Okay, there could be an upside.* Without Spring Faeries, you couldn't trust the water and without the ignoble Farq Faeries— he shuddered and dismissed the vile thought.

He stepped over a sheepdog snoozing in a patch of sunlight, around two children playing in an imaginary port they'd sketched in the floor's sawdust, and into his office. He tossed a piece of quartz to a Hinge Faery, effectively locking the door, set the message with the others and then removed the false wall-panel and crawled into his sanctuary. Turning to a blank page in the huge leather-bound, gilt-edged book, he dipped a quill in ink and recorded Loretta's name, the name of her semi-noble guest, a description of his position and holdings, and then, on the last line, wrote the date, nine months from today, and circled it.

He then crawled back through the passage, reset the panel, nodded to the Hinge Faery who let the door open a crack, and began composing messages of a more tactical than information-gathering nature than those he sent yesterday.

11.

Daffy fought a demon away from her husband's corpse. She cried out at the sight of him lying there, eyes open, staring at her, and pleading with her to go forward without him. Her own cry woke her. She struggled to sit up, but a weight held her down. Tiny hooves dug into her belly and the devil's eyes—brown orbs with rectangular pupils—bored into her guilt-ridden soul. She gasped and, when she exhaled, a piece of straw poked her nose and then disappeared into the baby goat's mouth. Its jaw ground from left to right and back. It swallowed and nestled into her lap, warm and soft.

She almost laughed. Gledig would love the story of her waking to a devil. And then it all came back to her. Never again would she share a funny story with Gledig. She'd never hear his laughter again—except, maybe, in heaven. She pictured The King of Glomaythea on hands and knees with a tiny wooden bunny hopping from one child to the other. *Anything to be with you again.*

The peaceful crunching sounds of goats on the barn floor, punctuated by the occasional bleat, helped calm her from the dream. Hens cackled, and a dog snored. She scratched her ankles, behind her neck, sat up and found welts across her torso.

Two teenagers approached her from across the loft.

The lass said, "Who are you?" On the cusp between child and woman, she had dark auburn hair and light olive skin with six perfectly placed freckles.

The lad spoke in a man's voice. "What happened to your Sleep Faery?" He was a year or two older than the lass and had the same complexion but no freckles. He was long and thin but filling out.

Daffy said, "My what?" And scratched a series of bites on her shoulder.

The lass said, "It's down on the floor." She scurried down the ladder.

The lad dropped to a knee and said, "Who are you?"

"I'm Dafi-ee, Daffy."

"I'm Rusty, this is my sister Kaetie. You're new here, already have children or …?

"Yes, I do." And it came back to her. "I had a girl and a boy, but they're gone."

"Well, if Dewey's already got them working the field, I better help 'em. He won't show them what to do, and then he's just gonna yell at them for doing it wrong." He started to stand back up.

"The field? No, my children—" She tried not to whimper. "They're gone, passed over." She hugged the warm little goat.

"Oh, I'm sorry." He dropped to both knees, held out a hand in a motion so natural and sincere that she gave him her hand without a thought. "That's harsh, if there's anything you need, if Dewey gets on you or …"

Kaetie shimmied up the ladder holding the stick that Loretta had given Daffy last night. She recalled thinking it had seemed possessed. In the light of day, it was just a smooth wooden stick with polished pebbles decorating one end. It no longer glowed or vibrated.

Kaetie said, "It's empty."

Rusty said, "What did you do to your Sleep Faery?"

"My what?"

"It was a hummer," Kaetie said. "The nubs buzz too much for me, but my mom likes them."

"The What Faery?"

"Not a What Faery, a Sleep Faery." Kaetie looked at her as though she was an idiot. "Sleep Faeries protect you at night from bugs and wake you if there's danger, like a fire, and they keep goats and cats from lying on top of you."

* * *

Kaetie knew everyone who lived and worked at The Gold Piece Inn. She took pride in knowing something about them, too. "You came here the other night, didn't you?" She lifted the blanket and looked at Daffy's feet.

"And who are you?" Daffy made the sort of indulgent, condescending smile that infuriated Kaetie.

Kaetie stared back, silent burn.

Blechk

12.

D ewey set the messages on his desk the way he'd deal a hand of cards. He needed dirt on Lukas and the principal players in his coup, he needed to alert his network, and he needed to repel Lukas's focus from Crescent Cove. He dipped the nib of his quill and started a rumor that the Queen had boarded a ship home to Nantesse. He dealt it to his left, in the pile for Aenzio.

His office door was open so he could monitor the inn. He looked up and saw Kaetie and Rusty leading the Queen between them. She looked pale, even with her sunburn. Dewey basked in the irony of a queen being led by the Bastard children of a Gold Piece Inn serving-lass.

"We found her," Rusty said. "She's in a sad state."

"She scared the crap out of her Sleep Faery," Kaetie said. "The bugs got her."

"Have a seat." He motioned the Queen to a chair. "You two," he pointed at Rusty and then narrowed his eyes at Kaetie, "find something useful to do."

They slipped out of the office, grabbed cleaning cloths, and rubbed the redwood frame of the office door.

Loretta came out of the kitchen and glared at Dewey.

Kaetie said, "She scared the crap out of your extra Sleep Faery."

"What?" Loretta said.

Daffy turned in her chair. "I didn't know what it was."

"The pink one?"

"She wrecked it," Rusty said. "The faery left."

"Daffy," Dewey said, "it's important that you be kind to the faer. I have few rules here …"

Loretta scoffed.

"… and taking care of the house faer is right up there beneath profitize, monetize, waste not—" Dewey leaned forward. The Queen sat rigid, her eyes red and crusty. *A thousand Volunteers, I gotta get rid of her*—but that thought collided with the curse and exploded into fear.

She wiped an eye with a trembling hand.

Now standing behind her, Loretta mouthed, "Get her out of here!"

Rusty brought a wet towel. "She's not well, Dewey." He wiped her brow. "She needs Lylli's help."

"All right," Dewey said. "I want Lylli here at the inn, anyway."

Kaetie said, "I'll fetch her."

Something caught his eye, up in the rafters by the chandelier—a dove with a message wrapped around its leg. The damn cat was closing in. "Kaetie? Did you send any messages by dove?"

"No." She curled her lip into her not-at-all charming sneer.

"What birds did you use?"

"Seagulls, robins, and that mean raven—the ones you told me to use. If they didn't get there, it's not my fault. I've never enchanted a faery before. Why are you such a—"

"You're sure you didn't confuse a pigeon for a dove?"

"A pigeon and a dove? I'm not stupid, Dewey."

"Uh oh." Dewey tried to swallow the lump rising in his throat.

He rushed out of his office, held out a finger, and the dove swooped down. This message had been written in the last hour and came from a shepherd who lived on God's Thumb over the River Adductor where he had a clear view of barges from Glomaythea. A train of them were coming, each one packed with red and black clad Volunteers.

"Uh oh," Dewey repeated.

He checked the angle of the sun. They'd missed the tide and

come anyway? They'd have to row against the current. The thing Dewey hated about humans was the other side of what he liked about them: their passion made them erratic.

The others followed him outside. Loretta said, "Daffy has to go to Lylli's cottage."

"What?" Dewey said. He processed the words and the damn curse spoke for him. "No, she's staying here where I can protect her."

"She can't stay here! You have to protect *us*."

He bent down to Kaetie's level. "Tell Lylli that we have a lass suffering melancholia and despair. And don't lollygag in the hills."

Kaetie said, "I'm on my way."

Loretta grabbed her. "If you see any faeries, leave them be. Don't pester no elfs and don't believe anything leprechauns say."

Dewey grabbed a knit hat from a rack by the door on his way out.

13.

Dewey hurried down the hill.

What is Lukas's angle? A bunch of humans complaining about the faer over drinks is one thing, but if you upset the faer, your luck goes to hell. What is his game?

Just before he got to the marketplace, he heard the familiar wood-on-wood impact of a barge meeting the wharf down at the river turning basin. Ahead of him, sidestepping a mule-pulled wagon, he saw Spaedlie in a crisp new Volunteer uniform, black leather coat over a coarse white cotton shirt with crimson pants and black boots. A few others from the shipping guild accompanied her, all of them Gold Piece Inn regulars wearing new Volunteer uniforms. Buyers, sellers, and beggars all gave them a wide berth.

Spaedlie stopped and waited for him on the wharf near the pier where dozens had gathered.

"Oh, Dewey. Dewey the halfling." She had a condescending smile.

"Spaedlie," Dewey said. He made a point of looking at her uniform. "You're making a bad bet."

"No Dewey, I'm all in and can't lose—Lukas and I grew up together, you know." She spoke with mock-reverence, "My childhood friend is The First Human, and he's coming to appoint me governor." She ruffled one of the gold epaulets on her shoulders, features of her uniform that the other Volunteers lacked. "It will be my responsibility to protect all lands in view of The Fist of God from the disease of immortals."

"Sure, we've all seen how well it goes for humans who bet against the faer."

"Which is exactly why we need Lukas. The damn things—nothing personal of course—"

"Of course."

"—damn things need to be put in their place. We own this land, hardworking humans who are willing to sweat, willing to get the job done."

"Uh, huh. Not very convincing. What's in it for you? Give me enough to believe you haven't gone stark raving."

She stepped away from the others. "Listen closely. We can coexist." She had that cocky look that card players get when they're playing either a royal flush or a colossal bluff. "I'll need monthly reports, you help me track the faer, and I'll overlook your funny ears."

Dewey spit on the cobblestones.

"Come now, Dewey—we've always haggled our way to a bargain," she said, sincere now, his longtime colleague, if not his friend. "I'll take care of Crescent Cove."

Dewey knew Spaedlie to be competitive, greedy, bombastic, arrogant, and in every way infuriating, but he also knew her to keep her word. He whispered, "And the faer?"

Four Volunteers in worn-in uniforms passed by. She winked at him and then spoke at full volume, "Have you finally admitted that I always get the better deal?"

"Once. You got me to pay full retail once." Dewey spoke just as loud, playing along. "Since then I've owned you." Lukas scared him. He couldn't deny it, at least not to himself. Spaedlie would be a fair governor. Fair from her perspective, anyway, and since Dewey knew her, she would be predictable. The devil you know.

The Volunteers passed, and she switched back to low volume. "I'll have a budget. You'll have information and I'll be happy to pay. Keep that hat over your ears, learn how to behave, and we'll do just fine."

She got Dewey's attention with the word "pay." The thought of being paid for information that he could curate to suit his own aims might be something he could live with. Indeed, the thought of being paid and perhaps profiting from this surely short-lived rebellion resounded with the thought of being paid. But then he looked at her and felt intense disgust. Even if you ignored the inevitable bad luck, what kind of idiot would want to live without faeries? He could do without elfs just as they'd always been happy to do without him, and he didn't care a wit about leprechauns, but he loved his Card Faery, and his Truth Faery was his best friend. Still, being paid sounded good, too.

He heard a rhythmic pounding from the river, almost a drumbeat. A figure in a black uniform with a red sash across his swollen stomach led hundreds of troops wearing red and black Volunteer uniforms with tricorn hats, genuine steel swords at their hips, and crossbows slung across their backs in a perfect ten-man-wide column.

Spaedlie said, "We'll talk," and rejoined her Volunteer cohorts.

Facing an entire army of anti-faer fanatics, Dewey made sure that his hat covered his ears. He backed away, up to the marketplace. From the safety of the crowd, he zeroed in on the officer in the red sash. A short, wide fellow with a mop of misbehaving curls, he stopped at the pier and the soldiers continued marching past him.

Dewey knew that this was not Lukas of Glomae. The officer obviously had expensive appetites and Dewey felt a profit coming on. Once he determined those appetites, he could manipulate them. Add that to Spaedlie paying him to control the information relayed to Lukas, and things might not be so bad. As long as he could keep his ears covered and protect his faery friends—*no, it's trouble, nothing but trouble. An ill-boder is right.*

The soldiers came to a stop and the sound of their boots echoed across the cove. They stood at attention, lining the entire wharf, from the river at one end to the bluffs at the other, centered at the pier.

Dewey followed the direction of the officer's gaze and saw a low-slung, three-mast ship entering the cove at an unheard-of speed keeling into the wind. It had the stern of a schooner but the rigging of a clipper. The entire ship cleared a swell, exposing its smooth hull and sharp keel—no wonder it was so fast. The Flying Anvil flew at the stern, its edges already shredding in the wind. When it looked certain to collide with the pier, the pilot pulled the rudder, the crew dropped the sails, and a dozen Volunteers leapt ashore to tie her down.

Trumpeters blew a fanfare, and a man stepped from the ship to the pier. He waved his hat to the still-growing crowd and, even from here, Dewey could sense his charisma. He walked without guards, just one man in a perfectly tailored Volunteer uniform, greeting sailors and dockworkers like they were old buddies. He spoke to a fisher who had been cleaning a halibut, and she laughed—Codae, laughing with the man she'd scorned the day before.

When he reached the wharf, the row of soldiers at the end of the pier snapped their heels and turned to face the crowd gathered at the marketplace above them. The next row snapped their heels and rotated and so on, like dominos.

This was Lukas of Glomae. The officer with the red sash over his belly saluted, but Lukas was busy chatting with the troops. He continued along the wharf.

Dewey counted and sure enough, a hundred rows, each with ten Volunteers. A thousand troops, far more than necessary to occupy a rural port, but then it came to him. Crescent Cove had a huge faer population. Faer Reef was home to thousands, perhaps millions of faeries. The situation just kept getting worse. Dewey had to find a wildcard.

He spotted Spaedlie positioning herself in Lukas's path. She gave him a sharp salute. Lukas returned the salute and continued forward, but stopped, stepped back, and hugged her. She walked along with him for a few strides but lost his attention to his troops. Dewey spent a lot of time trying to see the world through human eyes. He wasn't sure, but it seemed like Lukas had played Spaedlie perfectly. By acting surprised to see her, he'd denied any commitment to appointing her to an official position, but by hugging her, he'd solidified her as an ally—pure profit at no cost. Dewey nearly swooned in admiration for Lukas.

Back where the wharf and pier met, soldiers had assembled a stage and were raising Flying Anvil flags at each corner.

Spaedlie moved to the opposite side of the stage as the officer with the red sash. Dewey could see that she was seething and took a moment to enjoy her discomfort.

Lukas strolled to each end of the thousand-strong column of Volunteers. To all appearances, he made a friend of each one. By the time he approached the stage, the marketplace above it was packed.

The trumpeters blew another salute. The thousand Volunteers stepped forward, their boots in unison, clapping the crowd to quiet.

Lukas drew his broadsword, and it shone like polished silver—the famous hardened Maekhane steel. He raised it in salute to his troops, as if dubbing them all knights. Then he hopped up on the stage, a natural athlete comfortable with this crowd of new friends.

Four Volunteers joined Spaedlie at the side of the stage. Their uniforms weren't as fresh as the others. Dewey recognized them, the King's executioners.

Speaking in a deep, far reaching voice, Lukas said, "I'm here to spread the good news." He paused, and a few people in the shipping and smithy guilds cheered. "The days of the faer sucking the life out of humanity have ended!" The soldiers' provided a synchronized ovation, joined by applause from those same guilds. Most people stood silently, but they were all listening. Lukas raised an eyebrow at the rest of the crowd but didn't lose the warmth in his smile. "Not to worry. We're all in this together."

If I had a smile like that, I could rule the world.

Lukas took a piece of parchment from his pocket and switched to a more formal address. "I'm giving you a new beginning, a chance to show what you're made of. You're finally free. Let the faer hide in their holes while we humans stand tall in the sun!" He presented a rosy future where humans pulled their own weight without relying on the faer. Dewey watched the humans take it in. Had they forgotten what it was like before Maentanglement? Had they no understanding of how the faer held the world together? He could see it in their faces. Of course, they'd forgotten. Everyone who had fought for the peace and prosperity of Maentanglement was long dead. These people had no idea what life was like two hundred years ago, but Dewey did, and he didn't want to go back. No one on any side of those battles wanted to go back. *Short-lived idiots.*

Lukas gave the impression of a man in a hurry, available but busy. His speech was brief. He put the parchment in a pocket and said, "I need you to do something for me. I'm looking for Queen

Dafina."

Dewey's legs felt weak.

"The Queen can help us. I'm sure that you don't need encouragement, but I recently came into some extra cash." The comment brought scattered laughter. "I'll give you a hundred gold pieces if you can tell me where she is. Do not hurt her, just let us know where she is. I need to talk to her, alive and healthy. After what happened to the King, I'm sure that she's frightened, but she has nothing to fear from me. Not one, not a single human being has anything to fear from me—if they put humans first. I'm off to spread the good news, but I'm leaving you in the care of someone that I trust to lead you in our worthy but challenging mission." He cocked his head toward Faer Reef as if to show from where the challenge would come. "Let me introduce the new governor of Crescent Cove." He reached into his pocket and pulled the parchment back out.

Spaedlie started up to the stage.

Reading from the parchment, Lukas announced, "Major Finaeus Blechk is here to serve as Military Commander and shall enforce my will." He waved his hat again and two soldiers helped the short, wide man in the black uniform with red sash onto the stage. Lukas hopped off the stage, shook hands with everyone nearby and jogged up the pier. Spaedlie managed to reach him and he stopped, leaned in, and said a few words to her. She turned back to the stage and Lukas made his way to his ship.

Blechk pulled a scroll from his vest and read, "Lukas will be known for a thousand years as the Great Liberator of humanity, the First Human to ascend to greatness. As governor of Crescent Clove, I will not tolerate resistance to the Liberator's generosity." One soldier said something, and he looked back at the scroll. "Cove, Crescent *Cove*." He chortled at his error, cleared his throat, and spoke in a bored monotone. "Citizens shall provide all information of the faer to the governor: breed, location, species, and race of both low and high faer. Withholding or concealing such information will be punishable by execution." He kept glancing back down the pier where Lukas's ship already had its sails raised. "We will divorce our lives from dependence on the faer. They are to be left to their own devices, whether the lowest GloFaery or a thousand-year-old elf, we discourage fraternization." He looked up from the scroll and added, "But it's not punishable by execution," in a way that indicated he thought it should be. He rolled the scroll up and tucked it back in. "You have now been informed of the law throughout Glomaythea effective two days ago on the fifty-seventh day of spring." He had a look of anticipation, as though he'd just done everyone a favor and expected thanks. "Simple enough?"

He looked back and watched Lukas's ship catch the wind.

The marketplace resumed business. Dewey checked his cap and worked his way down to the pier. At first, he avoided the Volunteers, but then he saw how young they were. Probably the first time they'd ever been away from home, probably be open to some laughs, a good meal, perhaps a hand of cards, and they might have a few extra ohzees to spend.

He watched Spaedlie approach Blechk the way she would a profiteer who hadn't paid his guild dues, calling him by name, demanding recognition and respect: "... said you're the *military* commander but I'm the *governor* of Crescent Cove. I'll govern trade, shipping, tax collection ..."

Blechk had his eyes set on the ship, watching it gain speed.

"... you'll report your findings on the faer to me and I'll do the record keeping. Do you understand?"

Blechk turned to her the instant that Lukas and his ship disappeared around the point.

"Well?" Spaedlie said. "Do you understand, or do I need a written order from my *close friend* Lukas?"

"I have a close friend, too," Blechk said. He reached into his boot, took out a dagger and rammed it into Spaedlie's chest. "His name is death."

She fell slowly, the dagger stuck between her ribs, and brought Blechk down on top of her. The four seasoned Volunteers helped Blechk up. One of them pulled the dagger out. Spaedlie lay there, eyes still open, never to close. Blechk wiped her blood from his blade on that red sash.

He turned to walk away. No one stopped him. He seemed to be the only one moving. Everyone had seen what happened. Everyone knew that Blechk would answer to no one.

Dewey stumbled up Reye's street, trying to comprehend what had happened. Spaedlie dead. Such short-lived creatures, but they had a way of getting under your skin. A sharp woman with unrelenting greed—a kindred soul. Dewey would miss her. Thoughts of revenge bubbled up. Major Finaeus Blechk, Dewey didn't recall the name. He'd check and, if he had no record of the Major, he would soon.

Dewey took the long way up Reye's Street instead of the alley where he'd been cursed.

It didn't help.

Thousands of tiny faeries swarmed around him, singing, serenading him into a daze. Visions of the past and future swarmed in and out of focus. The peace and joy that the faer had brought to Glomaythea since Maentanglement, the vision of Blechk murdering Spaedlie, and back, and forward until he saw how the delicate interdependence of mutual favors between human and faer would be destroyed. The warmth of the faeries held him in a maternal embrace. Their wings painted pastel shades in soft light of every color, and they sang a melody of hope, the cosmic hug of a faer hive.

And then, with Dewey all but hypnotized, that melody took on lyrics: "Will you help us, Dewey Nawton?"

"You little farqs! You're overreacting. He just wants you to register. No harm in that."

The warmth of the faery swarm went cold, and they sang, "He's coming to take us away."

Dewey responded as though the swarm was composed of bees and each one had planted a stinger in his thin halfling hide, "Will the suffering of this curse never end?"

Kaetie

14.

Kaetie walked along the bank of Knuckle Creek toward Lylli's cottage. This time of year, it was more river than creek. Hundreds of streams drained into it from The Fist of God. Like every spring she could remember, the bridge was washed out, and she swam across rather than take the long way to a hand-drawn ferry. The riveting cold felt like freedom against her skin, freedom from the oppression of Dewey and his chores and the constant wrangling of her mother.

She didn't notice the fuss down by the harbor until she was squeezing water out of her clothes. Cries and shouts came up from the marketplace on the tail of an ocean breeze. But that's not what caught her attention. Looking back at The Gold Piece Inn, she saw faeries floating in sunlight. Faeries from the harbor, The Fist, the bluffs, and Faer Reef fluttering toward the inn.

She shrugged it off in favor of the freedom of being alone on a trail in an oak forest. She peeked around corners, hoping to spot an elf or unicorn and hoping not to see a bear or lion, and saw swarms of Grass and Leaf Faeries floating on breezes in the opposite direction. As she climbed to higher, cooler elevations, the oaks blended with redwoods. She took the long way around Sempervaereen, the ten-thousand-year-old redwood Tree Faery who claimed the valley as her own. Kaetie liked the feel and smell of the soft redwood-needle carpet that surrounded Sempervaereen and loved the songs of the Redwood Faeries who cared for her, but Sempervaereen told stories that could take weeks, better to go around than risk offending her by spurning a story.

Another mile uphill, she rounded a sharp granite slab that poked straight up from the ground, and heard bees, frogs, and songbirds all in harmony with what sounded like popping bubbles that provided the song's percussion. In the thick of the forest, nestled at the top of the valley where the ring and middle fingers joined, she approached an A-frame cottage built of stone. The mossy slate roof sloped down, almost to the ground. Eaves emerged on both sides. Wisps of pink smoke curled out of the chimney, and the entire forest smelled like peppermint.

A shimmering rainbow disappeared into a window above the door. Kaetie couldn't decide between being quiet to avoid interrupting, or being loud, so she didn't startle Lylli in the middle of a difficult spell. She stood at the door, unsure if she should knock or wait.

And then the door opened.

A small woman in a smudged bonnet and apron danced out and said, "A child for my cauldron?" She had big hazel eyes that nearly closed when she smiled.

Kaetie stepped into her open arms. Lylli hugged her tight and then walked around her, stroked her hair, pinched her cheek, and poked her ribs. "Not a child at all—you're nearly a woman." Lylli kissed the tip of her nose and tapped her chin with a finger. "You're growing up much too fast. Fortunately, I have a potion for that."

Kaetie didn't know how to respond. Her store of sarcasm felt out of place.

Lylli guided Kaetie across the threshold. The wooden door matched the curves of the stone walls. They walked into a room lined with bookcases packed with both leather-bound books and pyramid-shaped piles of scrolls. A low table cut from a tree trunk had a crystal ball at its center.

A series of extra loud pops drew Lylli to the kitchen. She wore pointy-toed boots and seemed to glide across the floor. Kaetie had never worn shoes. Lylli called back, "I've got a stew simmering, but first I have to—uh oh!"

Kaetie ran her hand along the spines of books and peered into the crystal ball. Her own life felt so dreary. Her mother had it all laid out: Gold Piece Inn serving-lass until she could catch a petty nobleman and then die of boredom. Dewey's plans for her were no less tedious—faery gardener, merchant, or pirate. Kaetie wanted to be like Lylli: a druid who studied whatever fascinated her, enchanted faeries, and didn't have to deal with the boring people of Crescent Cove.

She stepped onto the kitchen's bare slate floor and Lylli took her hand. A cloud of peppermint steam enshrouded her. The fireplace was a stone cavern that included a system of rotisseries and skewers. A huge iron cauldron sat directly on the coals. Clear, viscous oil boiled in it; each bubble worked its way up through the viscous fluid and popped.

Lylli set a dish with steaming vegetable and root stew, a pot of spicy herb tea, and a plate of honey-drenched peppermint scones. They sat on opposite sides of a flat stone that stuck out of the wall.

"What brings you here, my dear?"

Instead of answering, Kaetie asked how she coerced oil from peppermint leaves. Lylli described the process from leaf to oil, gel, lozenges, sticks, candles, and soap. She explained its uses from gas cramps to bad breath to feeding Mosquito Wrangling Faeries. For once in her life, Kaetie felt that someone appreciated her curiosity. But then Kaetie noticed that Lylli's earlobes came to a point.

"You're an elf." She meant it as a question, but it flopped out like a confession of her own inadequacy.

Lylli said, "Not quite." She pulled off her bonnet and held her hair away from her ears. They were the size of human ears and mostly round but narrowed to a point at the tips. "I'm a quarterling. My father, Dewey, is a halfling and my mother was human." And then, as though she'd read Kaetie's mind, she added, "Kaetie, most druids are human. It takes decades of reading and study. When you're old enough, I'll take you as an apprentice, if you want, but first, please tell me what brings you here? Is everything all right at the inn?"

"Dewey's going crazy sending messages, and we didn't have enough Messenger Faeries."

"Why so many messages? Is he up to something?"

"Well, he's always up to *something*."

"What is it this time?"

"Like I said, we ran out of Messenger Faeries and there's this beggar—"

"Why so many messages?"

"Fortunately, I figured out how to enchant Messenger Faeries, so he didn't freak out."

"You figured it out?" Lylli leaned forward. "Kaetie, where did you learn thaergy?"

"I just sang the same thing that you do. And it worked!"

"Kaetie, you shouldn't fake maegic. You don't understand what can go wrong. Come to me or seek Paetel, the faer gardener, she has a shop at the end of Faer Street."

Kaetie sat lower in her chair, staring at a scratch in the stone table. "I didn't fake it."

"You sang to them without knowing the song."

"Maybe I'm a natural? Did you think of that?"

"Did the birds deliver the messages?"

"I guess. If they didn't, Dewey'd have me out in a field with a shovel."

Lylli stared at Kaetie for a few seconds.

Kaetie gathered the dishes.

"Leave them," Lylli said. "Come into my lab and let's train some Messenger Faeries." She stopped at her cauldron, stirred the even thicker liquid, and then led Kaetie into a room on the opposite side of the fireplace. The walls were lined with jars of herbs, two aquariums, piles of stones, crystals, and a long, moss-covered branch. Lylli hummed a few notes and a chorus line of Stem Faeries fluttered up from the moss. Lylli had Kaetie repeat the process several times and explained the lyrics of the song, a simple sonnet of awakening.

When they finished, Kaetie walked around the bench, pointing at Lylli's equipment and supplies. "I want to know all of this. Everything."

"Now, tell me what my father is up to with all of these messages—and a beggar? Could it have been an elf? Perhaps a thief on the run? A gambler? Pirate?"

"Your father?"

"Yes, Dewey."

"It's hard to think of him that way." Kaetie found a crystal pyramid embedded with a little old man bent over a cane with wings suspended. "Seriously, I want to know everything."

"Everything?" Lylli scurried into the front room. "I have just what you need, but then you're going to tell me about the messages and the beggar." She returned with a leather-bound book of at least a thousand pages. "This is the history of the world according to a five-thousand-year-old elf named Quercus. It's as close to *everything* as you can get in one volume."

Kaetie took the book. It weighed as much as a water jug. She couldn't bring herself to admit that she couldn't read, and that feeling came back: just another Gold Piece Inn Bastard, destined to be a serving-lass.

"Now," Lylli said, "tell me about the messages and this beggar."

"Her name is Daffy, really pale, like she's never stepped outside, and she looks like she's starving except that, well, she isn't." She described how Daffy arrived at the inn. "She cries a lot and her kids are dead, and my mom says that she'd suck as a serving wench, so she doesn't know why Dewey even lets her stay there unless he's hot for her or something."

"Is she hurt or sick?"

"Oh, yeah, melancholia and despair—whatever that means."

"It can be very serious, but I can help her."

"Dewey said that he wants you to stay at the inn."

"Why?"

"Everyone's freaking out about the King getting assassinated in the marketplace."

"What?!"

Kaetie reported an exaggerated version that she'd overheard in the saloon. "And then the Wizard conjured a Pegasus and flew away with Queen Dafina!"

"King Gledig?" Lylli stood, all traces of her relaxed nature gone. "There's only an hour of daylight—why didn't you tell me?"

"I just did."

"Oh, Kaetie. Your next lesson is how to set priorities. We'll cover that on our way down the mountain. But we'll have to wait until dawn."

Kaetie liked the serious version of Lylli even more than she liked the light-hearted version. Lylli kept her on her toes, stirring this, pouring that into there, packing herbs, lozenges, powders, tubes, diaphragms, and lenses into baskets and bags.

Kaetie slept on a cushion with her new book at her side. She wondered how the letters could combine into descriptions of the world as it was and as it might be—a maegic all its own. She'd figure it out, she promised herself.

Lylli roused her well before any hint of sunlight emerged over The Fist. Kaetie closed the shutters and reminded the Monitor Faeries to pay attention. They packed Lylli's small donkey until he started complaining and then made their way down the same path that Kaetie had taken up. Kaetie hugged that book to her chest, protecting it from the fog. When they emerged from the valley onto the rolling hill that was The Fist of God's middle finger, they saw more faeries floating toward the inn. Kaetie told Lylli what she'd observed the day before, and Lylli's brow furrowed.

Lylli told Kaetie to stand still and silent and then hummed a few notes. A faery landed on her finger, a tiny woman in a red coat carrying an even tinier suitcase. Lylli and the faery stared at each other for a few seconds, and then Lylli blew the little faery on her way.

She wrapped her arms around Kaetie. "Oh dear, you might have to grow up fast."

15.

Dewey paced a rut in The Gold Piece Inn's front porch. He couldn't believe Spaedlie was dead. She was an ornery woman with a talent for annoying him, but she didn't deserve a knife between the ribs. And in one day, Blechk had already taken her position as master of the shipping guild. At this rate, he'd hold every position of power in town. Either Dewey would have to work with him or— *no, I'll find a way around him. He will not profit from me or mine.*

A cloud of tiny GloFaeries woke him from that worry and alerted him to the next. Faeries were flying toward his inn from every direction. So far, just the tiny lower faer that could blend into the landscape, but what would he do if elfs sought refuge? Where the hell could he hide a unicorn? Or, gods help him, would he have to help leprechauns? Could the curse be that evil?

The fog had burned off and a few clouds floated down the coast like suspicious seagulls. The gold coin marquee swung overhead, and, on the plus side, a nice lunch crowd assembled inside.

On his next circuit, the reward that Lukas issued for the Queen brought that familiar sense of greed—more money than he'd ever seen in one place in exchange for an irritating guest—but it came with a foreign feeling of guilt.

Naelth, one of the teenage Bastards, stepped outside. It occurred to Dewey that he always managed to remember the Bastard's names. And even though they looked the same, and were all bothersome, stupid, and ugly, he knew them all, thousands of them over the years. Why would he waste the brainpower? Profit. With-out studying them enough to find their quirks, he couldn't mone-tize them. Except Naelth. Sure, he was one of the smarter of this generation, but the kid was a natural born philosopher, useless.

Naelth tripped on his own shadow, stood, and said, "Lylli has sent me for you. She's upstairs with the crying lady." He lilted his words as though he'd drunk a flask of rum, and then he sang, "I've run these seas for fifty years, I know every ship, every pier, every curved hip, every beer—"

Dewey pushed him aside and headed for the stairs. He stopped to dust errant sawdust from the luxurious red velvet stairway before continuing up to a guest room on the second floor. He stepped inside and saw Lylli examining the Queen. Loretta leaned against a wash basin between the Queen and Kaetie.

Lylli hugged him. He kissed her cheek and said, "You took long enough." Then he noticed that she had brought baskets of gifts and supplies. "Did you bring your own cauldron?"

Lylli held up a cask of Dewey's favorite blackberry wine, and said, "If you don't want it," she dropped her voice into a baritone that mimicked Dewey, "I can score ten copper ohzees for it at the market."

Loretta cleared her throat and when Dewey looked at her, she shifted her eyes from Daffy to her daughter and back.

Dewey said, "Kaetie, get out there and pull some weeds, dig up potatoes, and when you finish there are chamber pots—" She ran out before the tasks became dishonorable.

He watched Kaetie all the way downstairs and then shut the door. "Lylli, do you recognize Queen Dafina?"

She took a close look and bobbed her head in a simple bow. "Your majesty, I'd know you anywhere."

"See?" Loretta yelled at Dewey. "She needs to hide!"

Lylli resumed her examination. She rubbed Daffy's temples, ran her hands over her skull, held up a special candle with a bright white flame and peered into her eyes, listened to her chest with a tube, and then told Dewey to leave the room. He stood outside, pacing the hall until he decided that he owned this building and had a right to observe anything that happened within its walls. When he came back in, the three women were in deep discussion of intimate topics that made Dewey need to wash out his ears. At least Loretta was engaged in the conversation.

"Daffy's in shock," Lylli said. "Acute melancholia due to the loss of everyone she loves and the only life she's ever known. It will take months if not years for her to recover. She will need to sleep much longer than—"

Both Dewey and Loretta said, "She pissed off her Sleep Faery."

"Why would you bother a Sleep Faery?"

"For gods' sakes," Daffy said, "what will it take to get you people to stop bothering me about Sleep Faeries?"

Dewey said, "The usurper has offered a generous reward for her." He waited a few beats, because it hurt to think so much money was beyond his grasp, and then managed to squeak in the voice of a forlorn lover, "A hundred pounds of gold, sixteen hundred gold ohzees, more than I've ever seen in one place. Ever. And she's not worth it. The Princess and Prince were worth it, and the King was worth ten times as much—it's Lukas's ego. He can't stand that she got away."

Lylli glared at him.

"Don't you see?" he said. "Lukas is paranoid and irrational and that makes him hard to predict."

Daffy began weeping again.

"She shouldn't hide here, but I don't know what to do," Dewey said. "It's an inn, too many people pass through and most will do anything for money. Handing in a queen for sixteen hundred gold ohzees is a tidy profit for very little work. A very very good tidy deal of money and income. Don't you see? It's easy money and I can't have it."

Lylli's eyes narrowed. Dewey said, "I'll explain later."

Loretta said, "Daffy'll be safe with Lylli and we'll be safer without Daffy." She sounded desperate.

Lylli started to nod and then shook her head. "I'd be happy to have her, but they'll survey the mountain and my cottage is easy to find—everyone knows where it is." She looked at Loretta and realized her concerns. "She could hide in the forest. I know a hive of Leaf Faeries who would put up an illusion for a song. Daffy? Have you spent time outdoors? Hunting expeditions? Travelled without a coach to sleep in?"

"You mean … camping?" Daffy said the word as though it were vile. "No. I don't 'camp.'"

"She's a queen," Loretta said. "She can't actually *do* nothing."

Daffy pursed her lips as though to object.

"Send her home to Nantesse," Loretta said. "Aerrol will take her on *Avarice*."

"Wouldn't that be a sight?" Dewey said. "The First Princess of Nantesse hand delivered to King Louae by scurvy pirates."

"I require a ship," Daffy said. "My father will pay a generous fare when I make landfall."

"It's settled, she'll ship out on *Avarice*," Loretta said. "Don't worry, Daffy, Madog'll give you a clean hammock."

Daffy's mouth fell open. "Do you despise me so?"

Dewey liked the idea so much that he started planning, but a dagger of guilt buried itself in his side. "No. Lukas controls the Royal Navy, well, the Volunteer Navy." The disappointment came with a morsel of relief when the anxiety lifted. "I can't put her on a ship unless I know she'll be safe, and I won't know that until Lukas makes his next move—I have reliable word that he wants to control all of Glandaeff, and that means war."

Lylli asked, "Who else knows that she's here?"

"You, Loretta, and I are the only people who know her true identity."

"Not for long. Minstrels sing about that long, silky black hair," Loretta said. "She can't stay here!"

Dewey said, "What can I do with her?"

"Do with me?" Daffy said. "I'm not chattel."

"You were right up until the King died."

Her chin started wrinkling. He girded for the curse, but nothing happened. Apparently, the curse didn't extend to personal affronts, so he just might survive it.

Lylli said, "There's only one place for her to hide."

"Where?"

"In plain sight," Lylli said. "Suitably disguised of course, but the last place they'll look is right in front of them."

Daffy looked around the room and said. "It's a bit rustic, but so am I."

"No!" Loretta said.

Daffy said, "What have I done to earn your animosity?"

Lylli continued, "Dress her up as a serving-lass. No one on earth would conceive that Dafina, the First Princess of Nantesse, the Queen of Glomaythea, could be a Gold Piece Inn serving-lass."

"Look at her," Loretta said, "with the famous eyes and hair, and that skin—can't disguise that."

"The Queen serving pirates, whalers, and goatherds at my inn." He pictured the possibilities. "Taking a fisher upstairs, oh gods, Lylli—you've found the silver lining."

"Suitably disguised and trained," Lylli said. She dug around in her basket and pulled out a flask. "This tonic will leach the color out of her hair."

Loretta took the flask, pulled out the cork, and sniffed it. "Oh mercy, that stinks." She pushed the cork back in but eyed Daffy.

Lylli continued, "She needs to keep busy."

Dewey said, "She'll do chores like anyone else."

Loretta said, "She's too thin to be a serving-lass."

"She is dangerously thin," Lylli said. "Daffy, you have to eat every meal." And then to Loretta, "She fell for the latest fashion trend in Glomaythea. The royal court decided that skeletal thinness is elegant."

Dewey said, "Well, it doesn't sell around here."

"Keep her away from my kids," Loretta said.

"But why?" Daffy whined. "Your son is so kind, and dear Kaetie is—whatever I've done to offend you, I apologize."

"No!" Loretta took a deep breath. "No, it's not personal, it's just that," she looked around the room, "you're dangerous for them if anyone finds out who you are."

"I see," Daffy said.

Dewey saw her eyes start to leak. "Oh no. Not again. Seriously?"

Daffy choked out, "I don't want to endanger anyone."

Lylli said, "She shouldn't alone in this state of grief."

Dewey rubbed his hands together. "You can do the floors, shovel manure, empty chamber pots, work the fields, shake out rugs, laundry. You're not strong enough to carry water, but you might be able to stir the filters and maintain some ditches."

"Father," Lylli said, "you don't have to enjoy this."

Though still dripping tears, Daffy's eyes grew into wide open circles. "I am the Queen of Glomaythea—"

"Nope, not anymore."

"I am the First Princess of Nantesse, and I will not empty chamber pots."

"I guess we could see how you do as a serving-lass, maybe we dress you up as a boy." He looked her over with an all new perspective. "The gay pirates might not like it, but some sailors would enjoy the surprise. Yeah, this could—"

"No," Lylli said. "Don't, please …"

"Why can't I stay in this room?" Daffy said. "I'd be out of sight and comfortable. Perfect for everyone." She raised her voice. "Help me find patriots in the royal guard and I will destroy Lukas … or take me back where you found me and let me die. Give me a chance to return to my husband and my babies."

Dewey spoke to Lylli, "We can't afford to take this room out of service." Then to Daffy, "Special treatment will get you caught. You'll have to sleep in the barn, nothing I can do about it." He waited for the curse to pinch him but nothing. He felt a burst of hope. "Can you cook or sew?"

Lylli rubbed Daffy's neck and encouraged her to take a few deep breaths. Her eyes cleared and she said, "I can play the piano, and I can sing. That would be in plain sight."

"We have flutes, lutes, a harp, drums, but there are no keyed instruments for fifty miles. Do you know what they cost?"

Daffy said, "I can dance!"

Dewey laughed so hard he thought he'd piss himself. Even Lylli couldn't hold back.

"I trained in four different styles of dance by the finest choreographers in all of Great Nantesse. I may not cook or sew, but I can bloody well dance."

"Dance?" Dewey tried to regain control. "Listen, Daffy, I don't think you want to dance for The Gold Piece Inn audience. Don't get me wrong, they're good people, they'll care for you in a pinch—unless there's a reward I suppose—and they'll certainly pinch you for a care, but dancing generates certain, uh, expectations. Embroidery?"

"Father," Lylli said. "How many children live here?"

Dewey was happy to change the subject. "Fifty? A hundred?"

Loretta corrected him, "Thirty-three."

"Well they make the noise of a hundred."

"What if those thirty-three children all learned to read?" Lylli spoke in a conspiratorial tone. "What if they could read and write in different languages?" And then to Daffy, "How many languages do you know?"

"I can read and write Nantesse and Glo, of course, as well as Draef, Aenz, Naest, and Yarrow. I only speak Puaepuae well enough to order a fruity drink."

"So what?" Loretta said. "Everyone around here speaks Glo, and no one needs to read."

Lylli said, "Kaetie wants to learn to read."

"Well," Dewey said, "Bastards usually learn that sort of thing when they need to. It would be an extra chore for them, and I'm all for that."

Daffy said, "I'm well read in history, arithmetic, and music."

Dewey stroked his chin. "We can clear out the shed for a classroom. But she still has to do chores like everyone else. No special treatment." Every time he repeated this point, he felt glee that the curse didn't object.

Lylli stepped over and looked up at Loretta. "Please let Kaetie learn to read."

Loretta's face turned a pinkish hue. Her lips tightened into a straight line. "All right, then." She took the flask of hair color-leach from Lylli and shook it. She then took Daffy's hand and said, "Come with me." Dewey felt a pang of empathy for Daffy.

Dewey helped Lylli gather her things, and they went downstairs. She handed out the gifts she'd brought, an old vintage wine in a glass bottle for Daeffid the Chef, a clay pipe for Bob the bartender, colorful scented candles for the serving-lad Faernando, beeswax balm for the pregnant serving-lasses Laetifah and Maeggie, and then set out peppermint oil and soap for everyone and candy for the Bastards. When she finished, she pulled Dewey's hot seat alongside his chair and sat with him. He could never talk to her without thinking of her short lifespan. Her mother died almost a hundred years ago at the ripe old human age of seventy. Lylli, a quarter-elf, might live another hundred years while he, a half-elf, would probably continue for another three hundred after she died. He wondered if he could go on without her.

His Truth Faery took a seat on his knee. Much as he loved the little guy, it could be difficult to have a free-flowing conversation with him around. He told Lylli about the rumors he'd spread, and the information he was gathering.

She asked about the children of The Gold Piece Inn, especially the orphans.

Then he told her about the curse. "Can you do anything?"

"That's the reason you're helping the Queen?"

"What? Why else would I?"

Lylli looked crestfallen, and Dewey couldn't understand why.

"This curse is costing me a fortune," Dewey said. "And not just because of the reward. Did you notice all the faeries?"

"Swarming your fields?"

"Lylli, you won't believe what I've had to suffer."

"You're helping the faer."

"A whole hive asked me to help, and the curse is forcing me to do it. I've got them holed up in beehives—except they're not beehives, they're faer hives with a million damn faeries disguised as bees."

"Sounds like the perfect solution."

"Lylli! What do beehives produce?"

"Honey and wax."

"Exactly! To prevent Blechk and his Volunteers from catching me aiding and harboring faeries, those hives have to produce something. But they don't. I have to buy honey in secret so I can sell it in the marketplace."

"Oh," she said. "I see your dilemma."

"No, you don't! The honey costs more than I can sell it for." He dropped to a knee. The Truth Faery fluttered up to his shoulder. "Please help me, I'm operating at a *loss*!"

"Hmm," she said, "This curse forces you to do nice things?"

"No! It forces me to help anyone who asks, and I'm *losing money*!"

"Have you helped Madog win any card games?"

"No."

"Have you helped any of your colleagues cheat any of your other colleagues?"

"No."

"Have they asked you to?"

"Well, of course—they do that all the time."

"Huh. So, this curse forces you to help people in need."

"It's going to get me killed, or worse—I could go broke."

"Sometimes doing the right thing comes with risk."

"Will you help me?"

"No."

"My own daughter, plotting against me …"

Rustin

16.

Alate spring heatwave kept everyone in the barn awake and sweating that night. Like everyone else, Rusty started the day in a bad mood.

He spent the first hour of the day like every other day, carrying water jugs from the spring to the kitchen while Daeffid fired up the stove. He and Taevius, the oldest of the teens, divvied up the workload, ignored the other Bastards' complaints, got it done, and then everyone gathered for breakfast in the kitchen.

Rusty admired Taevius. At sixteen he was only a year older and already had the strength of a bear, but even when they were little, Taevius always seemed above the fray. Maybe it was his passion for the ocean. Taevius knew knots, rudders, and the ways of wind and sail. With his dark skin and trombone voice, everyone looked up to him. They'd all heard Dewey predict that someday he would be the captain of a great ship, a tough position for a Bastard to get, but Dewey had his ways.

After breakfast, Rusty led his sister and friends, the so-called gang-of-five—Caeph, Macae, Aennie, Naelth, and Raenny—back to the spring to cool off. Dewey's rules were simple: don't piss in the damn spring!

They walked through an opening in the willow trees where the dirt path gave way to the natural granite basin that formed the spring. It stretched fifty feet across, the water so clear you could see every fish and frog, even footprints in its sandy bottom. Water Faeries kept the surface rippling, and morning sunbeams filtered through the willow curtain, scattering tiny rainbows from the faeries' spouts. Rusty noticed something about the faeries. There were a lot more than usual, and their ripples weren't perfect overlapping circles, they were jagged and turbulent.

Rusty walked right into the water, let out a sigh, and back floated. The gang-of-five followed. Caeph, a wiry, pale lad with light stringy hair but eyes that could frighten a leprechaun into telling the truth, snapped a twig from the willow, stuck it in his mouth and plopped down in the shade for a nap. Raenny and Naelth debated the nature of Maentanglement. Naelth, who already had stray black whiskers on his chin, insisted that it was fixed by nature, unchangeable, but Raenny, a dark-skinned boy whose unruly black curls covered an arrow-focused brain, argued that the state of Maentanglement depended on the actions of both human and faer. Aennie, a tall girl with amazing dexterity of both mind and body, dove in and swam across.

Kaetie led the fifth of Rusty's gang, Macae, by the hand into the relative privacy of an alcove behind a short granite wall. Water from the brook dribbled over the granite and into the spring, leaving algae and dirt behind. Macae flashed a lascivious grin to the others. Rusty and Caeph provided color commentary to Raenny and Naelth's argument, and Aennie scratched out a scoreboard in the sand where she kept tabs of the quality of their wisecracks.

The biggest laugh of the morning came from the privacy of the alcove. The others heard Macae yelp, and then Kaetie say, "Don't touch me there!" Ten seconds later, Kaetie added, "Yet."

Two other teens, Vaence and Viviaen, stepped through the willow curtain amid the laughter. Still floating, Rusty said, "Come on in, so good!"

Vaence said, "Like I need your permission?" Vaence was a strong, barrel-shaped lad, with a bulb-shaped nose, hair the color of sand, and a high-pitched laugh.

Dainty Viviaen walked the perimeter of the spring.

Vaence said. "I don't want to hang out with these losers." He took Viviaen's hand and led her to the alcove.

Caeph said, "I wouldn't go over there if I were you."

Aennie added, "Unless you're kinky."

"I do not need your permission!" Vaence said.

Rusty tried to like Vaence, tried to give him the benefit of the doubt, but only because he had a soft spot for Viviaen, though if he looked at her too closely, that spot didn't stay soft for long. Viviaen and Vaence had been best friends from early childhood, and that friendship had become romantic a few months ago. Most of the other kids thought their relationship was borderline incestuous, but Rusty didn't think it was anyone's business but their own.

Vaence climbed the granite wall that shielded the alcove and said, "Get out!"

Rusty heard Macae say, "A little privacy, please?" and then Kaetie, "Come on in, there's room," and then, more quietly, "Macae, if you don't move your farqin hand, I'm cutting it off."

Viviaen said, "Vaence, come on."

"We're claiming the alcove, you had your turn."

"Hey Vaence," Caeph said, "I didn't see you carrying water this morning."

"Didn't want to, decided I needed more sleep because you wouldn't shut up last night."

"Real tough guy you have there, Viviaen."

"Caeph, do you have to?" Rusty said.

"Just think Vaence ought to carry his prodigious weight," Caeph said. "But I had to carry an extra jug for him, and so did you, and Naelth and Raenny had to carry—"

"I didn't carry nothin'," Raenny said.

"I didn't mind," Naelth said.

"—well, it pissed me off."

Vaence said, "Move!"

"Stop being an arse," Macae said.

"I'm not an arse."

Caeph said, "Yes, you are."

"Let me add it up." Aennie scratched in the sand. "And the total is … yes, Caeph is right, Vaence is an arse."

"Behaving like an arse?" Naelth said. "Or is he an actual arse?"

Raenny added, "Or does he just have a big arse."

The others laughed. Viviaen's hands covered her smile, and Vaence glared at her. She walked into the spring, one step at a time, her hands held above the cool water.

Standing on the granite over the private alcove, Vaence announced, "I am not an ass, I'm a dick." And then he pulled down his breeches, leaned back, and let fly an arc of pee that rained down on Macae and Kaetie.

Kaetie shrieked, "Ewww," swam out of the alcove, and dove to the bottom of the spring.

Raenny said, "Uncool, arse." Naelth, "That's disgusting." Aennie, "And we have a winner!"

Macae climbed out of the alcove, his eyes fixed on Vaence. He clenched his fists, stepped over the stream, and up onto the granite wall.

"Macae," Rusty said, "don't bother." He walked out of the spring. "Come on, everyone's a little tense. The heat. Dewey taking Spaedlie's death so hard. We're here to cool off, so let's just cool off."

An irate Water Faery surfaced a few feet from the granite. Except for his hat, the faery looked like a tiny dolphin. He spouted a yellow jet of fluid directly into Vaence's face.

Kaetie yelled, "The spring is peeing back at him!" Macae stepped away, laughing, and dove in. Caeph pointed at Vaence, said, "Tiny," and cannon-balled in. The Water Faery disappeared.

Now dripping in pee, Vaence looked shocked. Rusty put a hand on his shoulder. "Gotta admit, you deserved that."

Vaence turned and jabbed his right fist into Rusty's jaw. Stocky Vaence had twenty pounds on him, but lanky, agile Rusty took the blow without losing his balance. Vaence followed with a left to the body. Rusty blocked the punch with his left forearm and caught Vaence's fist in his right hand. Rusty'd had enough. He had been keeping the peace for a long time, and he wanted to unload on the bully.

But from behind him, Taevius spoke in that deep voice of command. "Break it up."

Rusty held onto Vaence's fist and tried to stop the fight without returning a punch. Vaence jerked his arm back and pulled Rusty with him. To keep his balance, Rusty had to push off. Vaence fell from the granite wall. His wrist hit a rock and snapped. He screamed and twisted away, only to hit his head on another rock.

Taevius grabbed Rusty from behind and caught his neck in a headlock. "You'll pay for that."

From where Rusty stood, Vaence looked inert. Rusty moved to dive in and pull him out. Taevius was older, stronger, and more confident, but Rusty's long body gave him a leverage advantage. He got one arm free and tried to jump into the spring.

Taevius jerked him back. "Enough!"

Raenny and Aennie pulled Vaence to the surface. His head lolled to the side, but he didn't gasp for breath. Rusty watched him inhale—he'd been faking.

Taevius said, "Macae, help pull him out. Caeph, go get Aenki." Aenki was Vaence's mother. "I'm taking this tough guy to Dewey."

The gang-of-five tried to tell Taevius that Rusty wasn't to blame, but Taevius had seen what he'd seen.

Once they emerged from the willows, Taevius pushed Rusty ahead on the path. Rusty was too angry to think. Taevius didn't say a word until he'd shoved Rusty into the hot seat. He explained to Dewey that Rusty had attacked Vaence, that the others had tried to defend him, and that someone had peed in the spring.

Rusty sat silently, trying to get control of his temper, so he could think of a way to explain the situation that Dewey would accept.

Aenki marched up with Vaence, who bled from a cut over his

eye and held his wrist at an unnatural angle. She said, "Lylli has to set this wrist and you need to put Rusty in his place and stop playing favorites!"

Dewey groaned. "I have one rule for the spring. One rule." He looked at Vaence and then at Rusty. "Who peed in my Spring?"

Vaence said nothing.

Rusty took a deep breath. He had it together now. But Aenki was cradling her son's broken wrist. She was worried, and why wouldn't she be? Her only child was the least popular Bastard and Dewey had no plan for him. Rusty didn't want her to suffer. He said, "I thought it'd be funny."

"Well it wasn't," Vaence said.

Rusty laughed at his own misjudgment. For some reason, he'd assumed that Vaence would confess. It would have earned his mother's respect, maybe even Dewey's, but Vaence could never get out of his own way.

Taevius stepped away in disgust.

Dewey sent Aenki and Vaence to the faery garden where they would find Lylli. Then he made sounds that conveyed anger and frustration. "You peed in my spring?"

"Whatever." Rusty knew that it was too late to explain. Once Dewey's mind was set, he had no patience for details.

Dewey looked over Rusty's shoulder and then shook his head. "If you're going to lead the Bastards, lead them all, especially Vaence, he's the strongest—you need him—and he's the stupidest—he needs you."

"Me? No. Taevius, he's the leader."

"Taevius should already be on a ship. He'll be a captain someday, and you can write that down."

"On a ship?"

"Aerrol wants him on *Avarice*, but Laetifah wants him on a ship that's legal and legit." Laetifah, a popular and very pregnant serving-lass, was Taevius's mother.

Aware his punishment was coming, Rusty stared out the window, resolved to spend a week shoveling night soil. "I can't control Vaence. You know how he is."

"I don't have enough human blood to understand why your kind follows leaders, but you do." Dewey stared at him for a few more seconds. "You need to make yourself scarce for a day or two. Come with me." He led Rusty to his office and handed him a small folded and waxed sheaf. "Take this to Jon-Jay and ask him to deliver it. Do not let anyone see it but Jon-Jay—you know who I'm talking about?"

"The big man with long blonde hair and a scar across his face? Sails a dragonship?" He looked at the sheaf and said, "Nantesse?"

"You can read that?"

"It's got an 'N.' What's it say?"

"Don't make me hurt you." Dewey flipped him a silver ohzee and said, "Pay him if he'll take it." He pulled another message, this one a scroll of cheap paper. "Take this one to Aelbert at the lighthouse."

Rusty tucked them both into his pocket.

Dewey motioned to the door. "I'll tell your mom where you are. See you tomorrow. And here's a copper, have some fun, become a man, get out of my sight."

Through the conversation, Rusty never saw Dewey's Truth Faery hovering over his shoulder.

17.

Rusty made his way through the inn, not sure what had just happened, hoping to get away before Dewey dealt him a degrading punishment. He stepped onto the street. Being clear of the inn felt liberating despite the heat. In no hurry to satisfy Dewey's mission, he hung out at the marketplace for a while, maybe meet some new people, perhaps even a girl.

The sun beat down on the land, but a thick fogbank sat off the coast. Every five minutes the low-throated foghorn blew like long-winded thunder from the lighthouse.

He took in the sounds and smells of the marketplace—goats and fish, herbs and tea, plenty of full-throated negotiation. He knew everyone and called them by name.

Something felt different.

People bought more than they needed, especially dry goods, grains, and preserves—the sort of purchasing people did in late autumn not late spring. The butcher had him hold a side of beef steady while he cut it with a saw. Rusty asked what was up. She canted her head in the direction of a cluster of Volunteers at the top of Wide Street where goods were carried up from the harbor, and another cluster at Profit Street where money made its way to the counting houses. "Uncertain times." Flies hovered over the meat and when a Carving Faery flew out to shoo them away, the butcher stepped in the way of the Volunteers' line of sight.

Rusty bumped into the cobbler and promised to buy some shoes as soon as his feet stopped growing, and he had enough money. The cobbler said, "I better start saving leather now if I have to cover those clodhoppers." They laughed, but it wasn't the cobbler's usual belly-rumbling guffaw, and he kept looking over his shoulder.

When Rusty finally made it down to the wharf, he jumped into the cool ocean. He brought a shiny rock and a speck of quartz to the surface. He gave the rock to the fisher's three-year-old daughter and leaned down to the pier's wooden decking. And then he realized what had changed.

Rusty flashed the quartz in the sun so that a facet reflected light into the wood. Nothing.

He saw Madog, Baertha, and Aerrol leaning against a piling. Madog slouched against a post, tapping a dagger against his teeth. Baertha stood with her arms crossed over her open vest, and her hands on the cutlasses that dangled from her hips. Aerrol fiddled with the crank of his crossbow. All three of them watched a large rowboat carry sailors to shore from the Volunteer corvette *Daefender*.

Rusty's eyes locked on the eel tattoos that ran up from Baertha's navel, between her breasts, to her neck.

Aerrol said, "Baertha, you have a fan."

Rusty made sounds but couldn't muster a word through his embarrassment.

Madog reached a long arm around Rusty's neck and pulled him into a tight embrace. "Ready to set sail then? Escape your mother's fine clutches and see the world? Join us and make your fortune?"

Indicating the transport, Aerrol said, "You're better off camping out at The Gold Piece Inn, but once this blows over, you're coming with us."

"I'd like to crack their skulls," Baertha said.

The transport, usually called a ship's tender, carried a dozen sailors in red and black uniforms, and with its painted hull bright white with red gunwales, was obviously the newest vessel in the harbor.

"We're better off at sea. Split-up and gather the crew," Aerrol said.

Aerrol gave Rusty a firm whack on the back and headed up to the marketplace. Baertha kissed his cheek and walked down the wharf toward the river. Madog ruffled his hair and Rusty said, "Where can I find Jon-Jay?"

"Jon-Jay?" Madog squinted. "Really?" Rusty started pulling out the sheaf but remembered that Dewey had told him not to let anyone see it. Plus, it was soaked from when he'd jumped in the water, probably ruined. He groaned at the thought of another scolding, certain that this one would come with a list of repulsive chores.

Madog pointed at eight galleys anchored on the opposite side of the harbor from *Daefender*. They had rows of oarlocks along their sides, a single mast in the center, and great carvings at the bow and stern. "Jon-Jay is the geezer in the *Dragonship*." Madog looked Rusty over. "Something for Dewey?"

Rusty nodded, not sure of the best way to approach a Viking.

"Arrh, don't worry about Jon-Jay, treat him like you would one of those kids that follows you around, not so much respect that he'll abuse you and not so little he'll kill you." He laughed and pointed at a black rowboat tied to the pier. "That's our tender, have it back in an hour."

Madog bumped his forehead against Rusty's, just like he would one of his mates.

Rusty ran down the pier and hopped into the black tender. He matched his rowing tempo to the swells well enough that only a bit of foam made it into the boat. When he got past the pier, clear of traffic within the harbor, he stopped to check the messages. The message for Aelbert was soaked, its ink smeared. He unrolled it and set it in the sun to dry. He took the one for Jon-Jay out of its waxed sheaf. A tiny faery pushed a tiny squeegee across it, and water dripped off its edge. She looked up and visored her eyes with a tiny hand. "Stupid boy, is too much water!" She pronounced s's like z's. Rusty apologized. She buzzed up and perched on his nose. "You can't immerse the document. Look at this? I'm ruined." She zipped back to the document, squeegeed another few drops, and began weeping.

"But you did it!" Rusty said. "The ink has hardly run."

She coalesced into the scroll.

Rusty held the message in the sun between his toes, pulling the oars toward the *Dragonship*. He glanced over his shoulder and saw a cluster of people on its deck watching. Tall muscular men and women wearing nothing but short breeches, their torsos golden brown and their hair long, some braided, all blonde. Rusty determined not to replay the embarrassment of gawking at the women's breasts.

The tallest stood near the bow and yelled, "Lean into it!" His beard blew in the wind. "There you go, son, power twenty." Then all of them yelled "pull, pull" matching Rusty's rhythm.

Rusty met the challenge with all his strength. The bow rose on the water, and a wake stretched out behind. He pulled with all he had, exhausted on the twentieth stroke. The giant man said, "Check it down." A woman yelled, "That's one strong lad right there!"

Rusty brought the boat to a soft stop alongside the ship, and someone dropped a rope down. He tied it to a cleat, and a powerful arm reached down with a clenched fist. He gripped the forearm, and the man hefted him aboard.

"Jon-Jay," he said. "You?"

"Rusty." He held the sheaf against his belly where only Jon-Jay could see it.

Jon-Jay said, "Nantesse? Might as well." He looked across the harbor at *Daefender*. "Good time to get out of here."

Rusty handed him the silver ohzee.

Jon-Jay said, "You a Gold Piece Inn Bastard?"

"I am."

"Good on you. So am I. We do well by each other. I'll remember you."

"You lived in the barn?"

"Every second of sixteen years. Worked the springs mostly, you?" Jon-Jay took the sheaf.

"I carry a lot of water."

Jon-Jay slapped Rusty's back. "I bet you do."

"Your mom still here?"

"Left when I did. She's a fisher now, out of Grindaenberg." Jon-Jay stepped back and looked him over.

Rusty realized that Jon-Jay was just a few inches taller.

"I'll take you on right now. I can talk to Dewey, I know the process—you in?"

"Naw, the sea isn't for me, just makes me barf." He hopped back in the tender.

Jon-Jay called from above, "What is?"

"Huh?"

"If the sea isn't for you, what is?"

"Not sure." Rusty pushed off the *Dragonship* and grabbed the oars. "Guess I'll know it when I see it."

"You better start looking."

18.

Rusty watched a ship emerge from the fogbank. The foghorn reminded him he had another message to deliver. He removed it from his pocket with care. Dry now, the ink was smeared, but the paper hung together. Maybe Aelbert could decipher it.

Down the wharf, he stopped to help Fin, a sturdy man with ruddy, wind-burned skin, and a rubbery nose who was struggling to secure gray whale flukes to a flatbed. Fin carved intricate scrimshaw that Dewey bought and resold. When the mule pulled the flatbed onto the road, Rusty turned to go on his way and almost walked into two sailors in red and black uniforms. The sailors struggled with a full barrel that had skull and crossbones painted across it.

Rusty knew that Lukas had the King assassinated and that everyone who lived at the inn opposed Lukas, but he hadn't quite made the connection between "Lukas, The First Human" and the sailors in their fancy leather uniforms. And they even included boots. Rusty leaned in to help the sailors with the barrel. They were just a couple of years older than him and seemed nice enough. They were both from Glomaythea. Rusty asked about life in the big city.

A deep voice from behind said, "Get that kid out of here."

Rusty turned around and saw a short man with a big belly and scraggly hair. His uniform included black rather than red pants, a red sash, and gold epaulets on the shoulders. "I'm already on my way."

"Who are you?"

"Rusty, from The Gold Piece Inn. Welcome to Crescent Cove." The greeting he'd been taught to give strangers, a sort of advertisement for the inn, but the words didn't taste quite right.

The man didn't offer his name.

"What are you, sixteen?"

"Fifteen." Rusty stood nearly a foot taller than the man. Normally, he'd engage in conversation, but something about the situation discouraged that.

"Fancy a life at sea?"

It being the third time today that someone had suggested he become a sailor, Rusty felt obligated to level with the man. "No. I don't mind the harbor, but open sea turns my stomach." Rusty wanted to finish with a declaration of great ambition but didn't have one. To compensate, he said, "My mate Taevius, though, he's sixteen, and someday he'll captain a ship. You can write that down."

The man turned his back to Rusty, farted, and yelled commands at the Volunteers, a dismissal that Rusty was happy to accept.

Rusty jogged to the end of the wharf and took a trail up to the bluffs. Gusts of cool air blew in from the ocean. From here, the fog bank looked like a shipwrecked cloud. He watched a three-mast clipper with a flying jib sprint out of the cove. With its black hull and silvery gray sails, *Avarice* reached up and grabbed the wind. Before it disappeared into the fog, a black flag rose up its mainsheet: silver cutlasses crossed below the face of a man smiling and winking. Rusty tried to picture himself at its helm, but it heeled away from the wind, and he felt a wave of nausea.

He continued around the point until he faced the open ocean. The foghorn blew another deep-throated bellow, and Rusty ran until he found the path carved into the rocky cape that led to the lighthouse. He rounded a small freshwater reservoir and heard Aelbert's over-loud voice and then a door slam.

Two Volunteers came around the corner. One carried a

clipboard and the other a butterfly net. Rusty stood out of their way and watched them go up the trail. They turned left, toward the Great Beach, rather than back to Crescent Cove.

Rusty knocked on the door of the tall cylindrical building and soon heard the familiar clip-clap of Aelbert running downstairs. The door swung open, and Aelbert turned around and rushed back upstairs, waving Rusty to follow.

Rusty passed through Aelbert's living quarters; a cot piled with blankets, a fireplace with a built-in rotisserie, a table with open books and unraveled scrolls, and a bundle of sticks. The entire building smelled like sea lion belches.

"Drat!" Aelbert pointed at the bundle with a wag of his head. "Quick, get me a Foghorn Faery! Damn Volunteers made me terminate the last one."

Rusty stopped in his tracks. "Terminate?"

Aelbert ran back downstairs and said, "I didn't kill it. They made me discharge it. The poor thing's probably on the rocks below organizing seals into a cooperative."

Rusty pulled a blue rod from the bundle. It resembled a Sleep Faery but was longer and cold.

"Bring it up here." Aelbert ran back upstairs and Rusty followed.

Aelbert stood at a closed door with huge hinges and a giant knocker. He fixed wax plugs in his ears and motioned to the stairs that spiraled farther up. He yelled in Rusty's face, "GO UP TO THE OBSERVATORY. THE FOGHORN IS DUE IN—OH SHITE!" He opened the door to a loud cacophony of barking and moaning sea lions.

Rusty leaned inside to greet the foghorn. Four rows of sea lions stood side-by-side perched on a choral riser, small cows in front and large bulls in back. Some clapped their flippers against the floor when they saw him. One bit a whisker off the face of his neighbor. The neighbor barked.

Aelbert stood in front of a huge brass horn that expanded out over the ocean. He held up the blue rod and tapped it against a bucket of fish. The sea lions went silent. Aelbert yelled, "UPSTAIRS, RUSTY—AND DON'T TOUCH *ANYTHING*."

Rusty shut the door and ran upstairs. He got inside the observatory just as the foghorn let loose another wail. The observatory had thick glass windows on all sides. Cabinets lined the walls below the windows, some wedged open by stray equipment. A grinding wheel stood poised over a chunk of glass surrounded by brass fittings on a table. Rusty picked up a brass tube, and a round lens rolled out of it, across the table, and bounced off other pieces. He scrambled for it, but it fell, rolled under a chair, and came to a stop against a cabinet.

Rusty crawled under the table. He picked up the lens and noticed that the cabinet it had stopped against was cracked open. He opened it just enough to get some leverage to shut it, but objects made of brass, wood, and glass avalanched out, including a sword. Not much of a sword—thin, light, and barely three feet from pommel to point, in a scabbard made of whale teeth.

The foghorn sang again.

Sitting on the floor, Rusty turned the sword over and looked at the carved scabbard: images of tall ships and whaling skiffs with sailors wielding harpoons—scrimshaw. He wondered how such a light weapon could be used against such a great animal. He tugged the pommel just enough to loosen it in the scabbard and the sword came out, making that incredible sound. He heard the clip-clop of Aelbert on the stairs and pushed the sword back into the scabbard, but the blade caught on something. He pulled it back out, set the little sword on the table, and tapped the scabbard. A tight-wound, crushed scroll slid out.

He unrolled it.

Aelbert stepped inside. He looked past Rusty, out the window, and yelled, "THE FOG SEEMS TO BE LIFTING." Then he sat next to Rusty and yelled right in his ear, "DID DEWEY SEND YOU TO TELL ME THAT THE FAERIES ARE FREAKING OUT?"

Rusty pointed at Aelbert's ears. He pulled the wax plugs out of them. "Sorry about that."

"No," Rusty said, "I have a message for you to transmit—what did you say about the faer?" He handed over the crumpled piece of paper with smeared ink.

"My faeries are a wreck." He still spoke twice as loud as necessary. "Those soldiers were horrible, threatened everyone, demanded to know how many live here, wrote it all down, I lied of course. My lead Horn Faery stood up to them, told him their ships would sink without his help—big fellah always did have a mouth on him. You notice the others packing? Those that haven't left are worried sick."

"I didn't see any Pier Faeries on the wharf, either."

"What's this?" He took the message from Rusty.

"It got wet, and the ink smeared …"

"The Sea Lions are even spooked."

"Will they bark without a Foghorn Faery?"

"No." Aelbert took a monocle from the table, jammed it into one eye and closed the other. He wagged his head down to his left shoulder and examined the message. "Huh. The smearing improved his handwriting. Maybe you should dip all of Dewey's messages in water." When he finished examining the message, his head snapped over to his right shoulder. "It's no good, Rusty. No good. Bad times coming in with the tide." His head went straight, and the monocle dropped into his hand. "Where did you find that rapier? Not your weapon. A big man like you will want a big sword."

"I found this, too." Rusty held up the scroll.

Aelbert took it. "What have we here?"

"I don't know," Rusty said. "It doesn't look like a treasure map. Is it a spell? Can you read it?"

Aelbert put the monocle back in and held the scroll close to his face. "To Be a Knight. Huh. Goes on about honor, integrity, dedication, self-discipline, fighting injustice." He ran a finger across the text. "Chivalry, solidarity among brothers and sisters of the order, blah blah blah, champion of the right and the good against injustice and evil." He set it on his lap and let the monocle fall out of his eye. "I don't see anything about navigation, meteorology, or astronomy—which reminds me—I used to pilot a brigantine. Fascinating work. I can show you how to use a compass and a sextant, navigate by the stars—a boy your age, you'll be fascinated by the sextant." His laughter wasn't quite contagious.

Aelbert's lecture leapt from one unintelligible subject to another. Each time he changed subject, he wagged his head to a different side. Rusty looked down at the scroll. He'd always thought reading would be pointless drudgery, but even though it wasn't a treasure map, for some reason he needed to know what this scroll said, and he wanted to read it himself. It felt personal and important, and he didn't want to share it.

"Rusty, tough times are acomin' and you need to choose something, or something will be chose for you. A career in navigation sets you above and apart from scurvy sailors. You can pick whatever ship you want, and when you've had enough of the sea, you can operate a lighthouse!"

Rusty nodded but didn't take his eyes away from the scroll.

"You can have it," Aelbert said. "Knights—who needs them? I mean other than the weak, the poor, the sick, the hungry, the old, and damsels and ladsels in distress—a pointless pastime."

19.

Rusty spent the night dozing between foghorn blasts, made breakfast of sardines and crabs with the sea lions and then meandered the long way home to The Gold Piece Inn, stopping to look at the scroll every time he found a rock or log to sit on.

He walked into the inn before the supper rush. He came in through the kitchen, of course. Dewey discouraged Bastards from entering in front. He could tell something was wrong the instant he stepped inside. Silence.

Three Volunteers stood at a table where Paetel, proprietor of the faery cultivation shop, sat with Baeswax. Like the Volunteers Rusty had seen at the Lighthouse, one held a clipboard, and another held a butterfly net. The third had manacles on a chain slung over his shoulder.

Paetel tried to speak but quaked and babbled instead. She'd always had a kind word for Rusty and everyone else for that matter. No one, *no one*, had cause to frighten her.

She looked around the room, her eyes pleading. Dewey walked toward her. Rusty followed. He didn't know what he would do, but protecting Paetel from Volunteers was at the top of his list. Loretta grabbed him from behind. He stood a head higher than his mother, but that didn't make her any less intimidating.

Dewey waved to the stage. A new musician began an old song about the days before Maentanglement. He started with a loud, wailing riff on an instrument Rusty had never seen before—a long-necked, horizontal, six string lute. The drummer set the backbeat on goatskins, and a large woman held a tiny lute between her chin and shoulder and rubbed its strings with a bow. It gave the song a keening melody.

Dewey pointed at Paetel's chair, and she sat back down. Then he motioned to Baeswax, and she moved to another table. He took her seat. The muscular serving-lad, Jaek, brought three chairs to the table, and the Volunteers sat across from Dewey and Paetel. Soon, Bob brought horns of ale and Dewey was deep in discussion with the Volunteers. With the band playing, no one could listen in. Paetel looked faint.

The other guests huddled over their drinks. Even the goats

looked tense.

Before the band made it to their second song, the three Volunteers stood and left. Once they were out the door, Dewey led Paetel into his office. From the color of his cheeks, Rusty could tell that whatever had happened at that table had cost Dewey at least a gold ohzee. If Rusty'd had any doubts that the world was being turned upside down, they disappeared when he saw Dewey pay to help another person and gain nothing for himself.

The instant the Volunteers stepped onto the street, faeries emerged from every corner and crack in the building. They clustered in groups on the rafters, under tables, along the wainscoting. Unlike at the pier or lighthouse, there were far more than usual.

Loretta hugged Rusty and then told him to bring water in from the spring.

He went into the kitchen, and Daeffid said that he had plenty of water. Rusty asked if he knew how to read. He didn't, so he asked Laetifah and then Faernando. He thought about asking Dewey, but not now. He went out the kitchen door into the Faery Garden and found Kaetie singing to Stem Faeries. He asked her if Lylli was still around.

"No," she said, as though she suspected her brother of stealing a favorite toy. "Why?"

"I need to read something."

"You? Read?"

He ignored her and walked to the other end of the garden and sat on a round boulder in the waning sunlight. He unrolled the scroll.

A nymph squirmed out from under him and hopped from the boulder to a birdbath.

A thin woman with short, light hair approached him. "I can read."

He did a double take. "Daffy? Is that you?"

"Yes, it's me." She ran a hand through her hair. "Do you like it?"

"Yeah. Okay. Sure." She smelled of lilac and something about the way she walked hypnotized him.

"Why this sudden interest in reading?" She sat next to him.

He lost the ability to speak.

"Rusty?"

"Um, yeah. I, um, something I found at the lighthouse."

She held out her hand. "I'll read it to you."

The warmth of her thigh next to his decided the battle between needing to know what the scroll said and wanting to keep it private. "Uh, huh." He set the scroll in her hand.

She unrolled it and within seconds her eyes started moistening.

"No, not if it makes you cry again. Really, I can figure it out." He leaned toward her and then away, not sure if he ought to comfort her but sure that he wanted to.

She took his wrist, steadying him. "It's making me happy, not sad."

"You even cry when you're happy? What the …?"

"It reminds me of my husband." She looked at him, really looked into him as though he wasn't a fifteen-year-old Bastard who lived in a hay loft with dozens of others just like him. "You need to read this, Rusty. You need to understand it. This is important." She held the scroll for him.

With the scroll inches from his eyes and the urgency in her voice, Rusty felt like she was scolding him. "Daffy, that's kind of why I need help. I don't know how to read."

She pointed at the scroll, "It's titled 'To Be a Knight.'"

Rusty knew most of the letters in the alphabet and could recognize the names of cities but didn't know that every letter came with a sound.

"I'll teach you how to read, but only if you promise to live up to what this scroll says."

"Okay, I promise."

"You need to understand what it says prior to making *this* promise."

"If you need me to promise, I promise."

"Be careful what you promise, Rusty." Her voice was soft again. "When you make a promise, it's your bond, it represents who you are, and if you break a promise you lose your honor—that's what this scroll is about."

"People break promises all the time. My mom promises to take us to the beach, but she never comes with us. And Dewey—well, Dewey …"

Daffy laughed and Rusty laughed with her.

She read the scroll out loud.

Rusty took in every word and asked her to repeat certain passages. In the few minutes it took, Rusty felt as though one weight was lifted from him as another, far heavier weight piled on. He pictured the terror on Paetel's face, just moments ago and never wanted to see suffering like that again. He wondered where Paetel would go, and what he could have done if he'd been a knight. But then Daffy read the last line, and it all wafted away like smoke from a snuffed candle.

"Rusty," Daffy said, "do you promise?"

"Nothing to promise. Says right there that I can't be a knight." He took the scroll from her and let it curl up in his hand.

"Why?"

"At the end there, it said that knights have to be dubbed by a king or queen—I don't think my mom and Dewey can swing that."

She looked at him as though she was reading his face. "Rusty." She let his name hang between them. "Most people who are called Rusty have red hair." She ran her hand through his hair.

He couldn't breathe.

She said, "You can still see the red in the sunlight."

His heart felt like it would punch out of his chest. He managed to say, "It turned brown when my voice changed. My real name is

Rustin, but people still call me—"

"Rustin." The word came off her tongue in a way that he'd never heard before. Her Nantesse accent rolled the R and emphasized the second syllable. "Rustin. A fine name for a knight."

"Well, except for the whole dubbing thing."

"Rustin, you keep your promise, and I'll worry about the politics."

"Really?" he said, trying not to betray his doubts. "You?"

"Just keep that promise and get to work preparing to be a knight."

"Seriously?"

"Promise?"

"Yes, Daffy, I promise that I will be a knight."

She stood and tousled his hair. "Don't lose the scroll, Sir Rustin, you've promised your honor."

Town Liar

20.

Every day there'd be something. Daffy would see the bloodhound foraging through the saloon and picture how little Prince Piaer would follow along. She'd step into the kitchen and expect to see Princess Maechelle pestering Daeffid with questions about cooking.

When she felt like drowning in grief, that forbidden feeling of freedom tantalized her. She'd spent her life playing a role that had ended. The prospect of finding out who she could become terrified and excited her almost as much as it made her feel guilty. Maybe Gledig would have wanted her to be happy, maybe not. It always came back to this. She couldn't shed the belief that, if he'd known, Gledig would never have loved her. The truth was, she betrayed him years before they ever met. All it took was one mistake on a hot April day in Nantesse. If she could undo one day in her life— no, she wouldn't undo that day. She tried to lie to herself but couldn't, at least not about that.

She cried herself to sleep every night and was slowly coming to appreciate the privacy the others gave her, even in the hayloft full of snoring adults, giggling children, and farting goats. She learned to appreciate the finer talents of Sleep Faeries, discovered a taste for peasant cuisine, and hoped that someday the serving-lasses and lads would befriend her. The Bastards already accepted her. It was Lylli, though, who showed her the way. She badgered Dewey about letting Daffy teach the Bastards, "Just an hour a day. Daffy can teach them things that will make you more than a few ohzees— pounds of gold, Dewey, pounds … of *gold*."

Dewey told Rusty to convert an old shed into a classroom.

Rusty said, "What's a classroom?"

Daffy described the castle library, where a series of tutors had educated her.

"We don't have any books," Rusty said.

Dewey said, "A classroom is like a bedroom except that instead of beds there are desks and instead of trying to sleep, you try to stay awake."

"Okay," Rusty said. He motioned to the kitchen and Daffy found herself walking ahead of him. They passed through the faery garden, a field of tomatoes, and stopped at a small building with a sagging roof and closed shutters. In no way did it resemble her concept of a classroom. Rusty opened the door, and she got a whiff of decaying grain.

He said, "We'll fix it."

The next day, Rusty gathered Daffy's students, all the Bastards over twelve. He had Daffy describe what she had in mind, and then he went to each Bastard and asked them to take on tasks. Rusty never raised his voice, and when a Bastard complained, he either found something else for them to do or commiserated, but said, "It needs doing, and you're the best at it," and got results every time. He went to Daffy with the smile that lit up his dimples and pointed to a bench that Caeph had just set under an almond tree. She sat, and Naelth appeared with a cup of tea for her.

They took the old grain out of the shed, cut a fresh layer of thatch for the roof, and began cleaning. Daffy had spent the whole time watching from the bench until Rusty held up a broom. She'd never used a broom before, but something about the way he asked, so certain that she'd want to do her part, made it impossible to decline. The children offered detailed criticism of her sweeping technique: Macae, "It helps if the broom touches the floor," Kaetie, "You're supposed to sweep the dirt away, not spread it around," and Aennie, "And if that doesn't work, maybe you can ride it." Raenny, the only one who Rusty had left to his own devices, cleared a wall, sanded it, and then disappeared for a day. He returned with a bucket of dark goo and a sack of chalk sticks. By the time Raenny finished painting that wall, the rest of the team had cleared and cleaned the room.

Nothing could distract Daffy from her mourning, but she lost herself in that week of hard work and camaraderie. She saw a lot of her own children in the Bastards. It amazed and humbled her, but then the kids left, and she found herself alone in her new classroom. The sense of accomplishment faded into a confused web of pain and guilt born of the infernal sense of freedom that she both hated and relished.

Just one more day, she said to herself every morning, *one more miserable day*. She wanted to go home, and she wanted to stay at The Gold Piece Inn, and she wanted to run away, but more than anything, she wanted to hug and kiss her children just one more time.

21.

Dewey sat at his desk sorting the tiny scrolls. Armed with new maekhanical weapons, Lukas had stormed across Glandaeff like a sword slicing through fog. He shrugged. Maybe if Lukas won, he'd leave well enough alone. *Sure, victory always makes autocrats* more *tolerant of their scapegoats.*

He unrolled a new message from the Bastard Jaenet and exhaled a sigh that let his belly fall over his belt. Jaenet's note provided extensive details of not just Major Blechk's business dealings, but his personal appetites, and how he preferred to satisfy them. It also listed his affection for torture and child abuse. Dewey could now prime the rumor mill. If he had any luck, Blechk might believe that a certain halfling innkeeper had the goods on him. It had always worked before.

Dewey leaned down to stow Jaenet's message in his safe. He opened it and gazed lovingly at the piles of silver and gold ohzees resting peacefully next to a small hoard of gemstones. Faeries flew out of the woodwork to marvel alongside him. He tried to shoo them away. Faeries always feel a birthright to stray shiny objects. He wondered how much of his gold had made its way into pots at the end of rainbows. The safe's lock included tumblers and a series of gears that utterly confounded the faer. A little winged arsehole stood on the safe with his hand out. If he didn't pay the Protection Faery, the lock would rust. Maybe the usurper had a point about the little farqers holding back commerce.

He flicked a ruby granule at the faery.

"I asked you to keep her away from my kids!"

Dewey banged his head on a desk drawer, looked up, and saw Loretta looming over him like a dragon over a shepherd. He straightened an ear and said, "She can teach them things that will make them seem highborn, more marketable, better opportunities. Mothers are supposed to want that sort of thing for their children."

"They are high born!"

He raised an eyebrow.

"They're MY children. That's high enough."

"Kaetie has to learn to read, or Lylli can't apprentice her. You don't know how, and I don't want to teach her."

"If Lylli wants her to read, she can teach her."

"Lylli's busy."

"But why Daffy? What if she figures it out? Then what?"

"Everyone is happy with the arrangement."

"Not me." She slid into the chair opposite Dewey's desk. "You honestly think that a halfling pimp has a chance with the First Princess of Nantesse?"

He laid his head down on the desk and groaned. He could almost hear her devising another tack.

"Major Blechk doubled the reward, two-hundred pounds of gold!" Her voice got louder with every word. "Dewey—I can't believe I'm saying this—take the money, or I will."

"Two hundred?" Dewey whined. Then mustered his self-control and said, "And get us all killed? No, you won't."

"Her disguise isn't that good. And she cries all the time, it's annoying."

Dewey leaned back and stared at her. "Loretta, I held you as a baby—I didn't want to, you were a barfer—and you have never turned on an innocent person. Never. I don't know how you got this nasty moral streak, certainly not from your mother, but we both know that you won't give her up."

"If Daffy figures it out—"

"Go away."

She said, "Fine" with an intonation that brought sharp objects to mind.

22.

Daffy thought teaching would be her only chore, but she was still getting to know Dewey. His malicious grin should have given it away.

"No special treatment," Dewey said. "It would be dangerous for the children. Really, I wish there were something I could do." He waved her over to Loretta, who stood with a bucket, a mop, and several rags.

Loretta said, "You ready to work?"

Daffy choked on the many ways that she could have expressed the injustice she felt. "This is not the first time that I have labored."

"Listen, honey, it's the first time you done anything like this." Loretta waved her ahead and then followed.

Daffy hoped that she heard a trace of compassion in Loretta's voice. Daffy said, "I cared for my pony when I was a girl—shoveling, brushing, feeding, everything."

"Your pony," Loretta said and offered her a full-length apron.

Daffy felt uncertain. And stupid. How hard could it be to make a bed, sweep a floor, polish wood, empty and refill a washbasin? When it came right down to it, carrying a chamber pot out to the field didn't qualify as torture.

She hadn't realized how much she craved Loretta's approval. Loretta was warm and fun, ferocious and outrageous. Her eyes danced when she smiled and when she laughed her entire body shook. She didn't let anyone mistreat her and would defend her friends as passionately as she did her children. Daffy had grown up with women who controlled their emotions, did their duty, and tolerated offensive behavior. In a way, Loretta was the person Daffy had secretly wanted to be. She smiled at the irony of a queen envying a serving-lass.

Loretta said, "You won't be smiling long."

Daffy surrendered to the fact that Loretta hated her and didn't want her near her children. She felt her eyes start to water. No, she simply would not cry today! But it was too late, Loretta had noticed.

Loretta clucked like a mother hen, "You'll be all right, dear," and put a reassuring hand on Daffy's cheek. "It's not that hard, but you better get started."

Daffy took a breath, lifted the bucket and mop, and stepped right in front of Faernando who managed to balance the six plates he carried by twirling around her. He said, "Watch yourself, new girl." Daffy apologized and, even balancing all those plates, he held the door for her.

Daffy made it upstairs without spilling her bucket. Loretta held the door, gave brief instructions, and left her to it. She opened the shutters to let in the breeze and polished the wood furniture until the room smelled of beeswax. She scrubbed the basin and emptied it into her bucket; pulled the sheets and blankets from the bed and attached them to hooks on the shutters to air out; and got down on hands and knees to scrub the floor. She thought of the maids who had cleaned her rooms. She had thanked them every day but never really understood what they'd done for her. Scrubbing a resilient wad of phlegm, she realized that everyone who had cared for her did so out of obligation—even the King had married her for peace and trade. Her best friend had been her maid, a distant cousin who helped her dress, combed her hair, and, yes, emptied her chamber pot.

She was deep in her thoughts when she heard a voice behind her, "What is taking so damn long?"

She turned and saw Laetifah—stout, obviously pregnant Laetifah.

"Why does it still smell like shit in here? Woman, empty the chamber pot *first!*"

Daffy had worked around the chamber pot, procrastinating, and she'd thought the room smelled of honey polish. She started to defend herself by saying that she'd never emptied a chamber pot but managed to clamp down. Instead, she said what every maid she'd ever scolded had said, "Yes, ma'am." She bent over and pulled the large round vessel from under the seat. She used a rag to wipe its rim.

"Don't use your clean rag on the pot! You stupid?"

"Oh, right. Sorry."

She tucked the rag into her apron pocket and lifted the chamber pot. Breathing through her mouth to avoid the stench, she held the pot outstretched, walked to the stairs, and took them one by one. The contents sloshed back and forth. She stopped halfway down, and let it settle. She took the next step, focused on keeping the pot steady but with less attention on her footing. Four steps from the floor, her left foot slipped on the soft velvet stair. Still focused on keeping that chamber pot steady, she fell. She held it level, but still, she fell.

Her elbows hit first. The chamber pot hit the ground and bounced out of her grasp. Nothing splashed out until it came down. And when it came down, it landed on her head.

Human excrement rained on her, dripping down her cheeks and

closed eyes. She started crying but sealed her mouth and eyes closed. With her head and arms on the floor, elbows and knees screaming in pain, she lay there.

And then she heard laughter. Great roaring laughter. Laughter in women's alto, men's baritone, and, loudest of all, children's soprano. People came in, and the laughter got louder. She then realized she was wearing the chamber pot as a hat. She couldn't stop the tears now, wishing they'd killed her along with the King and her children. Her sobs forced her mouth open, forced her to inhale. She couldn't keep it out of her nose and mouth, and no one at The Gold Piece Inn had ever seen anything so funny in their lives.

And then she heard a familiar voice. "None of you fools are helping her?"

She heard Rustin say, "But mom, look!"

"Son, you fetch your teacher a clean towel and a pail of fresh water. One, two, …"

Daffy lost control of her gag reflex and vomited. She felt two strong hands on her shoulders.

"Let's get you up," Loretta said. "The sea will give you a good scrubbing, and you'll be right as rain." And then, much louder, "If I look up and see anyone laughing—well, believe you me, it'll be your last laugh!"

Daffy felt a cloth wipe her face from forehead to chin. Loretta rubbed another clean cloth over her eyes and nose. Daffy rose to her hands and knees and slowly stood. She opened her eyes. People looked back at her. Children snickered. She saw Caeph and Macae doing their utmost to hold back their laughter. And then she saw Dewey.

Dewey stepped over, looked at the ground around her and then at the stairway, his precious velvet stairway. "Amazing," he said, "total dedication to the job." He turned and walked away.

She looked back at the stairs and saw that the contents of the chamber pot had fallen in a wide path forward but not a drop on the stairs.

"Rusty, Caeph, Naelth—where did Macae go?" Loretta said. "Clean this up."

Daffy looked up at Loretta and saw what made Kaetie and Rustin who they were. Loretta didn't smile or frown, she didn't step back, and she didn't flinch.

Daffy started to apologize but couldn't get two words out before Loretta hugged her.

"Come on Daffy," Loretta said. "A little tighter."

"But I'm covered in, oh no, …"

"There, there, sweetheart. You're okay. Come on, a little tighter, you'll feel better."

"I can't even hug correctly."

"Oh Daffy, I'll make a hugger of you yet." Loretta squeezed her against her warm soft body. "We'll have us a drink tonight, just you and me."

23.

Loretta guided Daffy outside and downhill. Daffy babbled apologies and excuses and hoped against hope that neither her words nor her accent made her sound too much of a snob.

When they reached the wharf, Loretta pulled her off the decking, and the two of them flopped into the trough of a wave. The cold knocked Daffy's breath away. A seal barked at her. Loretta scrubbed her hair and face with sand and then held her steady as wave after wave washed over her. She let the foamy saltwater flow into her mouth, between her teeth, gargled and spit it out.

On the walk back, Loretta said, "You might get us all killed, but you mean well." She blessed Daffy with one of her wicked smiles, leaned in, and whispered, "Besides, I've always wanted to be friends with a princess."

"And I've always wanted a proper friend."

"Daffy, it's your title that threatens us." Loretta kissed her cheek and added, "You're all right."

When they got back to The Gold Piece Inn, Loretta said something about horses and saddles that didn't make sense, walked her upstairs, and put her back to work. Daffy only cleaned three rooms that day, and that meant others had to help.

When she went into her classroom, the blackboard was covered in obscene sketches.

Using a rag to clear the board, she said, "No problem drawing, once you've learned some words, you'll have no trouble writing." She then wrote the words apple, almond, and so on, for all the trees that the kids tended. Macae made a farting sound. Raenny suggested retooling the language so that the written words would resemble trees. Caeph snored. Naelth insisted the letters should be purely abstract, independent of any specific application. Aennie asked if words could prevent chamber pots from overflowing. Vaence asked her how to write "shite keeps raining on my head, it keeps rainin'." Daffy tried to continue the lesson, but even Taevius laughed at the others' cracks. Pent up frustration threatened to burst into anger. She looked at every child in the room. Not really children, though. She saw Rustin, his long frame relaxed on the chair, looking at his knighthood scroll. Some of them wanted to learn, but they all needed to.

Daffy erased the tree names and then wrote the nouns for the likely contents of chamber pots. Things got raucous when she had each student conjugate the verbs for the actions that produce those contents.

24.

Daffy slogged her way from the classroom to the inn. She sat with Caepra, the goatherd. He had a soothing quality about him. A kid goat settled in her lap, and she listened to the musician pick little ditties on his strange lute, all the while arguing with his Tuning Faery about the pitch of his G string.

Her hands were chapped and blistered, her fingernails cracked and torn, and her elbows and knees black and blue. Loretta approached with two mugs.

"How do you do this every day?" Daffy said. "And then serve all night?"

"Eh, you get used to it." Loretta set a full mug of wine in front of her. "And I don't clean rooms no more."

She took a mouthful of the wine. Thick and red, it went down soft and smooth and danced around her empty belly. "I've never been this tired and sore in all my life. And hungry!"

"Good for your skinny bones and there's plenty to eat. Dewey got a bargain on halibut."

Daffy looked at the base of the stairs. "Thank you for this morning."

"You'd do the same for me."

"I hope I would …"

"You would." Loretta took her hand. "I know you would."

Aerrol, Baertha, and Madog came in. Loretta stood and pulled Daffy up with her. The profiteers, in their leather vests and spiked armbands with daggers and cutlasses at their waists, swaggered through the room. Madog waved Loretta over, and they took a table in the casino. Loretta set Daffy in a chair and went to the bar. Madog barely glanced at Daffy. Aerrol scanned her for a second. Baertha winked at her.

Daffy drank the rest of her wine. Loretta returned with drinks for everyone and sat on Madog's lap.

The profiteers talked to each other about commerce and gambling. The lute player had a reckless lassrechaun drummer and an elfin harpist with him that night. They played a two hundred-year-old ballad, the story of Elaene, the legendary knight who held Draefenglo Pass single-handedly for twenty-four hours until King

Graeglory's army arrived and won the decisive battle in the war for Maentanglement. The song's heartbreaking end, Elaene's death in the final battle, always brought a tear to her eye.

Just when the day's trials started fading away, a woman in a heavy red and black gown carrying a bell marched into the inn. She rang the bell until she had everyone's attention. "Lukas, our Great Liberator, calls on all fine humans to search for the traitor and enemy of all humanity, Queen Dafina." She unrolled a drawing of a woman with long black hair and a cunning, evil smile. "Dafina, princess of an enemy state, lover of the faer, hater of anything hard earned, will be weak and harmless but worth three hundred pounds of gold. She must be taken alive."

The crier rang her bell and said something about flags and Lukas's war of liberation, but Daffy's mind wouldn't let go of her desire to be taken dead rather than alive.

Baertha interrupted her thoughts, "Where do you think she's hiding?"

Daffy said, "What?"

And Loretta said, "Safe and sound in Nantesse, no doubt in her momma's arms."

Aerrol said, "It's easy money." Madog, "I'd rather keel-haul Lukas than hand him the Queen." And Baertha, "Too easy. Some bounty hunter already has her locked up, waiting for Nantesse to offer a counter reward so he can start a bidding war. A clever bounty hunter should clear five-hundred pounds for that fine royal flesh."

Loretta slid off Madog and picked up the empty mugs. "Daffy, gimme a hand?"

The two of them walked to the bar. Taevius wiped spilled beer from two stools, and they sat.

"I do love the faer," Daffy said, "but I love humans just as much and that picture she showed—please tell me I don't look like—"

"Quiet." Loretta turned and scanned the room. Taevius stood

next to them, his eyes wide and focused on Daffy. Loretta grabbed his shoulder, pulled him close, and whispered, "You! Forget what you just heard."

"Done," Taevius whispered. "Not a word. Ever." He put his palm over his heart.

Loretta let go, and he walked away.

"I'm sorry," Daffy said, "it's just—"

"You're a good one, Daffy," Loretta whispered. "Right in plain sight, no one even looked your way." She patted her thigh. "But they will look for you, and someday they'll see you. You should disappear."

Daffy averted her eyes, nodded, and walked toward the kitchen with lowered head.

Dewey intercepted her. "Follow me." He led her to his office, shut the door behind her, sat, and pulled the knit cap off his head.

"No one recognized me. The haircut, dye, and—"

"Lukas is in a three-front war, Aschaffort to the north, Aenzio to the south, he's drawn Custaello to the Aelpine Ridge—gonna cost me a fortune." He rubbed his forehead. "There's something you have to understand." Dewey had a way of looking straight into you. The points of his ears were level with the top of his bald head, and they framed his eyes in a way that felt wild and feral, like a mountain lion sizing you up. "My messages to Nantesse aren't getting to your father."

"My father won't give up on me." She swallowed. "Dewey, King Louae is waiting for a message!"

"He gets lots of messages, and mine aren't exactly hand-delivered by a knight with the wax seal of the First Princess of Nantesse. They're from an innkeeper in a dubious fishing village in Glomaythea."

Dewey paused, daring her to speak.

She said, "Did you include the code word that I gave you?"

"Of course. If they ever make it into the King's hands, he'll read them. But how many layers of bureaucracy would they have to go through?"

Her fear became resignation. "I'm a chamber lass."

"It could be worse."

"How?"

Elfs on the Run

25.

Daffy shed her apron in the kitchen. Daeffid offered her a plate of halibut and almond-crusted potatoes, but Dewey's news had killed her appetite. She thanked him and went through the stable to the alley. An ocean breeze blew across the nape of her neck, reminding her of the long black locks that had always draped shoulders, gone with everything else she'd ever known.

It wasn't the chamber pots or pirates and certainly not the Bastards that pushed her away from The Gold Piece Inn. It was freedom tugging at her, dangling just out of reach every time that she expected to see Gledig at the bar holding a stein, or her children playing in the sawdust with the others.

The sun had set, and the GloFaeries were hiding. She'd never seen a street so dark. Fish sizzled on a grill in the Trading Guild Hall and coins clinked together in the counting houses. A few merchants milled about the marketplace with lanterns. No one paid her any attention. On Low Street, she listened to the rhythm of ocean swells. On Profit Street, she lingered outside the fancy Snob & Whistle, taking in the smell of beef simmering and exotic spices. The hunger pangs returned, but something else drew her inside, a piano. A melancholy melody came to mind, simple notes thrown together with complex chords, a sad song about a drowned sailor and the maermaid who loved him. She wanted to sing and cry and let her fingers dance across the keys.

The only resemblance of the Snob & Whistle to The Gold Piece Inn was that both served food and drink. The Snob was much smaller, and the serving-lasses—all lasses, no lads—wore long lace skirts and starched white aprons with rigid bodices that revealed modest décolletage. No dogs, goats, or cats lounged on chairs or under tables, no children played in sawdust at the feet of their parents, no serving-lasses jiggled their assets, no serving-lads pitched their packages, and the guests wore fine attire from different kingdoms.

Daffy found a small round table in the nook of a stairway and sat. She felt invisible among her class of people. She'd never noticed how sterile her old life had been—except that one day. Oh, it had been glorious. A sunny spring day when she was fifteen and the whole world beckoned her. She escaped her role as princess and the expectations that came with it. After fighting with her mother over something she couldn't even remember, she stole a scullery maid's clothes and walked right out of her father's castle. Walking alone on the other side of the fortified walls, she saw him in a crowd of women and children laughing and splashing away the heat. He called himself Luke and, when he asked, she'd given him a fine peasant name: Jill.

She tried to let the music carry her back to that perfect day, tried to let the soft melody wash away the shame and picture herself as she might have been, a girl visiting the fountain on a hot day. But a gentleman in a velvet jacket at the next table raised his voice.

"Did you hear that the kingdom is being renamed 'Maythea'?" the gentleman said. "The Flying Anvil will replace the Glo flag."

Daffy had been fond of the Glomaythean flag since she was a girl: A green oak leaf on a white background with a sparking Glo-Faery perched on the leaf's stem.

"Let me guess," the woman said, "there will be a flag burning celebration on the anniversary of Gledig's assassination?"

"Then you have heard."

"Lukas has a way of conveying his message." She sipped her drink.

"That he does."

"And possession of Glo flags will be yet another executable act of treason?"

"Naturally." He speared an olive with a tiny fork. "One might prefer a slightly more sophisticated monarch."

"Have you heard about the Faery Tax?"

"How can he tax faeries?"

"Once the faer inventory is complete, businesses will be taxed for using faeries." She looked at the tarnish on her fingers, the telltales of a banker, grayed from manipulating tarnished silver and copper ohzees. "It won't be cheap."

"How many Counting Faeries did you report?"

"What difference does it make?" She sighed. "They're all leaving."

"Good in the long run, open up opportunities for human beings. Though the notion of a Tax Faery is amusing. I picture a tiny gentleman with an even tinier watch-fob and the cutest little abacus."

She chuckled, nearly choking on her wine. "But will that be the end of it?"

"Not to worry. I have been assured from on high that Lukas knows better than to harm the lower faer."

Daffy had been Queen of Glomaythea for seven years. She'd watched the good people of this warm and fertile land—both human and faer—compromise when they disagreed, collaborate when they were challenged, and unite under their flag when threatened. Of course, Daffy cried, but she didn't cry for Glomaythea.

Freedom? Independence? The sense of forbidden freedom that had taunted her since the King died wasn't freedom. It was vanity. That cloud of self-loathing overcame her again. At least this time she wept alone.

Or so she thought. A serving-lass took this moment to visit her table. Daffy cleared her throat, wiped her eyes, and asked for tonight's supper. The server said, "What are you doing here?" and looked her over.

"Would the pianist mind if I were to play a song during her break?"

"I'm not serving your type until you show me some money."

Daffy stopped. She pictured how she must look. Daffy had never had to pay for anything. She'd never needed to carry money.

The serving-lass said, "That's what I thought. Do I need to walk you out?"

Daffy gripped the table to steady herself.

26.

Daffy didn't remember leaving the Snob & Whistle, didn't remember walking down to the wharf, along the dock, or up a sandy trail. She found herself on a cliff watching waves smash into the rocks far below. The foam glowed in the moonlight.

Once she'd run out of self-absorbed tears, she cried for the end of Glomaythea, the land and people and kingdom that her husband's family had united and that she had sworn to serve. Glomaythea was far from perfect. The poor suffered, the sick died, the wisdom of the aged was not always heeded, but the royal family had worked every day, all day, to guide their part of this world to an ever more peaceful, prosperous civilization that cared equally for every subject. Far from perfect, but better than re-flagged Maythea had any hope or intent of becoming.

Daffy awoke in the shadow of The Fist of God, shivering in thick dewy grass on a hill above Crescent Cove. The first light she saw sparkled from the sea. The ships cast long shadows, a dozen pelicans flew low over the water, seagulls complained, seals barked, and Daffy finally stopped crying.

That childish sense of freedom felt ridiculous now. Yes, she was stuck here, but she refused to accept that she was helpless. She had insisted that Rustin keep his promises. Well, she'd made a few promises of her own. She rubbed away the crusty tears and vowed to herself, to the sea, and to the people starting their day in the town below that she would uphold the oath she'd made to Glomaythea the day she married the King. The sun crested The Fist of God. Its rays warmed her neck. She imagined that the rays came from King Gledig as he dubbed her a knight, of sorts: the rightful queen embedded behind enemy lines as a Gold Piece Inn servinglass who would find a way to care for her subjects. The resolution brought relief from her grief, and purpose pushed away her fear. Ideas for how she could help the resistance flowed into her mind. They all settled around Dewey and his uncanny sources of information. She knew people, too.

Finding purpose has a funny way of encouraging fate.

She heard a rustling behind her and whipped around—nothing but oak trees at first. And then a movement in the grass caught her eye. Two figures stood just steps away. Their clothes didn't camouflage them against the yellowing of the hill's late spring grass, yet they were nearly invisible. The taller wore a suede vest dyed a color between sky blue and grass green, and the other wore a long tunic of orange and pink like the clouds that framed the sunrise behind them. They moved with the shifting patterns of the wind, seeming to step between tufts of grass rather than on them, leaving no trail.

The skin of their bare legs had the rich reds and browns of redwood bark. The shorter had long, tawny hair that cascaded down to her waist. She wore a belt heavy with tools, a hammer and chisels and blades of different lengths. The taller had tan braids that laced down behind the quiver of arrows slung on his back and the longbow he carried over his shoulder.

The woman turned to say something to the man, and, in that motion, her hair parted around her ears. Ears the size of an outstretched hand with sharp peaks that added a full inch to her height and, unlike the skin of her face, legs, hands, and chest, her ears were the pale color of her hair, easy to overlook, until you noticed them.

Daffy had met many elfs in her life but couldn't say that she'd ever known one. Their long lives gave them a foreign perspective, a relaxed, unhurried outlook on life. They only needed to eat a few times a month and had no affection for possessions beyond the simplest of comforts.

If you ignored their ears, the sharp angles of their eyebrows, and their tall, willowy form, they looked a lot like twenty-five-year-old humans. Daffy had to remind herself that they could be anywhere from fifty to five-thousand years old. They could get sick or injured like any other creature but didn't age. You could try to reckon their age from their scars, but even the worst gashes healed in a few centuries.

They stopped in front of her. Daffy said, "Hello?" She couldn't remember if elfin etiquette favored eye contact, but it didn't matter. There was no pulling away from the diamond shaped pupils in those green eyes.

"Yes, madam, hello," the elfin lad said. He stood a foot taller than Daffy, but like a willow tree rather than an oak, tall but not imposing. "My name, it is Conifaer."

The elfin lass said, "I am called Lapidae." She stood with her legs at shoulder width and hands on her tools.

"Can you tell us, please," Conifaer said, "has usurp—that is, Liberator—has Liberator occupied Crescent Cove?"

"I fear that he has."

"Uh, err." He looked at Lapidae and spoke to her in Naest, a northern language that Daffy had studied as a girl. "I know not how to do this."

Lapidae answered him in the same language, "This far, we've come." Then to Daffy, in Glo she said, "Help to get out of Glomay-thea, prefer north to the Grindwael Mountains, is what we need. We'll board any ship."

Daffy looked down at the harbor.

Conifaer added, "More will come, more of us, more elfs I

mean."

Lapidae said, "Many, many more." She stopped talking but her clenched jaw and narrowed eyes spoke for her, hatred.

Conifaer spoke in Naest, "Be careful with what you say to her."

Lapidae answered in the same language. "We cannot emerge from forest to human village, board ship, and fare thee well. Disguises, passage, allies, all of these things we need, and every one of us needs same."

Conifaer said, "Hopeless."

Lapidae switched to Glo. "We find ourselves a difficult situation. I apologize for his rudeness."

Daffy nodded. She looked at Major Blechk's corvette *Daefender* anchored in the harbor, the sun just lighting the Flying Anvil. People and their beasts of burden moved about the marketplace. She could also see the orchard, fields, and spring behind The Gold Piece Inn, even her classroom. And then she got it. She started to laugh but saw a look that might be elfin fear on Lapidae's face. "Come with me, I have an idea. We can talk on the way."

She led them to a path that curled along the index finger of The Fist of God next to a brook in a sparse forest. When she looked back, she had to stop to discern them from the surroundings even though they were right next to her. She said, "I know little about your culture, so please excuse me if I'm rude. Do you get along with druids?"

Some tension left Conifaer's forehead. "We get along with druids that we get along with. Others, not so much."

The trail wound along a brook that emptied into the spring that fed The Gold Piece Inn.

"Halflings?"

Conifaer's face went sour. "It is the offspring of an elf and a human? Is what you mean?"

"I do."

Lapidae spit on the ground.

"Well," Daffy said, "I'm not sure that anyone gets along very well with the halfling I have in mind, so it doesn't really matter."

"Halflings. Envious creatures yearning to be elfs," Lapidae said. "Pathetic, spend life among beasts."

Daffy couldn't imagine a more egotistical statement under the circumstances. "This halfling will help you if you're in danger. He'll help anyone who is in danger."

"Generous," Conifaer drew out the word as though he expected a catch. "Lapidae, mmm, she is maybe narrow minded about these things. Many halflings I'm sure are generous, caring people."

Lapidae snickered.

"Oh, he's not generous or caring. He's cursed," Daffy said. "If you ask him for help, he has to help you." They emerged near the spring. "Dewey doesn't want to help me, either, but I owe him my life."

The elfs stopped.

"Dewey Nawton?" Lapidae said. "You are not taking us to Dewey Nawton?"

"Hard to believe, isn't it?"

"This curse," Conifaer said, "was it invoked by human or elfin maegician?"

"Crisiant, Wizard and truth-teller to King Gledig."

Lapidae spoke to Conifaer in Naest. "What else is it that we can do?"

Conifaer shook his head and then, in that same language, said, "Why Dewey?"

Daffy said, "At the very least, he won't hurt you. He relies on the faer for everything he does."

"But why Dewey? It is this much the gods hate us?"

"You only get one chance," Daffy said. "Ask for everything you might need before he can get away."

As they walked through the orchard, Daffy noticed how the elfs stepped around trails without disturbing plants, not even groundcover. They didn't step into the shade of trees or bushes so much as they walked along the boundaries of that shade. Naelth waved to her from a willow near the spring but gave no sign that he'd noticed the elfs. Rustin and Caeph were dueling with sticks held as swords and both greeted her, but neither indicated the elfs.

Daffy left the elfs in the faery garden. She stepped into the kitchen and looked back. They stood in the shadow line of a blooming magnolia tree, but she couldn't see them. She found Dewey in his chair next to the window. He looked uncomfortable, ornery. She said, "I need you to come outside."

He demanded to know why, but Daffy was well versed in manipulating people, and Dewey had a particular weakness.

She said, "I was sitting in the garden and I noticed a strange rock. I pushed the dirt around it and ..." She leaned over and whispered. "I think it's gold."

He rolled his eyes and looked over her shoulder.

She looked back and saw Dewey's Truth Faery frowning at her.

"You're lying," Dewey said. He turned to his Truth Faery. "I know that she's lying, but what if she just thinks she's lying but is actually telling the truth? If she found a nugget of gold, and I ignored her, I'd never forgive myself. Do you see how difficult my life is?"

The Truth Faery swooped down and disappeared in the windowpane.

Dewey followed Daffy out to the magnolia tree. Petal and Leaf Faeries fluttered by.

Before Daffy could discern them, Dewey said, "Farqin elfs? Really?" He turned back to the kitchen.

Daffy blocked him. "You're an elf-bigot? Self-loathing becomes you, but it's such a cliché."

"It's just that ..." He rubbed a hand over his eyes, up on his bald head, and scratched one of his pointed ears. He turned around and looked toward a mound of lavender. "... elfs are critical, pretentious, arrogant—"

"You sure you're only *half* elf?" Daffy said, and then, "There you are." Dozens of tiny, immature Stone Faeries clustered around Lapidae.

Looking at the elfs, she whispered in the language of the north, "Ask the question!"

Conifaer and Lapidae's eyes widened at recognition of Daffy's use of their native language.

"You think I don't speak Naest?" Dewey said. "Ask what?"

Conifaer said, "Dewey, maybe you don't remember me, but—"

Lapidae stepped in front of him and said, "Help us please. The usurper will put in prison all of our kind and yours too." She spoke so quickly that the words ran together. "Help us with disguises? Transport? Will you help us contact humans worth our trust? Will you help us, Dewey Nawton?"

27.

Among the many things that Dewey found intolerable, being tricked was right up there with paying full retail prices.

"Oh, shite." Dewey dropped to the ground and sat with his legs crossed, cradling his head in his hands. He groaned. "Daffy told you about my curse."

Daffy grinned.

"One of these days, Daffy. I swear to the gods, one of these days, I'll get you." He rubbed his chin. He picked his nose, looked at the booger, and flicked it into the dirt. "All right." He stretched the words into an expression of disgust. A pair of Farq Faeries fought over his booger.

Conifaer listed dozens of requests. He spoke in the conde-scending way that kindled Dewey's rage, but every request came prefaced with "Will you help us …" He asked for help constructing the infrastructure necessary to create a secret transit system capable of moving thousands of faer to any land that would have them. He asked Dewey to install hiding places and secret passages in The Gold Piece Inn. Dewey sat, mouth agape, while the elf rambled on.

"Is that all?" Dewey stared at his inn. It was one thing to hide a renegade queen, harbor a few hives of lower faer, even shuffle a few dozen elfs from The Fist of God onto ships. But thousands? And leprechauns? And who would pay? Total ruin awaited. He lay on the ground with a lavender mound as pillow and watched clouds pass. He'd die young. That simple. "What about leprechauns? Dragons? Yeti? How about dryads? Are you digging up Tree Faeries and shipping them out too?" His ears flared. "And how about halflings?"

"Yes, leprechauns," Conifaer said. "Not yeti, the humans cannot find them. The dryads of Glomaythea are to be cut down and nothing we can do. Dragons, they care for themselves."

Dewey said, "Don't tell me you believe in dragons."

"It's true," Conifaer said. "No one has seen a dragon and lived to discuss it, but—"

"Get it?" Dewey said. "It's a joke. There's no evidence for them, not even a charred damsel." He rubbed his eyes with his fists. "Damn it, Daffy. Elfs weren't enough? You had to bring stupid elfs?" And then to Conifaer. "You didn't address halflings …"

Conifaer exchanged glances with Lapidae. "Halflings? We are not certain about halflings."

"Seriously? You farqin bigots! And because of the curse cast on me by the arsehole whose head will someday swing on the chain above the entrance to The Gold Piece Inn, I, Dewey Nawton, halfing, am forced to protect thousands elfs from—wait for it … bigots!" He stood and marched back into the inn. Without looking back, he said, "Hide them somewhere, I'll be in my office trying to solve this puzzle before it kills us all. And thank you, Daffy, thank you so damn much. We're now walking dead."

Conifaer and Lapidae followed.

Conifaer said, "I am woodweaver."

A Stone Faery perched on Lapidae's finger—the little fellow looked like a gray bumblebee except for his tiny hardhat. Conifaer nudged her. She shook her head. Conifaer said, "Lapidae is cold-smith."

Dewey stopped and turned, "A coldsmith, you say?" A smile wrestled with his lips. He appraised her. "You can work stone as humans work iron?"

Conifaer whispered to her, and she said, "Humans always in a hurry melt ore. I work geometry of crystal, each facet has its own way, already polished, with my friends, here—" The Stone Faery on her finger tipped his hat "—I make of granite things that that cannot break, cannot lose an edge, and are as bird wings. I even can make as thin and clear like glass."

"I'll need a few favors from you." Before she could reply, he went to his office. The kitchen staff gawked at the elfs, as did the few people in the saloon and casino.

Conifaer surveyed the inn's interior from Dewey's office doorway. "Your building, she will need fast modification, very fast and quick."

Dewey made the sound of a donkey carrying twice its weight.

PART II

Resistance

28.

When a king is assassinated, his wizard almost always has to start a new career. Crisiant considered a few options like enchanting Burglar Faeries and collecting enough treasure to live the high life, but convincing faeries to steal requires coercion, not enchantment—pure thaergy, nasty stuff. He wondered if the faer's lack of support for greed was the basis for Lukas's bigotry. Plus, Crisiant couldn't live with himself if he broke his last promise to King Gledig: to preserve Queen Dafina. Fortunately, his backup plan gave him a chance to monitor her.

As a lad, his father apprenticed him to a glassblower. A respectable trade, but he had no interest in sales and marketing. He ran away with a group of musicians, carried their equipment, helped setup and teardown, and eventually learned to think in melody. He became a minstrel, but the poor accommodations, infrequent meals, and low pay wore on him. His musical talent ultimately led to his career in maegic.

After the assassination, he spent his last gold ohzee on a guitar—and cringed every time someone referred to it as a long-necked, horizontal, six-string lute—let his hair grow, traded his robes for leather and talked Bob the bartender into getting him a gig at The Gold Piece Inn. With the help of a Makeup Faery, no one recognized him, not even the Queen.

He played all the historic ballads for Kaetie—performers will do anything for the one or two people who pay attention to lyrics. Then, one night he saw Rusty reading his "To Be a Knight" scroll and added a big dose of heroic poetry to the playlist—the long forms, twenty to forty minute songs that describe how heroes are made, not the three-minute pop versions. They were mostly myths and he could tell that Kaetie didn't like them, but with every lyric that told of a sword wielded in defense of the helpless and every arrow notched to take down a tyrant, that fire in Rusty's eyes grew more determined. Kaetie asked why his stories contradicted her books. He gave her the old art for art's sake excuse, and she rolled her eyes.

* * *

The annual Summer Solstice celebration was a somber affair. The jugglers, sword swallowers, and fire breathers made an effort, but with Volunteers staking out every corner in town, no one was in the mood. The only excitement came when Laetifah gave birth right on the pier. Without a Midwife Faery, it was touch and go, but she delivered a healthy little girl and named her Bellae. The next day, in the safety of The Gold Piece Inn, the Midwife Faery delivered Maeggie a new son that she named Glaen.

Daffy taught school, fell in love with her students, and became part of the maternal community that ran Dewey Nawton's Gold Piece Inn. Serving-lads and chamber men came and went with the tides, but a core of women stayed at the inn at least as long as it took to raise their children.

Lukas promised utopia once humanity finally "shed its faery shackles" and he "liberated" every other kingdom in Glandaeff and blah blah blah. He ruled with the same old recipe of well-told lies, well-placed bribes, and well-publicized torture that has always propped up autocrats. Laws were forgotten, and every case of justice balanced on loyalty.

29.

Conifaer, the elfin woodweaver, presented Dewey plans to install secret passages and hidden quarters behind false walls in The Gold Piece Inn.

Dewey spread the drawings across his desk. Conifaer suggested that the inn would be a way station, but Dewey saw it as a warren crawling with oversized rodents. Conifaer admitted that elfs are creatures of the outdoors, uncomfortable with anything but open skies and stars overhead, and Dewey found a nugget of solace in the discomfort that they'd feel within his walls.

The cost of materials and loss of square-footage gnawed at Dewey's tiny soul until Macae looked over his shoulder and said, "You should have built it this way in the first place."

"Go away," Dewey said. But before Macae took two steps, he asked, "Why?"

"Outlaws come through Crescent Cove all the time, and hiding places will rent for a premium." Dewey looked at the lanky Bastard with new respect and suspicion.

Dewey apprenticed the gang-of-five to Conifaer. He had already taken advantage of Rusty's obsession with knighthood by assigning him extra chores in the stable. Rusty did all the shoveling, repaired tack, trained fillies and colts, and sharpened blades.

Without Rusty to keep them in line, the gang-of-five complained so much that Dewey had to summon them to his office. He told them that, if they didn't get the job done fast, they'd get caught and Blechk would torture them into betraying their dear mothers. Aennie laid odds on how long the average Gold Piece Inn Bastard could withstand torture. When Caeph predicted that Naelth and Raenny would be the first to talk, Raenny said, "If they withheld my morning tea, I'd tell them anything they needed to know." And Naelth, "Goes without saying. How can I concentrate on self-preservation without tea?" After a few days he assigned Rusty to Conifaer, too, and the gang-of-five finally got to work.

Between his work in the stables and helping Conifaer, Rusty managed to find time to carve training swords of oak and redwood.

He asked Conifaer for help and learned a lesson that would serve him the rest of his life. Conifaer seemed to ignore the request, but when Rusty left one of his "swords" in a field, he saw Conifaer examine it and then snap it over his knee. When Rusty held up the two pieces, he saw that Conifaer had marked the break to show Rusty how to use the rhythm of the grain.

During the dog days of summer, when teenage boys feel like fighting and middle-aged halflings feel like being left alone, Dewey took Rusty up The Fist's middle finger to a clearing hidden by live oaks covered in moss and mistletoe and surrounded by dense manzanita. "If you're going to beat each other with sticks, do it here where I can deny all knowledge of your stupidity."

Rusty and his Knightlets whiled away hours training in their "arena." Rusty tried to recruit Taevius, but the strong, silent Bastard spent his free time sailing in a single-mast dingy.

* * *

An early Autumn heatwave brought louder arguments. Supporters of the usurper, led by Grindaer the miller and members of the blacksmith's guild, were outnumbered but tried to make up for it in volume and self-righteousness. "Lukas is leading us to a thousand years of prosperity. Forget all that claptrap about first humans, just line up and let him lead. It's going to be incredible!"

"Go ahead, kill your brothers and sisters for treasure and then give it to some arse and call him your 'leader,'" Dewey said. "Stupidest species on earth, and you think you're superior."

"You can't understand!" Grindaer said. "You're not one of us."

When Lukas spent his treasure faster than he could pillage it, he issued "Acquisition Receipts" in lieu of payment. Anyone who complained was branded a traitor. Merchants who asked to be paid in ohzees were guilty of treason, and treason was punished by death.

When the autumn winds blew the leaves off the orchard trees, and made way for winter, the ships that once brought exotic goods—woven rugs, fruit, jewels, teas, and herbs—stopped landing in Crescent Cove. Major Blechk took whatever the fishers and whalers caught. They soon had enough Acquisition Receipts to wallpaper their boats and stopped catching more than they needed for their own families. Crescent Cove's marketplace became a desolate square where seagulls and crows congregated as though in mourning, guarded by a squad of Volunteers. Pirates stopped coming too, and the absence of Madog Grwn broke Loretta's heart, but worst of all, rumors swirled that Lukas had begun conscripting every child age sixteen and over into his so-called Volunteer army.

But in Dewey's eyes, Lukas did something far more appalling. One dreary day, the Town Liar made a proclamation that brought tears to Dewey's eyes: the rumor of a Faery Tax came true. The use of faeries for labor would be calculated in human-hours and taxed accordingly. The pain started in Dewey's stomach, worked its way up and settled in his chest. He couldn't draw a deep breath.

At the Winter Solstice celebration, a frenetic affair with refugee Yule Faeries instigating drinking games and the fallout that comes with them, four serving-lasses announced their pregnancies. Dewey took news of the next generation of Gold Piece Inn Bastards the way he did most news. "We're short on food and drink and now we're short on serving-lasses and damn it, I need Daffy to start serving."

"Someone will recognize her," Loretta said. "I'll train Kaetie."

"Kaetie? She'll drive guests away." With every report of Lukas's wars—increasing body counts, stagnant fronts, and sieges—Kaetie's need to understand became more ravenous. How had the Liberator obtained so many followers? Why hadn't King Gledig seen the discontent and acted? When had history presented a people such a situation before and how had they responded? "How many times do I have to tell her that human history is nothing more than a bunch of drunk people walking aimlessly through time?"

"More reason for her to start serving."

"She wants to be a druid."

"Where's she going work in The First Human's faer-less society?" Loretta said.

"Loretta, I hate to be the one to say it—no, actually, I'm quite happy to be the one to say it—your daughter is not friendly. She doesn't tolerate fools and look over there." He motioned to the saloon and casino beyond it. "They're *all* fools. Kaetie would make a horrible serving-lass. No. She's better off tending the faery hives and learning the tricks of a different trade than yours." He paused long enough to interrupt Loretta. "It's settled, start training Daffy."

"What'll you do when someone wants her upstairs?"

"No one wants to take that skinny lass upstairs."

30.

Dewey sat in his favorite seat on a dark winter day, watching icy rain through his glass window and worrying about the Faery Tax. The fire roared next to him, and his Truth Faery napped on his lap.

Loretta dodged a running child, bleated a reply to an inquisitive goat, and set a bowl of watery, salty, anchovy soup and a roll the size of a faery's fist in front of the goatherd.

"That's it?" Caepra said, dropping the wooden spoon on the table. "The Gold Piece Inn isn't what it used to be."

The band played a rousing ballad that didn't rouse anyone: the story of a sailor who fell in love with a maerbutler. The maerbutler followed her ship for years. Eventually she jumped overboard and into his life. He brought her to his grotto and, so the legend goes, she's still there.

"True story," Bob said. "Happened to my mom. She eventually drowned, but she drowned a happy woman." He didn't even get a chuckle.

Daffy delivered more weak soup to the arguing table.

"You have to trust him," Grindaer said. "Lukas is a genius. Normal people like you and me can't expect to understand the intricacies of his plan."

"Uh huh," Baeswax said. "Trying to invade an island a thousand miles across the sea while he can barely hold the front in his own backyard—that's genius?"

Codae said, "Putting thousands of our kids into battle because the Queen got away. Right. Genius."

"You'll see, he'll win this damn war," Grindaer said.

Fin sat a table across the room and bellowed as if he was trying to be heard above a storm at sea. "My son died fighting for that farqin usurper!" He marched to the arguing table. "That third-rate human thinks he can storm Nantesse Castle during winter?"

"It's called laying siege!" Grindaer said. "He's got a beachhead. Whose side are you on?"

Daffy stopped. Her shoulders slumped, and she stared into the fire.

Fin yelled, "Thousands into ambush after ambush on the eastern front. You can't fight Yarrow Cavalry on foot! He's got supply lines up the Aelpine slopes in *winter*. The troops who aren't killed by avalanches will freeze to death!"

"Are you talking about the Volunteers' glorious victory over bareback savages?" Grindaer pushed out his chair. "Don't you people get it? We're this close to taking our proper place in the world." He motioned around the room. "But we have to do our part. Lukas can't liberate us as long as we're surrounded by traitors."

Fin said, "Tell me you're not blaming faeries for the deaths of thousands of our sons and daughters."

Grindaer stood and seemed to realize that he was alone in his loyalty. The three young men in the Volunteer's red and black leather drank from their mugs, listened to the band, and wanted nothing to do with politics.

Grindaer turned to his old friend Dewey as though he might find an ally. Dewey removed his hat and scratched an ear. Grindaer walked out into the cold, driving rain. The wind held the door open and ice flew in and melted in the straw.

Bees

31.

One morning, as usual, Dewey was on the porch at dawn watching for messenger birds. His Truth Faery, wrapped in a heavy blanket, well, a fluff of wool, leaned out of the windowpane and wished him a good morning. A flock of geese honked their complaints at the icy fog, and Dewey sensed a major storm on its way. The nut and fruit trees had started budding a month early. He wished he had the luxury of worrying about a freeze destroying his crop, but with an inn packed with faer, survival made everything else seem petty. Plus, what really ate at him was reselling the damn honey he had to buy as cover for the faery hives.

Back inside, he heard the Bastards clanking their water jugs into the kitchen and the cracking of fresh logs as Daeffid got the stove going. He took a cup of steaming tea into his office. A Monitor Faery paced back and forth on his desk, a muscular little guy about the size of your pinky toe with mosquito wings wearing a tank top and shorts on a day like this.

Dewey sat and confided in him. "It's broken me. I wish I'd died with the King."

The faery stood a few inches from Dewey's nose, feet shoulder width apart, poised for Dewey knew not what.

Dewey continued, "I'm cursed. Everyone knows it, and no one cares. Oh, the pain and injustice."

The faery looked at his tiny watch but didn't say anything. Dewey knew that this Monitor Faery was sensitive, and that sensitive people tend to be shy, but his troubles distracted him. "Lylli, the fruit of my loins, laughs at me. You know Lylli, didn't she enchant you?"

The faery nodded, eyes wide, now tapping his foot as though he had to pee.

"She never did have a sense of commerce." He turned to a stack of Acquisition Receipts. "We should counterfeit these things. Do you know any Printing Faeries?"

A crack of thunder shook the inn down to its foundation.

"Uh, sir?" the Monitor Faery said

Another resounding crack.

"Shouldn't you be monitoring something?"

"The inn is surrounded by Volunteers, and I fear they're breaking down the door."

Dewey launched out of his chair and into the saloon.

Volunteer boots clanked on the porch boards. Another clang and the front door flew from its hinges, battering into a table. Two Volunteers holding a battering ram stepped aside and a stocky woman stepped in. She pointed a broadsword at Dewey and told him to freeze.

Dewey looked at the peg where he kept his knit hat. It wasn't there! He touched his head. He'd put it on before going outside. He took a breath and let his elfin blood calm him.

He held out his hands to the woman and said, "Why ruin my door? It wasn't locked. It's an *inn* and you're welcome any time." He hung his head. "All part of it, I suppose. Come in, have a seat at any table you like, we'll be serving an oyster omelet for breakfast." He pushed the splintered door off the table and held out a chair.

She had sergeant stripes on her right sleeve—a sleeve that lacked an arm—and used the broadsword in her left hand to direct soldiers into position. Some soldiers carried shovels, others had spears, and they all had butterfly nets attached to their belts. Their uniforms had patches, and the bright red and polished black had faded to brown and gray.

"Already ate?" he asked. "The bartender won't be here for hours—hard to get good help—" he indicated her motley crew of soldiers "—I'm sure you understand. But I'll be happy to fix you something, Leprechaun coffee?"

"Nawton?" The sergeant spoke with a guttural rasp, more air than voice.

"Perhaps a game of chance?"

She slid her broadsword into the scabbard across her back. "Sergeant Taelerson, here on Major Blechk's orders. Faer inventory." She motioned to Dewey with her sword. "Step out of the way." She rasped in the monotone of an efficient but unenthusiastic laborer.

Dewey looked at her again. She'd been there that day. She was the one who landed the blow that killed King Gledig and she'd lost the arm that had wielded the sword.

"Faer inventory?" he said. It didn't add up. Among the pile of tiny scrolls on his desk, Dewey had reports that described plans for Lukas's "Faer Centers."

Centuries ago, before Queen Graegloria and her father, King Graeglory, brought human and faer together in Maentanglement, humans used to fall for the rants of charismatic lunatics. The lunatic would blame everything from stale bread to poor harvests to outbreaks of disease on a group of outsiders and put them in prisons he called "camps" or "workstations" or "cubicles." The persecuted group was never guilty of anything but being different from the nut-job's followers. The lunatic starved and tortured his scapegoats at these camps. Like tides ebbing and flooding, the pattern repeated every few generations. Dewey was anything but proud of his elfin ancestry—*bunch of lazy snobs*—but he preferred it to his human lineage—*paranoid, smelly idiots. Damn humans line up like sheep to follow orders. Sure, they're a productive lot who know how to make a few ohzees, right up until they kill each other and everyone with them.* Craziest of all, from the perspective of a business-halfling like Dewey, the lunatics always ended up destroying whatever they bought with their profits.

But are elfs any better? They live long enough to see it happen over and over again, all the while clinging to the belief that their kind would never become the maniac's target. And here we are.

Stroking his chin, Dewey looked up at the ceiling in time to see the shy Monitor Faery disappear into a redwood rafter. "Faer inventory? I haven't seen a faery here in—well, I'm not sure that we've ever entertained a faery. What do they look like?"

The sergeant pushed him aside. She ordered Volunteers into the casino, the kitchen, and upstairs.

Dewey bowed to them. "Good luck." He emphasized the word luck.

The sergeant had the audacity to glare as if Dewey were to blame for the Volunteers' notorious bad luck in all forms of gambling.

Loretta stepped out of the kitchen and he heard Rusty and the Knightlets grumbling.

Sergeant Taelerson stopped and ran her eyes up and down Loretta's form as though digesting her.

Loretta crossed her arms over her breasts.

"No, no, don't cover up." The sergeant raised her eyebrows. "When my job is done here, maybe yours begins."

"Maybe," Loretta said, "but I don't take Acquisition Receipts."

The sergeant laughed, a low throaty rumble that shook her shoulders.

And then Daefer walked in. Tall and thin with skin that only seemed to reflect different shades of gray, Daefer wore a dirty brown tunic, breeches, bare feet and, like Dewey, he also had a knit cap pulled down over his ears. Dewey had known Daefer for over a century. The two looked at each other and Dewey felt a little burst of humiliation and shame similar to the effects of his curse. Even as outcasts, halflings share little camaraderie. They either join human society in the role of perpetual oddity or live on the outskirts as loners and hermits.

The sergeant said, "Have you met my faer hunter?"

"It figures," Dewey said. And it did. Daefer would do anything for money. He'd pimp his grandmother and steal candy from babies. Daefer once kidnapped an orphan and sold him to a wealthy pedophile. The description of Daefer that ran through Dewey's mind made him uncomfortable. Dewey cherished revenue, and if not for the curse, he'd profit when possible—except for the orphan thing, he'd never do that.

Daefer turned to the sergeant and pointed at Dewey. "Here's one."

The sergeant ignored the comment. Dewey's human side relaxed. He'd done his homework and felt reasonably immune. If anything happened to Dewey, Lukas would learn enough about Major Blechk's hobbies and sideline businesses to assure his execution, but the sergeant's reaction was the first tangible evidence that Blechk was aware of the situation.

More Volunteers streamed in and she ordered them to search the barn, bunkhouse, and fields. Two of the Volunteers were Gold Piece Inn regulars, soldiers who stayed out of trouble and tried to survive the war by avoiding anyone who might complicate their lives.

Dewey said, "Watch your step," half a second before a Wood Faery pulled a nail from a floorboard. The sergeant stepped on the board and it flipped up, capping her knee. She stumbled, and her ankle caught in the gap.

"Macae, Caeph," Dewey called. The two boys rushed in. "Caeph, help the sergeant up. Macae, fix the flooring."

Caeph kneeled and reached for the sergeant's right arm. He grabbed a handful of empty sleeve and nearly pulled off her tunic. He began a long-winded chain of apologies that delayed the sergeant another minute. Macae held the floorboard up long enough for the Wood Faery, along with dozens of others, to slip into the crawl space.

32.

Rusty had been tending horses when the Volunteers came up the hill. He ran out to the faery garden. If he hadn't known where to look, it would have taken hours to find Conifaer and Lapidae. They perched on a rock in the scattered shade of a sleeping apple tree. Lapidae worked a long thin piece of granite and Conifaer rubbed a piece of walnut against a piece of oak for no reason that Rusty could comprehend.

"They're coming," he said, "it's time to use the secret rooms you built."

Conifaer cocked his head and listened for an instant.

Rusty said, "Volunteers, and they're searching for faer." He ran back to the kitchen and let the door hang open, grabbed two five-gallon water jugs, and held them in a way that he hoped blocked the Volunteer's view. He resisted the urge to look at the false wall where, hopefully, Conifaer and Lapidae had already slipped into a passage. Daeffid held up one finger. Rusty set one jug down and took the other outside. He let the door slam behind him.

33.

Kaetie stood next to the faery hive under an almond tree between the classroom and the faery garden. The cutest little cherub you ever saw in your life, his wings just sprouted, stood on her palm. She looked him over and confirmed that he was a Stem Faery. Though his parents had been Leaf Faeries and Dewey wanted her to enchant the Stem Faeries into Monitor or Alert Faeries, Kaetie wanted him to become a Bricoleur Faery, good at almost anything, master of nearly nothing. Someone who would turn pages when she read, help with her chores, maybe even double as her Sleep Faery.

She blew on the little fellow. He spread his wings and rose on the warmth of her breath.

A rhythmic buzzing sound with varying pitch carved a complex melody across the field. Kaetie looked up and saw thousands of Monitor Faeries fly out of the inn. They spread into a cloud that looked like dust on the breeze. She concentrated on the sound and the buzzing coalesced into maegic words, "Frolic a mortal attitude; dust an eye, pebbles in boots, buzz an ear, smoke in a nose, loosen belts, tickle and trip. Hide sweet faer, in shadow, shade, or light; drop into earth, puddle, leaf, or fly." Kaetie had to fight its hypnotic allure.

She sang to her little friend. He drifted down to the bottom of the hive and disappeared. She sang again, and hundreds of faeries wearing striped black and yellow jumpsuits emerged from the honeycomb.

From the corner of her eye, she saw Rusty carrying a jug to the spring.

The door slammed behind him and then opened again. Five Volunteers walked out. A woman growled, "Destroy the garden."

Dewey was right behind them.

The woman pointed her sword at him and said, "Faery gardens are illegal. I can charge you for this."

Dewey said, "But you won't."

She didn't respond.

Above them, Kaetie saw a ladrechaun leap from a tree to the roof and slip through a shuttered window on the inn's third floor.

Volunteers worked in pairs. Plants flew from the earth, rocks tipped over, statuary fell, and birdbaths crashed to the ground. Like butterfly-hunting maniacs, they swept nets back and forth above the feats of destruction.

The breeze carried the scents of fresh lavender, rosemary, and mint to Kaetie, the same breeze that carried the barely audible cries of captured faeries.

And then she saw her brother spin around, but that's not what made her run after him at full speed. Kaetie saw that look on his face—one eye squinted, his jaw shifted to the right, and his dimples had disappeared.

He dropped the water jug. It broke into clay shards. Fists clenched, he dashed toward the garden. Kaetie dove at his legs, caught an ankle, and brought him down. She heard the classroom door slam behind her, and someone rushed up.

Clinging to Rusty's ankle, she told him he was stupid. He tried to break free. His foot hit her in the belly, and she lost her breath. From behind, Daffy piled on. The two of them held him down. Kaetie explained the idiocy of a fifteen-year-old boy fighting trained soldiers. Daffy said something about honor, integrity, and the value of strategy. She used formal language and spoke in a posh accent, and it seemed to work.

The three of them stood and watched the Volunteers. The one-armed woman who directed them collected the captured faeries into a leather pouch.

Dewey stood on the threshold between the kitchen and the remains of his faery garden. Kaetie had known Dewey since she drew her first breath. He seemed angry most of the time, but she'd never seen his jaw set quite like that.

The nearest Volunteer, a slender man with long brown hair, leaned over and picked up his shovel. When he stood, his hair flopped into his face. He tried to brush it aside, but his hand got stuck in it. He dropped the shovel and tried to untangle his fingers, but both hands caught in his dark locks. Then his belt came undone and his pants dropped slowly.

Daffy said, "We can't do anything right now."

Rusty said, "We can fight."

"Someday, Rustin, someday." Daffy stood between them. She wrapped an arm around him and took Kaetie's hand.

Kaetie knew he'd calmed down, though. His jaw was straight, and though his dimples weren't lit up by a smile, she could see where they belonged.

Daffy said, "If you fight today, you'll lose. Find the courage to wait until you're ready."

Kaetie said, "I have something in mind," but they didn't hear her.

The Volunteers took their tools and headed into the fields. None of them showed any satisfaction. They looked worn to Kaetie.

As they passed, she said, "Why?"

A woman a few years older than Kaetie who had a scar that ran from her temple through what was left of her nose mumbled, "Orders."

Kaetie looked up at Daffy expecting the obvious, but instead of crying, she stared past the Volunteers into the horizon. The sun shone on her face; her perfect skin contrasted with that of the Volunteer.

"Dewey's waving us inside," Rusty said.

"I have to tend the bees." Kaetie spoke loud enough for the Volunteers to hear. She walked away from the garden, up the path to the faery hive. Standing in the shade of the almond tree, she tapped the hive with a thin stick to get the disguised faeries' attention. Each one carried a pin, needle, or tiny pitchfork. She sang instructions and hundreds swarmed in the shape of a piece of fabric blowing in the wind, reaching up and over the tree.

She twirled around, amazed at the trust of so many faeries. Some were hundreds of years older than she was, and some were born yesterday. She held out her arms and gathered them into a ball. She teased it from hand to hand and more faeries joined. Finally, she unfurled it, casting the growing ball into the breeze.

"Watch out for the bees," she called out. "They sting."

The swarm dispersed over the faery garden. Volunteers screamed and swatted their arms, legs, and faces. They ran across the field, downhill toward town, or back to the inn. They tripped on the ground, stumbled over pebbles, ran into trees, got back up, and went in another direction.

The scarred woman straggled behind, trying to bat away the faeries.

Kaetie said, "I told you they sting."

The woman said, "Why don't they sting you?"

"Just lucky, I guess."

34.

Rusty held the kitchen door for Daffy. A smiling Crop Faery in overalls and a straw hat flew out as they stepped in. A Volunteer stood in the kitchen sneezing. His cheeks had swollen his eyes shut. Daeffid gave him a cup of tea that scalded his throat but would quell his allergies.

They heard someone upstairs yelp when a door snapped back in his face. Everyone in the saloon, even Grindaer, laughed when they saw the Volunteers run past, chased by bees.

A Volunteer working his way down the stairs, step by step, hand on the banister as though he didn't trust his balance, yelled, "I got one!"

Dewey walked over. "How can I run an honest inn without a Monitor Faery?"

The sergeant passed Rusty and Daffy and said, "You could hire a human being to do an honest job instead of one of these bugs."

The Monitor Faery stood on the banister. The little guy rubbed his eyes and adjusted his spectacles. His wings stretched out, and he tucked his shirt into his breeches.

Dewey said, "You're a *Monitor* Faery."

The faery shrugged. "I was on break."

More Volunteers came in. They reported from the barn, orchards, and spring. One had a bloody nose—"stepped on a rake"—another had a limp—"horse stepped on me foot"—and all of them had mussed hair.

The sergeant said, "Where's the Card Faery?"

Laetifah brought her a deck of cards and said, "She left weeks ago, bored by the honesty of our guests."

Rusty followed the sergeant. He rounded the bar and stopped in his tracks.

Conifaer lay on his stomach, knees bent under him, and wrists pulled behind and tied to his ankles. The halfling, Daefer, crouched over him.

Rusty looked at Dewey, who was still arguing with the sergeant, and then at Daffy. She took his hand and tried to pull him away. Conifaer looked back, the diamond pupils calm, his face passive but somehow not resigned. Rusty said, "Conifaer, I won't let them take you."

"Don't do anything stupid," the Volunteer with the scarred face said. "Please."

Loretta stepped in front of him. "Son! Out. Now."

"Conifaer," he said and couldn't resist glancing at the wall behind him where they'd built a hidden passage together.

"Rusty," Conifaer said, "I have survived worse."

"One," Loretta said, "two …"

Having a mother whose greatest asset and most egregious flaw is passion for the people she loves programs certain responses in a boy. When she started counting, Rusty found himself halfway to the barn. Before she could get to three, he'd stepped into the scene of destruction that had once been the faery garden.

The gang-of-five leaned against the wall.

Rusty said, "Get your weapons."

Minutes later, the Knightlets strode through the kitchen and into the inn carrying sword-shaped sticks. Rusty held his as though he'd wielded it for a decade after pulling it from a stone. Caeph held his *en garde*. Aennie's rested on her shoulder. Raenny and Naelth hid their "swords" behind their backs. Macae set his on a chair.

Led by the sergeant and her halfling faer hunter, two Volunteers carried Conifaer through the door.

Rusty said, "Not on my watch," and lunged forward.

Caeph moved with him. Rusty went toward Conifaer. Caeph whipped around, covering Rusty's back, a move they'd practiced a hundred times. Rusty almost made it to the halfling before the woman with the scarred face slapped his legs out from under him with the side of her sword.

Caeph's blue eyes expanded with his smile as though he'd been hoping for a moment dire enough that he could let his raw courage shine. He stepped like a dancer; his smile so sinister that the sergeant took a half step back. Caeph lunged at her, a strong riposte from a tough, wiry kid. The sergeant flicked her wrist and her broadsword cracked Caeph's wooden sword in half.

The Volunteers laughed, and the sergeant said, "How old are you?"

Caeph looked at the pieces of his sword as though he couldn't imagine it would let him down.

From the floor where he lay, Rusty looked up at the sergeant. He'd never felt so angry or humiliated in his life. He started to answer, but his mother interrupted him.

"Twelve! He's twelve." Loretta pushed the Volunteer away, knelt over Rusty, and rammed her elbow against his mouth. "They're just children."

"Lukas is always looking for a few brave Volunteers," the sergeant said. "If that kid's twelve, I'm thirteen."

"He's too young to serve."

35.

Seated at the arguing table, Grindaer the miller said, "You missed one."

The sergeant examined the Knightlets. Dewey noticed that her eyes fixed on Aennie. Rusty must have noticed it too. He went to move in front of her, but Aennie held him aside. She looked so calm, but Dewey knew better. Aennie found delight in just about everything and always seemed happy to watch the world pass by. Her expression right then could be mistaken for amusement, but Dewey knew that look. She wanted to break things.

Grindaer added, "Another Monitor Faery just flew out the door."

Dewey gaped at Grindaer. Tolerating arguments, even to the point of fisticuffs at the cost of broken furniture, was all part of running a tavern but allowing a guest to betray an employee crossed the line. Grindaer had been edging up to that line for months. Dewey went to the bar and whispered to Bob, "Mix some water into his drinks that hasn't benefitted from the work of a Spring Faery." Bob leaned forward in the exaggerated nod that made his long hair bounce across his shoulders.

Word would work its way into the kitchen and Daeffid would fix him an equally special dinner.

The sergeant told a Volunteer to catch the fleeing Monitor Faery. The rest of the Volunteers left the inn, headed downhill.

Baeswax was the first to break the silence. "Grindaer! Unacceptable."

"I'm sick and tired of the faer stealing our way of life."

Dewey moved back to his chair by the window. The argument faded into the background noise. He looked away from the flames and noticed a mug of ale on the windowsill next to him. His Truth Faery hovered over the mug on yellow and black swallowtail wings. He dipped his hat into the ale and drank from it. Dewey picked up the mug, had a sip, and noticed Rusty seated in the hot seat.

"Why didn't Lapidae fight?" Rusty asked. "At least I tried." Leaning forward with his elbows on his knees, Rusty held his head in his hands. "We tried, Dewey, my Knightlets—we tried. We just don't know how to fight."

Dewey said, "I know where you can learn to fight."

"Where?"

Lost in his worries, Dewey didn't notice Rusty's enthusiasm. "Become a Volunteer. Lukas will give you weapons, teach you to fight. He'll take you to the mountains, the sea, the plains, and you can kill people you don't know, people who would be your friends in any other circumstance, and then others will kill you. Done. End of another short human life."

"Dewey, I made a promise."

Dewey laughed, a deep howl that ended in a cough.

Rusty said, "We can't fight injustice with wooden sticks we don't know how to use."

"That's special." Dewey slapped Rusty's knee. "You stupid well-meaning farq. Ever hear the concept of 'choosing your battles'?"

Rusty seethed.

"Sorry, kid. There might be honor in keeping such a hopeless promise, but I doubt it."

"Why do elfs tolerate it?" Rusty sat up straight. "They have the maegic of a million faeries. They never waste an arrow with the longbow—"

"You get pretty good with a bow after a thousand years of practice."

"Then why? Why don't they fight back? Ten elfs could beat a hundred Volunteers."

"You don't get it," Dewey said. "Humans are herd animals. You hunt in packs. You follow leaders, usually straight to your graves. Elfs aren't like you. When they hunt, they hunt alone. When they fight, they fight alone. They aren't capable of working in teams. Elfs don't take orders. Even if they're tortured or promised treasure. Orders, commands, none of that registers with them. They don't recognize leadership. I've got half their blood in me, just enough to know that humans will do what I tell them because I provide food and safety. But elfs? Sure, they love and hate, care for their young and all that, but there is no 'elf' in 'team.'"

"But Conifaer and Lapidae didn't even resist."

Dewey grunted. "Did you hear me? Elfs are different than you. They can live forever, and that changes everything. If you're going to be a knight who practices chivalry with elfs, you better understand them, or you'll see just how dark their hearts really are."

Rusty's jaw shifted to the side.

"Keep your cool," Dewey said. "Messing with the faer brings bad luck because the faer are patient. They wait to get even until people forget. They're immortal, they'll wait forever—literally."

Rusty stood. Frustration shook him from his shoulders to his knees. He tried not to grind his teeth. "Well if Madog and the pirates were here, things would have been different."

"Don't count on it, kid." Dewey saw Naelth and Raenny laughing in a corner. Macae and Kaetie sat next to them making googly eyes at each other. Caeph paced back and forth, his eyes set, and shoulders hunched. "Rusty, you need to get out of here. Find Taevius, take the Knightlets, get Vaence and Viviaen, and go up to your arena. I'll send someone for you when it's safe to come back. Now. Go."

"Why?"

"Did you hear the farqin sergeant? They're just called 'Volunteers'—no one actually volunteers to join Lukas's army. Now!"

"I'm not running away."

Dewey hollered, "Loretta!" She got the message in two syllables and cleared The Gold Piece Inn of teens.

Serving Blechk

36.

The faery garden would take a season to recover, but so many faeries hid within the inn that Dewey could wait until tomorrow to care. He glanced out the window where the sun hung over the cove, an hour or two from sunset. The first dribbles of the dinner crowd arrived, more quiet than usual. Loretta, Daffy, and Laetifah rose from a table and carried mugs into the kitchen. The band opened with an old elfin song that told the tale of Queen Graegloria winding the lives of humans and elfs together. Dewey's Truth Faery fluttered up and took a seat on his shoulder. The two of them stared into the flames, dozing.

When the inn went silent, Dewey's eyes popped open. He heard boots on the floorboards. His first response was to tug his hat down over his ears. He fought the feeling of defeat—Dewey-the-halfling, lord of The Gold Piece Inn, man of information and intrigue. It all felt so far away.

The door swung open all the way and a gust of icy wind blew inside.

Dewey cupped his Truth Faery in his hand and slipped him into the windowpane. *Just when I thought this day couldn't get any worse.*

"Singing praise to the Liberation?" Major Blechk said in that deep, official sounding voice. "Nothing but good wishes to the First Human and so on?"

Grindaer the Miller said, "Hear, hear!"

Blechk passed Dewey, glanced at him, and continued to the arguing table. He stood over Grindaer, facing Baeswax, Codae, and Fin. Dewey moved to a spot in the shadows between the casino and saloon where he didn't stand out. A dozen Volunteers stood just outside the closed door.

Blechk bit off a fingernail and spat. Faernando tried to pass on his way to the bar. Blechk grabbed his bottom. "Get me something wet and fermented."

Faernando rushed to the bar where Bob poured a mug of mulled red wine.

"Everyone feeling patriotic?" Blechk bellowed and his belly shook.

Isolated grunts of approval came from a table near the casino entrance where two blacksmiths, Ferrous and Smithae, sat.

Caepra mumbled, "So obvious, why didn't I see this in the stars?" His Crook Faery slid down the staff and jumped under Caepra's robe. One of his dogs raised a lip and let out a low growl.

The room went dim as the GloFaeries sank into knots in the redwood beam ceiling, leaving the room in pure candlelight.

"Sergeant Taelerson told me about some courageous young warriors who want to help Lukas liberate humanity." Blechk raised his drink and said, "Let's drink to those young men and women who will Volunteer right here tonight!"

Speaking just as loud, Loretta said, "No one old enough to volunteer here."

"Tired, dried-up old woman," he smirked at Loretta and let his tongue sweep across his teeth. "Hags like you always deny the next generation's need for adventure and triumph." He turned his mug upside down and a few drops fell out. He threw it at Loretta.

Between them, carrying her baby in one arm, Laetifah reached up with her other, intercepted the mug and took two steps to the bar. Bob had a dipper poised and filled the mug. She delivered it to Blechk in one seamless motion.

Blechk took it. "Now here's a handsome serving wench."

"Lass," Loretta said, "we don't have wenches here."

Blechk spoke over her, "I've come for the famous Gold Piece Inn Bastards!" He scanned the room. "Where are these famous warriors? Or are they all cowards hiding in their momma's be-hinds?" He tapped his forehead. "Yes, I remember now. It was months ago, a hot day last summer." He made eye contact with every serving-lass before continuing. "I spoke to one of these Bas-tards and he told me of others. Good thing I brought recruiters." He turned about and pointed at the Volunteers. "Fetch me the boy called Rusty and the lad named Taevius who he said would some-day lead a Volunteer ship into battle." He rotated to Dewey and added, "I wrote it down."

The Volunteers fanned out in different directions.

Blechk raised his mug again. "Drink to their glory!"

Dewey saw Taevius's mother, Laetifah, look at Blechk. Her eyes brimmed with horror. She held her baby tighter.

The guests of the inn stared in silence. Blechk knocked back his mug as though everyone in the bar were joining his toast.

"Music!" Blechk said. "Play that ballad of the Volunteers' vic-tory over the Yarrow at Aelpine Ridge."

"I don't know that one." The guitarist slurred his words and launched into a romantic ballad about the sturdy nomads of the Yarrow plains. The song described an ancient battle of the unifica-tion when King Graeglory and elfs rescued a tribe of Yarrow horse riders.

Blechk sat at a table near the stage with his back to Dewey.

Daffy emerged from the kitchen with plates. Dewey waved to get her attention. She delivered the plates to a table with a hunter, a trapper, and a merchant. They said something to her, and she laughed, but never looked in Dewey's direction. She turned to take an order from another table. Blechk's table.

She pulled up short. Dewey thought she'd run like a terrified hare. Instead, she smiled and leaned forward.

37.

Daffy had trained most of her life for that terrifying instant. A queen must be capable of not just interacting with rivals of the state but manipulating them.

She caught her breath, pasted on a smile, and asked Blechk if he'd like more wine.

"I'd like a lot more than wine."

Leaning across the table, her hair fell over her eyes. She brushed it aside, took his mug, and headed for the bar. Two steps away, she looked back and, yes, he was watching her. She tipped Blechk's mug up and let the last few drops of wine drip onto her tongue. Blechk clapped his hands together three times and said, "Bring yourself a drink, too."

At the bar, Bob asked if she could handle it and she replied with greater confidence than she felt, "Finally a chore I already know how to do."

"What will you have?" Bob said.

"Wine," she said. The tension in the room now made sense. The word "conscription" chewed at the back of her consciousness. "Make it brandy." She scanned the room and felt reassured that the older Bastards were out of sight.

She brought the drinks to Blechk's table. He invited her to sit on his lap. Fortunately, his belly already occupied that space. She sat next to him. He pulled her close. His hair was so oily that the curls hung like dead seaweed. His forearm lingered against her and felt like a hairy spider. She needed to distract him, anything to keep his mind away from conscripting the Bastards. She described the soup as if it were rich and filling, with fresh bread, butter, and honey.

"Perhaps," he said, motioning at the velvet carpeted stairs. "We should go upstairs."

"Upstairs?" She looked at the stairs. Loretta slept upstairs a few

nights each week, more when Madog was in town. Daffy's grandmother had told her horror stories of how gossip had destroyed the
tenuous fabric that held kingdoms together, and she learned to
mind her own business. But, now that she thought about it, she
realized that all the servers took guests upstairs now and then.

Blechk leaned forward. His breath smelled like a dead skunk.
She resisted leaning away, but he farted and settled back in his seat.

"Are you a boy?"

Daffy said, "What?"

"You look like one."

"I'm wearing a dress."

"That's good, too. Innie, outie, I don't care." He sipped from
his mug. "Take me upstairs, I'll give you a pile of gold, I'll take you
on a sea cruise—"

"You say that to all the girls." Sure, it was a cliché, but she had
to say something to stop him without making him angry. "Let me
fetch your supper." She stood, and he reached for her chest. She
didn't pull away then either, even as his hand slid from her sternum
down to her navel on its way to her thighs—a path that felt so slimy
that she felt the urge to scrub herself in icy waves and sand.

"Huh," he said, "So you are a girl."

38.

Daffy went into the kitchen.

Loretta looked up from her seat near the fire and said, "He still
here?"

"Where are the Bastards?" Daffy said.

"They headed for the hills. May the gods give them the sense to
stay there." She rose from her chair and adjusted her bodice. "I'll
go help Blechk forget about them."

"Don't worry, I'll distract Blechk."

Loretta dropped back in her seat, and Daffy sat next to her.

"Don't worry?" Loretta's hands trembled. "You're the reason I'm worried. That stupid promise my son made—nothing but a Gold Piece Inn Bastard. The crazy ideas you put in his head, he's gonna grow a hair on his arse, decide to be a hero, come down that hill with his stick, and get himself sent to war."

"Rustin won't do anything to risk anyone's life."

"To keep the promise he made to you, he would. Can't you see the boy is smitten?"

"I think he can do it."

"What?"

"Be a knight."

"Right. I can see it now, a king tapping the royal sword on my barefoot son's head and shoulders, dubbing him a knight." Loretta looked away and wiped spittle from her lips.

Daffy leaned close and whispered, "Or a queen."

"What?"

"Dubbing Sir Rustin would be the proudest moment of my life."

"Why do you call him that?"

"It's his name."

Loretta pulled away, her brow furrowed, and lips pouted as though she was adding up a guest's tab. "You could do it. I mean, if Lukas falls and a million other things, but you could."

Daffy nodded. "But first I have to distract Major Blechk."

"Let's kill him."

"He'd be replaced, and that sergeant would come for them."

"What we gonna do?"

"When you take someone upstairs, what do you do?"

"You're kidding, right?"

"You take guests upstairs all the time—why? What do you do up there?"

"Dewey never explained it?" Loretta's voice took on the strained tone of mock patience she used to correct children. "When a guest asks you upstairs, you decide if you want to. I only go with men I like, men who make me feel, well, you know …"

"No. Loretta, I don't know." Daffy threw up her hands. "That's why I'm asking."

Loretta took a breath, mumbling about naïveté in high places. "You can make good money taking guests upstairs, but you have to find out what, umm, services the guest wants first. If anything makes you uncomfortable the Monitor Faeries will send in Screaming Faeries, Scratch Faeries, and Tooth Faeries—that lot could stop a yeti in rut." She sighed. "But there's not much I won't do for a night on a feather bed in a private room."

"Services?" Daffy's brow furrowed. "What are you talking about?"

"Really?" Loretta said. "If you want to sleep upstairs, you got to sleep with a guest."

"In the same bed?"

"Yes."

"But isn't that?" Daffy felt her face heat. "No. Oh gods. Really? I'm such a fool!"

"When you're with a guest who's kind and gentle, on a feather-bed with sheets and a glass of wine—Daffy, it's the only time I ever slept on sheets! With the right guy, I love to go upstairs."

"And you …"

"What?"

"You …" Daffy's eyebrows went up and down.

"Honey, that's the best part."

"The King was an ardent lover." Daffy's eyes grew wider. "Are they all like that?" And still wider.

Loretta looked away. "I wish."

Daffy's eyes were steady at wide open. "Have you ever done it with someone you'd just met?"

"I trust the faer to watch out for me."

"You have!"

Loretta winked.

"But what happens if …"

"If what?"

"If you get with child."

"How do you think I got Rusty and Kaetie? That's how we got Tifenae and Macae, Taevius and Bellae, Naelth and Caeph—haven't you noticed all the pregnant women around here? Why you think they're called 'Gold Piece Inn Bastards'?"

"Do they know their fathers?"

"That don't matter."

"Rustin and Kaetie? They must have been sired by a great man."

"That's not the point. We get all the joy that comes with them."

"Oh." Daffy tried to see the world through Loretta's eyes. "Is that what you want?"

"Want?" Loretta said, her voice rising. "Want? No, Daffy, I want to be a farqin princess and have grapes peeled for me by men who grant my wishes." She clenched her fists. "Want. Let me ask you this, how many children you got?"

"You know that I had a girl and a boy, I also lost a son to sleep sickness."

"How nice. Where are they?"

"You know what happened."

"Didn't work out so well? Guess what? I have a boy and a girl."

Daffy couldn't speak.

"I didn't mean it," Loretta said, and pulled Daffy into a hug. "I'm sorry."

"It's wrong," Daffy said. "Their fathers have a right to know."

"I'm a Gold Piece Inn Bastard. Never knew my father."

"My father would want to know about me. And the King, the King would have been horrified to have children in the world that he didn't know. King Gledig was a wonderful father."

"Would he want to know? You really think so?" Loretta pushed away and pointed at Daffy the way she did when scolding a child.

"My mother was a wise woman, and you know what she said when I asked her about my dad?"

Daffy didn't understand what she'd said to upset Loretta, so she didn't respond.

Faernando passed through the door and said, "You better get out there!"

Daffy stood, but Loretta took her hand. "Momma said that you can pretend to care, but you can't pretend to be there. Daddy was never here, neither is Rusty and Kaetie's."

"Does he know about them?" She had to get back to Blechk but couldn't bring herself to pull away.

"He's not here, is he?"

Daffy said, "They have Dewey."

"What? Dewey?" Loretta laughed and pulled herself up to hug Daffy again. "Dewey. That's funny." Her laughter stopped short. "And right now, our children are sitting around a campfire on The Fist of God's middle finger. Rusty's probably reading that damn scroll and you know that Kaetie's reading a book. Why'd you teach them to read?"

"No, they're not," Faernando said.

"What?"

"That's what I've been trying to tell you," Faernando said. "You *have* to get out there."

Daffy looked back at Loretta and tried to steel herself. She'd flirted kings into signing treaties but take Blechk upstairs? "If that's what it takes," She said, and repeated it, trying to convince herself.

39.

Dewey cringed when he saw Volunteers push the Bastards through the door. They looked at each other, at the Volunteers, and then at Dewey. The band stopped playing. The silence exposed the sound of huge winter swells barreling into shore, rocking the wharf, and vibrating the inn's foundation.

Seated at his table and facing the stage, Blechk pretended not to notice the commotion behind him. The Volunteers pushed the Knightlets between tables, shoving chairs aside, scraping the sawdust and raising dust that would have been secured by Dust Faeries if they weren't hiding.

Dewey would remember the look on Kaetie's face for a long time. Caeph, Aennie, and Vaence seethed, wanting a fight they couldn't win. Macae and Raenny scanned the Volunteers, the walls, the door, searching for an escape route. Naelth stood silent and proud, his head bent slightly and his lips moving, no doubt preparing a speech. Taevius stood stiff and stoic with all the emotion of a rocky outcropping immovable in the storm. Viviaen was the only one with the good sense to be terrified. Dewey couldn't quite make sense of Rusty. He had that look; the dimples were gone, but at least he wasn't grinding his teeth, his temper was under control.

But Kaetie. Kaetie's expression betrayed a thousand plans for Blechk's destruction. She had a leather-bound book tucked under her arm. Dewey recognized it: *Glandaeff Faer and Beast*, the five-thousand-year history written by the elf Quercus who had witnessed the entire epoch. Dewey looked between Kaetie and Rusty and realized that he might have miscalculated which of this era's Bastards would be the greatest of all.

Blechk didn't focus on Kaetie. Dewey relaxed in his chair. If Blechk didn't have the sense to kill Kaetie on the spot, he didn't have what it would take to beat Dewey.

"Rusty, isn't it?" Blechk said in that deep voice that resonated across the room, perhaps his only attractive feature. He pointed at the chair across the table. "Sit."

Rusty motioned to the other Bastards and said, "Everyone pull a chair over and have a seat."

All but Taevius reached for empty chairs, but the Volunteers restrained them. Rusty turned to the woman whose face had been scarred in battle, the Volunteer who had knocked him to the ground that morning. "Give us a hand with the chairs?"

The Volunteer said, "You're not helping anyone."

"If my sisters and brothers have to stand, I'll stand with them," Rusty said. "I'm sure you understand."

Blechk said, "Gigi, now."

The Volunteer kicked the back of Rusty's knees and shoved a chair under him.

Rusty landed on the seat and crossed his legs.

The exchange almost gave Dewey the impression that Rusty controlled the encounter. Almost. True to form, Blechk broke that impression when he leaned to the side, tensed up, and cracked a fart.

The kitchen door opened with a bang.

Daffy rushed in with Loretta on her heels.

Still leaning to the side, Blechk looked back and said, "Weren't you bringing my food? A man could starve in this inn."

Daffy stopped short. Loretta pushed past. Everyone in the inn had experienced Loretta's rage, it started with deep rouge on her cheeks that promised an eruption of criticism and correction— Loretta's moral compass had sharp points.

For an instant Dewey thought she could intimidate Blechk and his ten trained soldiers.

"Just who do you think you are?" Her voice came out as a growl. "Get away from my boy."

A Volunteer grabbed her from behind. With his arms around her waist, he lifted her. Her bare feet kicked the air. She rammed an elbow into the Volunteer's belly, but he didn't even flinch.

Loretta released a stream of epithets regarding Blechk's ancestry, his appearance, scent, preference for farm animals as intimate companions, and, as she spoke, the Volunteer put her over his shoulder and carried her to the back of the casino where he set her on the floor and hog-tied her. The last winding of rope wrapped through her mouth and around her head, tight enough to prevent her jaw from moving. She didn't stop scolding Blechk, but her words became moans and she drooled a little puddle in the sawdust.

"Wench," Blechk said, still to Daffy, "assemble your tiny arse on my lap." He reached to grab her wrist.

She looked back at Dewey. He expected her to run for the door. What else could she do? It would have been a bad move. Instead, Daffy wagged her tail at Blechk and said, "Take me upstairs. You promised."

A genuine grin spread across Blechk's face. It changed his entire complexion. For that instant you could imagine Blechk being pleasant company. But then he sucked in his gut, pulled her onto his lap, and the grin evolved into the more fitting lecherous smirk. "I'll finish here in a jiffy and get you upstairs in no time." He rotated her to the side, to get an unobstructed view of the Bastards. His protruding paunch held her thighs to his lap, and he put an around her waist and pawed at her torso. The angle of her eyes, the warmth of her cheeks, her relaxed brow, and pouting lips—none of it screamed revulsion.

Dewey didn't know what to make of this. Upstairs? Daffy? The curse wasn't without its amusements. Daffy had shown grit and adaptability, but she couldn't possibly stand this. He shuffled to the other side of the fireplace to get a better view, and then he couldn't believe his eyes or ears.

Daffy wrapped her arms around Blechk's neck and spoke loud enough for all to hear, "Come on, big boy, let's go upstairs. Mama's ready."

Nervous laughter came from different tables, including Bob's slow, low-throated har, har, har.

Rusty's dimples disappeared.

Blechk said, "I'll pop your tiny butt when I'm ready."

Daffy choked out a girlish giggle.

Blechk spoke to Rusty. "It's been months since we chatted on the wharf. Do you remember?"

Rusty took a deep breath and looked away from Daffy. He said, "I remember" in an unhurried tone as though Blechk didn't bother him, that his mother's precarious position on the floor was just another inconvenience on a blustery day, that this treatment of Daffy was the sort of thing he saw all the time. But there was still no sign of his dimples.

"You welcomed me to Crescent Cove and told me you'd rather be a soldier than a sailor because you get seasick."

"I said that I like the harbor all right but not the open sea. I never said anything about being a soldier."

For an instant, Dewey feared that Rusty would add some nonsense about becoming a knight.

"Ahh, that's right." Blechk looked at Daffy. "The young seem to remember every detail."

Blechk held a finger to his lips as though pondering a thought, and Dewey was reasonably certain that Blechk wasn't burdened by many.

Blechk continued, "Don't I recall you describing someone who did want to serve? Didn't you mention a young man—what was his name?"

Rusty's face went pale. Dewey had never seen confidence evaporate so fast.

Blechk tapped his teeth with that finger, and then the finger moved from his teeth to his nose. He dug around and then pried a bit of congealed phlegm, inspected it, and scraped it from his finger with his teeth. Daffy looked aghast.

"Taevius, wasn't it?" Blechk said.

Laetifah shrieked. She stood twenty feet to Blechk's left, holding little Bellae to her breast.

Taevius finally moved. His head turned slowly, eyes squinted at Rusty in disappointment but not disbelief.

"Didn't you say that someday your friend Taevius would be a

ship's captain? A tall ship? A frigate in the Volunteer Navy?"

Rusty looked down at his hands. He looked more like a boy than a man. A boy who had broken a mother's heart.

"You did say that, didn't you?" Blechk cracked his knuckles. "Answer me, boy!"

Rusty's chin quivered. And then he looked Blechk dead in the eye. "Someday Taevius will be the greatest captain on the sea, but he won't serve the usurp—"

"Which one of you is Taevius?" Blechk looked at the Bastards lined up behind Rusty. "It's your lucky day."

Aennie said, "I'm Taevius." Caeph said, "I'm Taevius." Naelth, "Someday I'll sail a great ship, for I am Taevius!" Raenny, "I'm not Taevius," and Macae, "Never met him." The others stood silent, though Taevius had turned to his mother. She shook her head, silently begging him to stay quiet.

"I'm the one you want," Rusty said. Loretta cried out, struggling against the ropes.

Daffy pulled Blechk's head close to hers. He turned to her with a broad smile and said, "Control yourself, horny wench, I will pile drive you into the floor when my work is finished." She bit his ear. He cried out but didn't lose the smile. "I like your attitude."

He turned back to Rusty. "You? I don't think so. You let a couple of Volunteers who aren't good enough to fight in the war destroy your home. Lukas has no use for cowards." He turned to a Volunteer and added, "Can you imagine that, Haery? This weakling thinks Lukas would make a spot for him." Daffy's wedged her mouth against his neck. He leaned into her and said, "Just a few more minutes, morsel."

Blechk nodded to the Volunteer and Haery pulled Daffy off his lap. He twisted her arm behind her back and held her tight. Her eyes flitted in every direction, finally showing fear.

Blechk stood. He looked at Rusty and shook his head before stepping to the line of Bastards. He poked Caeph in the ribs, "Too much ego, too little strength." He looked down at Raenny, "Too scrawny." He scowled at Naelth and moved on. He looked up at Macae, "You'll just blow over in the wind, maybe next year."

He stopped at Kaetie and cupped her breast. She jabbed at him, going for the throat, but a Volunteer grabbed her arms from behind and held her. Blechk pinched her. "Too ugly and fat. No one wants to see this in uniform." An Alert Faery screamed from the rafters, swooped down, and into Blechk's face. Kaetie squirmed away. Macae launched himself at Blechk, but a Volunteer caught him. Trying to evade the faery, Blechk almost fell over a chair. Gigi, the scarred Volunteer, trapped the faery and held him in her fist. The little guy's brown and orange wings stuck out between her fingers.

"Give it here."

The Volunteer held the faery out to Blechk. He reached for it and it either got away or she let it go. Blechk grabbed the Volunteer by her neck. "Catch it. Tear its wings off and give it here." She saluted.

Blechk straightened his tunic and stepped to Aennie. She tried to swallow a sob. Blechk said, "What are you, sixteen?" She nodded. He looked her over and added, "Ugly enough to freeze a maermaid." He leveled an index finger at her. "I'll take this one, too. She can be my valet."

Aennie looked at Dewey and yelled, "Please help me!" A Volunteer pulled her toward the door.

The curse stabbed Dewey in his figurative heart, as though the love of his life had been raped. His mind rebelled, certain that the curse would get him killed this time. But then ideas for how to get her released started boiling into consciousness, blackmail, threats, cons, coercion, even diplomacy, but nothing spurned him into suicidal action. Dewey thanked the gods for sensible Curse Faeries.

Blechk then pointed at Vaence. "Lukas will love this guy, big, strong, and stupid." He paused at Viviaen and said, "No. As cowardly as Rusty and as ugly as the fat one."

He stopped at the next Bastard, looked him up and down and said. "Rusty was right, you'll make a fine officer—you prefer the navy then?"

Taevius looked straight ahead.

"What a specimen," Blechk said, "built like a frigate."

A pair of Volunteers stepped to Taevius's sides. One said, "Come with us. Please don't make it a big hassle." And the other, "You should do okay. The rations suck, the pay sucks, the work's boring, but if you follow orders, you'll learn how to sail a tall ship."

Bellae started crying.

Blechk spun around and said, "Ooo, a little black one." He walked toward her, taking his time, looking first at Laetifah and then back at Taevius.

Dewey saw Blechk's expression change. He'd just solved a puzzle.

When he got to Laetifah, he said, "You are a sad case, aren't you?"

"Please leave my boy," Laetifah said. "Take Rusty and his sister, they'll serve you well. My Taevius is stubborn, hardheaded, won't take—"

"Give me that," Blechk said.

"What?"

"I want the little black baby. Is it a boy?" He motioned for a Volunteer, but they all managed to be occupied with the newly conscripted Volunteers. "Oh." He said with mock disappointment. He spoke to Daffy, "It's a girl. I prefer old women and young boys."

"You can't take my baby!"

Laetifah rotated the baby against her belly and raised her other arm to shield the child. Blechk punched Laetifah in the stomach. She staggered and doubled over, and Blechk tugged the screaming baby into his arms.

He said, "Yes, I can."

Goateye

40.

Loretta was released and ran to her children. Kaetie hugged her and Rusty pushed away, his eyes fixed on Taevius, imploring. Taevius didn't falter.

The Volunteers assembled the conscripts on the inn's front porch. Blechk had Gigi carry Bellae.

Laetifah chased them out with Loretta close behind. Loretta demanded the baby's return. Laetifah got within a step of Gigi, but a Volunteer popped the back of her head with the thick edge of his sword.

She fell to her knees.

Taevius stopped and looked at his mother. One of his guards tried to push him. Taevius didn't seem to notice the shove. He showed no hint of fear, no sign of dread, just self-respect coated with discipline and acceptance. He didn't raise his voice, but it carried into the inn.

First, he looked down at Gigi and said, "You will protect my sister."

Gigi said, "I follow orders," and held the baby tight in both arms.

"And I just gave them to you."

Gigi started her automatic "aye-aye, sir" response but stopped after one "aye."

Second, Taevius turned slowly on the Volunteer standing over his mother and said, "Sheath your sword and help the woman up."

The Volunteer reached down, took Laetifah's hand and pulled her to her feet.

Third, Taevius said, "Mother, don't worry about Bellae or me.

Take care of yourself and Shaelie. We'll be fine."

His stolid response conveyed the message his mother needed, and with that assurance, Laetifah's fear and loss became anger.

Laetifah slapped Loretta. "It was your Bastard. Blame him for this." She pointed at Rusty and trembled, sputtered, unable to summon words to express her anger.

Taevius's head rotated from his mother to Rusty. Rusty's face showed both shame and determination. Taevius the man stared at Rusty the boy as though sending a message—a threat? a promise? forgiveness and understanding? Dewey couldn't tell, but he pitied anyone who made an enemy of Taevius.

Taevius then looked down at the Volunteer who had tried to move him and said, "We can go now."

The Volunteers, their conscripts, and baby hostage made their way down the hill into the twilight.

Inside The Gold Piece Inn, silence rested on the sounds of crying seagulls and wind howling through the eaves until the band broke into a taut, driving melody.

Blechk and the long-armed, low-browed Volunteer named Haery were the only Volunteers who stayed behind. They looked pleased with themselves.

Rusty walked out.

Daffy told Blechk that his supper was finally ready and then followed Rusty.

Kaetie took her usual seat to the side of the stage.

The band played on. They tried a light ditty but got no response and switched to a heavy ballad built on ancient legends from before Maentanglement. Kaetie read her book. Dewey stared into the flames. Bob poured drinks and the serving-lads and lasses delivered them.

The door opened with a blast of wind and four scurvy pirates swaggered in.

Loretta dropped a tray of mugs and goblets. Dogs moved in like a cleanup crew. Loretta ran across the room and leapt into Madog's arms. Baertha announced her return and reached out her arms as though hugging The Gold Piece Inn. Jon-Jay demanded a mountain of food, "An entire roasted whale won't satisfy this hunger!"

Aerrol glanced at Blechk and came straight to Dewey. Even in this weather, Aerrol wore an open vest and breeches. He leaned down and whispered, "Where can we speak freely?"

41.

Dewey closed his office door, yanked off his hat, and threw it on the desk. Aerrol pulled a chair around.

"Import anything interesting?" Dewey asked as he dropped into his desk chair.

"Fairly conventional cargo." Aerrol belied his words with a raised eyebrow. "Sugar, dried tropical fruits, spices, tea, coffee, rum—lots of rum." His voice trailed off, but that eyebrow begged for questions.

"I'll give you a silver ohzee for three casks of rum, but you didn't need to come in here to tell me that."

"Had to get ashore before the storm hit. We barely stayed ahead of the front the last two days. We're in for it tonight." He paused. Dewey hated it when people teased his curiosity but played along anyway. "The rum is two silvers per cask, I'll take five for the three."

"Volunteers give you any trouble?"

"They watched us unload. No trouble. A sorry lot, at this point. Tired looking."

"Prices high enough to be worth your while?"

"Five silvers for three casks of rum is about twice what I got two years ago." Aerrol then told Dewey that they'd spent the last few months sailing beyond the usurper's no longer expanding borders and got word of the conditions in Glomaythea while sailing from island to island in the tropics. "You and me, Dewey, we have that in common."

"Profit is a universal desire."

Aerrol leaned back and put a boot on Dewey's desk. A Desk Faery appeared with a tiny broom and swept the dirt that fell from it. Aerrol pretended not to notice. "Lukas is overextended. The blockade has caused shortages," Aerrol said. "Prices are peaking in Maythea."

"Glomaythea."

"They renamed it."

"Bullfarqs."

"It's good to be back, Dewey, there's money to be made here."

"Aerrol, tell me you didn't ..."

"Didn't have to." Aerrol then explained that the usurper had given a wink and a nod to piracy if supplies made it to his soldiers at the front. Shortages had to be met somehow. Aerrol described the additional bribes as a tax. The black market remained illegal, another convenient crime for Volunteers to use against citizens suspected of treason. It sounded like reasonable rules of commerce to Dewey. Since profiteers don't burden themselves with much introspection, he wasn't surprised when Aerrol said, "Lukas has promised a lot of business, a lot of treasure, and his message about the faer standing in the way of human beings goes over with natural born rebels like pirates."

Dewey said, "You forget what keeps you afloat?" All sailors are superstitious, and ships without faer have bad luck.

"The Volunteer Navy floats without faer help. New ways to operate, new weapons, times are changing." He looked Dewey in the eye. "I might have to banish the faer from *Avarice*."

"But you haven't?"

"There's some disagreement within the ranks, but we will. Nothing personal, but the day of the faer is over."

Then, as though to placate Dewey, and Dewey hated being

placated, Aerrol added, "But there is one other thing." Aerrol's eyebrow went back up.

Even with disgust rising in his throat, Dewey's curiosity begged for satisfaction.

"A little thing. You're probably not interested." Aerrol pulled a small herb box from his vest pocket and opened the hinged lid. "Ever seen this?"

"Looks like dirt from here." Dewey held out a hand and Aerrol handed him the box.

Aerrol grinned like a bad poker player with a good hand.

The box held a red-hued resin. Dewey pinched it and it stuck together like tar. He sniffed it and set it down. The scent brought memories, most of them bad. "How much do you have?"

"A barrel."

"Are you kidding?"

"You heard me."

"A barrel." Dewey fidgeted with a quill while he did the math. "You're telling me that you have four thousand ohzees of goat—"

"Whoa, Dewey, don't say it out loud."

Dewey shook his head. The numbers fell into place, but so did something else. The Curse? He said, "You're either the stupidest or smartest person who's ever sat in that chair."

"It's a fine line, isn't it?"

"You realize how much gold you're sitting on?"

"Double it," Aerrol said. "Whatever you think it's worth—with soldiers around? Double it."

"And you have this *deal* with the usurper."

Aerrol winked and rose from the chair. "Just think about it."

Dewey tapped his forehead. "The wheels are turning, Captain." And they were. In Dewey's mind, everything was a game and Aerrol had just dealt him a joker.

42.

Rusty walked to the school shed and shut the door behind him. He sat for a second and then paced around the room. If only he could go back and just not say it, go back and just not do it. Go back. The taste of blood ran from where he chewed the inside of his cheek.

He had failed in his first chance at honor.

The excuse that he'd betrayed Taevius before he'd discovered what it meant "To Be a Knight" made him cringe. Rusty looked inside and knew that he craved the approval of other people, especially authority. It ended right then. From that day forward, Rusty would judge every statement, every word and action, on the merit of decency and honor.

The door opened behind him. Daffy stepped in, the last person he wanted to see. He moved toward the door.

"Rustin, I don't have time for children." She wouldn't let him pass.

The words cut into Rusty's heart. His head hung lower.

She said, "Don't waste your time crying."

He clenched his teeth and clamped his eyes shut. He summoned anger and then pride and put up a fight, but his cheeks rose, his lips folded, and his chin crumpled.

"Knights cry when it matters," Daffy said.

He turned away.

"Knights cry in moments of joy or grief, and they cry at memories of wonderful times and wonderful people that they knew and lost, but knights do not cry during a crisis."

His shoulders fell, and he gave in to a sob.

Her thin arms reached up, and he felt her tiny hands on his back. He pulled away, but the arms tightened.

"Okay," she said, "a bit more and then you will fix this."

His breath caught in his throat. He coughed and she let him go.

"Fix it?" He snorted at the absurdity. "It's too late. I betrayed

Taevius. I couldn't defend Conifaer. I couldn't do anything, not even protect the farqin faery garden."

Her eyes looked inside him. He feared what she saw in his cowardly soul. Thank the gods she didn't offer sympathy.

He mumbled, "I'm not a knight."

"Too late, Rustin. You promised."

That word hit him in the throat. He took a breath and said, "Well, I guess I broke—"

"Nope. No, you haven't broken anything and you're not going to. You will fix it."

"What can I do? How can a Gold Piece Inn Bastard undo betrayal? How can I rescue the baby or Conifaer? I can't fight trained soldiers—how can I possibly fix this?"

"I'm just a serving-lass, how would I know? I need to go back in there and serve that pond scum Blechk. I have to disgrace myself so that maybe, just maybe, I can distract him long enough to protect the children." She shuddered.

Rusty finally broke out of his self-absorption and saw Daffy's fear—a damsel in distress scolding him, not exactly consistent with a ballad of knighthood.

"You're the knight. Fix it." She turned to the door, opened it, and looked back. Rusty would not forget that look. "And grow the hell up. Your name is not Rusty, it's Rustin." The wind slammed the door behind her.

With no plan, no idea of what he was doing, Rustin walked to the stable. He couldn't go through the kitchen, not with Daffy there, and he couldn't bear to see her with Blechk. He knew these were not the thoughts of a knight.

He went into the stable, passed horses in the stalls and some goats that poked their heads out of a pile of straw. People were talking up in the loft. "Hey," he called, "have you seen Laetifah?"

No one answered. He climbed the ladder and saw Laetifah with Shaelie, Taevius's six-year-old sister, packing their blankets and extra clothes in a knapsack.

"I'm sorry," he said. "I didn't know who Blechk was when I told him about Taevius." A harpoon of shame hit his heart when he heard himself use that excuse. He tried to suck it up. "You know how much I look up to him." He paused, but Laetifah ignored him. Shaelie kept her eyes on her mother.

He said, "I don't expect you to forgive me. I made a huge mistake. I don't want you to forgive me until I've fixed it."

Laetifah turned to face him. "Fixed it?" She stood up straight with her hands on her hips. Shaelie slipped behind her. "Taevius doesn't need you."

Rustin walked between blankets and hanging tapestries until he stood within arm's reach of Laetifah. He wondered if she'd slap him as she'd done his mother. He'd welcome it.

"You're right," he said, "Taevius doesn't need me. Someday I'll make it up to him. I will. Someday."

"You don't know what you're talking about."

Laetifah was a large woman, two hands shorter than Rustin, but the tallest of The Gold Piece Inn women, strong, immense in spirit and with a powerful beauty that commanded attention. She'd held Rustin as a baby, she'd scolded him when he misbehaved, and she'd praised him when he'd done well by her. A wave of affection and debt filled his heart. He looked into those dark eyes and said, "I promise, Laetifah, I will bring Bellae back to you."

"Just like you rescued the elf?"

"I will rescue him, too."

"You promise that?" The scorn in her eyes withered him.

"I do. I promise. I swear I will fix this."

"Rusty, I don't need promises from a child."

She turned away.

"My name is Rustin. And I keep my promises."

Another voice said, "I accept you of your promise." A thin, airy voice that came from the rafters or the floor—Rustin didn't know where, but he recognized Lapidae's elfin lilt.

She seemed to appear out of nothingness, but Rustin had worked with Conifaer long enough to know how elfs could stand motionless at the edge of shadow in a way that made you overlook them until they moved or spoke.

Laetifah had no such experience with elfs. She shrieked, lurched away from Lapidae, and stumbled. Rustin caught her. She pushed off and grabbed Shaelie, looked back for an instant, crammed the rest of their things in the bag, and the two of them backed their way to the ladder, down, and out of the barn.

Lapidae said, "You promise to help Conifaer?"

"I promise. I will bring Conifaer back to you."

"I will hold you to this promise."

"Thank you."

43.

Daffy took her time in the kitchen. She tried to convince herself that she could do it. She'd dealt with brutes before, calmed them, primed them to be better than their natures.

Daeffid put the tray in her hands and held the door open. "He'll be worse if he's hungry."

"I need a second."

He let the door close and put his hands on her shoulders. "Daffy, you don't have to do this."

"They're destroying Glomaythea, upsetting Maentanglement—it's my duty." The words helped. Major Blechk was just a misbehaving child. She just had to clean him up and put him in his place.

"He's already done his worst. You tried. You don't have to go up there with him."

"He's not finished. People like him never finish torturing innocents." She stomped her foot. "Taevius, Aennie, Vaence—my students. He took Laetifah's baby."

"It's too late."

"What if he catches Lapidae? What if he changes his mind about Rustin and Kaetie? No, my dignity isn't worth that much."

"You'll be on your own. The Monitor Faeries and Alert Faeries, even the Hinge and Farq Faeries are hiding."

Daffy shrugged off Daeffid's hands. "I'm ready."

"Keep him drinking, get Bob to spike his wine with brandy, maybe you can get him drunk enough that he won't be able to—"

"Don't say it." Daffy looked up at Daeffid. "I'll drink too, hopefully enough that I won't even know what he does to me." She hesitated. "If it comes to that."

"Right. If." Daeffid opened the door.

"Thank you."

Daffy carried the tray into the saloon. She saw Loretta and Madog on the porch in each other's arms, oblivious to the icy gusts. She set a plate of smoked herring and a bowl of thin whale-broth soup in front of Blechk. He blew his nose in his hands and said, "I'll eat you in a second." She tried to smile and when that didn't work, she took his goblet for a refill. Baertha and Jon-Jay leaned against the bar. For an instant she felt rescued, but then realized what would happen if anyone tried to stop Blechk.

Baertha hugged her in that not-quite maternal but protective way she had. Baertha also seemed unaware of Blechk. If she found out what Blechk had in mind, there would be trouble.

Bob poured mulled wine into Blechk's mug.

"Could you top it off with brandy?"

He looked at Blechk and his shoulders shook with that low-throated laugh. He stirred in brandy and poured Daffy a mug of ale. "This will help."

Daffy said, "Could I have brandy?"

Bob pulled out a cup.

"A whole mug?"

Baertha and Jon-jay were deep in conversation.

Daffy quaffed the brandy. It went down hard, and she coughed. It also went down warm and she could already feel it softening the world's jagged edges. Bob topped off her mug again.

Daffy took the drinks to Blechk's table and sat next to the creep before he could put her on his lap. He raised his mug in a toast. "To your tight arse" and tipped his mug back. She guzzled more brandy and pointed her eyes at him but visualized the castles she used to call home in Glomaythea, Nantesse, even the warmth of her blanket in the barn.

The band played long, sad songs about loss and grief, hunger and despair, punctuated by hard-driving riffs that sounded violent to Daffy. People didn't dance. They fell into their thoughts and worries, and sometimes they argued. The guests drank more than they used to, and the ale wasn't as good as it had been before the war.

Rumbling thunder brought Loretta and Madog inside. Twilight had turned to darkness. Daffy watched Loretta smile, glad that she was happy. She wondered what disgraces Loretta had survived to guarantee the safety of her children. If Loretta could do it, then farq it all to hell, so could Daffy.

She tried to ignore Blechk's groping and failed. Worse than disgrace, nothing like manipulating a courtier's ego, no one could be prepared for this treatment. Except, of course, Loretta, Faernando, Donnae, Aenki, Daeffid, and all the *real* serving-lasses and lads, they were prepared. But Daffy was Dafina, the First Princess and—even in her own mind the thought brought a wave of disgrace.

Blechk pinched her. She squealed and Blechk seemed to like it, so she squealed a few more times. She looked up in time to see Baertha step toward their table with her hands on her sabers and an expression of pure violence on her face.

"I'm empty," she said to Blechk, wiggled out of his grasp and took their mugs to the bar.

Daffy pushed Baertha back. "Baertha, let me do this."

Baertha said, "That swine?"

"I'll explain later."

Baertha let go of her sabers. They clanked against the bar and she pushed her way around Loretta to Madog.

Daffy felt abandoned, but at least Baertha would be safe. She set the mugs on the counter. "Fill both with brandy, please."

Bob filled a mug from a small wooden cask. "That's the last of it."

Daffy couldn't decide whether she'd be better off taking the brandy for herself or giving it to Blechk. Passing out sounded nice.

Baertha appeared at her side and said, "Put a spoon of this in his mug." She set a small tin of brownish resin on the bar. Bob stirred a scoop into the mug and stirred. Baertha said, "And give some to his lackey, too."

Daffy said, "Poisoning him will only make it worse."

"It's this or I gut the farqer, but either way, you're not going upstairs with that. No. Way." Baertha then leaned against the bar, looking pleased with herself.

Bob said, "It's not poison. Well, for some people it is." Then he scooped a tiny bit onto his pinky fingernail and snorted it up his nose. "Hoo hoo!"

Baertha took the tin back. "Bob, you're hopeless."

Bob shook his head as though trying to loosen brain cells. He then poured mulled wine into Daffy's mug. She knocked it back, said, "I don't care," and asked for more. "Okay," she said, "I'm ready."

She picked up the mugs and took a trial step away from the bar. She staggered a bit and laughed a little. It almost sounded sincere.

Blechk drank without noticing anything. The band played and the morose mood dragged on. And then, half an hour after drinking the spiked brandy, Daffy noticed Blechk swaying in time to the music. He leaned farther back in his chair and his cheeks gained a rosy hue.

He turned to Daffy. The lines in his forehead had disappeared, and his devious smirk had turned to a contented smile. He looked like a genuine guest of The Gold Piece Inn—but that's not what stopped her.

Above that grin, Blechk had the eyes of a goat. His pupils had elongated into rectangles and the whites of his eyes had turned the gray of his irises.

He clawed at her thighs and she leaned out of reach. He told her he loved her and then told Haery that he loved him. Haery had goateyes too. They laughed hearty belly laughs that echoed with the vibrato of a goat bleating.

For an instant, Daffy's drunken haze cleared and disgrace came rushing back. She saw herself sitting in the inn of an outlaw port, trying to seduce a repulsive animal. No, she couldn't do it. Not in a million years. She drank more wine.

Blechk leaned into her, his face against her chest. He opened his mouth and chewed on her apron in the general vicinity of her breasts, all the while bleating like a kid goat.

Daffy turned to look at Baertha. Could she go through with it to protect Baertha? *For Baertha, I can do it to save Baertha's life.* But as she turned, the world rotated faster than she expected, and she lost her balance. She hung onto Blechk to keep from falling out of her chair.

He made a happy sound.

She felt stable for an instant but then a wave of nausea overcame her. She wouldn't be the first person to barf at The Gold Piece Inn, indeed, she wouldn't be the first person that night, but she'd never drank so much in her life. She tried to move away from Blechk, tried to lean between her chair and Haery's so she could barf into the sawdust and straw. Blechk hung on.

Daffy's throat spasmed, and she hurled brandy, partially digested chunks of herring, and bile on Haery's leg, the floor, and some other guest's leg too.

She pulled Blechk from his chair onto her. His balance was no better than hers. Her chair teetered. Haery pulled himself away. Blechk pulled her toward him. The chair tipped over. It took seconds to descend but descend it did. Daffy fell into the foul puddle.

She looked down, drool hanging from her mouth, her eyes defocused. The world swirled around her and her guts recoiled a second time. She heaved again and again, releasing less with each convulsion. Blechk descended on top of her.

Dafina had always carried herself with dignity and poise. And now she lay in vomit with Major Blechk.

Blechk sat up. Daffy pulled herself to her feet but slipped and fell. Aenki helped her up. Blechk stood, still wearing that goateyed smile as barf dripped from his sleeves.

Haery stood in the pool of vomit. Blechk bowed to Daffy and said, "I have to go to the Crab and Anchor now because," he stumbled, "because, umm, barf and sex."

Truth Faery

44.

Blechk and Haery stumbled out of the inn, arm in arm, humming the chorus of *Nuts O'er the Fork of the Maiden River.*

From his chair, Dewey watched a Monitor Faery clinging to the windswept sign of The Gold Piece Inn. On the backswing, the little guy drifted inside before the door slammed. He had an injured wing, and his spectacles had a cracked lens.

Serving-lasses and lads brought drinks and collected dinner dishes. The warmth and companionship of the packed room kept everyone inside. The guitarist argued with his Tuning Faery, a tough little thing with spiked hair, a safety pin through her nose, and a few choice words about playing untuned guitars. Dewey watched profits accumulate in the casino and hoped he wouldn't run out of ale. For a few hours it felt like things were almost back to normal, as though surviving that long day of persecution had brought everyone together. But drink loosened tongues and tempers.

The band finished a ballad that everyone knew, the story of how the Earth God left her fist over Crescent Cove, and how that fist would come to life in Crescent Cove's darkest hour. Baeswax grumbled, "Should be here any minute."

"We don't need God's Fist to sort out Blechk," Caepra said. One of his border collies sat on a chair between him and the leader of the blacksmith guild, Smithae, and another blacksmith, Ferrous. His long, braided beard dangled like a pendulum and his voice quaked. "How much longer will we tolerate that lot? Lukas pisses off every faery, low and high. When will his luck fail?"

"Luck has nothing to do with it, don't you see?" Smithae said.

She set her mug down with a clank. "Lukas is liberating us from that shite. The man has vision!" She leaned back in her chair, her arms around her barrel chest. "Taevius, Aennie, Vaence—they're just doing their bit—people have to do their bit, we're at war." She added, "I hate to be the one to tell you, but you better get on board or there will be trouble for you."

From a nearby table, Codae said, "Vision, my stinkin' arse." Sitting next to her, Fin pounded the table in agreement.

"If this is winning," Fin said, "I shudder at the thought of what will come of this land when his luck turns. Lukas is doomed and we all know it, and we're all going down with the farqin bastard."

Dewey mumbled, "We wouldn't be in this mess if he were a Bastard."

Fin added, "No offense."

"The losses come heavy, but the glory will be great." In myopic contrast to Fin, Ferrous hunched over the table. "You fools!"

Grindaer stood waving a fist. "I can't believe how you behaved for Major Blechk! He's just doing his job. The faer have to be monitored." He motioned around the inn, though not in Dewey's direction. "The only way that we can lose is if we're betrayed—and we all know who the traitors are."

Eyes turned to Dewey. When he appeared to have his patrons' attention, he pulled off his hat, letting the knitting catch on the points of his ears. He then tossed it in the general direction of the coat and hat rack. His Truth Faery flew out of the windowsill, pulled his derby tight on his head, caught Dewey's flying hat, and carried it to a hook on the rack.

"Looks dangerous to me," Dewey said. "Little guy could pull a thread if he isn't careful."

"Our children are dying in this war while the faer reap the benefits and risk nothing."

"The benefits?" Fin bellowed in a voice huge enough to be heard over wind, sail, and waves. "Benefits? The destruction of our way of life, centuries of good luck ended. We've never known rotting ships, stinking sewage, but we will! You fool, our soldiers are dying for nothing."

"Lukas is a thief! Demands we accept Acquisition Receipts for our crops and bounty."

"What the hell could a faery do in a war, anyway?"

"You saw what they did to the Volunteers today—traps, tricks, distractions—it adds up and demoralizes."

"Those arseholes were rude to the faer. For a little courtesy and a few shiny grains, the faer do all the worst work! How fast will the wharf rot without Pier Faeries? Any of you know how to stop a ship from rotting without Hull Faeries? Anyone?"

Grindaer shouted over the growing tumult, "You know I don't mean the lower faer—the higher faer could make formidable fighters. Elfs, dwarves, and think of what the maer or yeti could do!"

"One unicorn could wipe out a hundred savages."

"Maermaids and maerbutlers fight? You'd corrupt the kindest creatures on earth?"

"They're too damn lazy to fight."

"Then why are you worried about them?"

"Because they're holding us back. Benefitting while our children die."

"Hey!" Baeswax whistled and held her hands out. "A little respect for each other! Grindaer's upset because his daughter died in the battle of Aelpine Ridge. How about some compassion for our friends and neighbors?"

Grindaer, now red-faced and beginning to belch and flatulate loud enough to be heard across the room, said, "Maybe Millie would still be alive if the elfs had done their bit."

"Humpback shite!" Graey jumped up on a table. "Your damn Liberator has banned the faer from Volunteering."

Dewey watched Caepra hurl a steaming potato at Smithae. It smacked her in the back of the neck. Siotwo attacked Grindaer with a baguette. Paefid the stevedore threw the first actual punch. He cold-cocked Ferrous, broke his nose, and blood made the floor slippery.

Smithae yelled, "Maythean patriots don't tolerate faer."

Saelmon, a stout old fisher, popped Smithae in the solar plexus. "Glomaythea only exists because the faer rescued us from ourselves."

The drummer pounded his stones. The guitarist strummed his guitar hard enough to get his Tuning Faery to slam dance a Monitor Faery. The flutist blew on a long bass flute. Together they created the perfect brawl ditty.

Curses and threats were exchanged. Fists, mugs, stools, and then finally tables flew. Neighbors broke each other's bones, clawed each other's eyes, and friendships ended. Dewey sat and watched, keeping a mental tab of the damage done by each guest. He'd never charge anyone, though. How could he demand payment from the guests who returned to the inn each night when he couldn't charge the people who would never return?

45.

Thunder, hail, and icy winds drove livestock and people alike into the stable and barn. The crowd annoyed the screech owl but made the loft cozy. Daffy snored in her spot near the shuttered window.

Kaetie sat next to Macae, just to the side of the other Knightlets beneath a swirling cloud of GloFaeries. Caeph and Raenny had nicked a cask of ale from the bar and were drinking away their sorrow and humiliation with Naelth and Viviaen. Rustin paced around them, occasionally voicing ideas for rescuing the baby Bellae and the elf Conifaer. The others pointed out the obvious flaw, "Getting yourself—and us!—killed won't rescue anyone."

Wind howled inside, goats and sheep bleated, a horse nickered, and the collie barked. Dewey stomped up the ladder. From the landing, he said, "Bring tools."

The Bastards groaned but headed for the ladder. Dewey glowered as if they were the source of all his troubles.

Kaetie came last. Dewey said, "Ever seen a saloon after a brawl?"

"I've lived here my entire life, what do you think?"

"You've never seen one like this." He put his arm around her shoulders. "Don't let the mess bother you. A post-brawl saloon, late at night with just the core of us, you'll like this."

The floor and walls of the saloon were splattered with food and drink. Broken chairs, stools, and tables were heaped with mutilated benches. Serving-lasses and lads sat at the edge of the stage. The half-drunk Knightlets sat on the floor and began reassembling furniture. Kaetie had a team of Leaf Faeries weaving the fibers of broken boards back together, and Macae sat next to her, carving new legs from destroyed tables.

Dewey leaned against the bar facing the Bastard workers and drinking from a wooden mug. Madog and Baertha were in the casino arguing with Aerrol, captain of *Avarice*. Jon-Jay, the big blonde-haired pirate from the north, stood by, the pommel of a sword mounted on his back sticking up above his head.

Kaetie listened to the adults and got a sense of what had happened. Rustin listened, too, and she saw his jaw shift.

He said, "The Volunteers have no honor."

"Faeries!" Kaetie said. "Cute, playful, and more helpful and guileless than any human."

Macae said, "Guileless?"

Kaetie had learned the word from one of Lylli's books. "Exactly."

By the time she and Rustin and the Knightlets finished resurrecting what furniture could be saved—about half—the floors and walls had been scrubbed clean, the children were back in bed, and most of the serving-lasses were in the loft with them. Even the storm had blown down the coast.

Dewey, Madog, Baertha, and Jon-Jay were at the bar in heated conversation. Aerrol, who had already gone back to *Avarice*, seemed to be the central topic.

Rustin went to the bar and interrupted in a way that the adults welcomed. Kaetie didn't get how he did these things. And Jon-Jay greeted him with a fist bump and told the others how fast Rustin could row and what a great sailor he'd be if they could just get him aboard ship. Kaetie could only marvel.

When Rustin came back, the Knightlets talked him into a late-night visit to Aelbert at the lighthouse. The storm had left behind a crystal-clear moonless night that made every star a beacon. Aelbert would have all his optics pointed to the sky and would tell ghost stories until sunrise.

Kaetie watched Rustin weigh the idea.

"Aelbert, huh?" Rustin said.

Raenny said, "He's always got a fresh perspective, and we could use one."

Kaetie swept her thick auburn hair out of her eyes and looked at Macae. She said, "I'm staying here." She puckered her lips and cast him a seductive smile.

He gathered with the others.

She said, "Farq the lot of you."

When the Knightlets walked out, Kaetie slapped Macae on his bottom as he passed. Then she went to the bar.

Loretta dozed with her head on Madog's shoulder and his arm around her. Kaetie went straight to the center, between Madog and Dewey. Just walked up as though she belonged, and as she approached, she became more confident that she could contribute to the conversation.

Madog said, "Hey kid, 'tsup?"

Kaetie asked Bob for a glass of pinot. Bob chuckled the way he did, with his eyes squinting and hair bouncing around his shoulders.

Kaetie said, "Have they forgotten everything about this land?"

Bob handed her a wooden goblet of thick red wine from the bottom of a cask.

Madog said, "Do you know what she's talking about?"

Loretta said, "Kaetie, get on to bed."

"This land has had nearly two centuries of peace and prosperity, skirmishes but no wars, sickness but no epidemics, hunger but no famine, and do you know why?"

Dewey said, "I reckon we're about to find out."

Loretta said, "Get a move on, Kaetie."

"This idiot Lukas—"

"Kaetie, don't talk like that, if they hear you—"

"—blames the faer for holding back humans." She turned to Dewey. "Don't buy any of that crap about faeries being traitors, that's all smokescreen. He wants—"

"Kaetie. To the loft. Don't make me start counting."

Jon-Jay, in the deepest voice Kaetie had ever heard from the largest man she'd ever seen, said, "She's got something to say, and I want to hear it."

Baertha said, "I do, too."

Kaetie saw jealousy in her mother's eyes and couldn't believe how wonderful it felt.

"Well, I'm going upstairs," Loretta said. And then to Madog, "You coming?" He said that he'd follow in a while.

Jon-Jay leaned down, way down, close to Kaetie where she could see a long, jagged scar across his forehead. He said, "I got your back. We Bastards gotta stick together. Will you cover for me, too?"

"What could I ever do to help you?"

"I got a hunch, Kaetie."

Baertha said, "You're one of his?"

"And you thought you knew me."

"Only in the religious sense."

Kaetie cleared her voice. "Two hundred years ago, the land was in turmoil, all of Glandaeff. Crops barely grew from soil so exhausted it might as well have been salted. Villages fought other villages for food, horses, tools, and females—they actually treated women like chattel. Bandits ruled the roads and pirates—real pirates, not free profiteers like you lot, real pirates, the kind who murder, rape, and pillage—controlled the oceans."

"Whoa," Madog said. "We're real pirates."

"When did you last rape and pillage?"

"We don't do that," Baertha said.

Madog added, "Your mom wouldn't let me go upstairs with her if I did that. So, no."

"How many ships have you sunk?"

"I've sunk two," Baertha said. "They were trying to board us, though."

"You're traders, not pirates."

"Free-profiteers," Jon-Jay said. "We are traders. We work for no one but ourselves, and if someone comes between us and our booty, we will fight—doesn't matter if they're royalty or merchants, we enforce our own justice."

"And if something of value is left out," Baertha said, "say, on a ship with a docile crew unwilling to keep track of their belongings, well, we're not above relieving them of the burden."

"Before Queen Graegloria the Uniter ruled, you would either have been true-to-gods evil pirates, or you would have had to work for wages set by nobility—no share of the booty, just a seat at the oars, a mast to climb, and a boss to obey, all to make a rich man richer. Tyrants ruled everyone, women were essentially slaves, but so were farmers, fishers, whalers, everyone except royalty. And every village had its own petty tyrant who called himself a king, duke, or baron. Before the unification, disease killed almost half the humans. Do you know how Graegloria changed all of that? How she and her father King Graeglory the Great made life in Glandaeff peaceful and prosperous, not to mention decent and just?"

Now she had Madog's attention.

"Dewey," Kaetie said, "don't you remember? You were there."

He nodded and said, "It was different for us, for elfs, I mean."

"Exactly," Kaetie said. "Queen Graegloria invited the faer to live among the humans. She promised peace and respect. Up to that point in history, the faer only interacted with thaergists, and almost never willingly. Thaergists trapped lower faer and enslaved them in spells. The faer were as afraid of humans as humans were of the faer. People think the 'unification' was about bringing villages together and making peace, trading, benefitting from each other instead of pillaging, but that's not what happened. No, it was Maentanglement of humans and faer that led to the unification of people across the land and sea. Peace and prosperity have prevailed ever since. The usurper wants to go back to life without the faer, when the faer are the only things that keep humans from killing each other. Damn humans are too stupid to remember the horrors of the world before Maentanglement."

Madog had always been kind to Kaetie, brought her presents and played with her, made her laugh, and stuff like that, but this was the first time that he'd ever looked at her as an equal. Kaetie liked it. He said, "That's so farqed. I didn't even know. And I do feel stupid."

Jon-Jay said, "You and me both, brother."

Dewey said, "So now you understand why you have to do what you have to do."

"But he's our captain," Madog said. "Last five years, a damn good captain."

Baertha said, "He picked sides first."

"I wouldn't sail on a ship without faeries," Jon-Jay said.

"The open sea is about the worst place for a run of bad luck," Madog said.

Dewey turned to Kaetie. "Good stuff, kiddo. I need you to go to bed now. Or wherever you want to go, but the four of us need to talk about something that is none of your business."

Kaetie's temper simmered. She could feel herself turning red the way her mother did.

"It's not like that, Kaetie," Baertha said.

She marched away from the bar like a pissed off two-year-old and plopped down in Dewey's chair next to the window. She'd never sat here before and realized that sounds bounced around the room in such a way that she could hear everything they said.

* * *

"They know where the gold is stashed," Baertha said.

"It's not at the end of any rainbows—I've checked," Dewey said. "You'll make a hundred times what you're doing in the black market."

"The risks are low enough," Madog said, "and the profits high enough. But they hate ships. How can we get them aboard? Will they pay their debts?"

"They'll pay, or someone will pay for them," Jon-Jay said.

"Let's not talk about that. It hurts me. You have no idea," Dewey said. He looked wistfully at the chandelier, covered with radiating GloFaeries, and cleared his throat. "There are thousands hiding on The Fist of God. Hundreds more arrive by barge every night."

Baertha asked, "How do they get past the Volunteers?"

"They come on the night tide."

Madog spoke with skepticism. "Through the Haunted Passage? At night?"

"Yes," Dewey said, "the flesh-eating ghosts don't like faer meat."

Madog said, "But the hills are crawling with Volunteers."

A distinct voice came from behind the bar. A woman's voice with a peculiar lilt said, "Have you ever tracked an elf?"

"Lapidae?" Dewey said. "How long have you been there?"

"Since Blechk went away." The elfin woman stepped into the light.

"Right there?"

"Yes, in the gap of shadow." The elf's diamond eyes focused on Kaetie for an instant.

Kaetie felt certain that a message was contained in that look.

Baertha said, "Will it work?"

"It must," Lapidae said. "We are so many in the hills and nowhere to go. Hundreds of us are caught already."

Dewey asked, "Will you pay?"

"I don't have to pay. Your curse will provide." She smiled.

Baertha stepped back and took a long look at Lapidae, as if she'd never seen an elf up close. She held out her hand to close the deal with a shake, but Lapidae took a step back. For a few seconds, Kaetie couldn't see her.

"They're not like you," Dewey said. "They're not punctual, they're not nice—but they can be caring—and they won't take orders, so don't even bother."

Jon-Jay said, "Not exactly ideal passengers."

Baertha said, "Then fares won't be cheap."

"And it'll be tough to get them aboard," Dewey said. "You'll need humans on shore who can cozy up to the faer and coerce them onto tenders and to your ships."

"We can do that."

"No, you can't," Dewey said. "They'd drive you crazy, and you'd end up killing them. Trust me, you'd gut every one—they ignore suggestions." He turned to Lapidae. "Am I right?"

The others took a few seconds to find her, even though she stood less than two steps away.

"Suggestions from humans?" she said. "Would a bird take

orders from a worm?"

"How can we evacuate the faer if we can't get them on our ships?"

"In our own time, we will mount these ships."

Baertha said, "Not on my ship, you won't."

"Lapidae," Jon-Jay said, "when I drop anchor, I'm an easy target, like a duck in the middle of the lake. The only way this works is if I can sail in, drop anchor, collect my passengers, and weigh anchor in less than an hour. Otherwise it's not worth the risk."

"It won't work," she said.

"I have an idea," Dewey said, "but you might not like it." He stepped in front of Lapidae and she disappeared. Dewey glanced where she'd been, scanned the room and when he looked satisfied, he said, "First, we'll need a lot more of that resin you put in Blechk's drink."

"The goateye?" Madog said. "We got it in Puaepuae."

"And saw the whole picture, too," Baertha said. "Not pretty."

"Then a shipload of faer will land on Puaepuae in a few weeks. The second thing, we have to move the faer—we're talking about elfs and leprechauns now, snobs and arseholes every one—from the River Adductor, across The Fist of God, to the Great Beach, and onto ships. The timing is key, so humans have to run the show."

"If not us, then who? You?"

"Not me, personally, but ..."

* * *

Something outside distracted Kaetie. A flash. At first, she thought it must be Lapidae, but elfs don't flash. Nor was it the flash you expect from faery wings reflecting light, and nothing like a GloFaery.

Then a crack, a crash, and shards of glass blew into the room. Dewey's prized window shattered into thousands of pieces.

Two shards hit her foot, one went in deep. She screamed and fell. The pain wasn't so bad, but the pool of blood scared the crap out of her. Kaetie glimpsed someone, but in the dark and with her foot leaking blood, she couldn't tell who it was.

The pirates ran through the saloon and out the door. Baertha already had both sabers out. Madog had his dagger in his left hand and a throwing knife in the right. And Jon-Jay held a huge, straight sword, a sword longer than Kaetie was tall.

Dewey lowered himself next to Kaetie. He reached under her and lifted her foot by the heel. A triangle of glass stuck out of it, two inches long and half an inch wide where it entered.

He leaned down and examined it. "Didn't go through." He sat down next to her and slid over so that her foot bled onto his lap. He snapped his fingers and about twenty different types of faeries flew over and landed on his knees and thighs and her ankle and shin.

The faeries looked at her foot. A tiny woman Monitor Faery tut-tutted and wiped away a sharp line of blood along the glass-skin boundary. Blood seeped back into the gap. Kaetie had never seen faeries so serious.

Loretta ran down the stairs yelling pointless shite like, "my baby," "you're such a good girl, not even crying," and "I'll murder the farqer who did this."

Dewey yanked the glass out of Kaetie's foot and Loretta jammed a clean cloth into the wound. She held it tight. So tight that Kaetie screamed, but Loretta didn't let go and after a while the bleeding slowed.

"She needs Lylli," Dewey said, and then he scanned the room. He's eyes landed back on Kaetie. "When you finish here, go release the owl to fetch Lylli."

Kaetie liked nothing more than a visit from Lylli, but with her foot cut nearly off, how was she supposed to make it out to the aviary? She said, "Would you do it? I've got an owl roosting in the box in the almond tree, all you have to do is tap the box and it'll go straight to Lylli."

But Dewey wasn't listening. He was staring at the sill of his broken window.

"Oh no," Dewey said. "No, no, please, no." He was looking at the window where pieces of glass still stuck out. "Not him, oh please. Please?"

Kaetie had never seen Dewey cry. She honestly didn't believe that Dewey could care about something enough to cry. But then she saw it and it was too much for her, too unjust, too mean, too wrong.

A tiny creature lay unmoving on the windowsill. A swallowtail butterfly wearing a tiny suit with an even tinier wand next to him, and the tiniest bowler hat on the floor below.

"Why? He never hurt anyone, wouldn't know how." Dewey lifted the dead Truth Faery in his palm. The tiny suit it wore looked strange on the body of the dead butterfly that remained. "Please, gods, please don't take my Truth Faery. I'll be decent and good. Curse me again, anything, please." He set the tiny bowler hat on the dead butterfly. "But not my dear Truth Faery, please, not my little Truth Faery …"

46.

Dewey greeted another winter day seated in his chair. Icy breezes blew through the open space that had held his cherished windowpane. The space looked as empty as Dewey felt.

His eyes shifted, and he saw Raenny sitting in the hot seat. "How did you get there?"

"I've been here for an hour."

"What do you need?"

"I need Aennie back."

The curse hadn't let up on him since she'd asked for help.

"Can you arrange something?" Raenny said. "Isn't that how you work?"

"You don't know how I work." As the words came out, Dewey caught Raenny smiling. Of all the Knightlets, he thought Macae would have figured it out, not Raenny. Maybe they all knew. Since the damn curse—but now he felt it relenting. Of course! He could outsource it to Raenny. He said, "You're volunteering?"

"To get Aennie home, yeah, but I'm not, like *Volunteering*, you know."

Then a loud familiar voice came from upstairs, "You have to do something!" Loretta rushed down the stairs ahead of Madog. "Taevius knows everything."

"Office," Dewey stood. She started to speak again, and he repeated, "Office. Now. Close the door behind you."

She harrumphed but did as he said.

Dewey pointed at Raenny. "I can arrange for Aennie to appear in a certain spot at a certain time." An avalanche of unwelcome thoughts and emotions cascaded through him. "But she's not safe here. I have errands to run and a hysterical serving-lass to deal with. Meet me this afternoon and have a plan."

Raenny stood and walked out.

Dewey said, "And don't say any—"

Raenny's glance made finishing the sentence irrelevant, even inane. Dewey made a mental note to keep track of this one. The only thing that surprised Dewey about The Gold Piece Inn Bastards was when they didn't surprise him.

Raenny held the door for Daffy, who carried in a tray of steaming potatoes and eggs. She set the plates on one of the surviving tables.

Dewey motioned Madog to a chair at the table. Madog tossed him a silver. "She woke up with a hive buzzin' in her bonnet."

Dewey said, "How does that make today special?"

Daffy followed him into the office and sat in one of the two chairs on the receiving side of the desk. Loretta stood with her arms crossed and her foot tapping. At least she waited until the door shut. "Taevius knows everything," She said. "Everything!" This time it came out as a shriek. "He worked at Conifaer's side, he knows every hiding place in the inn, and he knows that Daffy is the queen."

"What?" Dewey said. He pointed at Daffy. "How did he find out?"

"He overheard us while cleaning behind the bar."

Loretta said, "He hates my son and you let Blechk take him. And now Laetifah is gone! Gone, Dewey, she's gone, she knows everything, and she hates you." She held out her arms to Daffy. "You can't stay. I love you like a sister, but don't you see? She's probably already told them who you are."

Dewey plopped into his chair. "If they knew about Daffy, they'd already be here." He knew what she would say. "Quiet, I'm thinking." He reached inside to feel for the curse. His appetite to check on Aennie had been slightly subdued by Raenny, but he felt nothing for Taevius or the baby.

Loretta interrupted his thoughts, which was just as well because he wasn't exactly bathing in brilliant ideas. "He hates Rustin, and he knows—"

"Don't you see what Blechk is doing?" This time Daffy interrupted her. "He's driving a wedge between us. Why announce to everyone that Rustin mentioned Taevius? Why didn't he conscript Rustin? Why take the baby?" She took Loretta's hands. "Don't you see?"

"It's all he can do," Dewey said. "He can't touch me, but he can plant the seeds of doubt and watch them bloom." Dewey rubbed his hands together. "It's a good move, but he doesn't know Taevius." He stood and worked his way around the desk, past Loretta, to the door. "I'll talk to Laetifah."

Loretta said, "She's gone!"

"Stop yelling."

"Daffy has to go."

"I'll decide that."

He opened the door and motioned for Loretta to step out. She did.

Daffy said, "I'm coming with you."

"I don't think so." Dewey laughed in her face. "What if Taevius spilled to Blechk? What if we walk down to Low Street and some bored Volunteers throw a net on you and collect a reward that by all rights should be mine? How do you think that would make me feel?"

"Dewey, you can pretend that we're not friends, but you won't convince me."

"You're probably right—damn this curse, what has happened to me?" He pushed her back into his office. "Stay here, right in here, find something to read." Before closing the door on her, he shuddered. Then leaned down near one of the door hinges and said, "Keep the door closed until I return." A Hinge Faery poked her head out, and Dewey flicked a grain of quartz to her.

Dewey was halfway to the door when Aerrol stepped in carrying a basket woven from river reeds.

"You see?" Aerrol held the basinet out and, sure enough, tiny Bellae snoozed away swaddled in thick wool with her little tongue sticking out. "Being on good terms with the Volunteers has its advantages. Blechk had to choose between surrendering his post or surrendering his plaything, else I send a note to Maedegan."

Dewey scoffed at mention of Lukas's right-hand man. He didn't trust this situation. There's good luck and bad luck, but dumb luck was never free. He called Loretta. She stepped in from the kitchen with the same angry fix of her eyes and arms—Dewey wondered if her gizzard looked angry. And then she saw the baby, and all that fury melted.

She reached into the basinet and lifted the infant.

Dewey's office door let out a beer curdling shriek and Daffy appeared next to the baby. And then Maeggie carrying her baby, Glaen. And then Aenki, Manuelae, and Donnae.

Aerrol raised his voice, "King Gledig respected Maedegan. If Maedegan supports Lukas, then he can't be all bad."

Dewey continued past Aerrol. He reached for the hat rack, took the beige knit hat, turned his head to the side and scratched behind his ear so that Aerrol faced the entirety of that elfin appendage. Dewey pulled on the hat. "If Maedegan does business with flotsam like Lukas, then he should suffer for it." Then he looked Aerrol square in the eye. "Feelin' lucky after making friends with the Volunteers? How about you and me, one-on-one poker? A few hands of Yarrow hold 'em? What do you say?"

"Halfling arse-biter." Aerrol spoke through clenched teeth. "Last time I do anything for you."

"For me?" Dewey said. "For me. You didn't take the child to her mother, you brought her to me. What, you need a favor? You need money? You need …" but Aerrol was already out the door and across the street.

Daffy cooed at the baby; she sounded like a pigeon in orgasm. The baby started crying and the mothers nearly stampeded.

Loretta said, "How do we find Laetifah?"

"You think one of my serving-lasses left without my knowledge of where, why, what, and how? Really? She's in the boarding house on Low Street."

Loretta said, "Low Street?"

Dewey nodded.

"Is she …?"

"… serving at the Crab and Anchor?" Dewey said. "Laetifah? I don't think we have to worry about that. She'll take up whaling first. That one wouldn't need a harpoon, either."

Loretta pulled a wool cape and scarf from the rack. "I'll carry the baby," she said. "You carry the basinet, Laetifah will need it."

"No," he said. "I have to do this alone."

"Hold on," Daffy said. "Wait here."

Dewey would have ignored her but for her expression—conniving self-satisfaction. It looked good on her.

A minute later, Daffy returned with Rustin.

* * *

Rustin and the others had gotten back from the lighthouse before sunrise. They'd taken the long way home, through the hills and along Knuckle Creek. Even in the moonless night they'd seen elf and leprechaun camps—if you can call a few creatures huddled in and around trees camps. They'd even stumbled into some sprites. Rustin had never seen so many faer before and knew that for each one they saw there were at least a hundred unseen. When Daffy came in, he pretended to sleep, hoping she'd go away, but she was learning more from his mother every day. She started to count, and he followed.

The covey of women meant one thing. He moved into the gap between Loretta and Dewey. "You have the baby!"

Dewey said, "What's it to you?"

"How did you get her?" The relief didn't mix well with the realization that he couldn't rescue the child himself. So far, knighthood wasn't working out very well. The baby looked perfectly sound. She smiled at him and wrapped her tiny hand around his finger and washed away every feeling but joy.

"Take the baby to her," Daffy said.

Rustin didn't know what she meant. She held the baby out to him, and he took her. He cupped the back of her head in his palm, set her body along his arm, and tucked her tight against his chest.

"Me?"

"I like it," Dewey said. "Laetifah can't hate you if you bring her baby back. Daffy, you're starting to catch on."

"Who rescued her? I'm not takin' credit for—"

"Farq sake!" Dewey said. "You'd fold on a straight flush? I thought you were smarter than that. Take what luck you can get."

"You'll have plenty of defeats and hard-won victories," Daffy said. "Let yourself have an easy one."

On the walk back from the lighthouse Rustin had talked to Naelth about right and wrong, and Naelth had said that sometimes the best thing might not be the right thing. Taking credit for rescuing Bellae wasn't right, but he could return the baby without taking credit for it. And he wanted to see Bellae back where she belonged, in Laetifah's arms.

* * *

Dewey and Rustin walked down to the boarding house on Low Street. Rustin winced at the stench from the Crab and Anchor next door. "Are you sure she won't have to work there?"

"I don't get a say in what Laetifah does." He pushed the door open and they went in. Rustin held the baby inside his cape. Dewey motioned for him to stand to the side of the fireplace. Sand and dirt covered the floorboards. Sailors, shipwrights, and dock rats shuffled across the floor, many still in their nightshirts. The lack of faery helpers left the room smelling like rotting fish, spilled ale, and night soil. Dewey went to a woman seated across the room. Rustin had seen her around town but had never talked to her. Dewey then led him up a flight of rickety wooden stairs, down a corridor, and past a fowl smelling privy.

Dewey knocked, and the door cracked open. "We have Bellae."

Laetifah frowned at Rustin until he pulled his cape back and put the baby in her arms. Shaelie hugged her mother's thigh.

Dewey stepped into the room and pulled Rustin with him. Laetifah was too absorbed in her child to notice.

Rustin said, "Aerrol rescued—"

Dewey interrupted. "I owe you money."

When she finally looked up from the baby, she said, "It was you." The child suckled at her mother. "You let him take my baby." Then she turned to Rustin. "And you sold out my boy."

"I did," Rustin said, "and it'll never happen again. Taevius is my friend, my brother, and always will be."

"Never was. Never will be."

Shaelie had been watching Rustin but looked up at her mother, confused.

Rustin said, "My loss."

"No," Dewey said, "Blechk took Taevius and Rustin brought back your baby." He cleared his throat. "I owe you eleven silver, and eighteen copper ohzees." He held the coins in his open palm.

She spit at Rustin. He felt it on his cheek but didn't wipe it off. He cocked his head so that it wouldn't run down his face. If it would make Laetifah feel better, he didn't mind carrying that mark of shame.

Dewey started babbling about how word would spread if he didn't pay her and he'd lose his staff. He seemed to be apologizing to the coins. She reached for the money. He withheld it and tried to talk her into returning to The Gold Piece Inn.

"I'd rather whore at the Crab and Anchor than do anything for you." She pointed at Rustin. "Or you."

"Laetifah," Dewey spoke in an impatient tone, "Taevius will be in the Volunteer Navy. I'll pull a few strings and make sure he starts at second mate, maybe pilot."

She shifted Bellae to the other breast but never stopped glowering.

"Laetifah, your son will be the captain of a ship and soon. Think about that. A Gold Piece Inn Bastard captain in the Glomaythean Navy, not bad."

"You're a snake."

Dewey shrugged and stepped out the door.

Laetifah said, "Give me my money."

Sempervaereen

47.

Kaetie's foot throbbed all night. Limping out to the aviary to send the owl for Lylli didn't help and climbing the ladder up to the hay loft had been an ordeal. But Lylli arrived in the afternoon and summoned faeries that went crazy on her foot. Through most of the treatment, Kaetie was convinced that they were amputating. Lylli assured her that the faeries were doing their job. When they finished, Lylli wrapped Kaetie's foot in honeycomb and melted the edges to seal it against her skin. Now, along with the throbbing pain, her foot felt bruised and twisted.

"You have to stay off that foot for weeks."

Then Lylli had the Bastards carry her down the ladder, into the inn, and next to a fireplace off in the corner of the casino. She set her foot on the hearth. A border collie curled up next to her, then a sheepdog, and all three of them had a nap.

Kaetie awoke to Dewey arguing with Daffy and Lylli.

Dewey said, "How am I supposed to run this place?"

"You can't stop Blechk from conscripting them," Lylli said. "They have to go into hiding."

"Who will carry the water and firewood?"

"Poppa," Lylli said. It always threw Kaetie for a loss when Lylli referred to her father that way. Not only did it seem inconceivable that they could be related, but the concept of Dewey as "Poppa" was like mistaking a Farq Faery for a Star Faery. Lylli continued with an underlying spark in her voice, "What are you hiding?"

Dewey let out a long groan.

Lylli laughed, turned to Daffy, and said, "He's got a plan."

"What?" Daffy said.

"He does this," Lylli said. "Look at him, everything is going according to his plans, but he doesn't want anyone to know."

"Why?"

"Because my father doesn't like to share."

"All right," Dewey spit out the two sharp syllables. "It's true. I have a plan for the Knightlets."

"Will it get them killed?"

"These are dangerous times."

"Are they going to serve in the Volunteers?"

"No."

"What about Kaetie?" Daffy said.

Lylli said, "She can't stay here."

"She annoys everyone," Dewey said.

Kaetie didn't want to leave that unanswered, but when she started to sit up, her foot throbbed, a dog harrumphed, and she realized that yelling at him might not make the best case.

Dewey continued, "She badgers people with questions, practically interrogated the pirates last night."

"She could stay upstairs," Daffy said. "She has a lot of reading."

"Those rooms are not available!" Dewey said.

"It's all money to you, isn't it?" Daffy said.

"Yes, what else could it be?"

Lylli interrupted, "Kaetie is ready to apprentice."

Kaetie sat straight up when she heard those words.

"What?" Dewey said. "And how many times have Volunteers showed up at your cottage?"

"It's true," Daffy said. "She's starving for knowledge."

"I have Alert Faeries," Lylli said.

"I can picture it. An Alert Faery flies through the window, you throw Kaetie over your shoulder, and run out the back door—she weighs more than you!"

Kaetie stored the crack about her weight for later. Dewey would pay.

"I can protect her and get her the best education imaginable."

"Then do it."

"I will," Lylli said, "but *you* have to convince Loretta."

"Lylli, you've always been so sweet." Dewey's voice took on that sarcastic tone that Kaetie associated with long lists of chores. "Always happy to send your dear aging father into the dragon's breath." He pointed at Daffy. "You do it. She likes you best."

"No. Way."

"All right." Dewey looked across the room at Kaetie. She faked asleep. "Fine. Send her in."

The room went quiet and Kaetie's fake sleep became real. When she woke, she heard her mother and Lylli. "You swear it's safe?"

Lylli said, "It is probably the safest place in the world."

Loretta said, "And it might get Kaetie to stop hassling everyone?"

"No one can promise that."

"But why would this, this, *thing* protect my Kaetie?"

"The only thing that Sempervaereen wants in the world is for someone to listen."

"Kaetie'll badger her with questions!"

"Sempervaereen has the answers."

"Will weird things happen to her?"

"Knowledge changes people." And then Lylli said something in a hushed voice that made no sense to Kaetie. "Loretta, you have to understand, Kaetie needs to be trained. You have a responsibility."

Loretta's voice bristled with confrontation. "Promise she'll be safe?"

"She'll have plenty of good food, fine shelter, and constant protection."

"But she'll be with the faer the whole time."

"Yes, her foot will have time to heal completely and then she can join me at my cottage and begin her apprenticeship."

48.

Kaetie's foot was wrapped in fresh honeycomb, a layer of fresh-sheared wool, and an oilskin. She struggled on crutches—sticks, really. Lylli carried her clothes bundled in her blanket along with her favorite food, smoked salmon in lavender honey. They took a trail up the forested valley between The Fist of God's middle and index fingers.

Lylli said, "Have you ever listened to one of Sempervaereen's stories?"

"I've heard bits of them. She takes a while to get to the point, so we go around her."

"She has been here through our entire history."

"She's a big Tree Faery, right?"

"A dryad. As much of a person as any of us, but she is also most certainly a tree. The thing you have to understand about trees is that they live vastly different lives than people."

"Okay, she can't move. Does she have a brain?"

"She's rooted to the ground but can move her limbs, and she's a deep thinker. What we experience as a year, she experiences as a day. It's more complicated, but that's the gist, and she loves a violent storm. Trees are big fans of weather."

Kaetie's crutch caught in the root of a buckeye and Lylli caught her. They crossed a bridge over Knuckle Creek and walked up a grassy hill. Kaetie saw Caepra and one of his dogs ran over for a scratch behind his ears.

"Her stories are neither long nor boring, it just takes her days to tell them."

"Sounds tedious."

"Maybe they're boring when you stand next to her trunk, but that's not how she works. She's a mighty redwood, over three-hundred feet tall, and for her to teach, you will have to live in her canopy."

Kaetie stopped. "I am not climbing that tree."

* * *

Lylli had known both of Kaetie's parents. Along with her father's dark skin tone, she had his spirit and ambition. She had her mother's eyes, a few of her freckles, and she'd soon have her mother's luxurious curves, but it was when Kaetie showed her mother's unrepentant passion that Lylli fell deeper in love with this child.

Kaetie smiled back and mouthed the words, "No farqin way."

"You will love Sempervaereen's canopy. It has little bowls of the freshest water you'll ever taste. Birds and frogs, salamanders live up there, and faer! Kaetie, you'll meet baby faeries who will remember you for the rest of your life. When I was your age, my father sent me up there for six months."

"Six months?" Kaetie sounded appalled. "How long do you want me up there?"

"Until your foot heals."

"Six months. Dewey can really be an arse."

"Yes, he can but not that time. I was like you. My curiosity was about to get me in real trouble—"

"I'm not getting in," Kaetie did a poor impression of Lylli's higher pitched voice, "real trouble."

Lylli stopped. "The questions you've been asking, challenging Volunteers, you're this close to being arrested for treason." She pointed at the mighty redwood still a mile uphill, near the ridgeline. "Without Sempervaereen, I'd have never become a druid."

"Will she make me a druid?"

"She will help you with Druidry, but I wonder if the world might have greater plans for you."

"No, I want to be a druid. I've wanted to be a druid since the first time I looked in your crystal ball or saw your kitchen—and especially the first time I enchanted a faery. I've got the talent, you know."

"Oh yes, you do. But your questions—you're more interested in history than nature."

"I'm interested in nature."

The path drew them through a forest. About halfway up god's middle finger, the oaks gave way to redwoods. Among those trees, Lylli felt like a pixie. Some of them had trunks that were forty steps around.

Sempervaereen grew in the center of a wide clearing that she showered in shade. Too dark for grass to grow, the clearing was carpeted in thick auburn needles that had accumulated over millennia. Each step released a waft of fresh pine scent. Her lowest branches were thirty feet above their heads.

"There's no way I can climb that—her."

They went around a ring of perfect white mushrooms.

"Sempervaereen won't let you fall."

A sunbeam penetrated to the ground, like a single thread of light.

"Go ahead," Lylli said. "Step into the light and let her see you."

Kaetie struggled with her crutches on the soft floor. A slight breeze shifted the branches and that single ray crossed her face.

Sempervaereen's trunk was made of thick earthy brown and red fibers. Many-colored lichen grew in the deep groves of the bark.

Lylli began to sing. She reached up in the scale and then lower, zeroing in on the right frequency. When she found it, the needles above them started vibrating complementary notes, and Lylli and Sempervaereen's voices formed a heavy, soothing chord.

Sparks of light appeared around Lylli. They built in number and formed a fabric, like a long scarf that blew on a breeze around her, but the air was still. The ribbon of light wrapped around Lylli's head like a halo. Her eyes opened and she danced in a way that made her smile reach up to her forehead and down to her toes. She laughed for a few seconds and then her smile faded, and she moaned in grief, nodding, agreeing with the tree.

Sempervaereen and Lylli's duet included rhythmic flashes of light, a bass line from branches rubbing together, and rhythm from the sound of her tiny needles in the wind. The orchestra washed Kaetie of concern for the mortal world.

Sempervaereen's needles were less than an inch long and ranged in color from the fresh yellowy green of spring to a rusty red when they dried. Pinecones not much bigger than Kaetie's thumb decorated her branches, and even tinier faeries inhabited them.

Lylli's faery halo unwound and swarmed up out of sight. She relaxed with a great sigh and turned to Kaetie. "I knew she'd love you."

"To know me is to—"

"Kaetie."

More threads of light poked through. Lylli said, "It's time."

Kaetie said, "How do I ...?" But before she could finish her question, thousands of redwood needles fell from the tree. As they reached Kaetie, their wings spread, and they swarmed into the shape of a hammock.

The sound of children playing emerged from dozens of nymphs. About the size of her forearm, they wore sheer gowns of green, silver, and gold, and their skin matched the auburn of Kaetie's hair. They fluttered about on delicate, barely visible wings.

"Watch yourself," Lylli said. "They're loyal to Sempervaereen, they don't like sarcasm, and they don't appreciate irony."

"Sound like a barrel of laughs."

A little fellow with curly green hair poked her in the butt.

Kaetie turned to look at it, and the hammock rotated with her.

Two muscular nymphs flew into Kaetie's chest and pushed her over. Others took her crutches away. She fell into the hammock and a crowd of nymphs assembled below her and pushed her up.

Kaetie shrieked with glee and the hammock maneuvered her in a spiral that led up between branches. The canopy was made of limbs woven together in concentric bowl-shaped layers several feet from the top of the tree. The lowest had a diameter of at least twenty feet and the highest about ten feet. From here, Kaetie couldn't see the forest floor without climbing out on a limb.

The sun shone bright up here, though there were plenty of shady nooks. Mushrooms grew in the shade, some tiny and bluish, others bright red and large enough to form a soft seat. Frogs croaked, bees buzzed, and ferns and flowers grew from thick, wet branches. She cupped her hands into one of the puddles and drank. The water tasted like honeysuckle nectar.

Kaetie had seen more faeries in one place before, but never so many types, and they were all children, all naked, and they knew how to have fun. They played hide and seek, they coerced each other into attempting flight on their fledgling wings. They laughed and told jokes and teased each other without mercy. When Kaetie crawled toward them, they hid within the boughs. Some peeked out at her, but most disappeared.

She settled onto the cap of a mushroom and felt relaxed awareness. Three nymphs lifted her injured foot and set it atop a soft fungus pillow. The sounds of the young faeries meshed into a background melody. A subtle light show played across the sky. Fog wrapped around her, reached into her lungs, and a bright star warmed her.

As Kaetie adjusted to Sempervaereen's timescale, the low-pitched branch-on-branch rumble became a discernible voice, the voice of a kind old lady with secrets she lived to share.

Kaetie felt her own intelligence the way a musician feels an instrument. Her first question came out as though her fingers wove it of fog in the wind, "Why?"

Sempervaereen laughed. The world shook.

Knightlets

49

N o one ever found out who broke Dewey's glass window-pane.

A few days later, the water wheel that powered Grindaer's mill broke loose from its axle and rolled into Knuckle Creek. It seemed impossible for such a huge wooden object to float over the rocks, around the bends, across the shallows, and into the River Adductor, but it did.

The huge wheel reached the river as the tides pushed a hill of water out to sea. People gathered on the wharf and watched Grindaer dive in and swim after his precious wheel. The ferocious waves of that late winter day battered, crushed, and splintered the grinding engine into thousands of pieces, and every piece had rotted clear through.

While Grindaer treaded water among the remains of his wheel, back at the mill, the gears that turned the millstone corroded into a single knot of iron and the two-ton stone developed a crack.

Grindaer, his mother before him, and grandfather before them had grown wealthy serving a vital role in Crescent Cove. After the water wheel rolled away, he lost his business, his savings, and his wife, who left him and took his surviving children.

The Volunteers, most of the blacksmiths, and the glass blower blamed the faer for the odd sequence of events that destroyed the mill. Grindaer had a different explanation. When Major Blechk asked him what happened, Grindaer said, "Just bad luck."

Without a functioning mill to grind grain into flour, the good people of Crescent Cove had to go without bread for the year it took to build a new wheel and smith new gears.

Thank the gods you don't need milled grain to brew beer.

50.

Using the skills Conifaer taught them, the Knightlets combined pieces of walnut and oak into sturdy tables and chairs that locked together. The work had a somber feel. Everyone knew things had to change.

The Town Liar made her announcements every day, reports of glorious victories that contradicted the sorry state and sorrier moods of the Volunteers assigned to Crescent Cove. But the day the Knightlets installed the new furniture in the inn, the Town Liar brought a different message: "Lukas, the glorious Liberator and First Human, announces with great sorrow that the faer menace is taking a toll larger than the Humans of Maythea can afford. The faer will no longer be tolerated."

To the Knightlets it was the same old same old, but Dewey knew better. Blechk's troops had spent the last week fanning through the forests, the hills, and across Faer Reef with nets and traps. They flushed little people—pixies, nymphs, leprechauns—from their homes in flowers, ponds, and at the ends of rainbows. They hunted elfs deep in the forest and high on The Fist of God. Empty barges arrived with the morning tide and returned with captured faer on the evening tide, headed for Lukas's Faer Centers. Thousands of innocent creatures were enslaved, but for every captured faery, a dozen remained free to taunt the soldiers, and Dewey was certain that every one of them was hiding at The Gold Piece Inn.

Once the furniture was installed, Dewey sat the Knightlets at a large round table—the masterpiece of their carpentry. Bob brought pints of ale and their mothers set out bowls of hearty goat stew. The mothers hovered over their Bastards as they ate.

Dewey took Rustin into his office. Loretta tried to follow, but he shut the door in her face.

At the round table, Macae said, "This is it, Dewey's selling us." Naelth, "We knew this day would come." Viviaen, "I better a fetch good price."

Raenny, the only orphan among them, walked out as if to use the privy, but didn't return.

When Rustin emerged from the office, he looked serious but confident and older.

Caeph said, "He's not selling Rustin." Macae, "Maybe Rustin bought us." Naelth, "I don't like being on this end of a bargain."

"Close to the truth," Dewey said, and then explained that every Bastard over fourteen had to go into hiding. "But that doesn't mean you're getting out of your chores." He turned to Rustin and said, "Good luck."

Rustin led them into the kitchen, where they found their few things rolled in heavy blankets. They attached their dinner knives to their belts, and Daeffid handed out parcels of bread, nuts, and smoked fish wrapped in dried kelp.

The Knightlets kissed their mothers' goodbye.

They took the trail that started in the faery garden and led up The Fist of God. Dewey accompanied them as far as the gate.

Lapidae stepped onto the trail and into the light. She reached down to what looked like a pile of rocks at her feet and lifted a long, thin piece of granite. She tossed it into the air. Nearly four feet long, it spun perfectly about an axis two inches from the guard. The pommel shone like glass, the grip looked like a rotating shadow, and the blade was the mottled white, gray, and black of the granite that reached into the sky like calluses on The Fist of God. The sword rotated five times and then stuck in the ground in front of Rustin, vibrating a perfect note.

"Yours," she said.

Rustin touched the grip, and it slipped into his hand the way that his wrist fit his arm.

In reverent silence, she set weapons with elk-skin scabbards in the hands of each Knightlet. She then gave Rustin a long bastard sword and two long, double edged daggers. He asked what they were for and she answered with an arrogant elfin glance that said if he needed to ask, he was too stupid to deserve the answer.

Rustin accepted them and thanked her.

Dewey marveled at the coldsmithed granite weapons. He'd never seen one before. The legends described them as eversharp and unbreakable. If he hadn't known what they were, he'd have mistaken them for tarnished castoff bronze worn too thin for use.

Caeph said, "They look kind of fragile." Macae, "Better than our sticks." Naelth, "Not much."

"Humans," Dewey mumbled, "Lukas has it backward."

51.

In the invisibly subtle way of elfs, Lapidae found a moment when no one was watching and leaned close to Rustin. "Bring my Conifaer back to me. This is your vow." She kissed his cheek. When he looked up, she was gone.

A cold wind blew down from the north. The sky was clear, and the sun felt warm on his face, but when they passed into the shadows of trees, under rocky outcroppings, or into the valleys between god's fingers, his exposed skin chilled to the gristle. Caeph and Macae tried to trip each other and laughed at every success and failure. Naelth stuck a finger up his nose when he caught Rustin's eye. Viviaen shivered under her cloak.

Rustin wondered how they would be welcomed when they made it to the Great Beach. He was deep in his thoughts when he noticed Raenny and Aennie on the path waiting for them.

"Aennie?" He said. "Where did you come from?"

Naelth said, "It worked?"

Macae said, "Looks like it worked pretty well." His eyebrows bounced up and down, and Rustin noticed that Aennie was holding Raenny's hand.

"Nice work," Rustin said.

"I've deserted the Volunteers," Aennie said. "Just as my naval career was set to take off, he seduced into committing treason."

Raenny shrugged. "Helping the faer will pay better long term."

"If I'm not hanged."

Rustin said, "How'd you do it?" They stood where the paths crossed.

"Lured her away with my good looks and charm."

Aennie's eyes didn't leave Raenny. Rustin looked back at The Gold Piece Inn. "Now if Taevius and Vaence can get away, we'll be complete."

"Well, Taevius," Macae said. And then, "Sorry, Viv. Vaence is a tough guy, he'll be all right."

Viviaen shook it off.

"How did Dewey know you'd escape?"

"Could have been the curse," she said. "I asked him for help, but Raenny would have gotten me, anyway."

Rustin pulled the daggers from his belt and handed them to Aennie. "Lapidae made these for you."

"Is something wrong with the blades? Not exactly shiny."

"Farq me running," Raenny said. "Coldsmithed granite."

"And she still hasn't let go of his hand," Macae said. "You two are going to be insufferable, aren't you?"

Caeph said, "They'll have ugly children."

Naelth sang a particularly explicit stanza of "Barnacle Balls the Sailor."

Rustin said, "Keep it moving."

* * *

They had just come out of a valley. Caeph stopped and shushed them. He pointed up the hill at a lone oak tree and whispered, "Ladrechaun."

Rustin saw him too. About three feet tall in green and white checkered pants with a black hat. "He's afraid of us."

Caeph said, "Thinks we're Volunteers." Aennie, "How can we help them if they're afraid of us?" Naelth, "Perseverance and integrity." Macae snickered.

Caeph, "He's hiding something." Macae, "Yeah, burying it." Viviaen, "What a cute little shovel."

Rustin said, "He needs to get out of sight before a Volunteer sees him. Come on." He led them off the trail and sent Caeph and Macae to outflank him. It felt like hunting. Helping the faer might be tricky.

They ran up the hill. The ladrechaun had disappeared.

"A rainbow!" Macae said. A spectrum shimmered in the clear sky, arcing up over the hill.

Caeph said, "One end of that rainbow is right where he was digging."

Rustin circled the oak. Macae and Caeph ran to the disturbed dirt, just beyond the oak's shade. They started digging.

Raenny said, "You know what's missing from that rainbow?" And Aennie, "Rain?" The two of them stopped fifty steps from the tree.

Rustin heard buzzing. It started faint, like mosquitoes but grew louder and more distinct.

Macae said, "Uh oh."

There was an instant of silence … broken by the ladrechaun's hooting laughter. Macae and Caeph sprinted away with a cloud of bright yellow wasps in pursuit. The cloud splintered into strands that pursued every one of them. Caeph and Macae ran back down into the valley. Rustin ran uphill in the general direction of Lylli's cottage. Naelth and Viviaen ran down the path, and Aennie and

Raenny ran up.

The sun had set by the time they regrouped. They put together a modest campfire against a rock face.

Macae had the most stings, but Caeph's swelled into bright red hives. Raenny was the only one unscathed. Aennie insisted that leprechauns and wasps respected heroes. Even Raenny groaned at that one.

"I was being sarcastic."

Macae said, "No, you weren't."

Viviaen said, "Do we have to help leprechauns?"

"I don't," Macae said. Caeph, "Me neither." Raenny, "They don't seem so bad to me." Naelth, "They don't deserve to die because of their twisted sense of humor." Macae, "Doesn't make them deserve our help either."

Rustin poked the fire, rolling a log over to expose the hot edge. Everyone huddled closer.

Macae whispered to Raenny, loud enough for all to hear, "You two aren't going to do it tonight, are you?"

"Leprechauns might be easier than elfs," Rustin said. "They don't fear water. Getting elfs onto ships ..." He exhaled through his teeth.

They spent the night huddled with their capes spread around each other's shoulders. Their teeth chattered, their jokes soured, and their wasp stings itched.

The next day, Caeph's face was red and puffy. Macae scratched himself against trees, rocks, bushes, anything in their path. Viviaen couldn't stop shivering. And they complained about everything. Except Raenny and Aennie who were in a world all their own.

52.

The Knightlets followed the trail north, every step accompanied by grumpiness from lack of sleep, complaints of the icy wind, and itchy wasp stings. They glimpsed signs of elfs in trees, shrubs, and crevices in the granite that seem to grow on the fingers of God's Fist. Like seeing a wildcat that didn't want to be seen, the abrupt visions disappeared when the Knightlets focused on them. Sometimes they caught sight of a family, but elfs didn't form what humans considered communities.

Macae said, "There's one!" But it disappeared before the others could turn their heads. "I swear, there were five of them—and one of them was good looking, I mean legendary elfin good looks. The whole container, mmm mm."

Aennie said, "I wonder why they hide from us."

The trail wound through oaks and buckeye whose branches reached over the path. Still leafless but budding and shrouded in moss that hung like lace, they cast patchy, skeletal shadows.

Raenny whispered, "There's one in the tree to my right." He faced forward but pointed with his elbow.

Without moving his head, Rustin peered from the corner of his eyes and saw her. She shifted into the shadows, crouching among the branches of a sturdy bear oak. Long, white hair cascaded around her ears and over her shoulders. Her skin was the color of shadow, a soft darkness framed in that white mane.

Macae whispered, "That's her." Aennie, "And she's got Rustin's number." Naelth, "Wow."

From another direction, Rustin heard the scrape of an arrow and vibration of a bowstring, followed immediately by the thwack of an arrow piercing the ground between his feet. The angle of its shaft pointed back at a tree where a branch wavered in the windless morning. Another arrow zipped past his ear, so close that it took a few strands of hair and then shattered in a rock behind him.

Raenny said, "Let's get out of here."

Caeph moved off the path and pulled his coldsmithed sword from its elk skin scabbard—Lapidae had made him a scimitar with a long, gracefully curved blade. Everyone had agreed that it fit

Caeph's sense of drama. With his back to a tree trunk he whipped the sword in a figure eight. The thin granite blade sliced through the air with a satisfying twang. Rustin saw something flash from the blade to the hilt, maybe a GloFaery.

In half a heartbeat, six arrows stuck in a semi-circle in front of Caeph. He leaned against the tree, his back straight, holding the sword upright. "They're good. What do they want?"

"Be still," Rustin said.

Raenny stopped in his tracks and Aennie with him. Naelth huddled in his cloak, though Rustin could hear him pull his new sword from its scabbard. Lapidae had made a rapier with an extra broad blade for Naelth.

Macae said, "They don't seem to want our help." Aennie, "On to the next ones?"

"If they wanted to hurt us, we wouldn't be standing," Rustin said. By instinct, he'd put his hand on the grip of his sword. "They think we're Volunteers. Stay cool. This is what we're here for." He held his hands out and took five measured strides away from the trail. He scanned the trees and spoke with more courage than he felt. "My name is Rustin, and we are the Knightlets of The Gold Piece Inn."

Naelth whispered, "Badly in need of a better nickname."

Rustin waited for a response, even a bowshot to the ground, but got nothing. "We can get you away from the usurper." That thick white hair caught his eye. He shifted and saw her reach for a branch, so graceful that it looked more like she was dancing than climbing. She wore brown leather and green cloth wrapped tight around her frame. Her legs seemed too long for her torso, but her shape defined feminine.

Thwack, thwack, thwack. Arrows drew a line at his feet.

"You can shoot me where I stand," he said, "but I'm not leaving until you're safe." An arrow hit the ground between his feet, and then another that came from a different angle. "We'll guide you to a ship that can take you to a land free of Lukas the usurper."

He heard murmurings behind him. Raenny, "He's nuts." Aennie, "He's brave." Naelth, "He is more than that."

"I'm with you, brother," Caeph said, and then at a higher volume. "No more arrows for me? Even with my sword drawn?"

Thwack, a foot over his head into the tree trunk behind him.

"Now you're just showing off."

Naelth rose from his crouched position. He swept his cape to his back, exposing the rapier in his hand. An arrow creased his cape and stuck in the ground between him and Viviaen. He flinched but said, "I dedicate my sword to your safety!"

Raenny mumbled, "How did I end up with a bunch of stupid Bastards?" But then, he, too, pulled his sword, slowly, deliberately from its scabbard. Lapidae had given him a simple, not quite aptly named bastard sword. "For no reason I can imagine, I'm in, too."

"You're just trying to impress me," Aennie whispered, "and it's working."

Farther up the trail, dozens of crows complained. A loud voice said, "Freeze!"

A squad of Volunteers in red and black leathers rounded the corner. An empty mule-driven cart followed. Annoyed crows swooped around the Volunteers.

Rustin whispered, "Sheath your swords." And then, "Elfs, we'll cover you." He watched Raenny and Naelth sheath their swords, noticed that Macae, Aennie, and Viviaen had the sense not to draw their weapons in the first place and hoped that Caeph would at least hide his.

A high-pitched voice up in the trees said, "You lie. You led them to us, but you'll not be rewarded." She all but sung the words.

He looked in the voice's direction but didn't see her. "We'll distract them long enough for you to get away. And I would never, ever lie to you."

The Volunteers closed in. The cart held an empty cage.

Rustin whispered, "Play along." He stepped toward the Volunteers, motioning the others to follow. Caeph stayed off the trail, moving from one tree to another, holding his sword against his leg where the Volunteers couldn't see it.

"Now would be a good time for a few bars of 'Barnacle Balls,' Naelth?"

Naelth said, "What?"

Raenny sang, "Come on in and let us dance ..." Naelth joined in, "... cried the fair young maiden."

"Really?" Aennie said. "You listen to the minstrel every night, ballads, ditties, old favorites, and all you have is Barnacle—"

A tall man with lieutenant stripes on his shoulders yelled, "Do NOT move."

Rustin didn't pause, only Naelth slowed for a fraction of a heartbeat.

The other Volunteers surrounded the copse of trees, one on each side of the path, surrounding the elfs but also the Knightlets. All but the lieutenant and the soldier driving the cart dropped to their knees and wound their crossbows. Rustin followed the line of sight of one soldier and saw a figure wrapped around a thin branch.

Caeph stood behind the trunk of an oak, several steps from both the lieutenant and one of the crossbow wielding Volunteers.

"I said, don't move."

"Oh, you're talking to us?" Rustin slowed and looked back. "Why?"

The lieutenant stepped up and gripped Rustin's shoulder. He pointed at the arrows embedded in the ground, now several steps behind them. "Did elfs attack you?"

"Elfs don't attack," Rustin said.

Aennie said, "Those arrows were here when we walked up." Raenny, "Why are you guys pointing crossbows at trees?" Macae, "They're hunting squirrels." Naelth, "I've heard that Lukas loves squirrel fricassee." Raenny, "Well, who wouldn't?" Aennie,

"Lieutenant, will you share your fricassee with us?" Even Viviaen got into it, "What do you put in the sauce? There's a bay tree right behind you." Caeph remained silent and hidden.

The three soldiers shot their crossbows. Bolts thumped into separate branches.

The lieutenant pushed Rustin.

Rustin didn't budge. "Oh, tough luck. Try again, you'll get a squirrel this time for sure."

The lieutenant drew his sword. "What are you doing out here?"

Raenny said, "Enjoying a brisk winter day." Naelth, "Hoping for a slice of your squirrel pie." Macae, "I'd prefer a curry." Viviaen, "Bird watching—you do attract your share of carrion—maybe you should eat crow." Aennie, "Line of the day goes to Viviaen. Unless the lieutenant here can offer some wit?"

"Fraternizing with elfs is treason," the Lieutenant said. "Faer are enemies of the state."

Stepping out of the shade, Caeph said, "Not my state."

The lieutenant jerked around, his sword in a defensive posture. "You're coming with us."

Caeph set his legs shoulder width apart. The gentle curve of his scimitar pointed at the lieutenant's neck. He flexed his knees twice, gauging his balance, and then smiled at the lieutenant. "I don't think I will."

Rustin saw a glimmer on the hilt near Caeph's thumb, swaying this way and that, and wondered if it was some sort of faery. "Lieutenant," he said, "you're looking for faer and we're not faer. You have no business with us."

The lieutenant said, "I got business with you, faer lover."

Two of the other Volunteers grabbed bolts and started reloading. The third dropped her crossbow and pulled her sword.

The Knightlets had practiced being surrounded by rivals. It had been good fun when those rivals were figments of their imaginations. They'd practiced positioning, footwork, and how to coordinate their attacks, but all they knew about fighting came from ballads of heroism and barroom brawls among drunken pirates.

The memory of a maimed Volunteer slapping his legs out from under him came to mind. The granite sword looked less foreboding than the oak stick he'd had that day. If they survived, he'd have a long talk with Caeph about discretion and honor. He yelled, "Ring of defense!"

Raenny shifted to Rustin's side and faced a Volunteer several steps away who was arming a crossbow.

Aennie pivoted, reached into her skirt, and drew the two long, vicious, granite daggers that she wore against her thighs. She was the most agile of the Knightlets and still the most adept at hand-to-hand. The wooden versions of the short swords had become foot long extensions of her fists and these cold granite daggers were lighter and edged, double edged. Something on these, too, caught Rustin's eye, a shadow dancing along the blades.

Behind Rustin, at the end of the line, Macae drew the cold granite cutlass Lapidae had given him. Its long, curved, nearly sickle-shaped blade fit Macae's lack of patience; it could be used for fencing but was better fit to simply gut an opponent. He whirled around the other crossbow-arming Volunteer, drawing him closer to the Knightlets. The Volunteer had the bolt in place and was bracing the crossbow, about to wind it. Macae swiped at him, a move Rustin had never seen him try before. The cutlass caught the end of the crossbow and knocked it to the ground. The Volunteer dove for it.

The lieutenant advanced on Caeph.

Caeph faked a lunge and dropped back when the lieutenant moved to parry. Then Caeph moved in.

Rustin cringed at the thought of Caeph using his most practiced and clichéd maneuver against a seasoned veteran, but this time, instead of pulling up short and thrusting at his opponent's heart, Caeph took a hard swing at the lieutenant. Rustin had never seen

Caeph hold a practice sword with such finesse.

The lieutenant shifted his blade for an easy parry, but Caeph's scimitar cut right through the steel. Half of the lieutenant's blade fell at his feet. He stared at the broken weapon in his hand.

Caeph stepped forward, raised the blade above his head and, spinning, his blade traced a helix through the air. Rustin knew for certain that Caeph didn't know this move. The blade slashed into the lieutenant's waist, sliced through the leather armor, skin, and abdomen, finally coming to a stop against his spine.

Blood pooled around the fallen Volunteer. He tried to tug his organs back together and died without making a sound.

Caeph stared at his victim, the sword still wedged in the lieutenant's spine. His face turned white.

"Caeph!" Rustin yelled. "Run. Now. Run." But Caeph couldn't seem to move.

Thoughts tumbled through Rustin's mind. A strange inner voice told him he could panic later. Then it scoffed at him for letting his blade droop, complained about the position of his hand, corrected his footwork, and told him he didn't deserve the fine blade that Lapidae had made for him—all this in an odd brogue.

Rustin rushed the Volunteer, who had abandoned her crossbow and drawn her sword. She stood a foot shorter than Rustin, and her sword was much shorter than his. That inner voice laughed in Rustin's head and said, "Experience is over-rated when you outreach your opponent by a foot." Rustin nearly lost his balance when he caught sight of a grizzled looking faery standing on the grip of his sword, looking over his shoulder at Rustin. Dressed in a blue vest and red tartan kilt, he had a short beard, a judgmental scowl, and sported huge biceps.

The Weapon Faery spoke with utter disdain, "You don't need my help with this," and melted into the sword's hilt.

Rustin's pause gave the Volunteer the time she needed to back away. She held her sword up in a defensive posture. Her eyes fixed on Rustin's, she moved behind the mule and cart. He heard the Weapon Faery groan in disgust.

The Volunteer who had given up on his crossbow finally drew his sword, but Raenny was already close enough to poke that long granite bastard into his foot. The Volunteer fell and landed awkwardly.

Caeph finally seemed to comprehend Rustin's order. He stepped away from the dead lieutenant. A Weapon Faery in a gleaming suit of armor standing on the grip of Caeph's sword pulled back her visor, grabbed Caeph's finger and bit it. Caeph stared at her for a second. The Weapon Faery said, "You wouldn't leave your weapon behind, would you? Course not! What a fine battle, you'll be a great warrior, son." Caeph yanked the scimitar out of the corpse and started jogging into the woods, almost in slow motion.

The wounded Volunteer managed a jab at Raenny, but Aennie caught his sword in her daggers and it clattered to the ground. The two of them followed Caeph.

Above him, a flash of white caught Rustin's attention. She stood on the leafless bough of a black walnut. She had giant violet eyes whose diamond-shaped pupils devoured him. He heard wood bending under tension behind him. She moved to the side and Rustin lost sight of her but heard that gentle high-pitched voice say, "Watch behind you," every syllable carried on the wind.

Rustin realized his predicament, turned, and dove to the side in time to see a Volunteer shoot a crossbow. He clenched, certain the bolt would hit him. The Volunteer exhaled frustration. He'd seen the elf too, had shifted to aim at her, and shot the bolt above Rustin and below the elf.

Rustin hit the ground, rolled over his shoulder, got to his feet, and darted behind a bay tree. He stopped and looked back, searching the tree canopies for elfs. He saw her. She waved. He motioned for her to follow, but she disappeared again.

Rustin ran uphill in clear view of the Volunteers and then dropped into a creek bed and worked his way back toward the trail. He'd spent his entire life running around these hills. He knew the best hiding place for miles, and so did the other Knightlets.

53.

Over millions of years, ocean breezes had carved long, snaking tunnels through the blonde sandstone that formed the inside of god's pinkie finger. Wind whistled through each cave at a different pitch, combining into chords that united in melodies known as the Song of God. The haunting sound demanded quiet from those who took shelter here.

Rustin found the others in the highest cave. Raenny and Aennie pulled him inside. He lay on his stomach. The cave looked over the oaks on the lower slope of God's Fist. He could see the lighthouse and the ocean on the far horizon. The sun warmed the stone, but the wind chilled everything else. An eagle floated on the breeze inches from their faces and disappeared when it passed by the opening.

The angle of the sun indicated that it was just midday. Rustin mumbled, "On the longest day of my life." Aennie said, "And Caeph's." Macae groaned assent.

Rustin turned and saw Caeph sitting against the wall in the back of the cave. His fingers crumbled pebbles into sand and his eyes focused far away.

"Psst, over there." Macae pointed down at a copse of oaks. Raenny, "A deer?" Naelth, "A white deer?" Viviaen, "Maybe a unicorn." Aennie, "No, It's Rustin's new friend."

Rustin saw her for an instant. He focused on the horizon, detected motion in another tree, and saw her again. This time he saw two others with her. "They did follow." He got a feeling that he'd come to understand something but didn't yet know what. "Do you see them?"

Like solving an optical illusion, the Knightlets agreed one by one.

"Check out the slope of those branches?" Raenny said. "The bends look natural, but that's a stairway."

Naelth added, "Right into a hollow point in the trunk."

Raenny said, "Blocking cold ocean winds on one side and gathering warm sunlight from the south. You think the tree grew that way?"

"I bet they trained it," Rustin said. "Remember, they live forever, they don't mind if a task takes centuries."

"It must be their camp," Aennie said.

"Whoa," Macae said. "What's that smell?"

Just as Rustin began doubting his image of elfin perfection, the clip-clop of hooves, the clank of chains, and the sound of people talking came from around the corner.

Macae leaned out over the rock face but pulled right back. He whispered, "Volunteers."

A whip cracked, and a horse neighed.

"Twenty or thirty of them," Macae said, "and that path takes them right into the forest."

Rustin said, "How can we warn the elfs?"

"We can't," Macae said.

Caeph crawled over, sword in hand.

Rustin put an arm around his neck and whispered directly in his ear so that no one else could hear, "You'll be all right, brother, just don't learn to like it." Rustin saw anger, fear, and doubt in his friend's sky-blue eyes. Caeph shook his head as though trying to rid himself of a cobweb. He slid his sword slowly, silently back in the scabbard.

The troop of Volunteers trudged along the base of the sandstone and continued into the oak copse. The Knightlets watched cages drawn on carts, six of them, each packed with elfs and leprechauns. Rustin had never seen a leprechaun without a grin. He couldn't imagine anything more sad or wrong in the world. The elfs were beaten and bloody, but sat quietly, stoic, never taking their eyes away from their captors.

Rustin pried his eyes away from the carts as they turned into the oak shadows. The troop passed into the heart of the oak copse, close enough to touch the elfs. He used the trick of defocusing to detect motion. He saw her hair blowing in the wind.

"What?" Macae said.

"She's staring at me." Even from this distance, a good fifty strides, and her in the shade, he could feel her eyes on him, but he couldn't feel what they were trying to say.

"Oh no. No, no, no," Raenny groaned. "He's got to be stopped."

Two mules pulled the last cart into view. Instead of a cage, it carried the bodies of dead faer tossed in a heap and held in place by hay forks. Elfs and leprechauns, nets filled with thousands of tiny faeries, nymphs, and pixies.

No one spoke. A breeze blew the scent into the cave and the wind tunnels sang a song of sadness and loss. They watched the Volunteer pain train enter the forest and slowly disappear. They lay alone in their thoughts.

Rustin wondered how humans could be so horrible. He thought of his sister and the questions she'd been asking all winter. He hoped she never saw anything like this.

His eyes drooped from the horizon and he saw the elfin family standing on a single branch, out of shadows, in broad daylight, staring back at them.

"We're gonna rescue them." Rustin saw Raenny and Macae exchange doubtful looks, but he said, "Here's what we're going to do" and everyone shuffled over, and he sketched a plan on the sandy floor.

They climbed down from the caves and gathered in the shade.

Macae and Viviaen sat with Caeph on a patch of grass. Caeph hadn't spoken since he killed the Volunteer.

The elfin family came down from the tree, five of them. Rustin approached with Raenny, Aennie, and Naelth a few steps behind, close enough to listen.

Her hair shone in the light, subtle yellows, and hints of brown in waves of white that fell to her waist. She had high cheekbones and a narrow chin that looked delicate but not fragile. The flawless walnut hues of her skin amplified her nearly pink, heart-shaped lips. But these details only framed the masterpiece: the whites of her eyes made her purple and violet irises glow. When she looked at him, the black diamonds of her pupils contracted for an instant and then expanded like a warm pool in a purple forest.

"Do you not bathe?"

It took Rustin a few beats of his heart to gather her words.

"Are you all stupid, or just this one?"

Rustin finally took in the scene. She stood between an elfin woman and man. An elfin child held the woman's hand. The man and woman had the universal expressions of parents, except that their disapproval extended from their frowns all the way to the tips of their ears. The mother might have matched the beauty of her daughter but for her expression of pure disgust. Another man-elf stood a step back and to the side, in the shade of an oak. None of them looked old to Rustin's human way of thinking, but the man to the side looked somehow different. Not grizzled or aged, but distant.

"It talked before," the mother spoke again. "Did we scare it?"

From behind, Aennie said, "It usually speaks almost intelligently, but right now it's distracted—Rustin?!"

Rustin cleared his throat. "I, umm, what they did," he motioned at the trail the Volunteers had taken, "I won't let that happen to you."

The elf to the side laughed. "You speak large for a puppy."

"My name is Rustin."

"You have names?" The mother said. "Why bother? You'll be dead in less than a century."

"Naerium."

If he hadn't been focused on her every movement, Rustin wouldn't have distinguished the word from the song of the wind caves behind him.

The mother rebuked her in Naest, the language that Conifaer and Lapidae used. Rustin didn't catch any of the words, but the violet-eyed creature replied with the whine of a child.

"Rustin!" Aennie tapped his shoulder.

He recovered a hint of poise.

"You are foul creature," Naerium said. "And why do you not wear shoes? Is there anything about you that is not—coarse?"

There was something in the way she said it that ticked Rustin's hogwash meter. Her eyes swept across him but never strayed, and no matter the words she spoke, her voice sang each syllable as though she recited a verbal symphony.

The father said, "You possibly believe that a human boy can help?"

"Enough." The elder said, and in the time that it took for that one word, his bow slid down his arm, an arrow appeared from the quiver across his shoulders, and Rustin faced a skilled archer, cocked and loaded. "Back out or die."

From behind, Caeph yelled, "We farqin rescued you! I killed a man to protect you." Macae told him to calm down and Caeph added, "No. I've had enough."

Rustin didn't turn away from the elfs. "He's angry. He doesn't understand your ways, none of us do." Something in the way the father turned to look at the elder, the wordless glance they exchanged reminded him of how it had been with Conifaer. Conifaer taught purely by example. When they built the hiding warren, he'd never given instructions. He'd start tasks, make sure that his motions were visible to his Bastard apprentices, and then leave them to the task.

Rustin lowered his head in a subtle bow to Naerium. He then turned to face the northward trail that led to the Great Beach and the elfs' salvation. In his peripheral vision, he could see Macae holding Caeph to the ground, but kept his eyes focused in the direction they needed to go.

He described the route to the great beach as though giving an imaginary tourist directions. He explained that ships waited there to take the faer to safety, listed likely destinations across the sea, up or down the coast, away from the lands Lukas had conquered. He began walking as he spoke, and motioned with his hand to the Knightlets. They followed and he told of the ocean's danger and the length of the journey but said it was the only way to safety. He described how they would board the tenders that would take them from the beach, through breaking waves, to the waiting ships, and he told them how much they'd have to pay in gold or in kind for passage. He held nothing back, and he didn't know if they listened, until Macae whispered that he'd seen the elder elf moving parallel to them, off the trail.

When he finished explaining everything that Dewey had told him about the pirate's Ferry to Freedom, what Dewey had called the Profiteer's New Business Model, Rustin stopped talking. They continued along the path over god's pinky finger in silence. Rustin felt someone watching him, and the certainty that they were Naerium's violet eyes filled him with a strange blend of comfort, vulnerability, and joy.

They reached the bluffs that looked down on the Great Beach and the endless Narlzie Ocean. The elfs appeared several steps away. Naerium stood closest to him, close enough for him to taste her wisteria and lavender scent.

Fresh trails led down the sandy bluffs. Jon-Jay's *Dragonships* rested at anchor well past the cascading lines of curling waves.

Three white rowboats were grounded on the beach. Rustin resumed his monologue, describing the process. Clusters of creatures—leprechauns, dwarves, nymphs, and pixies, even two giants but not a single elf—boarded a tender. Rustin pointed out Jon-Jay rowing it. He explained how they navigated the tenders through sets of waves to avoid the most violent breakers. Still, this tender rocked through the heavy spray of a curling wave.

He heard the mother elf gasp, turned, and saw Naerium facing him, eyes set on his. He forgot how to speak. Naelth picked up the monologue but introduced danger and heroism that would frighten the already skittish elfs.

Rustin followed Raenny and Aennie down a sandy trail to the beach. Raenny said that he'd seen elfs in the redwood grove farther up god's pinky finger while Rustin was "hitting on the hot elfin-lass in front of her parents and grandfather like a horny doofus."

When they made it down to the beach, Rustin approached Jon-Jay. They gripped each other's forearms in greeting. "Expected you yesterday, what held you up?"

Rustin started to explain, but Jon-Jay cut him off, "How did you get elfs down here?"

Rustin followed Jon-Jay's gaze and saw Naerium and her family standing in the shadows of the bluffs. He wanted to explain, but Naerium was watching, and all he could squeak out was, "They followed me."

Jon-Jay laughed a bawdy snort and said, "Probably pointless to tell you that you don't have a chance. A maermaid, sure, but an elf lass? No, not a chance, lad."

"I'll get them onto your ship." Rustin spoke with the certainty of unearned confidence that only young men are stupid enough to possess.

"I hope so," Jon-Jay said. "If we can't get them on board, Lukas will slaughter them and us too, all of us."

Rustin turned back to Jon-Jay and realized that he was slightly taller than the pirate. He said, "No one will hurt any elfs while I'm here." He turned back to watch the sea and basked in the knowledge that Naerium had heard his words.

54.

Rustin let Jon-Jay examine his granite sword, but when he took it, the ornery Weapon Faery punched his fingers.

"I've heard about coldsmithed swords," Jon-Jay said. "Granite's brittle. You piss off your Weapon Faery and that sword'll be nothing but sand."

Jon-Jay put the Knightlets to work keeping watch, trying to persuade leprechauns to behave, rowing back and forth to the anchored ships, building trails and fire circles, and attempting to communicate with elfs in the forest. By sunset, the Knightlets were exhausted.

At twilight, the elfs disappeared. Rustin's shoulders relaxed, and he wondered how long they'd been tense. They ate grilled tuna, clams, and oysters and drank ale topped with rum, and the Knightlets harassed Rustin. Caeph said, "Rustin and Naerie's halfing children will be tiny versions of Dewey." Aennie, "You know what they say, boys always marry girls who remind them of their mothers—how high will Rustin jump when Naerie counts to three?" Raenny, "I just want to be there to see the elfin mother meet Loretta." Naelth even composed a new verse of "Barnacle Balls the Sailor."

Rustin didn't notice when Aennie disappeared but saw her rejoin the light of the campfire. Aennie flashed him a smile that said, "I know something that you don't know."

They wrapped themselves in their blankets and slept on the sun-baked sand.

Rustin woke when the crescent moon lit a shimmering path across the ocean. His mind wandered through fantasies of a future with his elfin wife. His dreams took a peculiar turn that made it difficult to believe he wasn't still sleeping when a warm hand touched his cheek. He sat up and found himself showering in Naerium's long white hair. Starlight and the flickering coals of the bonfire reflected from her eyes. Her lips shifted into a smile and his heart fell over a cliff.

She took his hand and led him to a tide pool. She sat in the warm seawater. He lowered himself into the water and she put her fingers on his lips. Perfect, long, exquisite fingers that smelled like jasmine blossoms. They sat close together, at first side by side. Her lips pouted in the suggestion of a smile or a kiss—his choice. She tasted like hot rosewater tea and her skin was softer than the sweetest dream. He didn't feel the need to speak and the only things that she said consisted of gently offered guidance. She moved with the grace of a willow tree in an ocean breeze and when the moment called for it, the frenzy of a trapped wolf. She opened herself to him and he fell into her like he would a field of mustard, wrapped in the tangy, verdant spice of comfort, joy, and pure pleasure. Her eyes, lit by the reflections of starlight against sea foam, burned diamond shapes into his heart and their intimacy left scars of joy and the desire to spend his life in her arms.

He returned to his blanket by the fire as dawn broke. Only Aennie seemed to have noticed, and this time she gave him a silent wink.

That day, he found Naerie in the shadow of a bluff with her family. He used the same technique to lead them as he had the day before. Standing several steps away, without making eye contact, he turned and walked to an empty tender. He felt Naerie's eyes on him and knew that the rest of her family was nearby.

He climbed into the empty tender. It rocked back and forth under his weight. He waited, and a few long minutes later, Naerie appeared on the bench behind him. And then her mother, father, and sister. Without the boat moving the slightest bit, the tender was soon packed with elfs.

Jon-Jay took his seat at the other oarlock and rocked the tender. Macae and Caeph pushed it into the water, and Jon-Jay called the rowing tempo. Rustin felt Naerie behind him, knew she was watching, and everything would have been perfect if he'd been even one step closer to keeping his promise to rescue Conifaer. He described Conifaer to Jon-Jay loud enough for everyone to hear. Surely some elfs would have seen him, but none said anything. Jon-Jay said he'd spread the word and get whatever information he could. It didn't feel like enough.

Jon-Jay timed the sets perfectly, and they rowed past the breakers with the tender barely rising and falling on the swell. Rustin and Jon-Jay tried to help the elfs board the *Dragonship*, but they wouldn't move. Rustin motioned Jon-Jay out of the way and then the elfs jumped to the ship's deck like deer leaping shrubs in a meadow.

Naerie let her parents and sister go first. When her family was aboard the ship and out of view, she took a leaf from inside her tunic, a large green walnut leaf, and gave it to Rustin. And then she was gone.

The leaf had two lines of script. Rustin had never seen letters like these. He tucked the leaf along his belt, intent on keeping it safe and dry, wondering if Daffy could read it to him, but he didn't want to share whatever it had to say.

When they returned to the beach, another cluster of elfs was ready to board. Rustin spent the day rowing. That evening, Aennie was waiting for him at the bonfire. She said, "Her mother told me that Naerium's 'only seventy years old' and 'that's hardly old enough to know the difference between a stirring in her loins and a wise choice.' When I told her you're only sixteen she freaked." Of course, she said it loud enough for everyone to hear.

PART III

The Book of Bastards

55

O ver that winter, Crisiant watched tension and fear grip The Gold Piece Inn. Only toddlers and puppies seemed to have any fun. As bandleader, he tried to keep spirits high, but how could he play silly ditties to parents who'd lost children and the faer that packed the inn's secret passages when he had caused their suffering? If he hadn't promised to protect Dafina, he'd have sunk into a goateye grave.

On the Great Beach, the Freedom Ferry evacuated faer to lands where they'd never been seen and might not be welcomed. Ships came every week and spent a few days teaching the Knightlets the tricks of their trade before setting sail with their faer passengers. The Knightlets fended off Volunteers with traps, tricks, and sometimes weapons. Lylli enchanted a forest with Leaf Faeries that created illusions to disorient them when they got too close. The Knightlets made mistakes, were scarred by them, and learned enough to start toughening into capable young adults.

The profiteers exported faer and imported goateye resin. Dewey used the oldest trick in sales: he bribed a Crab and Anchor servinglass to smoke some with Major Blechk.

The next generation of Bastards carried the water, tended the fields and livestock, and studied in Daffy's school.

Dewey chose nine-year-old Tifenae, Macae's kid sister, to take over Kaetie's aviary duties. He picked little Tifenae because he thought she looked like a bird, thin and skittish, and she had a strange habit of bobbing her head when she got excited. Plus, the kid could whistle. After a week tending the birds, she learned their songs and within a month, mockingbirds, seagulls, crows, and even hawks ate out of her hand.

Tifenae brought messages to Dewey, and he shared the reports in hushed tones, as though doling out secrets, but everyone knew that he loved being the source of news and producer of juicy rumors.

Lukas's enemies used the winter months to forge weapons and alliances, and stiff resistance met his early spring attacks. As tyrants always do, Lukas hoarded credit for victories and blamed others for losses. His need for fresh soldiers bled Blechk's thousand Volunteer force down to a hundred walking wounded in Crescent Cove.

Up in Sempervaereen's canopy, Kaetie absorbed ten thousand years of history. Her foot healed, and she came down and apprenticed with Lylli. When Volunteers came to the cottage, she hid in oak trees with the faer. Lylli taught her how to enchant faeries for healing, cleaning, and helping. The two of them even enchanted a Truth Faery for Dewey, a kindhearted, nearsighted lass who wore spectacles and flew on monarch wings. You should have seen Dewey's face light up when that adorable Truth Faery peered up at him through eyelashes made of butterfly antennae.

On the anniversary of King Gledig's assassination, Crisiant played a long ballad composed of the inside jokes they'd shared. Daffy sat still that night. If she'd given him a second glance, Crisiant would've revealed his disguise. He owed her that, but she turned inward, just another Gold Piece Inn serving-lass trying to get by as well as she could.

A week before the summer solstice, when the leaves began turning from the glowing green of spring to the waxy green of summer, two messages arrived. A dove brought a report from the Valley of the Glo River: Lukas had obtained an awesome weapon that would bring immediate victory. It frightened human and faer alike. Dewey told anyone who would listen that reports of invincible but invisible weapons was nothing more than the sound of imminent defeat, and he tried like hell to believe it.

The second message came from the Crab and Anchor: Major

Blechk and his faer-hunting Volunteers had been ordered back to Glomaythea. Lukas could no longer spare the soldiers. Instead of suing for peace, he was sending ever younger conscripts and walking wounded veterans to war.

56.

Every year, the people of Crescent Cove celebrated the height of the growing season on the summer solstice, that day in June when the sun spends more time in the sky than on any other day. With *Daefender* no longer at anchor in the harbor, the festival promised extra exuberance. It was safe for the Knightlets to come home!

People gathered in the market square wearing their finest clothes and carrying their favorite goblets filled with honey mead. At sunrise, they raised their goblets to The Fist of God and offered their own silent toasts for the long summer to come.

Children raced tiny sailboats, and a surfing competition occupied the older kids. The adults who weren't cheering their progeny took entertainment at the center of the market square, first a harpoon swallowing whaler and then a boot juggling cobbler. A harpist played the morning set, and then a team of drummers tapped out a percussive melody.

At high noon, elfs and leprechauns joined humanity in raising their horns and mugs in a toast to the south, toward Faer Reef. The sight brought a tear to Daffy. The remaining Surf and Sand Faeries played in the waves, and Cloud Faeries sprinkled faery rain that cast fluorescent rainbows. Even the shy maer performed a coordinated flip to raised goblets.

The Knightlets came down from the hills, and Naelth climbed a wall and bellowed for all to hear, "We have returned! Drink and yield to our pleasures! We have returned." Macae leapt on Rustin's shoulders and let out a whoop. Caeph stood at Rustin's side, silent, with his hand on his sword. Loretta screamed and ran to them.

Soon Lylli and Kaetie came down, too. Daffy saw no sign of a child on Kaetie's face. She even walked formally. At first, Daffy thought her foot had failed to heal, but she didn't limp. No, she carried the burden of understanding.

Smoked chicken and grilled halibut were served on skewers with ale but no bread. Not this year. The games resumed and Loretta finally let Kaetie and Rustin free.

Rustin called Daffy to a shady corner of the marketplace. He reached under his tunic and pulled out a rolled piece of leather and explained that he needed help to read it. Daffy watched the care that he took as he unrolled the leather. When he looked up, she saw the boy again. Color rose in his cheeks and he held out a walnut leaf, still green but dry and delicate.

Rustin's brow furrowed and his blue eyes widened with doubt, not fear, but a close neighbor. "A friend gave it to me. I think it's Naest, can you read it?"

Daffy took the leaf. "It says—oh my, it's so sweet." She smiled at Rustin, thrilled to share his special moment. "It says, 'Rustin, I will love you until the day of my death.'"

The furrows in Rustin's forehead smoothed away and his smile consumed him, making dimples like his mother's, and his eyes took on the joy that only returned affection can bring.

"The script looks elfin. Is she …?"

Rustin couldn't seem to choke out an answer, so he nodded.

"'Until the day of my death'—from an elf that is quite a promise." She stopped talking because Rustin wasn't listening.

The dinner toast came when the sun dangled over the sea. They raised cups to the west to toast the endless ocean and the horizon of hope beyond it. Faeries perched on many of the raised drinks and took bows that concluded with a sip of mead. In past years, dozens of faeries crowded each mug.

The band played the old songs that never failed, songs of bawdiness washed down with a sip of moral justice: serious enough to bring forth a tear and silly enough to raise a smile.

When the sun came down, people lined up to see the green flash the instant it disappeared into the sea that would promise a season of good luck.

The celebration's last toast, to the first starlight of summer, demanded a tiny glass of special brandy, the golden distillation of autumn honey, winter oranges, and spring honeysuckle nectar. But Dewey had left the jug of seasonal sunlight back at the inn. He turned to Loretta, of course, but she was glued to Kaetie and Rustin.

Daffy volunteered to fetch it.

She walked up to The Gold Piece Inn, around the stable, and through the kitchen door. She'd never seen it empty: Bob not behind the bar, Faernando not flirting with Jaek, Daeffid not stirring steaming pots and pans. The kitchen smelled like bacon and butter, goat and fish, laughter and tears—a smell as comfortable as any she'd known.

She thought of everyone at The Gold Piece Inn and, sure, she'd rubbed some people the wrong way and some of the kids still called her the crying lady. When she was queen, people used to get on her good side so they could squeeze a favor out of the King. Only here at The Gold Piece Inn had she ever known for sure who were her friends and who weren't. And right then, it felt like they were all her friends, even Dewey.

She passed the stairway and looked from the sawdust-coated floor up the red velvet stairs and had to laugh. She lived in a bordello and preferred it to a castle. She laughed her way into Dewey's office where he stashed the brandy.

Kneeling behind his desk, she pulled on the bottom drawer. It stuck, so she put her foot against the wall for leverage and tugged. Her hand slipped off, and she jammed her elbow into the wall behind her. Part of the wall collapsed, a square panel that reached from the floor to the wainscoting. Light showed through. She hadn't realized that Conifaer had built a hiding spot behind Dewey's office. Leaning down, she saw another room with a desk and crawled inside.

The light came from a GloFaery lamp. She stood at a large gold desk in a small room whose walls were covered in tapestries. A huge leather-bound book with gilt-edged pages lay open on the desk. Several fine quills rested next to the book near a covered pot of ink.

The page was nearly full. Each paragraph was marked by a date, clearly some sort of log or diary and five blank lines were left between each entry. The latest was marked by a date set nine months in the future and said, "Laelith: Waerner of Verdaent Plains, first son and heir of the Duke of Kaerlscrag whose holdings include a small estate on the outskirts of Draefenberg, business interests in Custaello."

She flipped through the book. Every entry had a date, the name of a serving-lass, and a man's name. Most of the entries also described the man's home, his holdings, and description of either his rank within the aristocracy or his business and social connections. Some just had the date and a man's name. She flipped through many entries with date-Loretta-Madog and the five blank lines.

She came upon an entry that had just four blank lines. The name Glaen appeared on the last line. The child's mother's name, Maeggie, was recorded several lines above, next to the date, not quite a year ago. She flipped back and found more entries that had a mother's name in the first line and her child's name with the date of the child's birth next to a date that had been scratched out.

Flipping back a few hundred pages to dates set decades ago, she found an entry that described who the child had become. She read a few more and even saw a name she knew. One of the King's squires was apparently the bastard son of the King's uncle and a Gold Piece Inn serving-lass who was no longer here.

The listings included a few people who had high rank in different kingdoms. One of her mother's ladies-in-waiting was a Gold

Piece Inn Bastard. Officers of every court she'd heard of, people who practiced every trade from pickpocket to pirate, fisher to goatherd, cobbler to money counter, and in every land she'd ever seen on a map. A surprising number had even been recognized by their fathers. She could imagine Dewey turning the screws on people in high places to make that happen.

The pieces jostled into place. She'd known that Dewey's network of contacts formed a wide web—he made sure everyone knew that—what he didn't crow about was that they had all grown up right here at The Gold Piece Inn. The first Bastard had been born 160 years ago, become King Llandow's fool, and died at the ripe age of seventy.

She flipped forward until she found Taevius. His father turned out to be Kekoa. Daffy wondered how Dewey would spin the web between Taevius-sailor-in-the-Volunteer-Navy, and Taevius son-of-the-legendary-Puaepuae-pirate.

She turned a few more pages and found Rustin.

Daffy collapsed into the chair. Her heart beat loud enough to echo off the tapestries.

She read it again and broke into a cold sweat.

Flipping back and forth through the pages, she looked for more instances of Loretta's name. She found Kaetie and saw that she had the same father as Rustin. Loretta took lots of men upstairs, but during a period starting seventeen years ago and ending just six years ago, she seemed to have been reserved for one man: King Gledig.

Daffy did the math. Loretta and the King had been together long before he married Daffy, before they'd even met, but also well after Daffy had given birth to a princess and a prince.

The King had cheated on her.

In fact, he'd been here at The Gold Piece Inn with Loretta while Daffy was pregnant. Both times she was pregnant.

She pulled herself together. She didn't know what she would do with this information, but she'd damn well do something. She left the book open to the page recording Rustin's birth and then crawled back through the passage, took the small cask of brandy, and walked out of the inn.

At least she finally understood what had drawn Gledig to come to this gods-forsaken place.

57.

Daffy set the brandy on the ground next to Dewey. Loretta and Madog stood nearby watching Kaetie and Macae. Kaetie looked impatient and Macae distraught.

Daffy dropped back to the edge of the crowd. Wisps of fog danced on the breeze, as frail as her life at The Gold Piece Inn. Dewey turned in her direction and she looked away. Lylli stepped around a group of fishers and joined her. She quietly watched the crowd. From her other side, Daffy heard a long and thorough but high-pitched sigh. She turned and saw a two-inch-tall faery perched on her shoulder. The little fellow wore gray robes, had droopy eyes, floppy basset hound ears, and the dusty wings of a moth. He looked back at her, solemn.

Lylli said, "You've seen a ghost."

"I suppose I have."

"I'm sorry."

"Can you read minds, or did you spy on me?"

"You can dispel the Sigh Faery with any word you choose. He'll get it. But he's not a bad guy to have around. You can trust him not to hurt you."

"Then he's the only one."

Lylli looked away but stayed where she was, a quiet presence.

How could she have missed it?

She watched Rustin and his Knightlets. He stood with Caeph at his side, said something to Aennie, and then they all ran up the bluffs, Rustin always in the lead.

At sixteen, Rustin was the tallest person in town. He had his father's broad shoulders and small waist, carved jaw line, and sleepy-looking eyes, everything but his coloring, brown hair to the King's black, blue eyes to the King's brown, and skin tone slightly paler than the King's. How could she have missed it? Rustin looked identical to the portrait of the King as a prince that Daffy had walked by twice a day for seven years. Of course, this child had taken her from their first meeting. Even the way he walked. She knew it wasn't his fault, but now she couldn't stand to look at him.

And Kaetie, too. Not so much her features, but her mind. Daffy had never known anyone but the King who could assemble facts and details into concepts so fast. Kaetie brought her mother's passion and wild spirit along with her father's brilliance. Six perfect freckles from her mother to complement her father's dark, penetrating brown eyes.

The betrayal landed in a confused pool of disappointment.

I'm a hostage. Neither family nor friend, a royal hostage stuck here until the liberator fails. If he fails. She exchanged a sidelong glance with the Sigh Faery. He looked up in the sky and she felt compelled to follow his example. They took deep, lung-overflowing breaths and let them go in a soothing sigh of acceptance. Another thought came to her, *I must find a new place, another new place.*

58.

The next morning Dewey had five prospects to record in *the Book of Bastards*. The solstice celebration always brought the lust and money out of the guests of The Gold Piece Inn. He sat in his chair next to the prismatic cold-cast glass window Lapidae had made for him, as transparent as glass, solid to the beast and permeable to the faer.

Each of the gentlemen took their time in the hot seat as Dewey mined their titles and holdings. Dewey's new Truth Faery hovered over the interviews, squinting through her glasses, and waving off lies and applauding the truth. Dewey then went into his sanctuary, where he found his book left open to his recording of Rustin's conception and birth. He put the pieces together and wondered if a pissed-off queen could dispel the curse. He doubted it, but a halfling needed hope.

In the kitchen, Daeffid told him that Daffy hadn't shown up for chores that morning.

Loretta said, "What'd you say to her?"

"Me?" Dewey said, "Innocent me?"

She crossed her arms and remained silent. So did he.

Daffy became more irritable and condescending every day. Even Dewey avoided her. And then, a week later, he heard Loretta talking to her through the kitchen door.

"I guess if your royal farqin high arse don't want to work, she don't have to. But the rest of us have to work for *our* supper."

He heard Daffy grunt, as though struggling. Dewey pushed through the kitchen door and reached them at full speed. Loretta held Daffy against the wall. Daffy pushed back on Loretta's chin. Loretta was stronger but spent her strength yelling.

He wedged between them, wrapped an arm around Daffy's waist and pulled her aside. Unwilling to let go, Loretta was pulled with her. Dewey lost his balance and the three of them fell in a heap, knocking over two water jugs.

Dewey said, "You're risking everyone. Everyone!"

"No, she's too full of herself to—"

"What she did to me? And I was stupid enough to believe she was my friend?"

"I took you in, protected your secret—you owe me everything!"

"You weren't protecting me, everything you did was a lie to protect yourself."

"Everything I done was for my children."

"Like all that time upstairs?"

"What do you know about providing for children, you had it—
"

"My children are dead, but at least they knew their father."

Loretta's eyes glued to Daffy's, casting unspoken threats.

Dewey pulled Loretta up by her wrist. He grabbed Daffy's wrist with his other hand and said. "You can't argue here."

He walked them into his office and shut the door. "Get it out of your system and find a way to get along, but if you raise your voices, you risk the lives of everyone who lives here."

"Then kick her out," Loretta said. "We'd be safe if you didn't have a crush on your farqin queen."

He stepped out and slammed the door behind him. Between breakfast and lunch, the inn was empty. Dewey pulled a stool over so he could listen and shut them up if anyone came by. They were quiet for a few seconds, but Dewey could feel the tension build.

Daffy spoke in a calm, reasonable tone. "You could have told me. Loretta, you know you can trust me with anything."

"Tell you what?" Loretta's tone made it a threat.

"That you had an affair with my husband and that Rustin and Kaetie are his children." Daffy's voice quivered, which Dewey thought was a big mistake. One should never show weakness to an angry carnivore.

"He should've been my husband."

"All this time—I thought you were my friend, the only friend I've ever really had. You don't know what it's like in a palace court—"

"Well, you thought wrong. I'll do anything to protect my children from you."

"You think I'm a threat? I've helped Rustin and Kaetie every way I can."

"Reading, writing, I've never needed it and neither do they. The ideas you fill their heads with, you'll get them killed."

Daffy didn't reply.

Loretta added, "You're a fugitive. If you care about anyone, leave."

"I'm trying to."

"Turn yourself in."

"You want them to kill me?"

"Beats them killing my children."

"Loretta, they assassinated the King. He fought bravely, and they murdered him. They murdered my children. Loretta, you don't know …"

"I don't care." Dewey could hear Loretta suck in a breath. He leaned against the door as though it were a dam holding back her rage. "Even though you stole the man who should have been *my* husband, I befriended you. I taught you how to live here." And then she screamed, "I shared my children with you!"

"Stole your husband? He married me. You were just his whore."

"Gledig loved me. He wanted me. He wanted to be with me." She took another one of those breaths and then out it came, "He asked me to marry him! I should have been queen, not you, me. He was my prince! His family forced him to marry you. He was stuck with you and you know it's true. He never loved you."

Dewey felt the door push against him.

Loretta piled on, "You stole my husband, damned if I'll let you steal my children.

Daffy shot out. Loretta tried to follow, but Dewey tackled her.

* * *

Dewey found Daffy alone in the orchard. "Loretta has a temper. She'll get over it, don't take it personally."

"She's right. As long as I'm here, you're all at risk. I need to go home. Please Dewey, please help me. I'll promise anything."

"You can't get through the blockade—a full-island siege, and it's the only part of the war he's still winning."

Escape

59.

And then, nearly a month after Daffy discovered *The Book of Bastards*, Jon-Jay bolted in. His eyes wild, his face dripping wet, and his muscles tense, he found Dewey and said, "They attacked, and I'll be damned if they didn't sink them!"

Loretta grabbed his shoulder. "Attacked? What do you mean attacked? Sank? A ship? What ship? Who sank who?"

He said, "Madog is okay. Aerrol sold them out, and they attacked during a mutiny."

"A mutiny? What are you talking about?"

Dewey stood and pushed Jon-Jay to the bar.

Bob had a brandy ready. Jon-Jay took a breath. "My *Dragonship* and seven galleys were carving the sea half a mile off the north coast. *Avarice* trailed us. I knew Madog and Baertha planned to mutiny—they'd had enough of Aerrol's anti-faer bigotry. But Aerrol saw it coming. Lukas's ships were waiting.

"Four of my galleys doubled back and I let the *Dragonship* drift so we'd be a few lengths ahead of *Avarice* when Madog gave the sign. Just as we passed Bodaega Head, a Volunteer Navy cutter marked *Conqueraer* darted between us at full sail and rained flaming arrows on *Avarice*. The crew manned buckets and put out the arrows, but that gave *Conqueraer* time to come about. They got alongside and launched grappling hooks, but they didn't count on me, did they?"

He tipped back his brandy. The saloon was silent for the three counts it took him to drain the mug.

"*Dragonship* is as much galley as it is sailing ship."

Madog, Baertha, and several others from *Avarice's* crew walked through the door. Madog limped, Baertha held her arm close to her ribs, and neither of them had anything approaching Jon-Jay's bluster.

"And if it weren't," Madog said, "I'd be counting ohzees in Davy Jones' locker."

Baertha made her way to the bar, staring at the floor every step of the way. Bob had mugs ready for all of them.

"But you're right here in The Gold Piece Inn, aren't you?" Jon-Jay said. "Now, where was I? Oh, right, I dropped the sail and maxed out the oars. We had a quarter mile to build up momentum, and we rammed *Conqueraer* broadside before the Volunteers could board *Avarice*. We sunk her, we did. But my prow tore off. *Conqueraer* was going down fast, and we had to get clear or be sucked down with her."

"We watched her go down." Baertha spoke softly. "The Volunteers that didn't drown swam to shore and waves pounded them into the rocks. You seen the waves at Bodaega Head? I never want to see a thing like that again."

Madog looked up in the rafters, his eyes unfocused. "And I threw Aerrol overboard. It sucked him down with the cutter." He rubbed his forehead. "I killed my friend. A stupid, wrong-headed, bigoted farqer who earned his just reward, but ... ah, shite. I'll miss him."

Dewey said, "Did any Volunteers survive?"

"It took a few hours to repair *Avarice's* rigging and set her sails," Baertha said. "When we took wind, we saw survivors on the beach south of Bodaega Head."

Dewey frowned. "Not good."

"Why?" Jon-Jay said. "We sunk the farqer!"

"You started a war."

"No," Madog said. "The war started the day they assassinated the King. We won a battle. I lost a friend."

"You think you can drop anchor in Crescent Cove, and the

usurper will go merrily about his business? How long do you think it will take Lukas to find out what happened to that cutter?"

"How long does it take to walk from Bodaega Head to Glomay-thea?"

"Walk? No. You think *Conqueraer* was the only Volunteer ship at sea? You think they don't have signals and birds?" Dewey rubbed his eyes. "Is *Avarice* seaworthy?

"She is," Baertha said.

"Set sail before you have the whole damn navy on top of you."

Baertha spoke to Dewey, now in the calm voice of authority, "Then I need Rustin and his Knightlets to get every elf, dwarf, and leprechaun aboard *Avarice*." She turned to Madog, "Puaepuae?"

"No," Dewey said. "Your destination is Nantesse."

Dewey then spoke loud enough to be heard throughout the warren of passages and hiding places in the inn, "Shipping out tonight! Get to the wharf right now. Forget secrecy, just get aboard *Avarice*."

Daffy looked at him with the obvious question on her lips.

"Yes," he said, "and hopefully you'll take this damn curse with you."

Baertha said, "What's this?"

"Your favorite serving-lass is coming with you."

Baertha said, "Daffy travels free." She held out her hand to Dewey. "But no one else does ..."

"What? I have to pay?"

"Should I wait until someone asks for your help?"

"Oh, the pain, will it never end?"

60.

Daffy ran down to the wharf with scores of elfs and leprechauns. Baertha helped her board a tender. She took a seat near the stern where she could look back at Crescent Cove. Leprechauns jumped aboard and elfs took their time, stepping from the dock to the little boat in time with the rolling swells. Rustin jumped aboard and lifted her into a tight hug that reminded her of his mother. She told him it was time for her to leave and he accepted that, though he made her promise to visit.

Daffy grew up among ships in the sheltered harbors of Nantesse. Good harbors are calm like lakes, but violent ocean waves threaten the shelter of Crescent Cove. The tender climbed up the front of swells and fell down the back of them. She wondered if she'd ever get to dub Rustin a knight. A deposed queen dubbing the rightful king? No, never. And she wondered what Kaetie would become. The tender finally bounced against *Avarice's* bumpers. Baertha boosted her up, and she climbed the rope ladder.

Seagulls swooped over the deck. The smell of wet wood, tar, and dead fish, the sounds of sails flapping in the wind and sailors calling to each other, and the constant roll of the deck brought Daffy face to face with the reality. She was finally going home.

She went below deck to claim a hammock. The elfs stood in separate families, so motionless and silent that they seemed to be in a different world. Daffy put her things in a hammock that stretched from the base of the mizzen mast to a cleat on the underside of the deck where the roll of the ship wouldn't bother her too much. She followed cackles of laughter to the lower hold and discovered that leprechauns had claimed it. Before she made it to the bottom of the ladder, a lassrechaun, offered to cut her hair. The lassrechaun wore white tights, a green dress, and had apple-red hair. She held up huge scissors that had a transparent quality that convinced Daffy they were an illusion. She declined the haircut, and, in an instant, her short hair assembled itself into braids.

"Better, ma'am?"

Daffy made the mistake of laughing and her fingernails turned a bright shiny purple. A ladrechaun cart-wheeled past and while she was distracted, another ladrechaun reached into her empty purse. She watched a juggler, declined several marriage proposals, and sang along to a ballad about rainbows and pots of gold. By the time she heard the windlass lifting the anchor chain, the leprechauns' boundless energy had exhausted her.

She climbed back to the deck. The crew stood at their stations, holding their lines, some taut, some slack. She found Baertha and Madog at the helm, a few steps behind the ship's wheel where the pilot stood. The anchor chains went silent and Baertha issued a command. Her voice bellowed over the wind, the waves, the birds, and the constant chatter of leprechaun pranksters. For a few seconds, the canvas sails clapped in the wind, and then the sails were trimmed, and *Avarice* pulled forward. Daffy watched little whirlpools form off the port gunwale and saw the wake form at the stern.

When they cleared Crescent Point, *Avarice* keeled to port under a harsh wind and took off.

"Braided like that, you can really see the black roots, love." Baertha stood next to her. "Going home then?"

Daffy went cold and silent.

Madog stood on her other side and said, "Hard to believe that a queen has been holding court at The Gold Piece Inn."

"Harder to believe that she's been holding court with scurvy muvs the likes of us."

Daffy stepped away. The pilot's eyes stuck to her.

Baertha caught the wheel and gave it back to the pilot. "You're safe here, you have nothing but friends on this ship."

"We always wondered," Madog said. "Your accent should have given you up."

"Serving-lasses don't read and write seven languages."

Daffy said, "Are you going to turn me in?"

"Love," Baertha said, "if we were going to collect your reward, we'd have done that a year ago."

"Aerrol wanted to, the stupid farqer."

"Why didn't you?"

"You don't know much about Dewey, do you?" Madog said. "People who get on his bad side have a way of, umm, suffering."

"Naw," Baertha said. "I'd have not let them take you from me, I love you so." She let out a big hearty laugh that Daffy could feel through the deck below her feet.

"Did you know then?"

"Well, love, with that much money on your head and not being able to access it without—" Baertha exchanged a sidelong glance with Madog, "what did you call it? Right, suffering—it was easier for me to convince myself that you were just another wayward lass in Dewey's collection."

"Until Aerrol drank the usurper's bilge water."

Daffy said, "It will be nice to go home and, I assure you, you'll be welcome in my court anytime."

"Which reminds me," Baertha said, "would you prefer to bunk in the mate's cabin?" She winked. Madog laughed and walked to the bow.

Daffy smiled and batted her lashes. "A hammock among the elfs suits me fine … for tonight." She curtsied to Baertha and walked to the stern. A cloud accumulated at the knuckles of The Fist of God, and the low-pitched wail of the foghorn reached out. The roll of the ship gave her the first drowsy sign of seasickness. She sat against the gunwale and pictured Dewey sitting in his chair reading tiny messages with his Truth Faery on his shoulder. The roll kept tugging her in different directions. She got up and ran to the poop deck to unleash her last meal.

61.

Avarice sailed into the wall of fog that accumulated off the coast on summer days. A Compass Faery stood on the wheel pointing due west.

When *Avarice* emerged from the cloudbank, she headed straight at a gaelleon with the red and black Flying Anvil.

The gaelleon sat in irons, waiting, facing *Avarice*. Baertha pushed the pilot aside, grabbed and spun the wheel. The rudder groaned under the force. The masts complained and *Avarice* turned downwind, south.

Avarice rode high on the water, her faer cargo lighter than the freight she usually carried and made the turn in half the distance she normally would have. Baertha gave orders to tighten some sheets, loosen others, and the sails trimmed to the new direction in seconds. They had the advantage of speed and maneuverability but were way behind on preparation. Still, in the time that it would take the gaelleon to raise sails, catch the wind, and come about to give chase, *Avarice* would be over the horizon.

But there was one thing that they could never have expected, much less prepared for.

Avarice completed the turn less than a quarter mile from the gaelleon, still well out of bowshot or catapult range, now aligned with the gaelleon's starboard side. The crew cheered and offered the gaelleon a variety of obscene gestures.

Eight large portholes opened along the side of the gaelleon. Seconds later, eight cones of fire blasted out of those portholes.

"Dragons!" The warning screams reached all the way to the poop deck where Daffy emptied her gut into the sea. She caught her breath. Her first thought was confusion—she didn't believe in dragons. After all, "no one had ever seen a dragon and lived to tell about it."

The streams of sparks were followed by a great pronouncement of might that echoed from the ship, roaring thunder and a splash off the starboard side of *Avarice's* bow. Steaming water blew hundreds of feet in the air. Ten-foot swells rocked *Avarice*. Seconds later, another jet of flame and sparks, blasts of thunder, and this time the tremendous splash aligned with *Avarice's* stern. The splash rained on Daffy.

Seconds accumulated. *Avarice* rocked but didn't lose her grip on the wind. And then the thunder returned. Had anyone possessed the wherewithal, they'd have heard eight distinct concussions within the thunderous orchestra.

The destruction came in a small fraction of the time it takes a heart to beat. Daffy heard the crushing sound of a hundred-fifty-foot redwood mast snap like a twig, the rending tear of molten iron balls punching through the hull—two above the surface and one below—the searing blast of boiling iron ripping into the starboard gunwale and exploding the deck in flames, and then a series of three more hits, one after another, cleaving *Avarice* at midship. Bodies flew, people screamed, faeries swarmed. The bow dove and the broken mast marked its grave. The stern lingered, bobbing on the surface.

In Daffy's experience, ships had crews that ushered royal passengers to lifeboats in an orderly fashion. *Avarice*'s tenders doubled as lifeboats, but Daffy had no notion of where to board one.

Baertha and her crew launched the starboard tenders. Madog moved across the remaining deck. He called below, and elfs and leprechauns streamed up. He directed them to starboard where Baertha pushed them into transports. But *Avarice* was going down fast.

For all his rambunctious ways, his lusty approach to life, Madog respected the code. He knew the risks when he pushed Aerrol overboard and asked the crew to accept him as captain. Searching the failing stern, he pulled mangled crew members from beneath broken masts, and encouraged them to swim with what limbs they had. He didn't see anyone down in the hold. Water boiled up through the hull and showered down from the deck. He climbed up what should have been flat decking and saw Daffy swept into the sea seconds before the hull shot to the sea floor, minutes too late for her to swim to safety.

Madog, comfortable with his fate, felt a surge of sorrow that he would never again fall into the generous, welcoming arms of that gregarious ginger, Loretta of The Gold Piece Inn.

62.

Daffy waited on the poop deck for someone to rescue her. It wasn't a conscious decision, just training. She saw Madog just as a wave pushed her overboard.

She swam for all she was worth but didn't know where to go. This business of the sinking ship pulling everything down with it didn't occur to her until she experienced it. The cold knocked the breath from her lungs. The hull reared above her. She pulled herself to the surface and sucked in a big breath.

She could have reached out and touched the rudder. Treading water in that instant of balance when the hull came to a stop, she saw a tender on the horizon. She took another breath and *Avarice's* stern came down. She might as well have been tied to the rudder. The vacuum that trailed it sucked her down, ever farther, deeper. Her ears felt like they'd explode. She held that last breath even as she collided with chunks of redwood that had formed gunwales, masts, and decks. A shredded sail caught her foot and flipped her over. Now diving headfirst, she experienced those last lucid thoughts. Rather than memories of joy or regret, she felt raw, unadulterated panic. She kicked and pushed away the flotsam. She held that last breath for nearly two minutes, even as the water pressure tried to collapse her ribcage, she clung to that air.

Something scraped her back. She tried to push off but got caught in it. Something else collapsed around her chest and tugged her down. The bubbles finally exploded from her nose and mouth.

The reflex to breathe overwhelmed her.

Whatever she'd gotten stuck in had a soft side and when she began to inhale seawater, something gentle pushed against her mouth, blocked out the water, and blew air into her lungs.

Daffy tried to push away, to break the grip, but she held on to that new breath. She exhaled a stream of bubbles and that soft warmth covered her mouth again and blew. It blew air into her, and this time she trusted it. She tried to exhale without disconnecting from the source of air, but the source pulled away. She exhaled bubbles and, in time with the rhythm of her lungs, the source blew into her again. It became a dance. She inhaled, exhaled, and soon caught her breath. She was conscious and, as far as she knew, alive.

The depths of the sea are too dark to see. With full lungs, she tried to swim to the surface, but it wouldn't let go. It pulled her down, ever deeper, providing breath the whole way.

Daffy felt a rhythmic pumping, powerful strokes. She stopped pushing and held on. Something scraped her. She breathed again, and now she recognized it. She ran her hands along the sides of the creature and felt strong shoulders and arms. The forearms had sharp edges from elbow to wrist. She breathed again and put her arms around its neck.

She yielded to the creature and continued deeper. Exhaustion eventually overwhelmed her.

When she came to, she was accepting another breath, and saw enormous eyes, iridescent as abalone shells, looking back from the distance of a kiss. She held her breath, and the maermaid pulled away. The creature's skin was green-tinted blue, the color of ocean water at about twenty feet—the very golden-haired miracle who had pulled her out of the Adductor River the day the King died.

She looked around and saw more of them, three maermaids and two maerbutlers. They smiled back and made all sorts of noises. They sounded like dolphins, but their voices were deeper and their clicks and whistles longer, almost like humming a tune.

At the end of another breath, before pulling away, the maermaid said, "Welcome to our home!" The words came directly into Daffy's mind. She tried to reply, but it came out in bubbles and meaningless syllables. The maermaid leaned in and she pulled away on impulse. The maermaid canted her head and smiled. Daffy needed to breathe, so she leaned in and took a breath of fresh air. Fresh might not be the right word. The kiss tasted like the ocean, like fish just caught, but warm and soft, a kiss.

They were in an underground cave, a sort of grotto covered in luminous plants that shed different colors of light that added up to a bluish shade of white. Smooth stones formed benches, sea anemone and starfish attached to the walls, floor, and ceiling. A wave flowed in from somewhere, jostling them about and cooling the water.

The maermaid made a genuine sound through the water, not telepathy. Daffy wrapped her mind around the sound, Zelda, a name. She tried to reply with her own name, but it came out as more bubbles and then she had to pull Zelda close to get another breath.

The maermaids and maerbutlers carried on a conversation. Every ten seconds or so, Zelda would lean over and share a breath. Daffy held out her hands and shook her head in what she hoped was a universal signal for, "What are you talking about?"

Zelda kept her eyes open and her tongue ran across Daffy's teeth. Daffy heard her say, "When the tide recedes, our grotto will fill with air."

Zelda pulled away and made sounds in that dolphin song that expressed joy. The next time she gave Daffy a breath, she put words in her mind, "We'll rest here, sharing air, until the tide ebbs. When you're all better, I can take you back to the world above the sea, if that is what you desire. Or you're welcome to stay with us as long as you like." She tugged Daffy to a giant green anemone, soft as a slick pillow. Daffy tried to sit, but her buoyancy pulled her away with every wave. She felt exhausted and, the next time Zelda gave her a breath, she yawned into Zelda's mouth.

Zelda pulled her close and carefully matched their lips together. Daffy inhaled and then started dozing, her lips against Zelda's.

When she awoke, she was still below water, still attached to

Zelda like lovers swimming in the rush of affection at the dawn of a new romance. Zelda pulled Daffy up and they broke the surface. A good three feet of air filled the top of the grotto and the tide was still going out.

Daffy took a fresh breath, introduced herself, and asked where they were. Zelda leaned in to kiss her, but Daffy no longer needed help breathing. Zelda laughed—squeaks and dolphin-whistles. This time, Daffy accepted the kiss and, noses touching, eye-to-eye, Zelda conveyed the story: the maer had been dining on a school of tuna when they heard dragons. Other schools of maer had rescued many of the elfs and leprechauns. The elfs demanded to be returned to land, and even the maer didn't relish bringing leprechauns into their grottos.

Zelda put pictures in Daffy's mind of the rocky outcroppings that lined the Glomaythean coast and told her of the maer grottos and communities beneath every rocky crag. With another kiss, she said that Daffy was welcome in every one of them.

Dragons

63.

W hen *Avarice* set sail, the day came to a lazy stop for Rustin and the Knightlets. A hot summer day with a nice cool breeze, perfect for lounging in the cool water of The Gold Piece Inn spring.

Caeph and Macae drove the younger Bastards away with a scowl. Raenny and Aennie sat behind the granite wall together. Caeph sat on a boulder in the shade of a willow, Naelth waded, and Macae skipped rocks. Rustin back floated in the shade, dreaming about the day he would find Naerie and they could be together. First, he had to find Conifaer, of course. He envisioned leading the Knightlets into Glomaythea, dispatching the Volunteers at the prison or camp or dungeon or wherever they held Conifaer, and then they'd—

"FARQ ME NOW!" Caeph leapt up

Raenny and Aennie were the first to climb the granite behind him. He said, "Amazing," and she said, "Beautiful."

Rustin jolted up the bank and around the boulder where Caeph stood within the willow branches.

A rider on a stark white horse trotted along Knuckle Creek about five hundred steps away. Rustin dashed back, pulled on his shirt and sword, and walked out to greet the rider properly.

The flagstone path was hot under his feet, good comfortable traction.

Taller than any horse he'd ever seen, with flanks more color-leached than cotton, the stallion pranced in the field, pointing the great curlicue lance that emerged from his forehead. An elf dressed in green suede that matched the summer foliage rode the unicorn but showed no sign of controlling the magnificent faery.

Caeph was silent. Naelth whispered thanks to Mother Earth. Macae claimed the first ride which brought laughter from the others. Aennie suggested that it would be Macae's last ride. Raenny exhaled an expression of awe.

The sight set off alarms for Rustin. Most myths and many legends turned out to be false, but some didn't. He called to the others, "You might want to go inside."

Raenny said, "No way." Caeph, "And miss this?" Aennie, "Once in a lifetime experience." Naelth, "I shall gaze upon the mighty faery." Macae, "I already called first ride."

"Unicorns sense evil," Rustin said. "If you've done anything that could be seen as evil since the sun last set, even a simple lie," he looked at Caeph, "theft of a slice of toast," a glance at Macae, "sip of someone else's ale," Naelth, "he'll know it, and he might kill you." Rustin thought through the last twenty-four hours and couldn't think of anything he'd done.

Naelth said, "I'm going in." Raenny, "Me too." Caeph, "I'm hungry." Macae, "You've seen one horse …" Aennie, "As long as we can make up a better story later."

The unicorn circled a field of wheat and then cantered toward Rustin, building speed. His elfin passenger pulled the reins, and at last prevented him from charging, but he still came straight at Rustin. The lance that grew out of his forehead was thick as a tree trunk and a good ten feet long. Rustin stood six and a half feet tall, and his head was barely level with the unicorn's withers.

The horn touched his chest, and the big faery curled his upper lip and snorted. The horn pushed against Rustin, and he felt judgment course through his veins. Thoughts of how he'd spent the morning sidling the faer into tenders—sidling, a nice term for deceiving. He felt a cold sweat on this hot day. The horn caught the rough cotton of Rustin's shirt and tore a small hole over his heart.

The elf declared himself Quercus. He described the sinking of

Avarice. "The dragons soared from their ship to ours, their roars louder than thunder, their damage greater than lightning." The description of death and destruction rattled Rustin. He couldn't imagine *Avarice*, the one ship he'd always admired, crewed by heroic figures like Madog and Baertha, being cleaved in two by a flying faery. And then the carnage, the drowning, and the survivors' struggle to shore.

"You have heard me, boy. Now. Now is when we need help."

"I will help you."

"You can repeat what I said by the word?"

"I can."

Quercus cast a look of contempt at Rustin. The unicorn raised its head, let out a neigh that shook the ground, reared, and galloped back up The Fist of God.

Rustin ran to the inn and burst into the saloon, where he found Dewey surrounded by locals. He knew better than to tell the tale in front of so many people but couldn't hold it in. "Dragons!" He yelled, "the usurper released dragons on *Avarice,* and they sunk her!"

Dewey grabbed Rustin. "Say nothing more—to my office." He hollered, "The boy has seen a ghost! Dragons, pshaw. Kids these days."

He shoved Rustin into the office and shut the door. He pointed at a stool, but Rustin couldn't sit and couldn't stand still. He walked back and forth, brushing against the desk, the wall, fingering the hole in his shirt. And then it hit him. *Avarice* had sunk. What of Daffy? Madog and Baertha? He could hardly imagine that woman built of stone dying, and it didn't seem possible for Madog to drown.

Dewey asked questions and Rustin tried to answer, but his words fell over themselves. Dewey waited, and when he could form a sentence, Rustin repeated what the elf had told him.

Loretta pushed through the door and grabbed her son. She

looked up at him, and he looked at Dewey and said, "The survivors washed up on Great Beach and need help."

Loretta asked what happened and Dewey told her the facts without sympathy: *Avarice* sunk, Daffy, Madog, Baertha all dead. She went silent and pale. He added, "Probably."

She slumped in a chair and covered her eyes.

"Rustin," Dewey said, "you have one day, maybe two, to get the survivors under cover. The Volunteers will invade. I'll arrange for another ship, but it could be weeks." He pulled the knit hat from his head. "If Lukas has dragons ..." His voice trailed off, and he rubbed his right ear. "Take your merry band and do what you must to help the faer. This is yours, son."

Loretta screamed, "You're sending him to fight dragons?"

"Dragons," Dewey said. "If dragons have allied with Lukas, then there is no hope." He scratched an ear. "But Lukas, he'll have lost something too. I don't know what, not yet. Lukas abhors the faer and dragons are the faer-est of them all. If dragons exist, why would they help Lukas?" He shook his head as though trying to dislodge a bad idea. "But I've been wrong about so many things since the assassination."

64.

A reckless hopelessness came over the inn. Only two regulars showed up, Codae and Baeswax—everyone else stayed home to prepare or cower or hide their meager treasures. Pixies took to the dance floor. The serving-lasses and lads indulged their absurd flirtations and kept mugs full. Tiny faeries danced from rafters to tables, on the edges of mugs and goblets, occasionally dipping in for an intoxicating swim. Dewey kept tabs but didn't collect copper, silver, or gold.

Kaetie arrived with Lylli, leading a donkey loaded with healing supplies and a full-sized cauldron. When they carried it inside, Lylli said, "If you're a witch in a land that hates witches, you want to be caught with your best cauldron before they burn you. Or drown you, I'm not clear on the current fashion."

The band was down to a single guitarist. While he argued with his Tuning Faery over the value of tuning to open C, Lylli stepped onto the stage. She cupped her hands together, held them to her mouth and whispered. When she pulled them apart, a stream of tiny faeries flew out—Stardust Faeries, dim cousins to GloFaeries—circled around the guitarist and returned to Lylli's hands. She held them to her ear.

The guitarist bowed to her, and she gave him a silent salute.

He played the old hopeful ballads that night, and Lylli sang. She sang of Queen Graegloria bringing faer and beast together. Songs of the euphoria experienced in unexpected commonality and the promise of hope, hope that had blossomed into reality almost two centuries ago and was now coming apart.

It felt like the last party to Dewey, the final celebration, a wake. He was in a bittersweet stupor when he saw Baertha limp inside. Her jaw was bruised, her vest torn, her eyes looked haunted, and her frown bode ill.

She slumped into the hot seat. "Madog is dead. Queen Dafina is dead." She continued a roll call of the dead and then gave Dewey the worst of all the news he'd ever heard. "It was dragons what sunk us. Dragons, Dewey Nawton, farqin dragons on his side."

Dewey stood and walked to the stage and sat on its edge to be close to Lylli. Baertha limped to Loretta, and he watched Loretta receive the news. He'd expected an outburst, a tidal wave of rage, but she slumped to the floor, her torso convulsing in sobs.

65.

Daffy settled into the tidal rhythm of the maer. The grotto was a cave among the tide pools in the rocky crags off Crescent Point.

The maerschool spent their time eating and talking, playing and making love. They had no rooms, nothing to separate each other, no concept of privacy at all.

Daffy slept at the highest point in the grotto where the tides only shut off her ability to breathe for a few hours twice a day. Everyone knew how helpless she was, and high tides became erotic celebrations of shared breathing. Daffy's vulnerability felt more like a gift that she willingly contributed to the school.

She swam along the reefs and flushed out fish for others to catch. Zelda and the matron of the maerschool, Annenone, took her under their fins and taught her the ways of the maer. They shared their food. Generosity and trust encompassed their lives.

Daffy swam around whirlpools, frolicked in the waves the instant before they crashed against the rocky crags, and learned how currents and wind formed the language spoken between the air and sea.

She had every intention of fulfilling her oath as Queen Dafina of Glomaythea, but not just yet. She also intended to apologize to Loretta. The maer taught her that love is never wrong and never wasted. From the grotto, Daffy found happiness in the understanding that the man she loved and the woman who was her closest friend had found love between them and that their love had brought Rustin and Kaetie into the world. Still, she had no desire to leave her maerschool yet.

She swam with dolphins and fish. But for her legs and need for dry air, she became a maermaid.

66.

Dewey slept on the floor of the inn with drunken pixies that night. He woke with his arms around Loretta and remembered how she'd cried herself to sleep. He eased away from her. The sun had yet to rise over The Fist, but its rays lit the fog bank off the coast.

The tide was turning from ebb to flood. They would arrive soon.

He went through the motions, as though it was just another day in Crescent Cove. The inn came to life as he made his market list. He had barely stepped off the porch onto Reyes Street when the Town Liar walked by ringing her bell and calling, "Hear ye, hear ye, the gaelleon *Faerbane* brings the return of Major Blechk, he will address the patriotic humans of Crescent Cove when the sun lights the wharf!" Repeating on and on in a singsong.

So much for pretending like it was any other day. He ran down to the square. Everyone was in a hurry. Fishers threw their catch to buyers, brewers and vintners rolled kegs and casks to the first bids, and merchants made reasonable counter offers. In light of the bargains, Dewey decided that Blechk's return wasn't all bad—until the town went silent and all eyes turned to sea.

A huge ship lumbered around Crescent Point. Not the longest ship Dewey had ever seen, but without question the heaviest ship that had ever entered Crescent Cove, a gaelleon three times wider than *Avarice* had been. Three square sails billowed from each mast, covering the area of ten standard sails. Even with a tailwind, it took a wide turn and had to double back into the harbor. The hull was painted red and had giant black shutters closed over great portholes that were evenly spaced along the hull.

Thirty minutes passed from the moment the ship appeared until it heaved to and dropped anchor. Nine tenders were lowered. Dewey saw Major Blechk standing at the bow of the lead vessel holding out his cutlass as though he was leading a shore assault. But for his ever-expanding belly, he might have looked dashing. As it was, he looked hungry, ready to use that cutlass as a steak knife.

Instead of tying down at the pier, the tenders pulled up on sand below the wharf in military precision. From the square, Dewey couldn't see Blechk emerge from the tender. He appeared to jump onto the wharf. With his cutlass now at his side, he held his arms out to the gathering crowd. A hundred Volunteers marched in a line behind him.

The soldiers in that line were not the injured and exhausted veterans he'd led a month ago. Nor were they young and green. No, the men and women behind Blechk were seasoned veterans in fresh uniforms with polished boots and freshly cast Volunteer-issue swords at their sides and crossbows mounted to their backs.

Nothing about this display signaled Lukas's imminent defeat. Dewey worked his way through the crowd, along the wharf, and up to Broad Way until he stood two rows from Blechk.

Just as the Town Liar had promised, the instant that the sun fully illuminated the harbor, Major Blechk pulled his sword from its scabbard. The cry of steel on steel carried across the marketplace. He held the sword above him while, behind him, the massive ship raised anchor.

Even from here, Dewey could hear the winches strain on the weight of the biggest piece of iron he'd ever seen.

Blechk lowered his sword and *Faerbane* trimmed its sails, caught the breeze, and cruised parallel to the wharf. It gathered speed and, when it passed the point where the River Adductor separates Crescent Cove from Faer Reef, the sails went slack, and it slowed.

Blechk addressed the crowd, "I am informed that this has been called Faer Reef?" He raised his sword again. The eight black shutters opened along *Faerbane*'s red hull.

The night that Blechk came to The Gold Piece Inn, he'd spoken in a deep voice with the precision of an official. He didn't sound that way today. Blechk's voice was just as deep, but his cadence now hinted vibrato.

Blechk bellowed, "I hereby declare it Liberty Shoals and this port, Liberty Cove." And Dewey noticed that his words ran together in a way that differed from a drunken slur. Dewey pushed his way to the front row and checked that his hat fully covered his ears.

Blechk scanned the crowd. His eyes passed over Dewey.

Dewey saw what he was hoping for: the pupils of Blechk's eyes were rectangular—goateye.

Blechk lowered his sword slowly, and as he did, great streams of fire blew from each of the eight portholes. Eight flaming comets trailing sparks as they flew from the ship. When the comets were midway between *Faerbane* and Faer Reef, a tremendous and sustained roar of thunder bellowed from the ship. Dragons arced across the sky, screaming into the reef. They destroyed granite crags that a thousand years of mighty ocean waves hadn't brought down. They boiled the water and cratered the reef. They skipped across, cutting chasms of destruction.

"Dragons!" shouted like a curse by hundreds of terrified humans—exactly what Lukas had in mind.

"These are dragons?" Dewey said to no one in particular. "Dragons attacking the faer?" He tried to focus on the portholes from which the dragons had flown. They were hardly large enough for the dragons of legend to escape. But legends have a way of exaggerating. He watched the reef, peeling his eyes the way a whaler does at sea, scanning for movement. And there was none. If these were dragons, they had disappeared into the reef. Dewey turned to Baeswax who stood next to him and said, "No one has ever seen a dragon and lived to tell about it."

Baeswax said, "Do you expect to live to tell about this?"

"I do," Dewey said.

Dewey stared at the reef as the others left. Laetifah passed by and glared at him. He broke his concentration to check the Volunteers—Taevius was not among them. He turned back to the reef and watched Blechk issue orders to destroy all faer, no prisoners, no quarter. He kept his eyes on the reef as the troops accepted their orders and began their mission. They advanced up the streets, into buildings, onto the bluff, over the hills, toward rivers and creeks, and Dewey watched the reef. He looked aside only long enough to see Blechk walk into the Crab and Anchor.

The sun was directly overhead when he saw them: swarms. Swarms of radiant creatures on the wings of butterflies, moths, bees, hummingbirds, and, yes, dragonflies too. Hordes of angry faeries flew from Faer Reef to the gaelleon *Faerbane*.

Dewey didn't bother to tell anyone. He enjoyed being in sole possession of powerful information. But he worried. The faeries that made up the swarms looked like they'd just emerged from the chrysalis. The work they had in mind required experience.

The Knights of Perpetual Poverty

67.

Since Kaetie came down from Sempervaereen, the world had felt different, like it had been a sketch but was now a complete painting. In every direction she looked, she recalled what had happened as if she'd been there. She saw the flash of the lighthouse and recalled how it was built. Where goats and sheep grazed, she saw battlefields. When she looked up at the series of four mountain peaks, the backdrop to her entire life, she recalled how The Fist of God had gotten its name. She laughed at how far the truth was from the legend and then laughed again at how the legends were always more complicated than the truth. She laughed at humanity.

She came to the Great Beach to reinforce the Leaf Faery illusion that Lylli had installed to mislead Volunteers.

The Great Beach ran ten miles from the Glomaythea coast to Lighthouse Point. Kaetie found the edges of Lylli's illusion. If it hadn't been on the verge of decay, she'd have been as lost as the Volunteers. The Leaf Faeries had gotten lackadaisical, and she spotted a seam in their curtain where sunlight reflected from the ocean on the other side.

The long stretch of white sand was littered with slices of mast, splintered, mangled, and burnt boards that had once formed *Avarice's* hull, gunwales, and deck. Two tenders were pulled up on the beach amid the wreckage. With no ship at anchor behind them, they looked like orphans.

And squalor, mostly squalor. Scores of waterlogged elfs and leprechauns, injured and suffering. Hundreds had boarded *Avarice* and dozens survived. Kaetie stood on the bluff, stricken, wanting to help but not knowing what she could do. Replenishing the illusion that kept away the Volunteers felt like window dressing.

She watched Rustin look over the scene with his brow furrowed, squinting in concentration. He nodded to himself and his brow relaxed. He went to Macae first. Rustin spoke, motioned at the beach, pointed to the bluffs, and Macae nodded. Rustin thumped his arm and Macae looked up and smiled in that amicable way of his. It still turned Kaetie's heart. Macae started down the bluff, stopping every few steps to position stones and expand the trail.

Rustin went to Caeph next. Caeph glared down the bluff, gritting his teeth at what he saw. Kaetie knew that look. He wanted to fight. Rustin took him by the shoulders. Caeph tried to shrug Rustin off, but Rustin held him steady without saying a word until Caeph looked at him. When they made eye contact, Rustin leaned close and spoke softly. Caeph rubbed his eyes with the back of his hand. Rustin stepped out of his way and Caeph jogged down to the beach to a tiny elf who looked like a five-year-old girl. He bent to his knees, took the child's hand, and walked her to clusters of survivors until he found her parents.

Rustin waved to Naelth, and he followed Caeph. Aennie called to Rustin, said they needed freshwater, and that she knew of a source. Rustin told her to go for it and asked Raenny and Viviaen to help her, and of course they did—even Raenny who she'd never seen perform a chore without questioning its purpose.

And then Rustin approached Kaetie. He asked her if the Knightlets could still make their way through the illusion when she'd finished rebuilding it.

She said, "No."

"We need to get the injured into the forest." He sighed. "And trying to get faer to move from one place to another is—basically impossible."

"I'll help."

"Perfect." And with that he went down the bluff to Baertha. He was taller than Baertha, but Kaetie'd never seen him that way before. She'd never seen them as adults before. She looked back at Macae. He rose from his task and made his eyebrows dance, a silly and lewd gesture, and he looked like a boy again. His advances were endearing but pitiful. She wondered how it would feel if he stopped trying.

Raenny and Viviaen came down a bluff and stopped a few steps from Rustin. He spoke to Baertha, and then she led Raenny and Viviaen to the tenders.

Kaetie felt a dawning, the feeling of the world turning. She listened to the waves on the beach and the ocean wind blowing into the forest behind her. Sandpipers pecked the waterline and she saw a whale blow on the horizon. Sempervaereen had taught her to watch for these moments, instants when the world was sensitive to change. She watched Naelth standing near a family of elfs, one of them lying on the beach roasting in the sun.

Her older brother had something here. Something important, but it lacked. If the Knightlets could join the rhythm of the sea, wind, earth, and stars they might help set Maentanglement back in place. She knew that it rested on her actions, could feel the immanence of her place in the world, but didn't know what to do—other than seal off the illusion.

Standing on that bluff, she watched how the waves record time in their rhythm. Black painted wood shards floated up and down, the corpse of *Avarice*—she gave silent thanks to Daffy, who had taught her to read and who had made Rustin a man. She pondered that last thought and let her mind wander. She could hear laughter in the cries of seagulls and decided it was none of her business.

It would be a few hours before she realized that Rustin had treated her the same way he treated the Knightlets. He'd assigned her a task as if she were any other follower. Yes, she said to herself, and with respect.

68.

What should Rustin have said to an elf who had just watched his wife of a thousand years die? He knew better than to offer a hug or a platitude or anything that might be appropriate among humans, and he knew better than to ask for information about Conifaer— the obligation that itched at his soul—so he stopped a few steps away. The elf didn't move; his eyes fixed on the body of his life mate. Another elf, dressed in the same redwood colored suede leggings and forest green tunic, approached and the two stood together. The one held out his hand and set it on the back of the other's. They stood the way they do, still as stone, eyes unwavering. Rustin waited, as still as he was capable, conscious of each breath and blink, aware without ever being told that even these tiniest movements conveyed disrespect, but even more aware that he had to stand with them through this moment, however long it might last.

What must have been hours later, the two elfs turned as one toward the bluff and the forest that ran along the heel of The Fist of God. Rustin felt their eyes pass over him, and he knew that this too carried a message. Without a word, he walked along the Great Beach in the direction Aennie said would lead to freshwater and dense forest.

Instead of following, they walked in the same general direction, but along the line where the bluff cast its shadow on the beach, sometimes ahead, sometimes behind. That is, they sidled. Rustin guided them to a pond in a clearing. They stopped, as he expected they would, and he circled around and returned to the beach where Baertha and the other survivors stood next to a pyramid of driftwood ready to be set on fire.

Rustin organized scouts to watch for the ship that Dewey had promised from the north. The tricky part would be distinguishing a friendly pirate ship from a Volunteer Navy ship.

Baertha spit in the sand. "Why would a ship come here?"

"Dewey sent messages up and down the coast by pelican and seagull," Rustin said. "Why wouldn't they come?"

"Facing dragons ain't worth faer gold."

Rustin felt her gloom. And who could blame her?

A salty pirate named Duncaen, whose pale skin seemed to repel sunlight but absorb and smear tattoo ink, said, "We might as well join the Volunteers."

Baertha brought her fist up hard and fast into his chin. He flew off his feet and landed on his back. She said, "Anyone else want to enlist with the Volunteers?" The others looked at their feet. Someone muttered that it might be the only way back to sea. The muttering got worse.

Rustin said. "If there's a ship within fifty miles, I'll get it here."

"Big words from a boy," Duncaen said from his seat in the sand.

"Want to wager?" Rustin said.

Duncaen spit a wad of blood at Rustin's feet.

Rustin could feel their eyes on him. He didn't mind being tested. He looked each of the pirates in the eye. "If I can't get a ship here in a fortnight, I'll introduce you to Major Blechk and join up with you. You in?"

Duncaen said, "Make it three days."

Rustin said, "Five."

"Done."

"Good. And I'll throw in a pet dragon for each of you." He toed a line in the sand near Duncaen's feet. "And when that boat gets here, you'll follow my orders."

He turned and walked up the bluff.

The pirate muttered, "Big words for a spindly boy."

And then Baertha, "I wouldn't bet against that one."

Rustin climbed the bluffs, thinking about the Knightlets and the situation. He headed toward the lighthouse. Thoughts of Daffy came in and out of mind, and he grieved for her, remembered her silky voice with that exotic accent saying, "When you make a promise, it's your bond." Even if he could leave, he didn't know where to look for Conifaer. And Naerie, always a vision of Naerie with him in that warm ocean pool.

A flash of white and two distinct thuds broke into his thoughts. He jerked his head to the side and peered into the thick forest through needles and leaves that whistled in the wind. He left the redwoods behind and walked in sunlight barely filtered by scattered oaks.

Something caught his eye again. He went to the base of a tree and leaned against its trunk. He heard a horse nicker and peered around the tree trunk. There, between two ancient oaks, stood a white horse.

Quercus sat bareback, staring at him. A thousand words came to mind, greetings, questions, even accusations—no one appreciates being shadowed—but Rustin remained silent in the way of elfs. The giant horse cocked his head and lowered his muzzle so that he looked straight at Rustin, not down at him, and his horn didn't look threatening. Dewey had given Rustin extra chores in the stable, and he knew that motion. He was halfway to rubbing the unicorn's muzzle when he caught himself.

Quercus held up a gloved hand. Rustin asked for help locating Conifaer the Woodweaver. Quercus responded by emitting a clicking sound from the sides of his mouth. The unicorn turned and carried him away.

No words, no message, nothing. The unicorn trotted around a granite outgrowth and Rustin continued on his way, another five miles to the Lighthouse.

Aelbert invited him in. The sea lion choir lounged on the rocks above the surf. Rustin described the predicament at the beach, waiting for a pirate ship that might not come.

"It all makes sense now," Aelbert said. His head wagged to the left. "My GloFaeries have been going dim the last three nights. Do they resist lighting the way for the Volunteer Navy?" Aelbert leaned his head to the right and answered himself, "The faer have to stick together. They've seen this before." Aelbert concluded, "So it is that we," he turned to Rustin, "and by 'we' I mean 'I,' will support the faer as they have always supported me."

Rustin then asked if Aelbert could direct messages to passing pirate ships without alerting Volunteer ships.

"Dewey's encryption," Aelbert replied. "Compose your message and the ships who see my light and know the code will receive it."

Rustin composed a short message. Aelbert commented on his handwriting, and it reminded him of Daffy again. He began the long walk back to the beach encampment. The sun set behind him and the lighthouse beam rotated about the point. He looked out on the darkening sea and, for an instant, hoped that Madog and *Avarice* would receive his message, but then remembered that Madog had gone down with his ship, and the hope dissolved into grief. He wondered how his mother would fare without Madog, wondered if she'd find someone else to care for.

He made it back a few hours after sunrise, wrapped himself in his cloak, and slept in the shade. Baertha woke him. The elfs needed help with their dead but would neither tell her what they needed nor do what she told them. He went to the elfs and stood with them. They spoke among themselves without acknowledging him, but after a few minutes, they switched from Naest to Glo and said enough for Rustin to understand how they honored their dead.

Rustin assembled the Knightlets and gave them somber instructions. They searched the bluffs and found a few dead cedars, an oak, and a redwood. They sidled the elfs to each tree and stood by as they set their dead children, mates, and friends in the branches. On the third tree, two elfs waited for Rustin to help them lift a child's body into a long dead oak. The honor all but brought him to his knees.

Rustin never knew whether his message by lighthouse or Dewey's messages by seagull and pelican did the trick, but the schooner *Happy Jack* laid anchor three days later. Sea-wary, terrified, exhausted faer kept coming. They packed this ship with far more faer than *Avarice* had carried.

The Knightlets sat leaning against each other, their feet in the sand, exhausted. Naelth said, "My blisters have grown calluses." Macae, "I should have stowed away—aren't they going to Puaepuae?" Aennie, "Viv? Have you seen the men from Puaepuae?" Viviaen, "Do they all look like Taevius?" Aennie, "Yumm." Raenny, "I thought you preferred crafty, swarthy, small men with big—" Caeph, "—noses." Rustin, "Another ship tomorrow." Viviaen, "Kaetie, your brother can really kill a party." Kaetie, "It's an art form."

Naelth started snoring. Lip-smacking sounds came from Aennie and Raenny. Macae whispered to Kaetie and eventually she laughed.

Rustin had just stretched out when Baertha walked up. She dropped into the sand next to him.

He said, "Have you heard anything about Conifaer?"

"Who?"

"The elfin carpenter—the woodweaver." The frustration caused him to speak in a sharp tone.

"Oh," she said, "last I heard Lukas was exterminating them—but a woodweaver, you say. He might make it through if the damn war ever ends. But listen, I have a request."

"What do you need?"

"I need you to captain my next ship."

"What?" Rustin sat up straight. "You're the captain."

"Naw, I'd rather be quartermaster. When people won't listen to me, I usually hurt them, not a nice quality in a captain, but you ..."

Rustin waited for a wisecrack from someone, but none came. Caeph gave him a nod of encouragement. Raenny, Aennie, and

Naelth sat up. Raenny said, "I could navigate." Aennie, "I'm not cooking." Viviaen, "Count me out."

Rustin said, "I get seasick from here."

"You'd grow sea legs."

Rustin thought about knights at sea and tried to describe his knightly calling.

Baertha started laughing.

"What? You think I could captain a ship but not lead chivalrous knights?"

"You can lead them," she caught her breath, "but as a captain you can make the money you'll need to become a knight. You see," now she spoke in a condescending tone, "knights are supposed to *start* with money, it's a key ingredient to knighthood."

He recited "To Be a Knight" from memory and concluded with, "Our goal is justice, not wealth."

"You'll be broke forever." She started howling again. She stood and faced them. "I dub thee The Knights of Perpetual Poverty."

69.

The Knights of Perpetual Poverty learned a lot that summer. The pirates who came and went whipped them into shape. Wary of the Weapon Faeries who possessed the knights' weird granite weapons, the pirates taught them to fight with wooden replicas. At the end of each lesson, the Weapon Faeries gave the knights an earful about their mistakes and hooted compliments to the pirates. They learned to fight with and without shields, how to board a ship with grappling hooks, and they learned the wrong way to drink rum and sing bawdy songs.

Sidling along with elfs, they learned how to fashion longbows and arrows of nearly elfin quality. The knights even learned their techniques for hiding, though humans don't have the agility or patience to ride the gap between light and shade.

Rustin spent his spare time among the elfs. He slept in trees near them—one doesn't do things with elfs so much as near them. He picked up a functional knowledge of Naest and asked about Lukas's faer camps. He described Conifaer and asked if they knew him. Many of them had met Lapidae at The Gold Piece Inn, but no one knew Conifaer. He swallowed the urge every time he wanted to ask about Naerie.

Jon-Jay took him aside one day. "You spend too much time with elfs. They're not our kind. Be careful, son. The faer are beautiful creatures, but they don't understand loyalty."

When Rustin looked away, Jon-Jay pulled his chin toward him. "Don't fool yourself, brother—elfs don't make friends."

Murder

70.

As he did on every Tuesday and Friday, Major Blechk pretended to survey the Volunteer Navy from the pier while waiting for his goateye. A fogbank sat on Crescent Cove like a fat man on a barstool, preventing the profiteer ship *Saetisfier* and its coveted cargo from navigating the point. If Blechk had to suffer, others would suffer with him.

He chose a young Volunteer who had never learned to swim. He unleashed a tirade on the boy and then pushed him off the pier. The lad thrashed and splashed. Blechk ordered the others to watch what became of soldiers who didn't follow orders—though how that boy could have lifted the fog bank was not lost on those who watched him drown.

But the boy did not drown. The boy came to the surface on a swirling bed of gold. He floated lifeless for the instant before she surfaced and locked her mouth to his. Her golden hair surrounded them, and her light blue skin matched his until she gave him enough breath to turn his skin mottled pink. She held the boy steady and waited for the humans to lift him from the water.

Blechk coughed an order, and the Volunteers scrambled down the pier, confiscated a net, and came back. By then, two maerbutlers had joined the maermaid.

Blechk cast the net and pulled her onto the pier himself. She thrashed around, tangling her flukes and the fins on her arms in the net. He waited, watching her strain for breath and try to return to the sea. When she got close to the edge of the pier, he kicked her in the head.

The Volunteers cast another net, and the maerbutlers swam

around it, surfacing a few strokes away. They cast the net again and again, and the maerbutlers ignored it. Blechk pushed another Volunteer into the water. She splashed in, surfaced, and treaded water. The maerbutlers watched but stayed clear. Blechk screamed at another Volunteer, told him to fake his own drowning and then pushed him in.

The Volunteer pretended to drown. The maerbutlers pushed him up and held him at the surface, until the other Volunteers could pull him out, but instead, they threw nets. Blechk shoved every one of the Volunteers off the pier repeatedly and every time, they caught a maer.

He faked a shipwreck and caught a whole school.

They stabbed the injured maer with spears and harpoons and locked manacles to the tails of the survivors, towed them to *Faerbane*, and imprisoned them in bilge water. They capsized a fisher's sailboat in the River Adductor and shot the maer who came to the rescue with crossbows. It went on for hours. A crimson arc formed around Faer Reef and by the time the fog cleared, blood covered the entire cove.

Saetisfier dropped anchor, and Major Blechk collected his goat-eye. He hefted a thrashing maermaid over his shoulder and carried her to the Crab and Anchor.

* * *

Grindaer, the guilt-ridden miller, rushed to The Gold Piece Inn, and begged Dewey to stop the carnage. "The maer!" he cried. "Of all the faer, everyone loves the maer—they've never hurt a soul, done nothing but rescue people from shipwrecks and folly. The maer are the best of the faer! Why would they hurt the maer?" He went on and on, a repentant sinner. "And why don't they put up a fight?"

"Have you ever seen a maermaid or maerbutler fight? Ever seen them show a hint of aggression, anger, or fear?"

"No, but—"

"Because they don't have it in them, you stupid Farq. Fight back? No, they'll go willingly into Blechk's traps, and you know why?"

"No, but—"

"What if one of the Volunteers actually needed help and they didn't give it? He'd suffer, and they can't abide suffering!" Dewey's frustration had long since turned to rage. "And your man Lukas brings suffering on the whole world. You disgust me."

Grindaer grunted partial words, stuttering until he managed, "Is there nothing I can do to help them?"

"Blechk will get ten gold ohzees each," Dewey said. "Buy a few and treat them well."

"Blechk's going to sell them as slaves?"

"Slaves?" Dewey said. "No. Curiosities of carnal entertainment. Now get out of here."

71.

Queen Dafina spent months rapt in the maer's world. They treated her the way they treated everyone in their school, like royalty.

She woke as the morning tide rose, dove below the grotto with her school, and swam around the reef. Part of something. Every hundred beats of her heart, a maermaid or maerbutler would come to her and offer a kiss of air.

The call came as a loud moan, like the song of a lonely hump-back, and the maer stopped as one. She bumped into Zelda. The school surrounded Annenone, a maermaid with hair as black as Daffy's. They swam to the harbor without a song or a tail flip. She'd never seen maer worry. They followed Annenone, stroking through the water too fast for Daffy to keep up.

She had to surface for breath.

Zelda curled out of the school, caught Daffy in her arms, and guided her to a tide pool nestled below the bluffs of Crescent Point. Daffy stood knee deep in a fog bank. She shivered and had the mundane realization that she'd been naked for months.

Zelda swam a circle around her in the frothy surf, beckoning. Daffy went in and joined her lips to Zelda's, and the mermaid set the words in her mind, "The usurper has come for us."

"Don't go."

Zelda's eyes, so huge they could see through acres of water, dimmed in response. "The innocent call as well as the guilty, and we can't refuse. The risk would be too great."

Daffy lost her balance and fell away. Zelda worked her tail flukes, rose above the surface, and pulled Daffy into their last kiss. "We are all victims of who we are." The maermaid disappeared under a wave.

Daffy knew this feeling. She'd lost her place in another world, and it cut her to the quick. Another life stolen from her. Once again, she was incapable of protecting those she loved. She climbed to land, found a rock to kick, and fell to the ground. She beat the sand and became the crying lady again—and hated herself for it.

The frustration encompassed her. She fought the blanket of humiliation, vowing that Lukas would never hurt her again. But what could a fallen queen, a failed maermaid, a useless serving-lass do to stop a king? That thought angered her even more—Lukas was no king. The kings she knew were made of honor and Lukas had none, not even decency. That so many humans fell for his lies angered her into a frenzy. She threw rocks at the bluff until a mini avalanche filled the tide pool where she stood. The harbor seals glared at her.

The fog burned off by noon and she heard the cries from across the cove, but on her little beach the harbor seals napped in the sun and Daffy paced a rut in the sand. From here, five miles from where the River Adductor meets the sea, Daffy could only guess at the horror.

Her anger dissipated until she ached with gratitude for everything the maer had done for her. She let her salty tears join the sea, and the first elements of strategy formed, an obvious goal surrounded by impossible details, like a puzzle she could see but whose pieces didn't fit together. The late summer sun beat down. She paced back and forth, combing her brain for fragments that she could put into a whole. She needed to find the pieces to this puzzle.

Dewey had connections. Lylli knew history, legend, myth, and, most of all, maegic. Even Loretta knew more about life, real actual life outside of castles and palaces. As hints of where to find the pieces accumulated. She realized that she'd have to face her own demons first.

The cries coming from Faer Reef faded as the sun set, and Daffy of the maer became Daffy serving-lass of The Gold Piece Inn again.

She waited until dusk became darkness and dove into the comfortably cold sea. She swam three miles without stopping. The exertion combined with grief into a fatalistic understanding that she lived on borrowed time, that whatever she did from here had to count, had to matter.

At the end of the pier, she surfaced and saw people in red and black uniforms. She dropped back in and swam to a kelp bed where she harvested a few long strands. She climbed out on the deserted part of the wharf, wrapped herself in kelp, and walked. The gritty feel of dry sand and cobbles gnawed at her feet, and the smell of humanity, smoke, and horses brought her back to the world from which she came.

People milled about the marketplace. Merchants tidied their stalls, assembled their wares, and headed off. No one laughed, no one hugged and kissed. Daffy hid in shadows when people passed, ran by the guild hall entrance up to Reye's street, and disappeared into the dark alley next to The Gold Piece Inn stable. She stopped at the gate and looked back. A sigh came up from her belly, and she let her head dangle for a few seconds.

She stepped into the stable and slid behind a barrel. A horse nickered as the door shut and she saw two kids, Maerk and Aelice, huddled over a game of dice. She walked through the barn and around goats chewing straw. The screech owl dropped from a rafter and hovered at eye level, welcoming her home. She emerged into the faery garden, sat behind a lavender bush, and waited.

72.

Daffy listened to the music that filtered into the garden, music for weeping, not dancing. The children walked from the kitchen to the barn, barely talking to each other. She watched Daeffid carry his dirty pots and pans out to the spring where they'd soak in water and sand. He moped his way both there and back. Even the dogs and goats looked unhappy. The only hint of glee came from a lassrechaun who tricked a pixie into jumping out of a window. From here she could sense that the faer packed The Gold Piece Inn's secret warren.

If Loretta took a guest upstairs, Daffy would be out here for a long time. Faernando passed by, then Jaek and Tifenae, and finally, Loretta walked out the door.

Daffy rose from the lavender, two vines of kelp around her shoulders, and stepped into the scattered lamplight that leaked from the kitchen window.

She said, "Loretta."

Loretta stopped. It would take her a while to adapt to the dim light.

"It's me, Daffy."

"Oh gods," Loretta whispered. "You live?" She squinted and leaned forward. "You live."

"I need to talk to you."

"Quiet." She held a finger to her nose and waited, listening. Comfortable sounds came down from the hay loft, people sleeping, talking softly, weeping.

Loretta opened the gate. "I'll get you clothes and meet you in the school-shed. Quiet, now."

Daffy walked into her classroom. It smelled different, like rose and mint. She shuttered the window and closed the door before finding a small oil lamp right where she'd always kept it. The hand-writing on the chalkboard was crisp and proper and accompanied by sketches of plants and leaves. She was happy that the school had carried on without her, glad that someone was teaching subjects that she wouldn't have covered.

From outside, Loretta whispered, "Down the light."

Daffy turned it down, Loretta came in and she raised it back.

Daffy dressed in the clothes she'd left behind and then stood with her back to the chalkboard and her hands clasped at her waist. Loretta stood against the door, arms crossed.

"Leave with the faer tonight. Wait in the orchard and then fol-low them to the Great Beach. You'll be in Puaepuae—or maybe they take you to Nantesse—you'll be there by—"

"I'm not going anywhere," Daffy said. "Not until we put an end to all of this."

"Oh farq." The words drooped out of Loretta's mouth and she slouched against the door. "Right. You and me, a dead princess, and an old serving-lass. And a greedy halfling. Sure, we can bring down the commander of the greatest army in the world." She straightened up. "I'll walk you to the orchard."

"No. I'm the First Princess of Nantesse, the rightful Queen of Glomaythea, and you are the mother of the direct heirs to the throne."

"Oh please."

"That's who we are," Daffy said. "Titles have value, and you and I have the highest titles in the land."

"Keep my children out of this!"

"Rustin should be King."

"Rustin is a bastard stable boy. A field hand and a fine young man, and you'd get him killed."

"I dare you to take one look at Rustin and deny that he's the King's son."

"I know who fathered him."

"Loretta." Daffy let herself sink onto a stool. "You told me you loved Gledig and that you should have been queen."

"It's true, and he loved me long before he knew you."

"I know." Daffy couldn't quite bring herself to maintain eye contact. "I've had a lot of time to think and, I know. He did love you. Gledig was a great man and the only man I've ever loved. He loved me too."

"He wanted me. He was stuck with you."

Daffy held her arms out. "The world wouldn't let him have you, the woman he loved. I was his responsibility, and he found it in himself to give me joy and affection. He cared for me." She took a breath, wishing it had come from a maer kiss. "And he still came to you."

"For a while."

Daffy saw that light in Loretta's eyes, that passion, the fire that made it so much better to be her friend than her enemy. She took Loretta's hand and pulled her away from the door. "You know that I have loved Kaetie and Rustin from the moment I met them. You know that I'd do anything to help them. You know it." She motioned at a stool near the blackboard. "Kaetie sat right there. Teaching her to read was one of the happiest times in my life. I know that you're angry with me—or at least you were—but when Rustin brought that scroll to me and we read it together and I saw him light up with purpose, I just—Loretta—and then when I discovered that Gledig is their father, well, I think that I knew all along.

Rustin has his walk, the same voice, people are drawn to him, they want to follow his lead, people believe in him—in every way, he is the image of his father. And Kaetie, if you could bottle Gledig's quick insight and grace under pressure, you would get Kaetie. But I think they're better than Gledig." Daffy had to catch her breath and swallow the growing lump in her throat. "When I found out, it was hard." She took another breath. "Loretta, they're yours. Just as I see Gledig in them, I see you. Add your spirit to Gledig's cool brilliance and—"

"And you get Kaetie." Loretta sat on the stool and took Daffy's other hand. "The first time Gledig came to The Gold Piece Inn, he was a prince and I was a young serving-lass. He had this knack. It amazed me. He'd walk into the room and befriend everyone there."

"Made everyone feel like the most important person in the room."

"Yes! That's what he did. That's right. Gledig, oh how he made you feel. He listened, and he cared, he really cared, and he had the power to help you, and he made me feel like I had the power to help him—me, a Bastard serving-lass. He listened to me, even took my advice."

"Rustin has that."

"Just like my Gledig, always fair, even when it hurts."

Daffy said, "He should be King of Glomaythea."

"And you took Gledig away from me," Loretta said, but she didn't pull away. She almost smiled.

"My family and his family took him from you. Not me."

Loretta's eyes wandered into the shadows. She spoke so softly that Daffy could barely hear. "He did love you. He told me so." She leaned back and whistled. "What a man."

"Oh! You mean …"

"Yes, that's exactly what I mean. And I been with a few."

"He put everything he had into it."

"And talk about making you feel important."

"I never felt more, I don't know—what's the word?"

"Special," Loretta said and then turned away. "That last time he come here, he told me about your children, told me he loved his life, loved you. Damn Gledig, he came to me and broke it off in person, came to me and broke my heart face-to-face. He sat still and let me slap him. Held me when I cried and waited until I told him to leave. And I never saw him again."

"He kept coming to you after he married me."

Loretta shared the story of the day they met. A drunk prince pulling a teenaged serving-lass onto his lap. Loretta had slapped him. "And then I yelled at his father, told him that his son was no gentleman!"

"You yelled at the King?"

"Can you imagine? I was sixteen, in my long apron with these bosoms bouncing about, and I slapped Gledig and scolded the King."

"Oh yes," Daffy said. "I can picture it. That's who you are, Loretta, that's why he loved you and why I love you and Dewey and Faernando—you have the biggest family of all."

"The King ordered Gledig to apologize, and he got on a knee and begged forgiveness. Scared the shite out of me! I'm standing there looking down at a prince with a king at me side. I ask him to forgive me. There we were, two dumb kids asking forgiveness, and do you know what Dewey said?"

"Oh no."

"Yes! He said, 'Go on Gledig, kiss her! Give her one for royalty.' I thought the King would kill him right then, but you know Dewey …"

"Everyone owes him something."

"Well, Prince Gledig looked at me and his father and around the room."

"I can guess."

"Go on, then."

"He kissed you for all to see."

"Oh, he didn't hide his love for the ginger-Loretta. He didn't bat an eye. Gledig was proud to be with me. How I fell for that man. And then I lost him."

"I lost him, too."

"And then I lost Madog."

"Madog tried to save me. It was the last thing he did before he went down with his ship." A smile tugged Daffy's lips up but her eyes down, "I wish you'd met my children. They were the King's too. Different from Kaetie and Rustin. Piaer never had a chance to develop Gledig's charisma, but Maechelle, oh, Maechelle was the charmer. How I miss them."

They sat together for a few minutes, holding hands but alone with their thoughts.

Finally, Daffy said, "I have a plan. It can work but not without you."

"You're not telling them."

"Tell them what?"

"That they're Gledig's heirs."

"Oh gods no. I'd never. Only you have the right to tell your children who their father was. And not until it's their time, not until it's safe for them to know. No one can know until then."

"Only Dewey knows."

"And Lylli?"

Loretta rolled her eyes, "Lylli, too."

"Loretta, I'm staying. I am the rightful queen, and I have a responsibility. We will defeat Lukas. I'm not leaving. I'm not leaving you or your children. I'll never leave the people I love again."

Daffy and Loretta spent the night trading stories of King Gledig. They laughed and cried and even waxed prophetic about what might have been and then they laughed again.

And they planned.

73.

The sun hid behind the fog that morning, so thick and wet you could feel it in every breath.

Loretta fetched Dewey from his chair and pulled him to the school-shed.

When he saw Daffy, he said, "I didn't think the world had finished with you." He sold it, too. He'd had no inkling that she could have survived.

Daffy stood at the chalkboard as she would for a lesson and described her plan. Dewey sat and tried to give the impression that he was listening. He scratched his ears. The oppression had gotten to him. Blechk practically lived at the Crab and Anchor, so the rank-and-file Volunteers spent every night at The Gold Piece Inn. Daffy showing up like this changed the game, not just the stakes, but the rules!

Daffy glared at him. "Well?" Daffy said, looking every bit the part of a schoolmarm.

Her game was simple, too simple. Ridiculous.

He'd been sitting on two royal down cards for a long time. *Kaetie's the key. What you see is what you get with Rustin. If he doesn't get himself killed, he can make his name as a knight—if the legends are told in the right places, and I'll see that they are. A self-made knight crowned king? Not a bad story. But Kaetie. A druid.* Dewey would bet on Kaetie in any game.

The room had been quiet for minutes. Dewey thought it through several different ways. He finally said, "Loretta, fetch Lylli."

Dewey stared at Daffy. Her face was flushed and skin tanned. Loretta returned and Lylli fussed over Daffy: checked her pulse, examined her eyes, and kissed her forehead to check her temperature. Daffy told her how the maer had taken her in.

"If humans and maer reproduce," Dewey asked, "would their children have flukes or feet?"

"You heartless farq," Loretta said. "Daffy lived with those people, loved 'em, and now they're …"

"Gone," Daffy said.

Dewey waited for the waterworks, but the Crying Lady's eyes went cold.

She said, "This time he'll pay."

"But could you be pregnant?" He looked at Lylli. "I'm just trying to make the best of this. Could she have a half-maer Bastard? It could live in the spring."

"No," Lylli said. "there are no legends of half-maer and there have been plenty of sailors who've tried."

Daffy described her plan to Lylli through Dewey's interruptions.

"We'll need help," Lylli said. Then she smiled. "Come with me. He's in the inn."

Dewey and Loretta looked at each other. "Who?"

"You'll see."

The Fifth Card

74.

By that time, Crisiant was ready to pack his guitar and hit the road. Making a living as a traveling minstrel had to beat playing sad songs to mourning parents and frightened soldiers.

Lylli walked in with a smirk that in no way fit his concept of the stereotype tree-loving druid. Dewey and Loretta followed, and then he saw Dafina. Her long black hair had grown in and she carried herself with that unmistakable grace.

She glanced at him on her way to the bar. He couldn't stop staring. The shock of seeing her return from the dead evaporated his disguise, and she looked back at him and came to a stop.

"Wizard?" she said. "Is that you? How could …"

He'd been sitting on the stage talking to Bob the bartender. The sight of her—so obviously the queen—plus her calling him out by his old title panicked him. It took a second to realize that the only people in the inn so early in the morning were the bloodhound, the cat on the chandelier, and Bob.

Daffy turned to Lylli. "Where did you find the King's wizard?" She turned back to Crisiant. "Has he been here …"

"Playing guitar right here at The Gold Piece Inn."

"Wow," Bob said. "I thought you were just a wizard on the frets."

Daffy walked up to him with her arm held out. "Crisiant."

He brushed his lips on the back of her hand.

"What?" Loretta said. "Who?"

Daffy said, "Crisiant, the greatest wizard on the continent."

"Well King Gledig's fool, now retired," he said.

"Hiding in plain sight," Dewey said, "a lot of that going around."

Dewey looked him over like a lion sizing up a hyena. He asked, "Have I done enough?"

"Enough?" Crisiant pretended not to get it.

"Yes, enough. Have I paid my debt to society, have I done my time, have I helped enough farqin beggars? Can you please release me from this curse?'

"No!" Lylli said.

"No?" Dewey looked stricken but not surprised. "Look what it's done to me." He groaned at a lassrechaun poking her head out from between two wall slats. "I live with vermin."

"That curse is the best thing that ever happened to you."

"How much must I suffer?"

Crisiant looked into Dewey's eyes until he caught sight of the Curse Faery. She looked content. He answered, "You can suffer some more."

"Good," Daffy said. "Forcing you to do the right thing is key to my plans."

"Nice to know you have faith in my character."

Daffy turned to Crisiant. "Do you know the royal succession?"

Dewey held up a hand. "We're a little public here."

He led them through the kitchen to the school shed. Daeffid grabbed Daffy in a big hug, and when Faernando saw her, he dropped a water jug and burst into tears.

By the time they made it into the classroom, Crisiant had sorted through the succession. He took chalk to the board and drew. "The Gledig line began running thin a few generations before your royal wedding. Kissing cousins make for high infant mortality rates. A wonder Gledig, his mother, grandfather, and great-grandfather coul speak without drooling. Though they humped themselves dry or limp, as the case may be, each hatched just one surviving heir." He pointed at Daffy. "You knew this. I badgered, I hounded, I hassled,

I pestered, I goaded and heckled until Queen Graenna and Prince Naevin decided that Gledig would marry outside the clan. They chose you." He sketched out the family tree from King Graeglory to Queen Graegloria, all the way to Daffy's children, Maechelle and Piaer. "The line ended in the marketplace of a pirate port."

"Fill in the indirect heirs," Dewey said. "Who are they, where are they, and what are their loyalties?"

"Bickering cousins, such fun, they keep it all in the family. Sort of." Crisiant added a prior generation on the board next to the family tree and drew horizontal lines. "The King's great-great-aunt and uncle were more prolific than the direct lineage." Vertical lines cascaded into four generations of the King's cousins, none closer than three times removed. "They are extremely loyal to yellow ore."

"I like gold, too," Dewey said. "Lukas pays them a fraction of the treasure seized by the Volunteers—like a royalty." Dewey chuckled at his pun, and Crisiant lost a bit of respect for him. "They added another false claim." Dewey took the chalk from Crisiant, wrote in the name of Lukas's mother, and connected it with a dashed line to a pair of the King's remote cousins.

"And this is how Lukas satisfies the aristocracy," Daffy said. "But is there a valid claim to royal lineage?"

"Lukas considers validity a relative concept," Crisiant said.

Loretta spoke in a soft voice, inconsistent with her usual bluster. "They're the last heirs."

Daffy said, "That's right."

"Direct heirs?" Crisiant asked, and then, to Daffy, "Did one of your children survive? Are they with the maer?"

Dewey stood and motioned for the others to be quiet, a motion he used frequently with serving-lasses and lads. Daffy spoke anyway, but he appealed to her, "Please let me tell him. I haven't had any fun since he cursed me. Please?"

Daffy sat back down.

Dewey spread his hands out, palms up. "What if—just for the

sake of argument ..." he waited.

"The world might be a better place if we accommodated argument a bit less," Crisiant said. "Or perhaps more, but whatever we're doing is doomed."

"Stop," Loretta said, "don't tell him."

"Consider this," Dewey said, "what if King Gledig had visited a certain inn, and what if in those visits he had interacted with a certain red-headed goddess, and what if—"

"Me kids," Loretta said. "Rustin and Kaetie—the King is their father."

Crisiant's head whipped from Loretta to Dewey and then to Lylli. A few hours later he'd suffer whiplash as severe as a rookie headbanger. "Is this true?"

Lylli said, "It's true but—"

"Can you document it?"

Dewey said, "Will dates of conjugation, confirmed by Truth Faery suffice?"

"It would, yes. Indisputable. Oh my. How can ..." And then it came to him. "His fishing trips. I'd always wondered what bait attracted Gledig to Crescent Cove." The Wizard bowed to Loretta. "And who could have blamed him, a mere human male in the face of this beauty." Then he bowed to Dewey. "And this conniving arse."

Dewey returned the bow.

"The portrait. Every day for years, I walked past that painting. Only a fool could miss the obvious. That's his hair color, spiced with a hint of ginger."

"Well, you played here for over a year and none of us recognized you."

"Cheated, of course. Used maegic." He covered his face with his hands. A Makeup Faery appeared with a paintbrush and palette on lace wings. She winked at Lylli and flew in a gap between Crisiant's fingers. A minute later, he drew his hands away from his face and revealed the younger, light haired, wild-eyed guitarist.

Daffy said, "Wish I could do that."

"That would be nice for all of us. Lylli?"

"I've never enchanted a Makeup Faery."

"They have to be seduced, and then they only possess the seducer."

"Well, I can seduce one, but enchanting a faery to possess someone else is a completely—"

"Stop talking shop," Dewey said. "We have a kingdom to salvage."

"Well?" Daffy said. "Do you think it will work?"

"Like any fishing expedition, it depends on how you bait your hook," Crisiant said. "Even with the right bait, you have to get him in the net."

"I have a way of placing embarrassing tidbits and well-timed facts in just the right places," Dewey said. "It's all about timing."

Crisiant said, "If we drop hints that the direct heirs to the throne are in Crescent Cove, he'll—"

"You listen to me, fool." Loretta moved on him like a mountain lion on a mouse. "You tell one person and I will skin you alive. No one makes decisions for my children but me. No one. Ever. I'll do it when I think it's right."

Dewey said, "The Bastard Prince and Princess can't be thrown into politics … yet,"

Loretta's face flushed an even deeper crimson.

Crisiant said, "Kings and queens, especially if they plan on ruling through loyalty rather than fear, require a good deal of preparation."

"Have you been paying attention?" Dewey said. "Rustin is becoming a knight and Kaetie a Druid—I have been preparing them."

"Rustin and Kaetie can relieve the world of all of this," Daffy said.

Loretta stared at Daffy. "When I say they're ready, Rustin and

Kaetie will rule together."

"Rustin's charisma and Kaetie's brilliance," Daffy said, "they'll need each other."

Loretta snarled. "You people can't whiff power without killing each other."

"I have no desire to rule," Daffy said. "I love those kids like my own. I swear, Loretta, I will fight for them."

"Rightful heirs, remarkable people," Crisiant said. "Kaetie and Rustin might be too good for politics." Loretta glared at him. "But I'll swear my allegiance."

"Write it down," Loretta said. "Right now, on cotton paper: 'Rustin and Kaetie of Crescent Cove, King Gledig's Bastard children of Loretta of The Gold Piece Inn, shall rule Glomaythea together.'"

"We can swear oaths carved in granite and drenched in blood, but it will be up to Kaetie and Rustin to decide how they rule."

"They'll rule together," Loretta said.

"Sure," Crisiant said, "teens love to satisfy their parent's wishes. Especially a darling like Kaetie, so sweet and amenable."

The thrill of the possibilities waned in the face of reality—two Bastard kids thrown into the politics of royalty and aristocracy? It seemed too obvious to say out loud.

"Kaetie studies with Sempervaereen," Lylli said. "Rustin studies weapon-craft with thousand-year-old faeries and skilled pirates. They have the desire to learn."

Dewey groaned. "Since she's been with that damn tree, Kaetie has lost the tiny shred of charisma she once possessed. And Rustin would rather spend his time with elfs than humans."

"It all depends on Lukas and me," Daffy said. "If you can get him here, I can do my part. I know I can."

"You need only offend Lukas's ego and he will come," Crisiant said. "If only we knew someone capable of offending people. Someone crass and impolite, a greedy Bastard. Hmm, if only we knew someone like that."

Loretta said, "What if she can't do it?"

"Then we will all die."

75.

The meeting went on for hours. They hashed out the details, the roles they'd have to play to support Daffy. Loretta would teach her the tricks of her trade. Lylli would support the two of them with the minor thaergy of fashion and sensory deception.

As the flaws in the essential plan became clear, Lylli's description of Crisiant as "the greatest wizard on the continent" went to his head. He made promises that he could keep only if he had the time and resources. He'd have to work faster than he ever had, and without his lab, he'd have to use what Lylli could offer and he could find. Crisiant hadn't practiced theurgy in over a year. Theurgist is one of those jobs like chef at a fine restaurant. The end product looks refined and delicate, and casts alluring aromas, but the production is difficult, smelly, foul work that leaves the chef with a dirty apron. The initial set of illusions had to reek of finesse, but try as he might, the only way he could accomplish his goal involved enchanting Farq Faeries. It's true that the ignoble Farq Faeries played perhaps the most important role in Maentanglement—but gods almighty they're filthy, stinky, ill-mannered, hideous-looking creatures.

76.

The two royal bastards, a queen, and a king's wizard—a lucky card that had come as a surprise. Dewey didn't like surprises and didn't trust good fortune. He'd seen it work both ways too often. And then there was the crux of the matter. The game rested on that fifth card: dragons. He still didn't believe in them, didn't believe that they existed in the first place, and if they did exist, didn't believe that they would align with Lukas, The First Human, Liberator, usurper, psychopath bent on destroying the world.

But what if?

It came to him while negotiating with a brewer at the market-place. The brewer tapped a barrel to pour Dewey a sample. Nothing came out at first, but then the bunghole popped open and some drunk faeries flew out. Two fell in the mug, one flew a figure eight and crashed into the brewer's face. The others flew off, arm-in-arm, singing all new verses of "The Phallus and the Egg."

The brewer raised a hand to slap the faeries. "Farqin faer!"

Dewey grabbed his arm and said, "Don't be one of them."

The brewer knelt to examine the keg. As he poked around, moving the lever back and forth, he said, "Faeries in the brew, double the alcohol for you." And then, "Ah, here it is." He pulled out a small valve made of brass and leather. "The faer destroyed the maekhanics."

Something clicked in Dewey's mind. He looked down at the harbor. The gaelleon *Faerbane* still lay at anchor. It hadn't move since The Day of Dragons. Everything Dewey knew about Lukas showed that his confidence lay in the power of his weapons. Even his hatred of the faer came as much from a preference for objects he could control as from visceral repulsion.

Distracted as he was, Dewey didn't get much of a deal on the maegic ale.

He returned to the inn and disappeared in his office. He didn't need to orchestrate rumors. *But that's the beauty, they're* not *rumors!* Spreading true tales put him in a strange position. It somehow felt like cheating.

Lukas had awarded Major Blechk a medal for all but wiping out the maer, but Blechk had allowed Crescent Cove to become the center of the resistance. The Freedom Ferry delivered hundreds of elfs to safety for each one caught. Blechk was too distracted by the demands of his appetites to do anything about it. Dewey savored the beauty of the business model. Blechk depended on goods delivered to the black market by the very ships that rescued the faer.

Lukas couldn't act surprised. He had to own it. He had to react.

It took two hours for Dewey to reel off the messages, and for Tifenae to summon a flock of seagulls and send them to the far corners of Glandaeff.

Word spread from frontline Volunteers and deck-swabbing sailors. Reports of Blechk's failure climbed its way up the power structure. Lukas couldn't afford to allow the small pirate port to be left rogue any longer.

Within a week, birds flew in and out with messages several times a day, and with every message, the pot grew. Dewey didn't mind waiting, after all, he could be wrong. Dragons. It all came down to dragons.

He sat next to his window talking to a young Volunteer who had just come downstairs with Lucith—the firstborn of a farmer, he stood to inherit a small parcel—when Tifenae brought him a message from Glomaythea. Dewey pocketed the note long enough to record the Volunteer's lineage in *The Book of Bastards*. First things first.

He unrolled the tiny scroll. The words brought sweat to his brow. Major Blechk would receive a message from Lukas that very day, but it didn't say when. The oh-so-human rush of adrenalin brought him to his feet. He had to see it. He had to be there. What if he needed to nudge the process along? He scurried up to his room, dug around and pulled out his fishing outfit, oilskin overalls and a floppy-brimmed otter-skin hat that tied below the chin. It still fit but smelled more like goat than fish, needed fresh oil, and chafed his thighs. It would have to do.

Dewey went back downstairs and sat at a table facing the kitchen. He waved Loretta off and the serving-lad Jaek came to take his order. He gave the order in a nasal tone. Jaek looked straight at him with no recognition and then went back in the kitchen. Perfect!

Dewey hurried down Reyes Street to Low Street and walked into the Crab and Anchor. The Crab had more of a gate than a door, like a pigsty. The floor had a thick layer of clumped sawdust that stuck to his feet. Redwood floorboards marinated in decades of lamp smoke, ale, wine, and brandy masked the most offensive scents. Dewey waited for his eyes to adjust. The smoky whale-oil lamps provided less light than the daylight that leaked through the doorway. He sat at a table with his back to the entrance so that anyone looking at him faced the glare from outside.

Barnaey, the Crab's proprietor, brought him an unrequested ale and held out a thick palm. That he didn't look at Dewey settled any question about the quality of his disguise. Barnaey would excrete a brick of anger if he knew that Dewey had entered his establishment. Some merchants handle market forces better than others. Dewey gave him a copper ohzee, and Barnaey waddled to the bar where he assembled his vast bulk onto a modest stool that complained bitterly of its fate.

The ale wasn't bad, not as hoppy as what Dewey served, and flat but strong.

Blechk sat at a table across the room in a well-cushioned, throne-like chair. His head lolled against the headrest and his arms hung at his sides. The only evidence that he was conscious was his ability to inhale smoke from a pipe and swallow ale from a mug. He barely reacted to the two serving-lasses who tended him. The women stood at his sides with their breasts hanging over their bodices at the level of Blechk's face. On his right, a young lass with black curly hair. She could have been beautiful in a better predicament. The woman on Blechk's left held his pipe. She had a gray tint to her skin, the sign of overindulgence in goateye, and blossoming red lips that framed a mouth designed to smile but destined to frown.

Blechk inhaled from the pipe and let out a weak goat-like bleat. He raised his hand and clawed at the gray-skinned woman's belly. She rotated so that a breast perched on his palm. Blechk lacked the muster to caress or squeeze. The curly-haired lass brought the mug to his mouth. He drank and then coughed bits of foam and phlegm on the lass's chest. She didn't bother to wipe it off.

Dewey had to turn away. These lasses needed music and laughter, animals and children. Dewey spent his life encouraging the guests of his inn to partake of decadence but couldn't understand why humans indulged to the point of depravity. He felt an urge to walk over and tell the serving-lasses how much better their lives could be. He wanted to hire them, take them away, and give them hope—he credited each of these charitable urges to the curse. He was halfway out of his chair when he saw Daefer, the faer hunter, sitting behind Blechk. Dewey downed the strong ale.

A Volunteer walked through the door. Dewey looked up at the face of the Bastard Vaence. He wore the uniform well, better than Dewey would have guessed. A sword gleamed at his side, its simple pommel and grip as nicely polished as his boots. He clicked his heels together and offered a tightly rolled scroll to Blechk.

Blechk pulled his head from the back of the chair and reached for it. His lieutenant, Haery, held up a lamp. Blechk fumbled with the scroll. Vaence caught it. Blechk managed to break the seal.

With the lamp held high, Dewey could see Blechk's eyes, gray orbs with long, narrow, rectangular pupils, no color, not even bloodshot. As he read, his rectangular goateyes grew wider and for an instant coalesced into circles. Blechk tried to stand. Vaence and the lasses struggled to hold him up. Daefer rose from his seat, went to the bar, and returned with two pitchers of what passed for water in this hellhole.

Daefer held up the pitchers. Vaence took the scroll away from Blechk. Daefer dumped water over Blechk's head. The serving-lasses jumped aside. Blechk shook like a wet dog and leaned against the table, his arms bracing him. He took the scroll, set it on the table, and read it once more.

He screamed at Haery and Vaence and pushed the young serving-lass to the floor, and ranted against the resistance, even mentioning Dewey by name. Everything he said was punctuated with that bleating sound, between hits on the pipe. He caught a breath of actual air and ordered Vaence to deliver orders to prepare *Faerbane* to sail.

Vaence saluted and turned to the door.

It was time to place a bet.

Dewey lifted his otter-skin hat.

Vaence's eyes widened in recognition.

Dewey pulled the hat back over his ears. He understood the thrill that gamblers feel when they lay it all on the line, but he didn't experience it. Dewey preferred to fix games rather than gamble. Everything rode on the value of that fifth card: his life, the Queen's life, the lives of everyone at The Gold Piece Inn, and, the way Lukas was going, the well-being of everyone in Glandaeff, both faer and human.

"You were thar, weren't ya?" Dewey said in his best fisher accent. "When the dragons attacked the faer. I seen ya, din't I?" He winked at Vaence.

Vaence looked confused. "But Dew—"

"Never seen nothing like it—oh, the faer got what they had coming that day, they did." Dewey looked back at Blechk. They had his attention. "That man right thar, the Major done it."

Blechk yelled, "Wait!" The first sound with no hint of a bleat. "Mate Vaence, wait for me."

Then, to Dewey, Blechk said, "I brought thunder that day. Today, I'll bring fury."

Dewey thought to himself, and I'll bring faeries.

Barnaey had the serving-lasses pour more water over Blechk's head, but he still couldn't keep his balance. Dewey wondered how a man could eat enough of the compost served at the Crab and Anchor to add an extra fifty pounds to his belly.

Vaence and Daefer helped Blechk walk and Haery held the gate open. When they passed, Vaence still looked confused.

Dewey yelled, "Unleash the dragons." And then whispered, "Do not get on that ship." He hoped Vaence heard and understood.

"That's right," Blechk yelled. "Unleash the dragons!"

77.

Dewey stood on the dock where he could see both Faer Reef and the harbor. The reef had changed without enough maer to tend it, and the dock had decayed without Pier Faeries to prevent fungus from eating it away. Dead kelp and logs accumulated in tide pools. Flies harassed a family of elephant seals who barked and whined. The smell of rot was new to Crescent Cove.

He saw Blechk step out on the pier wearing his black uniform with the red sash. It took three Volunteers to help him into a tender.

Dewey worried. If dragons flew today, could he live with the destruction of Faer Reef on his hands? He shuddered at how the curse would torture him. The knots in his shoulders tightened, and he tried to convince himself that it was just a bet. A gambler who can't lose shouldn't play. He tried to shrug it off, but his shoulders wouldn't cooperate.

Major Blechk's red and black tender rowed through the swells to *Faerbane*. Dewey waited. Rumors of dragonfire, dragonicide, and dragonthunder came from the lips of dockworkers, merchants, and pirates. The marketplace cleared. People clustered along the dock, on the pier, and around Dewey where the river emptied into the sea. Others headed for the hills. Fishers and whalers sought the relative safety of the sea.

The sun slipped behind a cloud. Dewey watched the reef. Waves rolled in and splashed against the rocks. A dozen GloFaeries, the smallest swarm he'd ever seen, formed a small brushstroke of purple, gold, and green. Dewey's belly cramped up.

He watched the reef and the gaelleon and then the gaelleon and the reef.

Faerbane finally raised her topsails and caught the wind. She sailed into position at the pace of an anchovy. Its port side faced Faer Reef; the name "Liberty Shoals" appeared on new maps, but Dewey had never heard anyone say it. The sound of chains and the groan of wood reached across the water. Those eight windows opened in sequence with military precision from bow to stern. Sunlight glinted from shiny black cylinders, the dragons' lairs.

Sweat dripped down Dewey's taught back. From neck to temples, his head pounded with each beat of his heart. Never had doubt so consumed him.

Major Blechk stood on deck above the dragons with his sword held over his head. He lowered it.

Sparks blew out of each lair.

Dewey's heart sank.

But they looked different. On the Day of Dragons, the dragons had flown on great streams of fire that soared across the harbor. This time, the flames blasted in every direction. The dragons roared, but none flew from the ship to the reef. Screaming followed the sound of thunder. Dewey watched the reef, but nothing interrupted the rhythm of the waves. The elephant seals looked at the ship for a second and returned to their naps. A single maerbutler surfaced. A long scar ran from his forehead to his chin. His eyes fixed on the gaelleon, his tail taut and ready to carry him upstream.

Dewey looked back at the ship. Smoke billowed from each of the eight windows and flames danced in the dragon lairs. He waited. So close. The smoke rose in the sky. When it matched the height of the bluffs, it met the ocean breeze and blew inland. He saw the first flames climb up the mainmast.

And then Dewey saw what he'd been hoping for. His shoulders relaxed and the pit of his stomach uncoiled.

Faeries.

Millions of faeries, their wings flashing sunlight, separating from the smoke in a great swarm of color, like a rainbow whose colors rearranged themselves in time to the waves washing the reef. A school of dolphins leapt out of the water, singing.

He turned and headed back to The Gold Piece Inn. Now the serious work could begin.

Lukas

78.

Lukas responded to the destruction of his dragons as Dewey predicted he would.

On The Day of the Dragons, swarms of faeries flew from Faer Reef to *Faerbane* and attacked the maekhanical with the maegical. Faery breath turned the explosive powders of the dragons' breath to dust. They corroded the ironworks that directed the dragons' flight, frayed fuses, chipped flint to splinters, sprouted fungus to consume the carpentry and infected the dragons themselves with tiny cracks, flaws that clipped their wings and made them shatter in their lairs. The sense of faer play required that none of these impairments be made visible to humans. Instead, when the Volunteers tried to unleash their dragon thunder, they encountered some bad luck.

79.

Dewey evacuated the leprechauns and elfs from The Gold Piece Inn. The tiny faeries laid low. There could be nothing incriminating to disrupt Daffy's plan.

Lapidae remained. She had a special job.

With his cannons destroyed by an incompetent officer, Lukas had to respond in person. Everyone waited, looking over their shoulders, pausing before entering buildings. Only a few knew what they waited for, but everyone felt the tension. It had been five days.

Daffy rehearsed with Ninja Faeries. She role-played with Loretta and Faernando to polish her skills and peasant accent. Loretta taught her dozens of ways to either stiffen a man's ardor or slacken it. Lylli leached her hair of color and cut it short. Lapidae made a mold of her right hand with muddy clay.

Daffy wondered if she'd need any of it, but the practice and preparation gave her something to do other than wait and worry.

Dewey found out first. Major Blechk would receive no warning.

80.

A seagull floated down to the beach. Thousands of them that argued over the dregs of food cast aside by the knights, pirates, and faer, but this one cried three times. Then three times again. Kaetie noticed it on the second series and had the scroll unwound from its leg before a third.

The last message they'd received had caused a celebration: Daffy lived. No one would celebrate this message.

Kaetie ran up the bluff, calling the others to follow. She slowed at a rocky crag that formed a huge, looming, natural lean-to. Quercus lived here.

Caeph and Macae stopped when they saw the huge hoof prints. Caeph said, "I'm not going near that thing." Macae grinned at Kaetie and said, "Will it kill you for evil thoughts?"

Sometimes, the attraction she felt to him confounded her.

Naelth, "I'll check." Aennie, "Naelth hasn't gotten any in a while." Raenny, "I'm not sure I trust the judgement of a horse, maegical or not."

Kaetie and Naelth circled the granite enclosure and found Rustin seated on a boulder. Kaetie glimpsed Quercus but only for a second. Rustin stood, looked into the shadows, and spoke softly in Naest.

Kaetie held up the scroll. "News from home."

"What's up?" Rustin said.

Kaetie walked back to the clearing where the others waited. Raenny sat on a low branch and Macae stood next to him. Aennie and Viviaen sat on a fallen log. Caeph stood with one foot on the log; if he'd had boots instead of bare feet, he might have achieved the dashing stance he sought.

"It's from Dewey. He says that Lukas is coming," Kaetie said. "Doesn't say when but soon, days, hours, not weeks." The others clamored with questions. She handed the scroll to Rustin. The others went quiet, except for Macae and Caeph who laughed at a joke regarding Lukas's manhood.

"He says that no more ships are coming until Lukas leaves. We have to hide the faer and we have to conceal ourselves." He handed the message back to Kaetie.

Caeph asked, "For how long?" Raenny, "That's vague, even for Dewey."

"It says enough," Rustin said. "The farqin usurper is coming. Lukas, The First Human of Maythea," he spit out Lukas's official title, "and he won't come alone."

Macae whispered something that brought giggles to the lads. Aennie and Viviaen moved closer to Kaetie.

"We can't match up with his elite guards—you listening, Caeph?" He then detailed a strategy for embedding themselves with the elfs, hiding in the dense forest on the other side of The Fist of God. He assigned each one an elfin family to sidle with and described a place for them to meet up each day.

Kaetie reread the message. Below Dewey's heavy scrawl, Lylli's tidy hand instructed Kaetie to release the Redwood Faeries from performing the illusion that had kept Volunteers from finding the Great Beach. After releasing the faeries, Kaetie was to take refuge in Sempervaereen's canopy.

Neither Dewey nor Lylli came out and said it, but Kaetie understood that the resistance was coming to its end. All she saw in that note was surrender. She watched her brother organize the knights—and they really were knights. With the help of their Weapon Faeries, pirates, and elfs, these six people she'd known since birth were no joke—despite their infantile attempts at humor.

Viviaen said, "I'm going home. I don't care. I can't stand another night sleeping in sand or dirt. I'm sorry, but I don't like elfs. I'm sick of eating fish and berries—I'd kill for a whale steak or goat sausage—and I want a beer."

The others rumbled agreement about beer.

"Take care of yourself," Rustin said, "and we'll see you soon. Hug everyone for us."

Kaetie called Rustin over and said, "You might have something here, but you need to study history. If you don't understand how you fit in the moment, you'll make the same old mistakes and fail. You're too naïve!"

"If I stand accused of being an idealist, I can live with it."

"Or die because of it—seriously, Rustin, what have you learned from Quercus?"

Rustin's eyes went wide, and he whistled. "He's over five thousand years old. He knew King Graeglory and was the first elf to make peace with humanity. He was there!"

"I know. I read his book. Did he teach you about Thaergists, Aempressifs, and Elementalists?"

"He's an elf, they don't talk much, but you know what he said?" Kaetie heard the boy in his voice. "He said—wait, let me try to quote him—he said, 'I see something in you, something that I've only seen in one other human.' And you know who it was? Graeglory. He said that I reminded him of King Graeglory."

"So, Rusty, you found an ancient elf who won't teach you history but will inflate your ego enough to get you killed before you turn seventeen."

"No, he—"

"Rustin, Quercus doesn't know how the words of a wise old elf affect a sixteen-year-old boy. He meant that you have leadership qualities, that people want to be with you, want to follow you. But that might just mean that you're a tall man with a deep voice.

You've heard the ballads. Graeglory was tall, with dark hair, blue eyes, and a voice 'that commanded others.' You've got that, but, Rustin—*listen* to me—that's not enough. To accomplish anything, you need to understand where we are in history, in the narratives of both faer and beast."

"He said that you remind him of Queen Graegloria, too."

"And without context, I don't what it means." The light faded from Rustin's eyes. Kaetie wondered if it was pointless to encourage him to study anything other than his scroll. The frustration built in her voice. "Graegloria was famous for her short temper, maybe that's it, or maybe she appreciated irony and sarcasm—that's a lot different from saying that I might be the type of leader who could help disparate peoples overcome their differences."

"Kaetie," he said, "you're right. I need your help."

"Me? No. No way. I'm not a knight. I'm going to live in a cottage with a giant kitchen and a great cauldron, a crystal ball, and hundreds and hundreds of books and scrolls. I'm going to—"

"What about Naelth and Raenny? They'd gobble up anything you could teach them."

"No, they need to study with Sempervaereen," Kaetie said. "Lylli told me to take refuge from Lukas and his thugs with Sempervaereen. I'll take Macae with me, She'll teach him."

81.

A raven flew down and perched on the giant wooden coin that spun in the lazy summer wind over the entrance to The Gold Piece Inn. Dewey ran outside and the bird dropped close enough to tease him but laughed and flew over the building.

He followed it, and Daffy followed him all the way to the aviary. They found Tifenae offering the raven a piece of walnut. When it had a mouthful, the bird lifted its leg. Tifenae removed the tiny scroll and handed it to Dewey.

Dewey read it, scratched an ear, and read it again. "Tomorrow," he said, "Lukas comes tomorrow, and he's bringing Maedegan." He handed the note to Daffy.

The message also said that Taevius was a corporal in Lukas's elite guard. A chill ran up Daffy's spine. Taevius knew everything. Was he just another strategically positioned Bastard in Dewey's network? Or had Rustin's betrayal turned him?

And what if Maedegan recognized her?

Daffy had never trusted him, but King Gledig had prized him as a sounding board. Gledig always valued the council of intelligent people who disagreed with him and thought they'd had mutual respect. Maedegan came to court every week for years, and he'd been there the night that Lukas had driven them from their home, Glomaythea Castle. A seemingly generous man, Daffy saw through him. Maedegan's definition of good and evil depended on what benefited him, and all the better if he could impose a touch of cruelty on others. She hadn't been surprised that he was Lukas's right-hand man.

82.

Kaetie led Macae along a deer path. He pointed to a shady spot blanketed in soft redwood needles. "There's a good spot," he said.

"You're tired already?" Kaetie put a hand on Macae's forehead. He had a goofy grin but might be a little clammy.

"Rest? Well, maybe, but you know, we don't get much time alone." He raised and lowered his eyebrows. She wondered if he would start drooling.

"That's a great idea, Mac, let's make out under a tree right next to the path that runs from Crescent Cove to the Great Beach. The Volunteers will never expect us to be that stupid."

She walked ahead.

The trail straightened out over god's ring finger and led into the valley.

Macae said, "We'll be up in a tree?"

"Sempervaereen's canopy."

"Comfortable up there?"

"Amazing. Cool, sweet water, shade, sun—"

"Enough room to lean back and relax? No one around?"

"On a clear day you can see the Aelpine Ridge—"

"As comfortable as that little mattress of redwood needles we passed back there but more private?"

"You realize that we're being hunted by Lukas's elite guard, don't you? Or does lust override both your sense of propriety and self-preservation?"

He whined like a spurned puppy but kept following.

She stopped most of the way up the middle finger where Sempervaereen towered over the land.

"Here she is," Kaetie said.

Wind blew through the giant redwood's branches, ruffling her needles and faeries into song, music so soft that it lulled Kaetie into a state of bliss.

Macae faced her, goofy grin in place. Now it seemed cute. She tugged his shoulders so he faced Sempervaereen. "Can you hear it?"

He looked around and said, "What?"

"Sempervaereen's song."

He closed eyes and concentrated. "No."

Kaetie didn't know what to say, so she leaned over and kissed him. He wrapped his arms around her and pulled her close. "We're still on the trail, Mr. Horny."

He stepped back, looked up at Sempervaereen. "How do we get up there?"

Kaetie hummed along with Sempervaereen's song and started twirling around. As she spun about, she lowered herself to the ground. Redwood Faeries flew from every branch into a swarm that circled them. She took Macae's hand and led him into the tree's shade. The thick, fibrous bark formed a wall in front of them. From here, the song sounded like a children's chorus.

Kaetie watched Macae react to the Redwood Nymphs that now surrounded them. His surprise gave her as much delight as she saw in him. She put her hands on his chest and pushed. She fell with him into the hammock formed by the swarm of Redwood Faeries.

She held him close, and the faeries raised them up between branches, ever higher, to Sempervaereen's canopy.

Kaetie's blanket and the clothes she'd left here had been folded and set on a dry branch. Macae investigated the bowl formed of woven branches and fungus. Kaetie felt Sempervaereen's touch and understood. Sempervaereen always had time for pleasure.

Kaetie relaxed on a mossy branch. Macae settled next to her, and she rolled onto her side, her nose inches from his. She said, "Now, what was it you wanted to discuss?"

Macae made several interesting sounds of approval, took her hands, and waited for her.

Kaetie caught sight of two nymphs in lingerie egging her on. She felt more than heard Sempervaereen suggest that she enjoy her youth and accept the comfort that Macae offered.

They had been making out for nearly an hour when sounds below reminded them of the world outside their embrace. Kaetie's clothes were in disarray and, but for one remnant of modesty, Macae's crumpled in a corner.

"You, up in the tree."

Macae sat up and searched for an opening in the branches. Kaetie sorted her clothes and sang two notes. The breeze blew an opening.

Ten Volunteers had gathered below.

"Time to come down." The man wore heavy chainmail instead of the red and black leather, had thick arms and stout, heavy legs, the body of someone who might carry cattle across his shoulders.

Instead of the standard-issue Volunteer sword, a heavy shaft connected by a chain to a spiked, foot-wide iron ball was attached to his belt.

"A flail?" Macae whispered. "Gnarly."

"Sempervaereen will protect us."

A tall, thin, barefoot man with a knit cap approached the trunk. Faeries flew out of his way. Kaetie didn't see any nymphs go near him. He touched the trunk and went back to the man in chainmail.

Macae whispered, "See the guy talking to the blowhard? That's Daefer, the halfling traitor."

"I see him." Kaetie's stomach tightened. The light-hearted song of pleasure transformed into the low-pitched sound of tree branches grinding against each other in the face of a storm, but there was barely a breeze. "The faer hunter who identified Conifaer."

Macae said, "He just identified Sempervaereen."

83.

How could Daffy sleep? Everything, truly everything, depended on her performance. Daffy lingered over that word: performance. She'd trained and practiced but had no experience at what she would attempt. Her adversary, on the other hand, played this game every day. Dewey had a web of connections, but Lukas's web wove further. Were they setting a trap or walking into one? By sunrise, she didn't care. She just needed to get it over with.

Loretta and Lylli curled her hair and added color to her eyes and lips. She put on skirts instead of her usual breeches, and Loretta tied the left edge at her hip, it gave her the same freedom of movement as her breeches and led the eye up her leg to the curve of her thigh. Loretta had her try on a small tight bodice. She tsked at it and fetched Faernando. Faernando whispered in Loretta's ear and they shared a laugh. They removed the bodice but left the nearly sheer white chemise beneath it.

The two of them walked around Daffy. Loretta didn't appear pleased. "No cleavage at all?" she said. "Not that the bodice gave her any, but without it he might think she's a boy."

Faernando said, "On a foggy day? I don't think so."

Loretta laughed, but Daffy didn't know why.

Loretta walked her to the cold-granite windowpane and tossed a shiny grain of quartz at it. The Glass Faery leaned out of the pane and caught it. Loretta said, "A few seconds of reflection?" The faery shrugged, popped the quartz into a tiny pouch, and the windowpane became a mirror.

Daffy stepped back. The woman she saw on the other side of the glass had suntanned skin with no royal pallor, her eyes looked bigger and perhaps even more innocent than the self she had known. She cocked her head and appreciated what she saw, a more complete if simple beauty than she'd had as queen. Her shoulders and legs looked strong and feminine, a woman who moved with the economy of someone accustomed to carrying heavy burdens, children on her hips, and tools in her hands.

She hugged Loretta, and they ate breakfast with the rest of the staff. Everyone worried over their own concerns. A few people said she looked nice, but no one seemed to notice her transformation or perspiration. She put on her long apron and tied it behind her neck. Loretta looked her over and pursed her lips. She said, "Take it off," and handed her a serving-lad apron, which covered her from the waist down. Daffy did her chores and then the lunch crowd started arriving. She managed not to spill any mugs, managed to smile and exchange small talk, correct children's behavior, and, most important of all, appear calm.

No one could have imagined that she was the black widow at the center of a web woven for Lukas. The only question was how long she could keep her cool.

She spilled a mug when the band played the ballad of the girl goatherd who grew tired of the darkness of night and decided to do something about it. She seduced the sun, and it has risen every day since. A Bastard named Billae stuttered apologies for getting in her way and used straw to soak up the spilled ale. Assuring Billae that he was doing good work distracted her, and Billae described how he'd spun the wool that composed Daffy's apron.

Dewey sat in his chair between the window and the fireplace with the hot seat pulled close. Fog swirled up from the harbor and cooled the saloon.

Daffy delivered mugs to a table of whalers. The way they looked at her caught her attention. She noticed Fin staring at her with a huge grin, but his eyes didn't focus above her neck. Daffy looked down and, for an instant, the tension evaporated. She pointed across the room at Loretta and yelled, "You scurvy wench!"

Loretta yelled back, "You got nothin' to work with," she squeezed her breasts together, "but we make do."

Daffy flicked Fin's forehead. "Don't get no ideas, whaler."

"You could put an eye out with those."

"Don't tempt me."

And then Daffy saw another Bastard rush in, Jaemie. She sat at the hot seat, leaned forward, and spoke to Dewey. She scratched a nanny goat behind the ears with one hand and pulled a tick from the bloodhound with the other and then rushed back out.

Daffy collected empty mugs from tables and took them to the bar. Bob refilled them. She wrapped her arms around them, twenty-seven, her previous record was twenty-four. She went to a table near the casino entrance first, figured that if she were going to spill, better to spill on pirates who wouldn't consider it impolite. Bending at the knees, she unlocked her fingers, and four mugs settled on the table with nary a drop overboard.

Another Bastard, Rachael, delivered a message to Dewey and then rushed back out. Dewey scanned the room. His eyes stopped on her. His face was blank. She bumped into a chair and caught herself without spilling.

Dewey moved toward her.

She delivered ale to the whalers. This time Spaerm complained that the mugs were blocking his view. She jostled herself in such a way that a tidy spray of ale landed in his lap. When she rose, Dewey was next to her. If balancing the mugs hadn't occupied her attention, his obvious fear might have freaked her out. Instead, she concentrated on her job. All she had to do tonight was be a convincing serving-lass, plus one simple action.

"Dewey," She said, "I've got to get these mugs to our thirsty guests. You can wait."

He followed without speaking.

Grindaer the miller came inside. "The usurper is here!"

Seconds later, Baertha came in. Baertha had no knowledge of their plans. She said, "Lukas sailed in on *Humanity*, went straight to the Crab and Anchor and killed Blechk in a five second duel."

Daffy went to a table of new guests to take their order. Anything to get the vision of a dagger against her throat out of her mind. Dewey stayed close.

A stevedore ran in and yelled, "Major Blechk is dead!" The guests cheered.

The band broke into a raucous tune about the death of a wicked witch. Lylli danced a jig. The celebratory air of the saloon continued for hours. The stress accumulated on Daffy.

When she passed Dewey on her way to the kitchen, he whispered, "The usurper might not come tonight, maybe not tomorrow night, but he will come."

She delivered more meals and more drinks, trying not to watch the entrance. When she set a pitcher of wine and three goblets at a table of merchants, the room went silent. She didn't need to look up to know who had come in.

84.

Crisiant played a special guitar. To say it was enchanted underestimated the amount of work he'd put into it. The band played songs to keep Dafina's spirits up, legends of Queen Graegloria The Uniter interspersed with bawdy tunes. From the stage, Crisiant had a clear view out to the street. When he saw them coming, he improvised a riff by picking notes up the neck where his little protégés hid within the tuning knobs. Dream Faeries were moody, temperamental creatures who didn't appreciate company. He plucked one for every Volunteer.

They flew on mosquito wings and lacked the good looks of so many other faer, though they weren't nearly as repulsive as the Farq Faeries who waited in the hollow of the special guitar. Each one buzzed to its target. Most slipped into the ear cavities of their hosts, a few lingered on the Volunteers' heads, unable to resist that favorite faery pastime, tangling hair.

Crisiant had thought about cursing Lukas, of course, but couldn't find a Curse Faery that would go near him. Something about Lukas repelled the faer. Crisiant had often wondered if their mutual repulsion—it bordered on allergy—explained Lukas's irrational faer-phobia. The Dream Faery that Crisiant targeted for Lukas came up short and tried to veer around him. Lukas slapped it against his cheek. He pulled his hand away and looked at the dead faery.

An instant of panic drove Crisiant to mis-finger a chord, but just one. He knew that the remains of dead Dream Faeries could only be distinguished from crushed mosquitoes with careful examination. Lukas brushed the corpse from his hand, and it fell. Crisiant dared not target another. The game would end badly if Lukas suspected enchantment.

85.

Macae and Kaetie looked down from Sempervaereen's canopy.

The soldier in chainmail yelled, "You have to come down eventually, and we'll be here to collect you." But then he and eight of his troops walked downhill and out of sight. He left two tough-looking veterans behind. A woman with a crossbow who looked like she could wind it tight enough to send a bolt through granite, and a sinewy man with a bow over his shoulder.

"Don't worry about them," Macae said. He tapped the hilt of his cutlass and a little fellow with glasses and buzz-cut hair wearing a suit and tie and spiked shoes popped out of the weapon—Macae's Weapon Faery. The little coach watched the Volunteers follow the trail down The Fist of God and said, "If you can accept losing, you can't win," and melted back into the sword.

The mood was gone, at least for Kaetie. "Could you just keep your hands to yourself for an entire minute?"

"But they're gone." He huffed.

"Sempervaereen has been here through all of recorded history." Kaetie said. She turned and set her hands against his chest. "Please listen to her. For me?"

"Listen to a tree?"

"You'll see what—" She heard a wagon and hoofbeats and saw the Volunteers coming back up the trail. The big man in the chainmail drove a horse-drawn flatbed that carried a huge geared maechine and a shiny metal tube.

Macae said, "We should have gone down when they left. I could have taken those two Volunteers."

"Sempervaereen has lived through worse than a few Volunteers and a halfling." She pointed at a tuft of yellow flowers. "Sit on the mustard and let her tell you about our world. Macae, I need you to care. Please care."

"Uh oh," Macae said.

Kaetie looked back down. The Volunteers had unwound the shiny metal tube into a long ribbon with sharp serrated saw-teeth lining one side. The wide man unhitched the flatbed and held the horse. A Volunteer assembled a platform several steps from Sempervaereen. They set the blade against Sempervaereen's trunk, maneuvered the horse onto the platform, and chained the horse to the maechine.

Kaetie started humming. Her nerves wouldn't let her reach the notes she needed to commune with Sempervaereen. A nymph flew up and hovered in front of her on lacy wings. Another settled next to her. One perched on her shoulder and rubbed her neck. More flew up and caressed her back. Her heartrate finally slowed enough for her to make sense of Sempervaereen. Kaetie queried the tree about safety and solidity and posed a question of how the great dryads had dealt with lumberjacks in the past.

The response shocked her. At first, she thought the sound was part of the answer. In a way it was. Below her, the horse walked on the platform, but didn't go anywhere, just walked in place. As the horse walked, the blade ripped into the great redwood fibers of Sempervaereen's trunk.

Sempervaereen lulled Kaetie and Macae into a trance. She started with the story of a fine hundred-year-old oak dryad who gave his all to provide warmth in both shelter and fuel. Cast to the wind as smoke and ash, he lives on in other trees, plants, and the ancestors of the people who sacrificed him. She described the death of a great, but diseased dryad, who starved himself to save the lives of a forest. And, finally, she told the tale of an ancient dryad who had lived a bit farther up The Fist of God and was poached for the maegic that a foolish man believed could be extracted from his wood. Every story ended with what became of the wood left behind. She concluded with "... you think the faer immortal, but we still die. Everything dies eventually."

Kaetie's brain stopped. Objections accumulated, outrage piled up, she tried to say too many things at once and nothing came out, neither by voice nor through the song of the Tree Faery.

Sempervaereen jostled her canopy in such a way as to muffle the sounds from below and form a more comfortable bed for Kaetie and Macae. She then said, "Now let me tell you the story of the Human Disease. Listen carefully because we have little time and it is perhaps the most important story that I must share. I'd been saving it for you, Kaetie, until—"

"While we still have time?!" Macae leaped up. "That's it? You're going to let them cut you down?"

"—the breadth of the symptoms of this disease so you would understand the importance of treating the symptoms, for it cannot be cured. It is only through Maentanglement that—"

Kaetie interrupted this time. All her objections tried to come out at once, and she stuttered. Sempervaereen waited for her and she finally chose what felt like the most important one, "Please don't let your story end now."

"Kaetie, my story is long, and I know that you won't let it end here."

"Do something!" Macae said. "Drop a log on the horse, anything to hold them off long enough for us to get a message to the knights. We can save you."

"Please, defend yourself, please!" Kaetie said. She tightened her grip on a branch as though she could wring sense into the ancient tree. "Use your branches like clubs. Wrap a root around them like a snake—stop them!"

She felt the tree's mirth, redwood needles dancing on a breeze. "I'm a tree. It would take years to grow such a root. And then what? Kill another being? Intentionally?" Sempervaereen's branches shook with the absurdity of the thought. "What if I were to gather all of my faery and nymph friends and we fought as you suggest? Then what? If we did that once, surely a time would come that would require that we do it again, and then we'd be no better than beasts." The shaking slowed to a stop and her limbs were peaceful again. The sounds of waves made their way to the canopy along with the cry of the saw as it dug into her. "No, better I die in peace than live with war."

Kaetie understood but couldn't help saying, "Please don't give up."

"Kaetie, you know better." A gust of wind blew up from Crescent Cove and shook the shroud above the canopy. Drops of dew fell on Kaetie and Macae and they felt quite small. Sempervaereen used that breath to sing, "There will come a day when a great leader will be forced to choose between fighting a war of total destruction or submitting to a peace of utter capitulation but will find another way."

86.

Lukas stepped into the saloon and took off his standard issue black felt bicorne hat. He wore a red waistcoat with polished brass buttons, white breeches, and black boots. An extra-long saber hung from his belt; Dewey saw the wear on the grip and a smudge of blood at the top of the scabbard. A long line of Volunteers stood at attention behind him. He had perhaps the warmest smile Dewey had ever seen. He carried himself with the power and authority of a king, but there was more to him than that. Dewey's reports told of a man who could raise other people's self-esteem with one word, destroy it with the next, and leave them begging for more.

Dewey looked away, trying to convince himself that he wasn't intimidated. He resisted the temptation to check that his hat covered his ears.

Lukas said, "Good evening, Dewey."

Dewey nearly swallowed his tongue. It shouldn't have come as a surprise. It was no secret that The Gold Piece Inn had a halfling innkeeper. A rush of human panic coursed through his halfling arteries.

"Fine crowd tonight," Lukas said and put his hat on the rack. "But are they always this quiet?"

Dewey's elfin blood finally caught up with his human blood. That or he fell for Lukas's seductive charm. In any case, he rose from his chair and pulled his hat from his head. When it passed over his sharp ears, he wondered how long he had to live. He held out his hand, welcoming Lukas, and said, "Quiet? No, just offering a bit of respect for the guvnor."

Lukas met his eyes and shook his hand. Dewey knew better, but still felt certain the man wanted to be his friend.

"Are my troops welcome?"

Dewey said, "if they have money."

Lukas laughed and about half of the Volunteers filed in. They didn't march, and they didn't maintain any formation, until they positioned themselves along every wall, in the kitchen, Dewey's office, and on each side of every doorway, perfectly spaced. They blocked every exit, and those outside probably surrounded the inn. The message was obvious. No one would leave and no one would enter.

Dewey saw Jaenet, the Gold Piece Inn Bastard who had left to find her fortune a decade before. She stood between the casino and saloon. He tried to get her attention without drawing anyone else's. She acted for all the world as if she'd never been here. She'd sent the messages over a year ago that had alerted him to Lukas's plans, but he hadn't heard from her since. If anyone could have turned her loyalties, it was Lukas. He'd lost the loyalty of Bastards before, and it drove him crazy. She'd grown up here. He'd fed, clothed, and sheltered her.

Dewey considered announcing Lukas as The Liberator, or The First Human, or even The Illegitimate Usurper. Lukas's smile conveyed goodwill for everyone—up to an ill-defined point. Oh yes, there was cruelty in that smile but hidden behind his playful mask.

Dewey said, "Can I buy a round of ale for the Volunteers?"

"A fine thought," Lukas said, "but they aren't big drinkers."

"You should see them when you're not around."

Lukas laughed and allowed Loretta to guide him to a table that had not been vacant seconds ago.

Dewey motioned to the bar and Faernando brought a goblet of brandy to his chair by the window. He quaffed it before his rump touched the seat. He looked around The Gold Piece Inn and wondered if it was the last time he ever would.

87.

Lukas was still the most beautiful man Daffy had ever seen. Gledig had the rustic good looks that, for her, described handsome, but Lukas was gorgeous and smooth, too smooth to trust. He leaned back, put a leg up on another stool, watched the band, and bopped to the music.

Loretta caught Daffy's eyes from the bar. She nodded in a way that said, "You're on."

Daffy checked her other tables. People peered in Lukas's direction, but no one stared. Except Baertha.

Daffy stutter-stepped, tried to tamp down memories of that night: the sound of Gledig's sword coming out of the scabbard, the door crashing to the ground, Lukas with the Volunteers behind him. Gledig jabbed his sword at Lukas, but instead of countering, Lukas had retreated with his eyes locked on her. And she had run away. How had she denied that look of recognition all these months?

She stumbled over a goat, caught herself, and continued to the bar. She set down four empty mugs.

He wouldn't recognize her tonight. She'd barely recognized her own reflection, and he'd only seen her that one time, over a year ago and, before that, well, she'd been a child then.

Bob nudged the full mugs against her arm. He whispered, "Maybe you shouldn't stare at him."

"Starin' at that? I think not." She laughed, and it sounded genuine to her, though Bob didn't look convinced.

She passed Lukas and set the mugs at the whalers' table. This time Fin and Spaerm kept their eyes on the stage. She sauntered to Lukas's table and leaned down, just as Loretta had taught her, and said, "What can I getcha, sir?"

When his eyes met hers, his lips parted in that perfect smile, rising just higher on the left than on the right, the imperfection that set off his good looks.

Did he recognize her? For a second, she was certain, but he gave no sign. Nothing, not a second look, nothing. And if he recognized her, surely, he'd arrest her or kill her or—Loretta walked by. Her bodice was tight and low and bouncing with bosom. Lukas tracked her every jiggle. He nearly fell off his stool.

Daffy said, "If you'd rather she served ya, fine by me."

"What's that?" He caught himself and settled back in the chair.

No, she concluded, he didn't recognize her. He was just another lusty soldier. "Ya hungry, too? Maybe for some food? Ya want a drink? I have other customers, ya know."

"Yes, I am hungry. You see, I just sailed in from Maythea and haven't eaten all day, could you muster something?"

"Halibut stew tonight, I fear it's more stew than halibut—rationing, ya know—would ya have ale or a white wine?"

"I'm sure I'll be happy with whatever you recommend."

Daffy went to the kitchen and conveyed the order to Daeffid.

She hadn't expected Lukas to order food. She discarded the thought of poison as soon as it came. Amateurs shouldn't get fancy. She'd have to stick with the plan until it worked or failed.

Daeffid filled a bowl with stew, cut a slice of sourdough and dipped it in olive oil. She reviewed her brief interaction with Lukas and admitted to herself that he'd offended her. She'd stood next to him with her bare leg at his eye level, leaned over, and offered him a glimpse of her small but, damn it, perfectly shaped breasts. And what had he done? Gawked at Loretta's overwhelming cleavage and then ordered a meal. Now she laughed out loud. She was a genuine serving-lass all right.

She took the food and, as she walked out the kitchen door, made a slight alteration to her plan.

She walked to Lukas's other side, denying him a view of her bare leg. When she set the bowl down, she bent at the knee instead of leaning ove, said nothing, stood, and went to the bar. The fish stew called for white wine, so she had Bob pour their cheapest ale in a small mug.

A certain delicious ire welled up. She brought the little mug of swill, set it down hard enough that specks of foam splattered on his waistcoat, and moved on to another table. She fetched Baeswax and Grindaer tall mugs of fine frothy ale and let her skirt brush against Lukas when she passed. His smile had disappeared. When she passed again, he no longer bopped to the music.

He said, "May I please have more ale?"

"Whatsat?"

"Have I offended you?"

She looked down at him.

His eyes were sheepish. It was hard for Daffy to imagine this gentleman murdering millions of faer, but she managed. She put her hands on her hips and took a breath, frustrated with a tiresome customer. She looked away from him and saw Loretta standing near Dewey. Loretta gave her a covert wink.

"Ya have, sir. A wee bit, yes, you have." She took his mug and went to the bar. Bob refilled it with the same watery beer, and she brought it back.

Lukas said, "I can make it up to you."

"Can you?"

He didn't reply, which surprised Daffy. To this point, she'd avoided looking directly at him since her first visit to his table. His left eyebrow was raised and playful.

"As ever," he said, "I am at your service."

She caught the twist in his voice. She said, "As ever?" but it came out too fast and she'd neglected to inflect her voice with the local accent.

"As," he said, "ever." His lips straightened but kept the playful twinkle in his eyes. "How can I make it up to you?"

"Don't know." This time she had the accent right.

"Can I buy you a drink?"

Back to the script. "A tipple might go some way in soothing me feelings."

"Please, sit. I'll fetch our drinks."

"Oh no, sir, if m' lord saw that I'd be on the street!" She took his mug to Bob and returned with two healthy mugs of fine hoppy brew.

She sat in the fashion of serving-lasses and lads invited to a guest's table, her bare leg pressed against his breeches and looked up through her lashes, another of Loretta's moves.

His gawked for just an instant before drinking.

She crossed her legs and the opening of her skirts fell aside so that both legs were exposed to the thigh.

The mug at his lips wavered and a few drops spilled down his chin.

Daffy said, "Do you have a name, sir?"

He said, "Lukas." But his eyes didn't leave her legs.

Daffy took her mug and raised it between them. She said, "Here's to you, Lukas, and a happy visit to Crescent Cove."

"You pretend not to know who I am?"

His choice of words might have thrown her, but she recognized his self-infatuation and knew to play him the way she would any other ego-driven aristocrat. "You just told me you're Lukas." She tossed aside her docile expression. "You come in with an army, everyone goes silent as if a king or a ghost walked in, and I can see that you're not a ghost but don't recall you being crowned, so I don't reckon you're a king either. I know who you are but am not sure what."

That threw him.

She held up her mug and continued, "But whatever you are, you're the cutest farqin man who's ever walked through those doors." She parted her lips with her tongue and repeated the trick with her eyelashes.

He pulled his eyes up to hers. On the way to eye level, they lingered where they were supposed to. He raised his mug to hers.

He said, "And you? Have you a name?"

"I do."

"Would you share it with a tired soldier?"

"No, I don't think I will."

"Well, here's to you, mystery lass."

He sipped his mug. She wanted to drain hers but remembered what happened last time. She rose slowly. He watched her leg straighten and kept watching as she collected his empty bowl and walked to another table to gather mugs.

Lukas pushed himself up, and with his eyes still glued to her limbs, turned, and walked toward the door. He left his mug nearly full—an action as unheard of as it was impolite at The Gold Piece Inn.

At the bar, Bob whispered to Daffy. "That one's getting away."

Daffy said, "Wanna bet?"

* * *

Dewey pretended to watch the band.

Lukas leaned down and said, "I would have that lass."

Dewey tried to look at him the way he would anyone who had

the decency to ask permission before inviting a serving-lass or lad upstairs. "A silver ohzee now, one in the morning, and—you quite like her, don't you?"

Lukas's eyes narrowed.

Dewey wondered if he'd gone too far but couldn't help himself in the face of profit. "At least two silvers to the lass, but something makes me think you'll give her a gold."

Lukas said, "I may well," and went back to his table.

Seconds later, Jaenet approached Dewey and handed him two silver ohzees. Looking at the coins, Dewey whispered, "Are you with us?" Jaenet gave no sign that she'd heard, that she knew him, or that she'd ever been here before. If Bob hadn't waved to her, Dewey might have thought he'd mistaken her. He couldn't remember her mother—was she an orphan? So many Bastards were born, grew up, and moved on. How did he remember them all? He couldn't remember how she ended up in the army and considered going to the book to look her up. Her eyes passed over him, and she returned to her post.

88.

Daffy returned to Lukas's table while he negotiated with Dewey. She pulled the seat out and crossed her legs. Lukas seemed fascinated by them.

Loretta passed behind and whispered, "You can still back out."

Daffy looked up and spoke in her full Crescent Cove accent, "Get off with you, lass, this one's mine." She didn't realize that Lukas was now close enough to hear.

He sat next to her and put his arm around her shoulders. "And you are mine, at least for tonight."

"We goin' upstairs?"

"I'd like that very much."

Daffy leaned against his arm and rested her head between his bicep and forearm.

He kissed her neck.

"Oh, that tickles just right." Daffy's physical response battled her emotional response. Could she do it? And if not, could she live with herself? And if she did, would she survive? But those were surface questions, and Daffy's sense of justice went far deeper.

She'd conceived this plan the day that the maer were murdered. From the start, it had been a suicide mission.

Lukas wrapped his other arm around her and pulled her against him. The shivers started cool on the back of her neck, warmed as they worked their way down, and were hot and moist by the time they made it down, around, and took refuge in her belly button. She said, "Ooooh," and Lukas cupped her chin and pulled her mouth against his. Beneath his hoppy breath, he tasted and smelled musky and healthy and strong, still the boy he'd been that day so many years ago. That one day of freedom, the one day she'd taken leave of her role.

Her body did its part, but could she bear the next step?

She stuttered and pushed far enough away to say, "Are we in a hurry?"

He said, "I have an empire to run in the morning."

"The sun has yet to set," she said. Fear and apprehension and dread collided in her heart. "I'd like one more drink."

"No."

She tried to stand but blood started to her head. Fainting would bring an end to the whole charade.

He stood and pulled her with him.

She grabbed his shoulders and hung on. Her consciousness dimmed. He held her by the waist, and her heart caught up to her brain. She let loose a breath. He placed a hand low on her back and pulled her waist against his. She hadn't felt a man against her in a long time. The words, "Oh my," launched out of her mouth unbidden.

That hand drifted south of her waist.

Her head rushed again. His other hand caressed the back of her neck and she got another shiver. Her mother's voice came to mind, "If you let them, they're all hands."

"Now." He moved toward the stairs. "Please come with me."

She clung to his muscle with her right hand and her left slid down to his waist and, across his pelvis. She said, "Oh my," again and felt stupid, naïve, and completely out of her depth.

"Nicely done," he said with that left eyebrow raised. "A good serving-lass needs to know when her guest is ready."

"And sir, you are ready." She managed a giggle and hoped that it sounded playful. She felt every eye in the room watch them head upstairs. Of all the things she'd worried about, embarrassment had never crossed her mind, but in that instant, Daffy worried more about what her mother would think than what she would be doing in the next ten minutes, or hour, or she didn't even know how long it might take. The King had never performed this act with brevity. Loretta had assured her that most men were more intent on the ultimate goal than the process. And then there was the entire question of whether an opportunity would present itself before the process began, during, after, or not at all. At least, for the moment, her embarrassment displaced her fear.

Three Wishes

89.

With each step up those red velvet stairs, Daffy felt another dose of foreboding. She was so caught up that she hadn't noticed Lukas ordering a force of Volunteers upstairs ahead of them. They lined the balustrade of the upstairs balcony. If she'd looked closely, she'd have noticed their dazed expressions and wilting eyelids.

Dream Faeries reassembled the random thoughts of bored people into scripts for the theater of dreams. If their hosts experienced even a few seconds of curiosity, it could undo their work. For instance, the Bastard Jaenet had been wondering what Dewey had up his sleeve. By watching every move of Lukas and Dewey, she frustrated her Dream Faery. But the little farqer kept weaving and re-weaving her thoughts, developing a variety of narratives to whisk her off to dreamland as soon as her concentration strayed. Eventually it would. Most of the Volunteers were already in dreamland.

Daffy clung to Lukas, not to play her role but to prevent herself from running away. Down in the saloon, Bob poured wine, Loretta flirted with pirates, the band played, and Lylli sang. Baertha looked straight back at her as though she didn't believe her eyes.

At the top of the stairs, Lukas said, "Do you have a favorite room?"

She pointed at the room directly over the kitchen. The passage behind the wall in this room had a ladder downstairs to an escape hatch that opened to the faery garden.

Lukas pulled her in the opposite direction. Three Volunteers went in.

"Security," Lukas said, watching the Volunteers search the

room. "But don't worry, as long I'm safe, you are, too." He looked down at Daffy and added, "I allow no surprises, walk into no traps, and have schemes for every possibility. *Every possibility.*"

Daffy's heartbeat was so fast that it rattled up to her throat. She could smell her own fear. She'd created a situation that she couldn't get through. Glomaythea, Nantesse, and the rest of the world would have to find another solution to the usurper. Simple as that. Dewey's fault. He should have known that a pampered princess didn't have the courage, much less the physical strength for this.

She felt her eyes water. Fighting back the tears, she saw herself: the crying lady. The First Princess. A woman who had never had a choice. Her father chose her husband, and her husband chose her life. She was nothing but a royal vessel.

The thought pissed her off.

She'd always been a confident woman, certain that she could play the roles that her father and husband assigned for her, roles that her mother had discouraged her from questioning. She'd faced many choices since the day that her children died at her feet, but instead of choosing, she'd let the wind of fear decide. It wasn't until she stood on that beach while her maer lovers were being murdered that she'd finally confronted her destiny and conceived this plan.

But failure still called to her, *just let it go, you're not made for this. You're not a princess or a queen, not anymore, you're just another serving-lass at an outlaw port. Your brightest future is to raise a Bastard or two of your own, right here at The Gold Piece Inn.*

The Volunteers stretched and yawned while they searched. It hadn't occurred to Daffy that they would discover the hidden passages. The wood grain of the openings and edges had all been matched by Conifaer, a woodweaver with hundreds of years of experience. Dewey had insisted that Lukas's prejudices made him doubt the faer's abilities. She still wondered if they'd find the weapon, though.

The weapon. She veered from failure back to fear.

The Volunteers left the room.

Lukas pulled Daffy in and shut the door behind her.

Loretta had been right, of course. Lukas was blind to her emotional turmoil. He pulled her into a tight embrace. She tilted her head back to catch her breath, and he licked her neck from throat to lips and then kissed her as though she might get away. He placed one hand down her back, lower and then still lower until he found what he was after and then his other hand worked its way down her side, pausing at strategic spots, all the way down to her hip, over the knot in her skirt and onto her bare thigh. His hands felt strong and warm, her leg even warmer.

She tried to relax into the sensations but went cold again. He pushed and pulled with no regard for her. Anger started pushing against fear, and anger has a way of focusing the mind.

She inhaled with moans just above a whisper and exhaled through opened lips as Loretta had taught her. It was when his hands were exploring her chest that she realized that he wasn't paying attention to her. Oh yes, he was consuming her, but as long as she made the right sounds and gripped him here and there, she could relax. Relaxing released her anger and fear made its way back in.

She had to try.

What was the worst that could happen? That answer jumped into her mind, so damn obvious that it pissed her off. Failure would be worse than death.

She sighed, and apparently it was a good time to sigh because Lukas responded with renewed vigor.

It would be worse than death to live out her life knowing that she'd had a chance to relieve the world of Lukas and everything he represented, and that she hadn't even tried. She might not be capable of completing this plan, rehearsed a hundred times or not, but she'd rather be dead than carry that burden. Death was okay. She was done. Ready. This man had killed everything she loved. She thought of Rustin and Kaetie and Loretta. She loved them, but for them to survive, Lukas couldn't.

With nothing to lose, fear lost its hold.

She groaned and writhed just a bit.

He stopped grabbing, probing, suckling, and so on, stepped away and removed his waistcoat and vest, and pulled his shirt over his head. One scar ran from his navel to his neck. Another formed a jagged ridge over his heart.

She stared with wide eyes, and mouth slightly ajar, a stance Loretta insisted would convey desire.

"Well?" he said.

Sitting up on the bed, Daffy pulled her chemise over her head. The air in the room was cool, but her skin was hot. He moved to her and, still standing, pulled her close. Loretta had suggested that this might happen, and she followed her instructions. Among other processes, it included the removal of his clothes. His boots and cutlass impeded the process. To this point everything had gone with a seductive progression, working in the obvious direction with appropriate attention to detail. But now she felt the time was ripe for the next act and that couldn't happen until his boots were out of the way and he was appropriately disrobed. She commenced the suggested procedure. At least he'd bathed recently.

He oriented her head this way and that. The rest of him pulsed in time to the rapid beat of his heart.

Everything was in place and at the proper angle, but she needed him to be completely, wholly, inextricably distracted for at least ten seconds. He was thoroughly distracted now, but from this position, any move she made, any distraction from her task—a task she didn't have much experience with, the King had always wanted to look her in the eyes and that was impossible from here—would attract his immediate attention, and he would kill her.

She and Loretta had role played. A Sleep Faery had been involved, a hummer. She knew what was necessary.

He began to make urgent noises and his thighs tensed. She stopped, pushed away, and wiped her mouth against the back of her hand.

"Very nice," he said. "Very very nice and good and nice." He struggled to catch his breath.

She looked from his belly to his chest and then at his eyes. He looked down at her with an intensity that she hoped could be attributed purely to lust.

Lukas, First Human, Liberator, usurper, murderer of her husband, children, and the Maer Nation stood before her naked but for the trousers around his boots with his cutlass on the floor in its scabbard attached to his belt.

"You have to pull them off." He chuckled. "There's no delicate way to do it."

Daffy stood, nude from the hips up. Her skirts fell into place, covering her legs; the knot on the side had come undone. She told him to sit and hold out a leg, she pulled off his boots one by one, he peeked under her skirts and then kicked off the rest of his clothes. The sword clattered to the floor. He looked up at the sound, glanced at the cutlass several steps away, and then pushed her onto the bed.

"Would ya like my skirts up or off?" Loretta had told her it was a question of taste. He answered by untying the rope. She let them fall to the floor.

Things happened so quickly that her body no longer had time to repeat the cycle from resigned failure to cold fear to hot anger. He pushed and pulled on her, placing her where he would. She found herself lying on the bed, her legs wrapped around his torso and Lukas looking down at her.

She remembered how this moment had been the night she married the King. A moment of truth. He'd taken his time, had asked questions, and taken care that she was comfortable in both body and mind. She wondered how he had been with Loretta. Had King

Gledig treated Loretta with ferocious desire like this? Had Gledig held back with Daffy out of politeness or respect? Had he wanted her?

Lukas pulled himself close to her, as close as two people can get. His nose touched hers. Now in control of her body, his eyes inches from hers, he said, "Dafina, we can rule together."

She tried to pull away, but there was nowhere to go.

"Or do you still go by Jill when slumming it?"

90.

The rhythmic whine of the saw cutting into Sempervaereen faded into the soundtrack to the story of how a world grew up on the forested slopes of this mountain range. The hearty folk who landed in Crescent Cove and made a home where they could hide from petty tyrants and would-be crusaders, the smoke from battles that raged every generation, and, much later, the songs of peace that the faer sang through the woods, over the mountains, and across the sea, the story of how the beast and the faer learned to live together, each making sacrifices that later came to feel like gifts.

The giant, gentle dryad shared simpler visions to tickle Kaetie. She saw her mother when she was Kaetie's age running across the field holding the hand of a young man who looked for all the world like Rustin, laughing and kissing, dancing and falling onto the bed of redwood needles, an emotional stroganoff of lusty joy. She saw GloFaeries fly above the lovers and heard nymphs cheer them on, and Sempervaereen intimated in the subtlest way that this was the vision of Kaetie's making. The compassion of the tree lent love to every image. And then she saw herself as a child with little boy Rustin when his hair was still a rusty mop. She remembered that day, playing on that redwood needle carpet. She felt the melancholy nostalgia of the old watching the young while preparing for the end.

Kaetie woke from that intimacy to the whining of the saw.

Hours had passed, and the sun was low over the horizon, lighting the few scattered clouds in purples and pinks that belied Semper-vaereen's suffering. The tree swayed too far with each gust of the ocean's breath and the images, scents, tastes, and sounds that she used to tell her stories grew faint.

Whatever stories Sempervaereen shared with Macae had a different effect on him. When Kaetie opened her eyes, he stood on the highest branch of the canopy where the tree tapered to a point. His cutlass in his hand, anger across his face, and that tiny Weapon Faery coaching him to choose his opportunities with care.

He looked down at her. His cheeks were flushed and his eyes moist. His head shook with rage and he said, "Do you know what we have done?"

"We?"

"People are horrible. They—we—torture everyone, everything in their way. Not just the faer but all the other animals. Did the tree show you what she showed me? They don't know what they're doing. They—" He bellowed his frustration. "We have to stop them."

The sawing stopped. The wide man who stood three hundred feet below yelled, "Either climb down or fall down—either way, you're mine."

Macae gritted his teeth and replied at full volume. "I'm coming down and I'm going to take every one of you to hell with me."

The wide man laughed and called him a tough guy, a brat, and, of course, a Bastard.

The Weapon Faery flew from the tip of Macae's cutlass to the tip of his nose. He shook a tiny finger in Macae's face and lectured him on how pride and poise brought victory, but pride and pretty much anything else guaranteed defeat. He finished the lecture with, "You need to make a difference, and this tree taught you what difference you need to make. Reel in your anger and store it in a safe place. You'll need it someday, but today it will just get you killed."

The sawing resumed.

91.

Daffy's back went rigid. Had he called her Jill? The name she'd given him when they were children playing at the peasants' well outside her father's castle walls? Her sweat turned cold, and her heart paused for an instant before restarting at twice its previous rate. "What did you say?"

"I know who you are. How could I forget you?"

"Must have me confused with some other lass, sir."

Lukas looked down at Daffy, his eyes serious, lustful of course, but more than that.

"It would take more than some face paint and hair leach for me to mistake you. Dafina, I loved you from the instant I first saw you."

It no longer mattered. The plan was shot, and she would die.

Why hadn't she told Loretta?

They could have planned for this, but her pride had gotten in the way. She'd barely been a woman that day at the well. Until she'd landed at The Gold Piece Inn, it had been her only experience of what it was like to be a normal villager. They'd splashed each other, flirted, and he'd chased her when she ran off. She'd let him catch her in a glade warmed by the spring sun. She looked nothing like that girl. He looked different too, but she'd recognized him. What a fool. But after Loretta had bragged about her affair with Gledig, how could she admit it? The story that Gledig was her one and only had cast her in a better light, and while it wasn't quite the truth, it wasn't quite a lie either.

Lukas slid forward. How could her body betray her by paving such a silky path for him?

"I'll give you power, too." He took his time, moving this way and that. "If you care so much for the faer, we can relax my policy. I have them under control, anyway. Once you understand the world I'm trying to make, you'll get it. I know you will! We can't fulfill our destiny with faeries dragging us down."

Now he moved faster. It became distracting—either the talking or the moving, she wasn't sure which.

"You can be Empress. And you'll have power. Anything that you disapprove of—we can fix it, Dafina, we can." He thrust quickly a few times, sucked in his breath, clenched his teeth, and then stopped. "Hold still. Don't move. Yes, that's it." He exhaled slowly and started moving again.

"You know?" She heard defeat in her own voice and hated herself for it.

"I can give you a better life. Better than anything Gledig could have done. We lost him in the lie of Maentanglement."

"Why should I believe you?"

"Why would I lie? Dafina, there's nothing you can do. I have complete power. I will have you either way."

She locked her legs around him and pushed against his chest.

"No, no," he said, "It won't be like that. I shouldn't have said that. I don't want you that way. You can say no, and I'll go away and won't come back. You can have Crescent Cove. I'll dam up the River Adductor, seal everything west of The Fist, and leave it to you."

"Why did you kill the maer? They never hurt anyone. They cared for us. They cared for me."

"If you disagree with my philosophy, I promise—I swear—then we'll change policy. We can liberate humanity without hurting the faer. You'll find a way."

"The faer help us."

"But they don't. They hold us back with their filthy tricks. They're thieves and swindlers. Humans are so far superior. Compare a man to an elf. Elfs' long lives make them lazy, no ambition, no fortitude, no heart or gusto—no reason to live, I say. And the others—all moochers and scum. Embrace who you are, a glorious human, the greatest creature that ever lived. Faer, filthy things!" His voice went up an octave, and he moved rapidly. Perspiration dripped down his temples. He stopped again and took a few breaths, taking great care to avoid moving. "Oh, gods, that's good. You are everything I ever dreamed. Please, Dafina, accept me. Let me be your emperor. Marry me."

His approach to this business seemed to prevent him from being distracted for more than a few seconds. Daffy needed him wholly consumed in the moment for at least ten. She rocked her hips.

"Whoa," he said.

She didn't stop.

He clenched his jaw. Every muscle in his body tightened.

92.

Caeph marched up to Rustin, his eyes too big, too bright, too blue in the forest shade. Rustin knew that feral look. "They're here." Caeph said it like a challenge.

Rustin had been talking to Quercus, sitting in the glade in front of the lean-to-shaped granite crag. He looked back and Quercus was gone.

Right behind Caeph, Raenny rushed up and said, "Volunteers on the beach."

The Knights of Perpetual Poverty watched the beach from the cover of the granite that grew out of the hillside. Cluttered with the remains of cook fires, campfires, makeshift shelters, and the flotsam left behind by sunken ships, the beach hid no secrets.

Caeph said, "We can take them." Naelth, "Go for it. See you back at the inn." Aennie, "Or on the other side."

Rustin said, "That's Vaence." He'd known that Vaence had been conscripted but seeing him in the Volunteer's red and black leather still shocked him.

Caeph said, "Where's Viviaen?"

Rustin said, "Back at the inn by now."

Raenny said, "She wouldn't sell us out." Caeph grunted. Naelth, "She knows not what she's done." Aennie, "But we're about to find out."

A heavy bass voice came down from the top of the granite crag, "Don't move. You're surrounded."

Rustin's hand went to his broadsword, he felt more than heard a tiny vibration from the tip of his sword and the gruff voice of his Weapon Faery, "Slide it out real easy and put your sword to work, lad."

Rustin took a quick look at his knights. None of them wavered. If preparation was a meal, his side was satiated.

"Hands over your heads, no quick motions."

Rustin knew that voice. He looked up and saw the Volunteers above. Two held crossbows cranked and loaded. He said, "Taevius?"

"Rusty."

"What are you doing?"

"Following orders."

To Rustin, it just didn't add up. Sure, the Bastards grew up doing more or less what they were told, but there was always a lackadaisical sense at The Gold Piece Inn that Dewey encouraged questions of right and wrong, good and evil. As much as he feigned annoyance and impatience, Dewey always made time to argue with a Bastard.

"Lukas's orders?"

"That's right."

"You must really hate me."

"That's right."

Naelth said, "They're coming up from the beach."

Rustin felt his Weapon Faery's nudge and said, "To cover."

Granite outcroppings, shards, boulders, and huge rock faces grew out of the ridge like the ancient oaks and great redwoods. On

Rustin's word, the Bastards rolled, fell, crawled, and shifted behind granite and trunk. A crossbow dart clattered from the stone, another stuck in the ground where Rustin had just been.

"Take it easy, mate, you could hurt someone with those."

"If you don't want to get hurt, do what I say."

"Really? For Lukas?" Rustin couldn't get his head around it.

Taevius didn't respond.

Caeph rolled over a rock, landed on his hands and feet and squirmed next to Rustin, his back against a tree trunk. He whispered, "We're ready for this and you know it."

Rustin could hear crossbows being cranked tight. He leaned far enough around the tree to see Raenny crouched next to a stone, not behind it but in the sun-shade boundary in plain sight of Taevius but so motionless, that he was all but invisible.

Rustin looked the other way and saw Aennie looking back. She motioned with her eyebrows. A cold-granite dagger in each of her hands and her Weapon Faery on her wrist. The tiny faery, dressed in a black cape and wearing a flat-brimmed hat, grinned up at her. Rustin nodded.

Aennie moved into the cover of an oak, negotiating the grass and stone without a sound.

From below the glade, Rustin heard the Volunteers coming up from the beach. Taevius and two Volunteers jumped and slid down the granite face. Taevius landed with his back to the lean-to-like opening of the granite crag.

Caeph said, "Damn elfs."

Rustin felt the same way—Quercus was right behind Taevius and would do nothing to help. He said, "They don't understand us either."

Taevius said, "Into the light, Bastards, hands up."

Caeph's scimitar slid out of the elk skin scabbard without a sound. Aennie now stood behind the crossbowlad. Raenny's bastard sword was within striking distance of the crossbowlass.

Rustin waited for Vaence to lead five more Volunteers up the trail. When they got to the edge of the glade, he nodded to Caeph and the two stepped into the light on each side of the trail, half a step from the safety of other tree trunks, boulders, and thickets.

"I thought you'd be with your elfin slut," Vaence said. He turned to the other Volunteers and added, "If she'd take him, she'll take all of us, right?" He got a chortle from one of the Volunteers, a pudgy man with a snaggle-toothed smile. "Your sister off servicing the navy?"

Rustin took two long, fast steps into the shade, raised his sword along the line of a tree branch invisible to the Volunteers, and hacked at the guard of Vaence's sword, sending it clattering against a stone.

"You want to shed blood?" Taevius said. "Because you and me, Rusty. You. And. Me."

Rustin watched the Volunteers spread around the glade, surrounding it, but they couldn't see Aennie or Raenny and Rustin had lost track of Naelth.

Taevius said, "We outnumber you two to one. I don't want to have to tell your mothers that you're dead."

On the word "dead," in a single fluid motion, Caeph butted Vaence in the back of the head, chopped into the hip of another Volunteer, and whipped around a third, stopping with the point of his sword against the center of her back. The two fell like candlesticks and the third dropped her weapon and gasped.

On the same cue, Aennie stabbed the wrist of the crossbowlad. The crossbow fell, its dart kicked up a cloud of dust, and Aennie flipped the Volunteer over her leg. He fell, clutching his cut wrist. She pinned him to the ground with a knee in his belly, one dagger at his neck, and the other poised over his groin.

Raenny used the tip of his long bastard sword to poke the crossbowlass in the forearm. The surprise that he'd been standing next to her shocked her into stepping back. She tripped over a granite shard and fell.

Rustin could taste victory and felt a yearning that he'd later learn to call battle hunger. He said, "You outnumber us, but we have the advantage."

"Not against me, you don't," Taevius said. "You owe me, Rusty." He stepped away from the Volunteers and used his boot to rake debris out of a smooth flat circle at the center of the glade.

"I don't want to hurt you." Rustin stepped to the edge of the circle. He saw Naelth on the granite crag above, where Taevius and his Volunteers had just been.

Taevius said, "But I want to hurt you."

Rustin looked at his knights. Their cold-granite weapons and the faeries that enchanted them plus, their knowledge of the terrain, not to mention the stealth they'd learned from elfs and tricks from pirates, added up to certain victory.

Taevius stood two steps away in the stance of a trained swordsman. In the red and black leather, and wearing boots, he looked all wrong to Rustin. Taevius should be barefoot on a ship with his hair blowing in the wind, waves crashing all around him, calling out orders to trim sails and alter course. He'd always known what he wanted to be, and this wasn't it. And it was all Rustin's fault.

Rustin had never meant to betray Taevius that day he met Major Blechk. And then again, the day that Blechk came to conscript the Bastards and took Taevius but left Rustin behind.

Taevius lunged. He'd have taken Rustin by surprise, too, if the Weapon Faery hadn't instigated an easy parry. The Weapon Faery conveyed Taevius's weakness and Rustin could see the simple move that would cripple him.

Taevius whipped his sword in an upward, backhanded motion that might have caught Rustin by the chin or even throat, but he left the opening Rustin's Weapon Faery had anticipated.

Rustin stepped into the opening at Taevius's side. His sword, perfectly balanced and all but weightless, moved effortlessly in a direction that would collapse Taevius's spine.

Rustin pulled the sword out of the arc. He stepped back and Taevius slashed through air where he'd stood. He took another step back. Taevius set his feet and glared at Rustin.

"You're right," Rustin said. He set the point of his sword in front of him and dropped to the ground. Kneeling with his sword standing before him and its pommel against his forehead, he repeated, "You're right."

Taevius stepped forward and raised his sword over Rustin's head.

"It shouldn't have been this way," Rustin said. "We're brothers and I betrayed you." He cocked his head at an angle that made his throat an easy target. He felt the vulnerability of his Adam's apple as he swallowed the rest of his pride. "I've always admired you, but somehow I can never seem to do the right thing when you're involved." He looked up at Taevius and added, "But I'll never stop trying."

No one moved except Rustin's Weapon Faery. The little geezer slid down the sword on his kilt, sat in the sand, leaning against the blade, facing Rustin, and said, "Six thousand years, laddy, I've never seen anything like this."

93.

Lukas sucked in his breath and held himself prone above her, struggling for control. Daffy let her right hand dangle down the side of the bed, but then his eyes opened.

He said, "I'll grant you three wishes."

She pulled her arm back. "Three wishes?"

"Sure. Isn't that the ultimate maegic? I'll grant you three wishes—you won't need faeries! I'm more powerful than any wizard. You'll be in awe of my power." Perched on his arms, looking down at her, he added, "If it's your wish, I'll even release the

Bastard heirs."

Daffy couldn't speak, couldn't breathe.

"Oh please, did you really believe that I didn't know about the King's Bastards?"

She stared back. Anything she said would backfire. Make a wish? Surrender to Lukas—even more than she already had? A wish? A real wish is like a choice backed by hope, and she didn't have any hope left. Again.

Hope had disappeared. Again.

"Dafina, I'm a better man than Gledig was, a better leader," he said. "I can say with total certainty that I am aware of every plot, every conspiracy, everything that opposes me." He rejoined her and moved forward slowly, ever slowly only forward. When he finally reached his hilt, he said, "My troops have already captured them. Rustin and Kaetie will be executed in the marketplace unless I issue new orders by midnight." He brushed her hair from her brow. "You can save them. Just make a wish."

Before she could answer, he withdrew and slammed back. Back and forth, her head bumped the headboard with each movement. "You need to choose soon," he said, each word spoken on a withdrawal, "before it's too late."

Choose? She'd never had an actual choice in her life.

She'd lost. Lost everything, including her dignity and whatever trace of self-respect she hadn't already surrendered. And on top of it, she felt like she'd cheated on her king. She assembled the remaining dregs of her strength and tried to come up with a wish that would preserve Loretta's children. Wishing to release them would do nothing. She had to be specific. Deliver them healthy and happy to Nantesse? She knew that Lukas would never allow them to stay in Glomaythea. But he'd perceive Nantesse as too close, too great a threat. It had to be far away, both geographically and politically, and somewhere that they could make decent lives for themselves. She'd also need to put in a time requirement, or he'd let them languish in a dungeon. She tried to remember how long it took to sail to Puaepuae or Maekindo—

"Dafina, hey! I'm still here. Be a good serving-lass and pretend to care. You have until I finish with you to decide. Either Empress and the Bastard heirs' hero or serving-lass—I can find contentment with you in either case."

She swayed her hips.

"That's better," he said. "Oh yeah, here we go."

It was too much to bear. Too much humiliation. Everything she'd done, regardless of her intentions, had led her deeper into disgrace. She remembered how it felt to wander Faer Reef, hoping only to die in peace. It would have been best. Memories piled up, every one of them died in shame, hiding in a brothel that called itself an inn, the chamber pot dumping on her head, thrown out of a restaurant as a beggar, surviving the sinking of *Avarice* only to become a burden on the maer. And now she was a whore. She wasn't cut out to be a hero, couldn't do it.

And now he wanted her to choose? Lukas had chosen every step of his path. It wasn't fair. She didn't expect fairness. She just wanted a choice.

Her skull bounced against the headboard. Lukas worked into a frenzy. He shifted a fraction of an inch and it sent tremors surging across her loins, up her spine, down her legs to her toes. Her body wouldn't even cooperate—how could her heart and mind?

Lukas moved even faster. He grunted and his muscles tensed again. Between clenched teeth, he huffed out, "A wish, Dafina, make a wish.

Spasms overtook her. His groans went up in pitch and urgency.

She opened her eyes and realized that she'd grabbed the back of his head and rammed his face into her clavicle.

No, she would not make a wish, but she'd damn sure make a choice.

She let her right arm fall down the side of the bed again. She opened her palm.

"Now, yes, now!" she screamed, and then released a long, loud, low-pitched, urgent roar.

She heard the passage open, barely a whisk of air, but loud enough for her to know.

She pressed his head against her and wrapped her hand tight in a faery tangle in his hair. Her roar became a high-pitched wheeze as she inhaled.

It took five faeries to carry the spike, a six-inch piece of cold granite carved by Lapidae to fit a cast of Daffy's hand, its point sharpened by thousands of years of wind and rain. It felt cold and heavy and fit the curves of her hand in such a way that she couldn't imagine dropping it. Not just the shape of her hand, but the lines of her palm. The spike nestled along her lifeline, aligned with her knuckles.

Lukas went silent, struggling for breath. His torso coiled back. He pulled his head up from her neck and uncoiled with neither control nor mercy.

With her left hand wrapped in the faery tangle, she rotated his face to her left. Her right hand brought up the spike.

His body went into a glorious spasm.

She rammed the spike into his throat.

94.

Dewey leaned against the end of the bar where he could see the Volunteers who guarded every entrance and exit, the bottom and top of the stairs, and along the balustrade. He heard Lukas and Daffy, but only because he had huge ears and was listening. No one else seemed to notice anything, and nothing sounded out of order. The clanking of the headboard sounded like a serving-lass doing fine work. It occurred to Dewey that if she survived, she could command a gold ohzee for each trip upstairs. And if she did, then

Loretta would demand it. The prospect of increasing prices almost distracted Dewey from the feeling of impending doom.

Baertha appeared next to him. She said, "I don't like it."

"She can work you into her schedule, maybe tomorrow night— or are you jealous?"

"Don't try to convince me that she's just a serving-lass upstairs with a soldier. I know, Dewey, we all know."

Dewey saw a flash. Way up on the ceiling over the Volunteers, it could pass for an errant spark from the fireplace. And then another, and another.

Baertha said, "Tell me what you're doing or I'm going up there."

"We're about to find out."

Five faeries fluttered over the Volunteers' heads and around the grand chandelier that hung over the center of the saloon. The cat reared back. One faery dove straight down and landed at the edge of the bar: a bright red, gorgeous, two inch-tall, stark naked, female devil complete with horns, a forked tail, and hooves instead of feet, plus iridescent dragonfly wings. The four other Ninja Faeries wore tight fitting black fabric from head to toe; they wafted down on blue swallowtail wings and perched next to her, two on either side.

Dewey said, "Well?"

The Red Devil grinned. Her teeth glittered, and she took a bow.

"Gods, I hate Melodramatic Faeries."

Baertha said, "What the hell?"

"Stay here. I might need you."

She said, "For what?" But Dewey had stepped in front of the stage.

Farq Faeries Rule

95.

Crisiant had played a long, driving riff to drown out the noise from upstairs.

Dewey jumped in front of him and gave the signal. Hardly covert, he yelled, "Now, now!"

Crisiant disconnected the strap and swung his guitar in a wide circle and sang the spell he'd labored over for the last two weeks.

Farq Faeries stumbled out of the guitar's sound hole. One-by-one, they fell and flapped like crazy, scattering in different directions. Some flew for the door, some to the kitchen or casino, everywhere that Volunteers stood. Several looked back at the Wizard, irritated at the prospect of flying all the way up to the balustrade. Each left its own foggy, toxic, smelly trail. They were small enough, and the inn was loud and smelly enough to prevent the crowd from taking much notice of them, and the Volunteers were absorbed in their own daydreams.

The Dream Faeries had reconfigured the Volunteers' thoughts much how your mind is altered while you sleep. Each Volunteer was lost in memories tangled together with fears and desires into that state known in the maegic trade as "being spaced out."

When the Farq Faeries closed in, some Volunteers tried to slap them away, but their motions were so sluggish that the Farq Faeries had no trouble hovering below their noses.

Prior to taking up residence within Crisiant's guitar—a guitar that was too smelly to be played again—the Farq Faeries' had produced a volatile liquid from the ingredients of their trade, human waste. With each flap of their wings, they farted a vapor called chloraeform. The Volunteers collapsed where they stood.

Baertha was the first up the stairs, Dewey followed, and then Lylli and Crisiant. Bob poured drinks and servers delivered them. It being the first time in the history of The Gold Piece Inn that anything had been given away for free, the guests were bewildered to a point of total distraction.

Baertha kicked Volunteers' bodies out of her way and pushed into the room. She pulled the usurper's naked corpse off Daffy and let it fall on the floor. Dewey gasped at the stain it would cause.

Daffy still lay there, naked, and holding the spike. Blood pooled on her chest and belly and drenched the bed. Her eyes were wide, and her skin was stark white and sweating.

"I didn't think you had it in you," Dewey said. When she didn't respond, he added, "You all right, kid?"

"No," Lylli said and gathered Daffy's skirts from the floor. She tore them into large rags and placed one over her nether regions and used the rest to blot blood from her skin. "She's not all right. But she did her part."

"She hasn't moved," Dewey said. "Daffy, you're supposed to be in the barn. Why didn't you go through the passage?"

Crisiant dropped to his knees and bowed. With his forehead touching the ground, he said, "Your Majesty, you have liberated us." It had been a long time since he last paid her proper respect and, to be sure, it was the first time that his respect was sincere. She'd sacrificed a lot for her people. That it was her duty made it more special.

Lylli said, "Get me towels and clean water."

Dewey pulled Crisiant aside and said, "I need you to rouse one of the Volunteers."

"For pleasure or pain?"

"Can you do it?"

"A bucket of water and a Farq Faery from the men's privy—but why?"

Dewey led him onto the balcony and pointed at a sleeping

Volunteer. "This is Jaenet, rouse her!"

"She'll come fully awake. You sure?"

"She's one of mine." Dewey leaned over the balustrade and gave Loretta his order. Lylli appeared next to them and added her request for towels and clean water.

Manuelae and Kaennie rushed upstairs.

"Let sleeping soldiers lie," Crisiant called out to them.

Lylli and Manuelae went back in Daffy's room.

Kaennie had a bucket of water in one hand and a chamber pot full of urine in the other. Crisiant relieved him of the burden.

He knelt over the Volunteer Jaenet. He brushed her dark hair aside and pulled up an eyelid. She snored peacefully. He spent an instant appreciating his handiwork. Any thaergist could think of using Dream Faeries, but a guitar full of specially trained and seasoned Farq Faeries was pure genius. "I still got it."

Dewey kicked him in the back. "Yeah, nice work. Undo it. We need her help!"

Crisiant pulled Jaenet away from the other Volunteers. While Dewey lifted her up, Crisiant hummed a noxious melody that summoned a Farq Faery from the chamber pot.

A little guy in a bright yellow raincoat flew up to Crisiant on horsefly wings. A fog of concentrated ammonia trailed behind him. "Oh gods!" Crisiant coughed and rubbed his eyes. "This one's ripe."

He had Dewey splash Jaenet's face with the clean water. Her eyes opened in shock, but almost immediately started wilting.

Waving his finger like an orchestra leader's baton, Crisiant hummed a few flat notes off key and the little guy buzzed in circles under her nose. Jaenet's eyes popped open. She took a deep breath and gagged. Coughing, but wide awake, she drew her sword from the scabbard, set her feet and looked around.

Dewey backed off. Crisiant leapt out of her range. The Farq Faery sat on the fine wood of the balustrade, caught his breath, and dissolved its lacquer finish.

Crisiant went back into the room where Lylli was treating Daffy.

Jaenet appeared in the doorway with her sword poised, her bicep bulging through the red and black leather.

Baertha stopped in her tracks and cutlasses appeared in each of her hands, held out to each side and ready to converge on Jaenet.

Lylli darted in. "Jaenet!" she said, "I barely recognize you" and hugged her.

"Oh Lylli, it's so good to be home." Then she untangled herself from Lylli and nudged Lukas's corpse with her boot. "And good to be rid of that vermin." She faced Baertha and slowly slipped her sword back in its scabbard. Baertha dropped her cutlasses back into her belt loops.

"Listen up," Jaenet said, "that's Lukas's elite guard asleep out there and when they come to, they'll obey their orders."

Crisiant said, "Surely Lukas ordered them to lie down with the lamb."

"We have to kill them now or they will kill us."

Dewey said, "You've been spending too much time with the usurper."

"That man lacked subtlety," Crisiant said. "The Farq Faeries' gas will provide a fine night of stinky sleep and when they awake, it will all have the evaporating quality of a dream."

Baertha said, "What the farq is he talking about?"

"That's Crisiant, King Gledig's Wizard," Lylli said. "He cast a sleep spell on the Volunteers and when they wake up, they'll forget everything."

"Forget everything?" Crisiant said. "No. They'll recall these last several hours the same way that they would recall a dream and then they will forget it the same way that, when you awake, you forget—"

"Get them out of here," Dewey said.

"—a dream. You know how when you wake up from an intense

dream, you can't remember—"

Dewey interrupted again, "If that spell didn't work on the Volunteers guarding the door, or who knows where they went? We could be in big trouble."

"—that combination of Dream Faeries and Farq Faeries is one of my finest—"

"Yeah, whatever," Dewey said, "Jaenet, get a keg from Bob, grab some Bastards, and drag the Volunteers down to the beach or up on a hill, pour some ale on them, and leave an empty keg or two."

"—the trick was teaching the Farq Faeries the recipe for—"
Loretta rushed in.

"I used all your tricks," Daffy said. She squirmed in Baertha's arms. "And I killed him—but what have I done?"

"You were brilliant," Dewey said. And then to Loretta, "She's in shock, go with Baertha, get her cleaned up and she'll be fine in a day or two."

"Wait!" Daffy said. "They have Kaetie and Rustin and they're going to kill them!"
Loretta shrieked.

"I'm sorry!" She wiggled out of Baertha's grasp, fell to the floor, and begged at Loretta's feet. "I couldn't let him keep doing that to me. I had to kill him. He had to die. But now—" She reached out and grabbed Dewey by the ankle. "Everyone! Get everyone. What have I done? It's too late, it's too late."

Lylli pushed Dewey aside. "Daffy, I need you to get a grip and tell me what you know."

She made Daffy close her eyes and take several slow, deep breaths. Daffy calmed enough to describe what Lukas had said. "They will be executed in the Marketplace at midnight—we have to get down there. We have to do something. Baertha, please, get the pirates, get anyone, we have to—"

Lylli said, "Kaetie and Macae are with Sempervaereen."

Loretta said, "Macae is up there with her?"

"I'll tell you later."

Dewey said. "Without Kaetie and Rustin, all of this is pointless."

"Daffy," Lylli said, "did Lukas tell you how they caught Kaetie and Rustin?"

"He knows everything, he told me that no plot could get past him, no conspiracy, no—he must have spies everywhere, how else could he know?"

Dewey said. "I need anyone who can hold a weapon at the marketplace right now."

"No," Loretta said. "I know men and I know my children." She pointed at Dewey. "You warned Kaetie and Rustin that Lukas was coming, didn't you?"

"They got the message within an hour of when I did."

"You listen to me," Loretta said. "The ego on Lukas? That man believes anything that comes out of his own mouth. The usurper might've sent Volunteers, but how could he know if they caught the Bastards?"

"The same way that I—"

"And let me tell you something, my children are no fools. Rustin is as tough a man as Crescent Cove ever saw. He led the resistance, he learned from pirates, elfs, and a master manipulator …"

Dewey smiled in the glow of recognition.

"… Kaetie knows the land better than any human. That tree put maps in her head. She knows every granite shard on The Fist of God, knows who put it there and when. The faer won't let nothin' happen to her." She sat down. "No. Worry all you want about whatever you want, but don't you worry about my kids."

96.

Rustin looked up the line of Taevius's sword into his eyes. A breeze blew through the forest. Leaves shuffled light and shadow, making late evening sunbeams dance along the blade. Taevius held the blade rock-steady, the edge a thumb's breadth from Rustin's neck. Taevius didn't look back. Those deep, dark eyes possessed aloof poise that made Rustin feel not inferior but awkward in comparison. When they were boys, every game came easy to Taevius, the fastest, strongest, most handsome Bastard. Until last year, Rustin's legs had been too long for him to control.

Taevius never needed the approval of the others. He led by self-assured example. The Bastards did what he asked out of desire for his approval, even though Taevius never granted that approval. Rustin earned his followers respect by supporting their aspirations and proving that he would never take advantage, never lead them astray. Taevius kept a silent distance and, when he spoke, his voice came from deep in his chest, a bass rumble that demanded attention. The knights knew they could laugh and complain with Rustin.

Right now, Rustin didn't care about any of that. He had set his sword point down before him and dropped to his knees because he had betrayed Taevius. In this fight, he was wrong, and Taevius was right.

From behind Rustin, Vaence said, "Surrender, cowards."

The sword at Rustin's throat wavered.

"Vaence," Taevius said, "one more word and I'll start by clipping your Achilles and won't stop until I've trimmed your eyebrows."

"Get on with it," Rustin said. "Kill me or join me, I'm not going to kneel here all day."

Taevius grunted. And then he laughed; short, distinct spasms from deep in his throat rising in pitch and lighting up his eyes, "Ha. Ha. Ha."

"How do you do this to me?" His voice echoed from the granite. "Every time. Every single time." His laughter was absorbed in a grin stupefied by irony. "I was two when you were born, too young to remember what life was like before I had to share the loft with you. How do you put me in these situations? Every time!" The tip of the sword scraped Rustin's collarbone. "Look at this." He pulled the sword away and used it to point at the knights and Volunteers.

The knights were in another well practiced position. Separated by two sword lengths, they could rotate through their adversaries. If a battle started, the Volunteers couldn't guess who they'd face next.

Aennie sat on the crossbowlad with one dagger at his neck and the other at his crotch. Raenny was a few steps behind Vaence. Caeph stood over two Volunteers, his sword *en garde*, daring them to stand. Rustin knew that the Bastards would drop them in seconds. He wondered if Taevius realized his disadvantage—no, Taevius was caught in the moment. If there was a battle, Rustin would be the first to die. *And farq it all, rightfully so!*

Taevius pointed his sword at Rustin. "Here I am, trying to get through this shite war, just trying to survive, just trying to make it home where I can get a job on a ship—any ship, any job—and I have to choose between you and Lukas?" He shook his head. "And the worst of it? You do it in a way that makes every bone in my body want to choose Lukas."

Taevius pressed the blade against Rustin's chin and then withdrew, flipped it in the air, caught it by the grip, and jammed it in the ground next to Rustin's.

Taevius reached out, Rustin gripped his hand, and Taevius pulled him into a hug. "I hate you like a brother."

97.

Sempervaereen sang to Kaetie and Macae about youth and age, when it's time to live and when it's time to die. Gusts of emotion battered Kaetie and soft redwood needles wiped her tears. She felt more than heard a lesson from the Tree Faery about how change requires change, and if she wanted to change things, she had to accept change.

She cried out, "Not this change!"

Needles leapt from the branches by the thousand and swarmed into a hammock. A row of nymphs lined up on a bough, solemn and proud, sad without pity. They lifted Kaetie and set her in the Redwood Faery hammock. Macae climbed in and knelt over her, his cutlass ready but his face composed. The Weapon Faery stood, arms crossed, on the hilt of the sword.

The hammock floated up and away from Sempervaereen and the ancient tree began falling. She didn't falter or teeter, she leaned downhill, toward the sea, savoring the view of Crescent Cove, the point, Faer Reef, and the endless ocean that she'd looked over for ten thousand years.

Kaetie felt Sempervaereen sigh. The tree exhaled everything she'd ever known or felt. Not just gas and sap, but all her stories, those she'd told and those she'd never found an audience for. Regret consumed Kaetie. How many times had she taken the long way around Sempervaereen to save time? A presence in her heart and mind scolded her for that regret, a scolding dusted with joy because wasn't it better for a little girl to skip through a forest picking flowers and hiding from leprechauns on her way to visit her favorite druid than to waste her time listening to the long boring stories of an old tree?

The hammock hovered where the canopy had been, and Kaetie watched her teacher fall. A tree so huge that her trunk couldn't be encompassed by the arms of forty men, took her time falling, dying. Her crown hit the earth, crushed an acre of forest, and broke pulverized walls of granite that had stood for a million years. A cloud of tiny faeries rose in her wake. So much of her bark and fiber had been composed of those little faeries that she left a corpse indistinguishable from a beastial redwood tree, barely remarkable in its length or diameter, ready for a lumber mill.

The faeries swarmed around the Volunteers and the saw that had cut Sempervaereen, though they left the horse alone. Lower faer have little capacity for independent thought, and Sempervaereen, ever the pacifist, offered no guidance. The saw would rust and crumble to dust by the next moon.

They set Kaetie and Macae down uphill from the Volunteers. Macae seethed and swore vengeance. His Weapon Faery said a word, and he took Kaetie's hand and they ran.

The man pursued them. A rotund fellow, his ample gut was firm with that mix of muscle and ale that only stalls a man's vitality later in life.

Macae tugged Kaetie onto a path. He slowed to catch his breath and said, "We're going home."

"We can't lead him to the inn!"

He ignored her, and she trusted him.

The path led around a knoll in the valley between god's middle and index fingers. The setting sun cast long shadows that blended into the trees and the granite outcroppings. Macae told Kaetie to run ahead, and she did what he said. He ducked behind a tree. Kaetie slowed and looked back.

The man had closed on them and when he saw Kaetie, he burst to higher speed. He held a crossbow in one hand and swung his flail in the other.

Macae stepped out behind him, and with a graceful downward swing of his cutlass, cut the back of the man's boot. The man sprawled forward.

Kaetie could hear Macae's Weapon Faery from fifty steps away, "Remember this lesson: subtlety can always beat brute force."

They left the wide man face down in the dirt. Macae smashed the crossbow against a tree and ran to Kaetie. They continued along the trail, through forests, and across creeks.

Around every corner and over every hill, Kaetie's thoughts returned to Sempervaereen. When she'd come down from the ancient dryad's canopy after her foot heeled, she'd carried the weight of knowledge without seeing its light.

They climbed a rocky crag, and a perception tugged at her. She knew that something important had happened here. If she'd had time to examine the crag, its cracks and scars, she was certain that she could assemble the perception into a memory. It confused her because, while it was in her mind, it wasn't her memory.

She looked in other directions and similar sensations overcame her, experiences that she'd never had.

The sun had dipped into the ocean for the night and understanding began to dawn. The moon had just emerged over God's Fist behind her, a thick gibbous with a bright star below it. She saw the moon and that star in a different way. Sempervaereen had planned to teach her about the stars but never got to it. Lylli had taught her the moon's phases, the seasons, and their relation to plants and animals, but not this.

Instead of a maegic nightlight, the moon looked like a cold, lonely world, and that star looked familiar the way that The Gold Piece Inn looked familiar—but why?

She stumbled and fell. Macae lifted her, and they ran along the path. When they reached Knuckle Creek, Kaetie laughed. Her heart filled with warmth, her mind with joy, love, contentment, and a good dose of mischief. She felt Sempervaereen laughing within her.

"She's not dead!" Kaetie yelled. "She's alive. Right here in me." Hilarity overcame her. "I'm possessed by a tree!"

98.

Rustin saw Macae and Kaetie coming toward them, downhill on a moonlit trail. He motioned to the others, and they waited at the bridge over Knuckle Creek.

Macae pulled Kaetie by the hand.

Rustin said, "Why is she laughing?"

"Your sister is seriously weird."

"I know, but—why aren't you up in a tree?"

"Why aren't you hiding with elfs?"

"Got a message from Dewey, we need to get back in a hurry."

Macae pointed at the red and black leather uniformed Volunteers and said, "What are you doing with *them*?"

"Taevius and his troops? It's a long story."

Rustin led everyone to the Spring. Traces of mist danced in the willow branches and the moon reflected from the water. The Bastards took their usual seats. Rustin told the Volunteers that he'd cover them, no matter what, and they found trees to lean against and rocks to sit on.

Taevius stepped into the cover of a willow tree. Rustin watched him, pleased that he'd finally managed an honorable deed.

Rustin then asked Raenny to scout the inn. "Find out what's going on and come right back. Macae, if you can't keep Kaetie from laughing, get her out of here. Caeph, put your sword back in the scabbard. Naelth, could you stand watch? And try to look scary. Taevius, what can we expect from the Volunteers?"

Taevius began his story. It started on the day that Blechk took him from The Gold Piece Inn. Rustin winced at the memory. Taevius described his military training and his first few missions. He stopped and looked at The Knights of Perpetual Poverty one by one. He told them how it felt to kill someone, how good people who become soldiers spend the rest of their days, and especially their nights, with the ghosts of the people whose lives they ended. How they worry about the suffering of the lovers and mothers and fathers, siblings and friends who are left behind and all the people who never got a chance to know them. He lectured in that aloof way that he had, "It may be necessary to fight, even kill, to protect the innocent, to preserve ideals and decency, but it doesn't bring glory. Glory is nothing, but a lie told by old humans to con young humans into killing other young humans for no honorable reason."

When he finished, the sounds of frogs, crickets, and the surf replaced his voice.

"Taevius," Rustin said, "we need your guidance."

Macae and Aennie both mumbled, "We sure do." Naelth, "Our lives for honor." Caeph said, "Glory would be good too, I mean, not as a goal, but you know, if we get some in the course of honor, then maybe we—" Aennie said, "Shut up Caeph," and he did.

Taevius stepped away from the willow. "No, I've had enough. I'd rather swab decks." He walked away.

Raenny shouted from the faery garden, "A little help over here."

Naelth said, "People are coming, lots of them, and they're carrying something. Something heavy."

The Bastards ran out of the spring and through the willow branches.

Ahead of the others, Bob the bartender rolled a nearly empty barrel of wine into a field. Rustin asked, "What the—?"

Bob pushed his hair out of his eyes. "Rustin?" He wheezed his strange laugh. "Should've been here, man. That Daffy, ho ho, did she put one on." And he rolled the barrel on by.

Then Caeph's mother and Daeffid the cook carried a body past. Donnae said, "Looks drunk to me, ha ha." Macae's mother and his older sister, Lucith, carried another, and Rustin could see the Volunteer uniform on this one. Faernando and Jaek carried yet another, and then a Volunteer dragged a smaller Volunteer behind her. She smiled at Rustin and said, "Nothing better than to be a Gold Piece Inn Bastard, am I right?"

The Bastards looked at each other. Dewey recited a litany of chores.

Aenki shushed them. "Don't wake the Volunteers."

And then someone ran at Rustin. He held open his arms and Loretta grabbed him and lifted him off his feet. Macae pulled Kaetie over and Loretta tugged her into the hug, too.

"Daffy, I knew it," Loretta called out. "I knew they could take care of themselves."

Rustin saw Daffy over his mother's shoulder and, even in the moonlight, saw that she had changed. Her eyes had a wariness to them. He didn't know what she'd been through with the maer, much less with Lukas. But she wasn't a ghost, and that made him feel better.

Morning After

99.

The Volunteers who composed Lukas's elite guard awoke in the orchard with headaches and dry, sour tongues caked with a putrid crust. An all but empty barrel of wine lay on its side. Jaenet groaned about the raging drinking and carrying on of the night before. She complained that Lukas should know better than to take a bunch of hard-up soldiers to a brothel and buy them a barrel of wine.

The Farq Faery farts provided the headaches, nausea, and bad breath that lent credence to the story, and the Dream Faeries cluttered their memories enough that few of them questioned the obvious. After Jaenet told stories of embarrassing behavior worthy of blackmail, the Volunteers stopped asking questions.

Days later, Lukas's corpse appeared on the beach well chewed by creatures of the sea. Rumors of Lukas's last night included the truth, but "the Queen posed as a whore and murdered him" couldn't compete with more reasonable stories.

The Autumn Equinox celebration came a week after the fall of Lukas, and Crescent Cove had never been more jubilant, but what happened in Crescent Cove had never been a measure of life in Glomaythea.

After his death, Lukas the usurper's fledgling empire began a slow, inexorable collapse. For all the confidence he'd shown, he'd never permitted anyone who could threaten his leadership into a position of authority. With no heir-apparent, his right-hand man, Maedegan, the stout veteran who had murdered Sempervaereen, claimed power, but defeat had left him bitter. While bitterness can unite people, it only leads them to more bitterness.

Fervent believers in the Liberator's cause gathered in the village along the Glo River where Lukas had been born and bred. The name of the village, known as Glomae for as long as anyone remembered, was changed to Lukasia, and flew the Flying Anvil. Maekhanes set to work building a small replica of Lukas's utopia. Mills were built, mines dug, and faer driven out. The Lukasians blamed any sign of rust or corrosion, any indication of maekhanical failure, disease, or bad luck on the faer, even though none ever visited them.

100.

The faer continued their migration over The Fist of God to Faer Reef and Crescent Cove. The Knights of Perpetual Poverty continued to protect and guide the faer to places where they could rebuild their long lives, but Rustin's promise to return Conifaer to Lapidae inflamed that instinctive itch to fly from the nest, leave the safety of home, and make a name for himself.

He asked the survivors of Lukas's camps about Conifaer—had he survived, and if so, where could he be found? But as he'd learned so well, elfs aren't like humans. It's not that they don't care. They just don't build communities beyond the few they love.

The knights were ready to right some wrongs, and if they couldn't rescue Glandaeff from the mess that Lukas had made, they could at least protect the innocent and help a few of the downtrodden. Rescuing Conifaer would be their first quest. They planned to leave when winter turned to spring. Dewey would be happy to see them off.

One afternoon, after the leaves had dropped from the trees and shadows grew long in the angled afternoon sunlight, a rider on horseback galloped up High Street and stopped in front of The Gold Piece Inn. Except that it wasn't a horse, it was a unicorn, a huge frothing unicorn, rocking his head back and forth, threatening anyone or anything with that long lance.

From his chair by the window, Dewey yelled, "Rustin, it's for you."

Crisiant was teaching Rustin the guitar. He wasn't bad and there was nothing like a few songs to ingratiate a traveler to villagers— gods knew he couldn't pay his way. He walked to the door.

You'd have thought someone came to deliver a sack of vegetables. Nothing ruffled that kid.

Rustin gave a slight bow as one elf would to another, and said, "It's good to see you, Quercus."

Quercus returned the bow from his mount. "Rustin, I bring the information of your request." He tossed a vellum scroll and Rustin caught it.

Rustin stood at the feet of the unicorn and read the scroll. The giant white horse shuffled this way and that, struggling with a desire to gallop, all but rearing, and Rustin acted like it was a sleeping mule. The scroll listed elfin woodweavers who had been held in Lukas's labor camps. It included a sketched map that led through Glomaythea all the way to the Aelpine Ridge. To Rustin it was a treasure map, the route to a promise kept.

Quercus addressed Rustin as a peer, "It is a small favor."

"I consider it a noble deed," Rustin said. "I will not break a promise in this life, and I promised to return Conifaer. Helping me keep that promise is no small favor."

"You delivered thousands of us to safety—you, a sixteen-year-old bairn."

"Madog Grwn died carrying the faer to safety. Baertha Dread and the Bastard Jon-Jay delivered thousands of faer to safety. I helped however I could, but the pirates deserve your thanks, not me."

Quercus looked down at him, puzzled. The unicorn stopped fidgeting and leaned his head to the side, eyes focused on Rustin, great horn pointed away and level with the ground, and his lips flared back. He snorted at Rustin.

"They did it for gold," Quercus said. "You asked nothing of us. Without you, no elf would have boarded ships. The Volunteers, they'd have captured us. Rustin, you earned our gratitude."

Rustin said, "I'll owe you for the rest of my life for the lessons you've taught me."

"The rest of your life?" Quercus said. His lips flirted with a smile.

His horse finally reared but with good humor.

Quercus stated, loud enough for everyone in the inn to hear, "When you're a thousand years dead and forgotten by your own, the faer will still speak of the nobility of Rustin and his Bastard Knights!"

With that, the horse launched up High Street, around the inn, and up The Fist of God.

101.

Kaetie said, "You don't understand."

"No," Lylli said, "I don't. No one knows what you're going through."

The two of them sat on an oak log watching Knuckle Creek flow by. Lylli massaged Kaetie's neck.

"I'm so confused." Half of her mind wanted to lash out.

"It will take time to digest what Sempervaereen has given you."

"How many times are you going to say that?"

"I don't know how a mortal can carry a ten-thousand-year-old soul, but I know you. And Kaetie, I know that you can do this."

"If I hear another farqin platitude, I swear, I'm going to—" Kaetie stopped and pushed her palms against her eyes.

Lylli sat quietly, watching leaves and tiny branches float past.

Sometimes Kaetie felt like Sempervaereen was digesting her. The patience that Sempervaereen had experienced as an immortal tree conflicted with the urgency of life in Kaetie's body and mind. The dryad had never been able to travel, not even a step. She'd never known a sense of smell. Her hearing had covered a totally different range of sounds. And sight, that sense that drives people more than any other, Sempervaereen had never *seen* anything. She experienced things and when she told stories her human audience reconstructed the descriptions into visions, but trees don't have eyes. Sempervaereen had never seen a color, never perceived the sunlight that she fed on as bright and yellow. She wanted to look at everything. She missed the feel of pollen blowing into her tiny blooms, the security of roots reaching deep into earth, and the wind in Kaetie's hair had nothing on a violent summer storm blowing through branches and bending her trunk. She loved the feel of Kaetie's lungs taking a breath, the sensation of her throat swallowing pure water, wine, or ale, and Sempervaereen had never felt flesh touch flesh, and she found it intoxicating. Sempervaereen still couldn't accept that Kaetie had broken up with Macae. "He has to learn the importance of being the knights' sage." To which Sempervaereen communicated, "Who cares? He's a man! We can be their sage."

"The hardest thing about this," Kaetie said, "is that I know you're right. Sempervaereen and I can be the person the world needs. We actually—damn it! I am that person. But how can I convince anyone? Why should people accept me? Should I walk into Glomaythea Castle and announce to Maedegan that I have ten-thousand years of experience? That I can solve all of the worlds' problems and he should get out of my way?" She grumbled at her mixed feelings. "I have two very different voices in my head, and do you know what they agree on?" Kaetie leaned close to Lylli. "The one thing that Sempervaereen and I both want to do?"

"When you and Sempervaereen have finished absorbing each other, meshed into one being, you'll find the harmony of Sempervaereen's wisdom and the strength of your spirit. You have no idea of your potential. No idea."

Kaetie tried to swallow the words. Not that she doubted Lylli's good intentions or her friendship, but what she wanted to say went against everything Lylli had taught her. She sighed and let the words out. "We want to be a serving-lass like my mother. I want to bring food and drinks to people. I want to sing and dance and gamble. I want to live and Sempervaereen wants to go upstairs. A lot. Like constantly. With anyone."

"For a few weeks, that might give you the routine you need to work through this."

"No!" Kaetie spoke with her mother's ferocity. "I've seen what humans do to each other, and I don't want to have anything to do with it. They can go to hell. Let Rustin save them. I'm going to live."

Lylli's face flushed. She swallowed the first words that leapt to her tongue. Kaetie watched her assemble a sentence. "This will sound like another platitude, Kaetie, but you have to believe me. There are things that I know that you don't know, that Sempervaereen doesn't even know." Her hand tightened on Kaetie's. "You have no idea of your potential. You don't even know who you are."

102.

Dewey sat in the chair next to his new window. The Window Faery worked her tiny squeegee and his Truth Faery rested on the sill.

It became obvious to Dewey within a month that Glandaeff would disintegrate back into the collection of skittish city-states that it had been two hundred years before the rule of Queen Grae-gloria The Uniter. Lukas had farqed things up that thoroughly. Famine, disease, war—it wouldn't be pretty. Humanity had forgotten what life had been like without the help of faeries, and as ever, would have to relearn history's lessons the hard way. But he'd be okay. The faeries owed him.

A new band played old songs. Baertha yelled in mock-outrage that the Card Faery had caught her again. A baby goat rammed a chair. Lucith complained that she wouldn't go upstairs with the goatherd until he bathed, but he held up a gold ohzee and she offered to share the bath with him. Kaetie carried a plate of salmon whose steam trailed the smells of dill and lemon. Bob poured drinks. A pirate stumbled on the bloodhound, and neither seemed to care. The damn cat lounged on the chandelier. A toddler crawled up on stage and Laetifah scooped her up without spilling a drop of the twenty mugs on her tray. More than everything else, having Laetifah back made Dewey feel that at least his world was right again.

Well, almost.

One thing ate at him—two things really. He watched Kaetie set the steaming plate at the arguing table where Codae, Grindaer, Fin, and Baeswax debated the merit of ambergris in aromatherapy. He could hear Rustin laughing with the Bastard Knights in the casino.

There had to be a solution. The rightful heirs to the throne, potentially the wealthiest people in all the land, lived here for free.

The rightful queen sat at the bar with the heirs' mother nursing a horn of pinot. When he told her that he'd received a message from the King of Nantesse asking his daughter to come home, she said that she'd also gotten those messages, and added that, one, she had unfinished business in Glomaythea—whatever that meant—two, she had no desire to be a spinster in an island castle, and, three, The Gold Piece Inn fit her needs for the next several years, thank you very much. When he tried to charge her rent, she argued that she did as much work as any other serving-lass. When he asked her to take guests upstairs, she said something about wombs, waiting for one thing or another, and love, but by then he'd stopped listening.

He just couldn't stand it.

He walked to the bar and stepped between Daffy and Loretta,

turned to Daffy and whispered, "It's yours for the taking."

Loretta said, "What're you on about?"

Daffy, shook her head. "Leave me alone."

Dewey shrugged. "I guess some people don't feel bound by their oaths."

Daffy said, "Dewey, bother someone else." She pointed to the arguing table.

"I understand," Dewey said. He waved Bob over for a mug and glanced at Loretta. She had her back to him and was watching Kaetie. He turned back to Daffy. "I know someone who takes promises seriously and when he finds out that he's bound by birth, he might feel an obligation. I might even point out that caring for his people is a prince's most sacred oath." Bob set a frothy mug in front of him and he took a sip. "But as long as you're happy."

Daffy tapped one of her long fingers on the bar. Dewey waited. It took longer than he'd expected. He'd nearly finished his ale by the time Loretta caught it.

"What?" She said. "Did you say *when* he finds out?"

"He has to be told."

"Don't you dare!" She started in a whisper but hit full volume in two words.

"Didn't mean to touch a nerve."

"He's right," Daffy said. "Rustin needs to know who he is."

"How dare you?"

Lylli rushed between Dewey and Loretta and said, "Knowing her legacy could give Kaetie the direction she needs. Right now, she's lost."

Daffy said, "We need to have this conversation in private."

"My office?" Dewey led the way, nearly skipping across the saloon.

Daffy and Lylli guided Loretta. Lylli closed the door.

Dewey took his seat and tried not to smile. "I feel it's my duty to tell Rustin that he's the rightful king." He tried to speak with regret but couldn't pull it off.

Loretta's voice came out ragged. "You will do no such thing."

"The land is without a king and Rustin is a king without a people, whether or not he knows it," Dewey said. "The curse is compelling me to tell him, I have no choice. I'm sorry."

"Liar!" Loretta sounded dangerous.

Daffy asked Lylli, "Is he lying?"

Lylli looked at her father. "The curse is triggered by legitimate requests for help."

"Glandaeff itself asked for my help just the other day."

"Yes, he's lying," Lylli said.

Loretta stood and pointed her index finger in Dewey's face. "The land can go to hell—"

"It is going to hell," Dewey said, maintaining his composure.

"—it's not bringing my son with it."

"Rustin will keep his father's oath, no less than he'll keep his promise to Lapidae. He didn't learn that keep-your-promise nonsense from me."

Daffy reached for Loretta's hand. "He has to be told."

"I'm so sorry," Lylli said. "For their own safety, Kaetie and Rustin need to know who they are and what they're up against."

Dewey had seen Loretta's eyes like this before.

"No!" she said. "It's over, Dewey. The reign of Glo royalty and their farqin Maentanglement is over. There are no heirs to the throne. It's over!"

"Lukas knew about them, and he had to have learned it from someone," Daffy said. "Someone knows. Word will spread." She sighed. "All Rustin talks about is taking his knights and following that elf's map into the mountains searching for Conifaer. He won't stand a chance in Glomaythea if he doesn't know who he is!"

"He's going nowhere," Loretta said. "He'll apprentice with the merchant's guild. I've already arranged it. They're thrilled to have him. He'll be Guild Master in a few years and have a wonderful, safe life."

"Master of the merchant's guild?" Dewey looked from Loretta to Daffy and back. "The lad has no interest in commerce. The kid's not even greedy—Guild Master?" He shook his head.

"And Kaetie is perfectly happy as a serving-lass."

"Loretta, please," Lylli said. "Kaetie has more potential than any of us can imagine, and she's lost."

Loretta said, "The world don't need another druid."

"Don't you see? Kaetie will soon know more than anyone on earth. She'll understand what separates people, what makes them hate, and what drives them to hurt each other and fight—you can't take that away from her. You can't take her away from the world."

"Oh yes I can!" Loretta stepped to the door.

Daffy said, "Rustin believes in honor and justice, he understands chivalry and what it means to be a knight—understands it better than any knight I've ever known. He will be a great king."

"Oh, come on," Loretta said. "He's a Gold Piece Inn Bastard."

"If the legitimate queen made her claim at the court in Glomay-thea Castle, Maedegan would have to accept it," Dewey said. "She would be regent and Rustin would be King in Waiting. There will never be a better time."

"Oh, don't even try," Daffy said. "I'd rather be a maermaid." She looked at Loretta. "I'd rather be a serving-lass at The Gold Piece Inn. What better place for me to raise my Bastard?"

"Enough!" Loretta said. "Kaetie will be a serving-lass and Rustin will start his apprenticeship. If anyone tells them they are Gledig's heirs, do you know what they'll do?"

Lylli said, "Kaetie won't believe it."

Daffy said, "Rustin will."

"They'll ask me, and I'll tell 'em it's not true. Who you think they'll believe?"

Dewey groaned.

"That's right," Loretta said. "They'll believe me because I never lied to them."

Epilogue

Promises and serendipity—do you ever wonder if they conspire?

Crisiant promised that he'd die at the King's side. Like most vows of self-sacrifice, it was an easy promise to break. He convinced himself that it conflicted with the King's demand that he preserve Queen Dafina's life above his or his heirs'.

And then serendipity stepped in. He cursed Dewey as compensation for his own failures. That curse, motivated by pure vanity, did more to protect Daffy and preserve the King's oaths to Glomaythea than anything he'd ever done or will ever do. Dafina, The First Princess of Nantesse and Queen of Glomaythea, was intelligent, skilled in diplomacy, and above all, sophisticated. But a hero? No one would have guessed she had it in her. But she wasn't finished, and the Princess and Bastard Knights hadn't even gotten started.

Taevius apprenticed with Baertha on *Daemned and Ugly*. The crew elected him captain in a month and she became quartermaster. Vaence apprenticed with Fin, and Vivaen became a serving-lass and then a singer, songwriter, and dancer.

Most of the Volunteers went home to their families and resumed their lives as best they could in a shattered land, but many of them had no home to return to, and others were so altered by atrocities that their villages wouldn't welcome them home. These Volunteers splintered into bands of mercenaries or brigands.

Several of King Gledig's distant cousins tried to claim the throne. Some brought lawyers with documents and made their claims in court. Others hired mercenaries and made their claims on the battlefield. Maedegan held the castle, but he used fear and terror to extract what authority he could and never achieved popular backing. In the countryside, greedy, power-hungry tyrants soon ruled most villages.

Travel along the rivers and roads that joined the ancient cities of Glandaeff soon required armed guards. Mercenaries profited at both ends as thieves or security; often as not, they were one and the same. On the sea and in the harbors, piracy, real cut-throat piracy, encroached on the comparative civility of profiteer sailors.

Short-lived, hopeful tales of worthy knights, wizards, and druids emerged from every festival and fair. Crazy rumors of renegade princes and princesses popped up now and then, usually following the narrative of one old myth or another. A favorite involved peasants kissing toads and being transformed into royalty, but most of the gossip followed the usual theme: orphans and bastards, in out-of-the way villages unaware of their lineage, being manipulated by unsavory halflings.

Acknowledgments

L et me use this space to thank some people for their help and support. My agent, Lauri Mclean of Fuse Literary, suggested I write this book, provided terrific feedback, and unlimited enthusiasm. I'll never forget her words after reading the first draft, "Ransom, you did it! You reinvented fantasy! You're the Terry Pratchett of your generation!" (She speaks with lots of exclamation points.) EJ Debrun, Julaina Kleist, Janine Love, and Ann Mannheimer provided in-depth feedback on early drafts. John Somerville, Ross Lockhart, EJ Debrun (again) (and about half of my Facebook friends—you should be one, just sayin') helped with the marketing copy. Lance Buckley created the cover art, with inspiration from EJ Debrun (yet again), Heather Stephens, and Karen and me.

The Book of Bastards was edited by the brilliant Alan K. Lipton (fictioneer.biz).

Crescent Cove comes from a daydream I had while staring at Drakes Bay from Chimney Rock in Point Reyes National Seashore, my favorite place in the world. Not too far from there, Black Mountain inspired The Fist of God, special thanks to Suzie Garbert for calling it that.

And, of course, I'd like to thank Karen, Professor Buckley, and Dear Abby because nothing happens without the steadfast support of your mate and your dogs.

Note to you

Thank you for reading *The Book of Bastards*. If you have a minute, would you please post a review at your favorite book site? Whether a sentence or an essay, I'll appreciate the boost as much as the advice.

I'd really like to hear from you. Seriously. To prove it, I'll resort to bribery. Send me a note and I'll send you a free copy of *The 99% Solution* or *Too Rich to Die*, whichever you want.

I'm at **paperbackwriter@ransomstephens.com**.

Or you can just sign up for my famous*, life-changing* Ransom's Notes, in which I provide amusement* and insights* into how* and why* we live, along with updates on my latest books, plus you'll get a link to a free copy of *The 99% Solution* (which I think is my best work). To do so, hie thee to **subscribe.ransomstephens.com**. Ransom's Notes hardly ever suck*, and it turns out that they're a really good way for us to stay in touch with each other.

Also, please let me know if I can support your book club or help with an event. Visit **www.ransomstephens.com** to get autographed print copies and to check out my other books and speeches on topics from fiction to neuroscience to physics to pursuing your dreams.

If it's ever relevant (and I hope it will be): beer not wine, tea not coffee, any topic you want*.

With gratitude and affection, I hope you're having fun!

Ransom

Petaluma, California, November 2020

Follow: @ransomstephens

Friend: ransom.stephens

Like: ransomsbooks

(* Results may vary. Sorry for the hallucinations.)

About Ransom Stephens

Author, speaker, and physicist, Ransom Stephens writes fantasy, science fiction, and popular science. He builds novels on big ideas with characters that make you laugh and cry and take you away for a while. His daughter once had a dream that he was a novelist hitchhiking across Europe, and he felt compelled to make her dream come true. He still blames her for the inconvenience—hitchhiking can be smelly.

With Dear Abby on her pillow under the desk and Professor Buckley on his couch, Dr. Stephens hacks at his keyboard striving to offer perspective, hoping it helps you along your journey in some small way.

Books by Ransom Stephens

Time Weavers: The 99% Solution

http://t99ps.ransomstephens.com

An intercontinental, inter-dimensional thrill ride.

Lucy Montgomery, a tiny woman with a commanding presence, is the 99%, buried in student loan debt and pissed off at a rigged system.

Francis Gordon Woodley, IV, is top of the 1%, heir to a corporate empire that can buy or topple entire nations.

Manipulated by anarchists, Lucy sets out to destroy corporate power so that classless democracy can bloom into worldwide utopia. With his oligarch friends, Francis sets out to destroy government, unleash free-market forces, and spawn worldwide utopia.

With Lucy and Francis on a collision course, the Time Weavers race to save the rest of humanity. Every future their computers predict leads to a hundred-year dark age except one. But for that one timeline to emerge into reality, Simon must encourage his daughter, Lucy, to assassinate his mentor's son, Francis.

Time Weavers: Too Rich to Die

http://trtd.ransomstephens.com

Love and money found, lost, and crushed beyond recognition.

San Francisco techie Eben Scratch becomes the world's first trillionaire on his 30th birthday. Like a high-tech Scrooge, Eben's greed has ruined his life and just might ruin the world if the Time Weavers can't rescue Eben from himself. Allison Anatolia created the app that made Eben rich and she'll do anything to bring Eben back to earth, even if it means tearing apart the world to do it.

Ranging from San Francisco to Paris, Mexico, India, and Vienna, Too Rich to Die melds Silicon Valley wealth, the French Revolution, and developing world sweatshops into a fast-paced story of love and money found, lost, and crushed beyond recognition.

The God Patent

http://tgp.ransomstephens.com

When electrical engineers Ryan McNear and Foster Reed co-authored two patents for company cash incentives, they thought it was all just a joke. One described the soul as a software algorithm and the other described the big bang as a power generator.

But when the company crashes, McNear finds himself divorced, broke, and estranged from his son. As he rebuilds his life, McNear discovers Reed has used their nonsensical patents to attract top-tier energy investors. A patent war erupts and McNear is suddenly immersed in a battle between hard science and evangelical religion. To prove himself, he will have to risk everything--his reputation, his livelihood, and even his sanity--to be with the son he loves and refuses to forget.

Set in the age-old culture war between science and religion, The God Patent is a modern story that deftly blends scientific theory with one man's struggle to discover his soul.

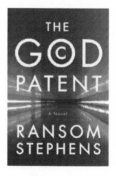

The Sensory Deception

http://tsd.ransomstephens.com

Can a video game save the polar bear, the sperm whale, and every other endangered species on the planet? Silicon Valley scientist Farley Rutherford thinks he has the answer.

His team has designed a virtual reality system that immerses users in the struggles of an endangered animal-and the astonishing experience leaves any who try it desperate to help. But the path to environmental salvation is not easy.

Luckily, venture capitalist Gloria Baradaran becomes Farley's most ardent advocate. Gloria and the team will have to fight for funding and their cause before facing the biggest obstacle of all: obtaining sensory data from the creatures themselves, including the biggest hunter of all-the sperm whale.

The cause is righteous, but the stakes are high. And while Farley fends off Somali pirates in pursuit of the ultimate sensory experience, a rift in the team puts Gloria's life in jeopardy, proving that idealism might just be the most dangerous game of all.

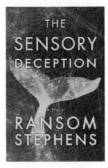

The Left Brain Speaks, The Right Brain Laughs:
a look at the neuroscience of innovation & creativity in art, science, and life

http://lbsrbl.ransomstephens.com

Neuroscience for lay-people that uses irreverence, wisecracks, and a physicist's eye for scientific accuracy to convey what makes us all tick and how we can tick better.

With as little jargon as possible, each chapter builds a background for the reader to understand the interplay between what we too often think of as separate topics. Starting with a new and improved left-brain/right-brain oversimplification, each chapter investigates the inseparable interactions of seemingly distinct concepts, all building to a working understanding of innovation and creativity in art, science, and life.

Using examples ranging from hanging out in bars to playing guitar to cave people hunting hippos to surfing to impressionist art to the most important failed experiment of all time, we address consciousness, value, hops and malt, why we mourn each other's deaths, and why we do what we do for money.

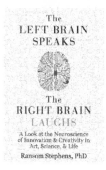

The
LEFT BRAIN
SPEAKS

The
RIGHT BRAIN
LAUGHS

A Look at the Neuroscience
of Innovation & Creativity in
Art, Science, & Life

Ransom Stephens, PhD

Made in the USA
Coppell, TX
25 September 2021